Caroline Cauchi is an international bestselling [illegible] seeks to give voice to silenced yet remarkable women, reimagining the stories of those erased from historical narratives. In 2023, her novel *Mrs Van Gogh* was published in multiple countries and selected as a 'Heather's Pick' title in Canada.

Currently lecturing in Creative Writing at the University of Hull, Caroline lives in the UK with her partner and their many children.

carolinecauchi.co.uk

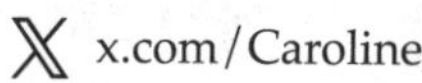

x.com/Caroline_S

instagram.com/caroline_cauchi

Also by Caroline Cauchi

Mrs Van Gogh

QUEEN OF THE MIST

CAROLINE CAUCHI

One More Chapter
a division of HarperCollins*Publishers* Ltd
1 London Bridge Street
London SE1 9GF
www.harpercollins.co.uk
HarperCollins*Publishers*
Macken House, 39/40 Mayor Street Upper,
Dublin 1, D01 C9W8, Ireland

This paperback edition 2024
24 25 26 27 28 LBC 5 4 3 2 1
First published in Great Britain in ebook format
by HarperCollins*Publishers* 2024

A catalogue record of this book is available from the British Library

ISBN: 978-0-00-871525-0

This novel is entirely a work of fiction. The names, characters and incidents portrayed in it are the work of the author's imagination. Any resemblance to actual persons, living or dead, events or localities is entirely coincidental.

Printed and bound in the United States

For my Cauchi women – Grandma Helen, Jaka, Poppy and Lauren – past, present, and soon-to-be.

CRUNCHING THE NUMBERS

THE ASTONISHING REALITY OF NIAGARA'S FURY – SEPTEMBER 10, 2023

Unquestionably, Niagara Falls is an awe-inspiring spectacle, yet its statistics are stark. They serve as a reminder that the odds of survival against its torrential backdrop have always been staggeringly slim.

Indeed, since 1850, more than 5,000 people have succumbed to its pull. Some were unfortunate accidents, some were deliberate attempts to end their lives, but, often, calculated decisions were made. Choices that resulted in more than 5000 people slipping over the lip and plummeting into its unforgiving waters.

Yet of those thousands who have taken that plunge, only sixteen individuals have escaped with their lives.

And of those sixteen, one name persists from the depths of history.

A name that beckons us to delve into the annals of human determination.

A name that holds the remarkable tale of the woman who went over Niagara Falls in a barrel.

Surely, it's time for Annie Edson Taylor's odds of survival to be crunched, scrutinised and for us to let her speak…

'… it has many times been intimated that women seldom know their own minds. But Mrs Taylor did. She had made up her mind to go over the Falls of Niagara, and she was going. It was do or die with her.'

Orrin E. Dunlap

Annie

PROLOGUE

24th October 1901

The barrel creaks and groans around me, its wooden walls whispering secrets of the mighty Niagara. Each breath I take feels heavier, laden with the roar of the Falls. My heart pounds, echoing the thunderous cascade outside. Louder and louder. I clutch the leather harness, knuckles white, palms slick with perspiration.

'Can't back out now,' I whisper.

Memories flood my mind: Tilda and Nora, the quiet moments at home with Mrs Lapointe. I picture Samuel, my dear husband, and David, our baby boy; his tiny face is forever etched in my heart.

'Can you hear me?' I call out, hoping their spirits linger close.

The barrel tilts and bobs a wild dance with the river. Every jolt and shudder's a test, a challenge from nature itself. The dark confines of this wooden cocoon press in on me. Every sorrow, every fear, is amplified. That weight pushes down on me.

The barrel pitches violently. Throwing me against its sides. My head strikes the wood. Dizzying pain shoots through my skull. The roar of the Falls deafens. A primal scream from the depths of the earth. I squeeze my eyes shut, bracing for the inevitable.

A sudden drop. My breath catches. The world spins. I'm weightless. Suspended in a terrifying freefall.

'Help.'

The word is swallowed by the thunderous water. Impact. The jolt is brutal. Bones rattling. Teeth clenching. Water floods in, filling the barrel, threatening to drag me down into oblivion.

I struggle to breathe, to hold on, but the darkness presses closer, consuming.

How in God's name did I end up here?

Part I: Adrift

DECEMBER 1900

Annie

31st December 1900

'What I'd give to be in my parlour with a cup of warm milk and comfortable footwear…' I say, shifting awkwardly.

Instead, I'm stuck in these torture devices for women with feet as dainty as their sensibilities, which clearly isn't me. With a slight pivot on the heel, I tap the sole lightly against the ground, hoping to alleviate some of the discomfort. It doesn't. They're Mrs Lapointe's dead husband's sister's shoes, and they're a size too small.

Whispers of a grand salon gathering hosted by Mrs Winthrop – a prominent figure known for her love of literature and the arts – had spread like wildfire through Bay City. The invite list boasted esteemed members of the community, and anyone with a spark of talent deemed worthy of recognition. The woman had a knack for finding artists, writers, and anyone who could hold a quill without poking their eye out. Naturally, she invited everyone except those she actually liked. My friend and boarding house owner, Mrs Lapointe, was always on the lookout for such opportunities. I've no idea how she secured an invitation for us, but she did. I was informed that it was an occasion I couldn't miss.

That's why I find myself standing in Mrs Winthrop's grand estate. My feet have been planted firmly on this spot for ten minutes already; I must resemble one of her weathered, stone statues. The imposing mansion looms and a muddle of annoyance and nerves stream through me. Its windows are aglow with warmth and invitation, but still I'm overly keen to flee back to the boarding house for a butter tart.

Letting out an exasperated sigh, I smooth the fabric of my dress nervously. I hate feeling out of place. I'm no stranger to opulence, but this world isn't mine. I'm literally in someone else's clothing.

'Are you knocking, or should I?' he says, stepping next to me. His tall frame's imposing against the wooden door. He gestures to it.

'I'd rather not,' I say.

'Let me.' He stretches his right arm across me, his fingers slightly curled and ready to rap against the door. With the move, his arm inadvertently rebounds off my bosom.

'Sir, this is neither the time nor the place,' I say, and I see horror leap across his face.

'I didn't … I wasn't,' he stutters, palms held up in surrender.

With a raised eyebrow and a smirk, I challenge him to question my authority or opinion. I see his fear. I'm wild and old; he enjoys his women young and tamed. The turn of the century may have brought us electric lights, but it hasn't yet cured the fear of a woman with opinions. He takes a step or two backwards.

My knuckles knock lightly on the door, and it creaks open within seconds.

'Welcome, Madam,' the butler intones with practised formality. 'If I could ask your name…' His voice is both crisp and professional. No-nonsense. I like him.

'Annie,' I say. 'Annie Edson Taylor.'

'Please, come in, Mrs Taylor.' He smiles and I step forward. 'Through there,' he says, pointing across the hallway before turning his attention back to the man who touched my bosom.

Ten short steps and I push my body against the mahogany door. It's heavy on my shoulder. A blast of laughter and chatter gushes as it edges open.

'Thank you,' someone says. 'Looks like I need to lay off pie if I'm going to squeeze through here!' A burly man, with a jovial demeanour; his presence fills the space with warmth as he wriggles past me and through the gap.

'Allow me,' a different guest says. A hint of grey streaks his dark hair. His pushing on the door appears effortless and the room opens before us.

The noise and vibrant atmosphere overwhelm instantly. Too many people, too much to see. I don't know where to look first. The room's a kaleidoscope of laughter, swirling gowns, and the kind of joy that feels almost tangible; like you could reach out and pocket a piece for later. Smoothing my eyebrow with the tip of my finger, I step into the ballroom. The room's abuzz with activity. I scan the crowds for a familiar face but see none. Mrs Lapointe was feeling a little under the weather, said she'd meet me here; I'll kill her if she doesn't arrive soon. I pat the skirts of my dress, keen to appear busy and to detract from how alone I suddenly feel. Indeed, this dress – Mrs Lapointe once wore it for an end-of-season ball – is tight and uncomfortable in its corset; a nagging reminder of the ageing I attempt to hide.

I risk a peek around, jumping my stare from person to person. My aim is to avoid eye contact at all costs. Women are adorned in jewels that glitter and materials that flow. Scarlet and emerald gowns shimmer. The men sport tailored suits in shades of navy or burgundy. Mrs Lapointe was right in her choice of dress for me; red and bejewelled. I'd told her I'd hate every minute of wearing it, yet here I am, blending in. The light from the chandeliers above reflects off the polished marble floor. A flicker of worry that I'll slip, but I push that thought away. Instead, I consider what it'd feel like to bend and stroke my fingers across its surface. This setting is beautiful, these people are beautiful, and maybe, tonight, I'm one of those people, too. I'm invisible because I'm merging and not because I'm ancient or lacking good looks. I shake my head to dislodge those thoughts; I find this relentless need for youth and femininity jarring.

I make my way to the refreshment table. One of the impeccably dressed servers points to bottles and says words I can't quite hear over the hustle and bustle and chatter.

'Dr-ink.' The server articulates the word as if I'm deaf. He gestures in front of him. 'Champagne, wine…' He pauses and then points to a bowl. His mouth twists as if he's having to force words through a pipe.

I shrug. 'What's in there?' My curiosity is piqued.

'Punch.' His tone almost apologetic. I open my mouth to speak—

'Been saying for years that something needs to be done about the alcohol problem.' I turn to two men behind me, their voices carrying over the ambient noise of the party.

'Absolutely,' the second man chimes in. Solidly built with salt-and-pepper hair; his voice has authority. 'It's high time we put an end to the excessive drinking that's plaguing our society.' Their words linger in the air, mingling with the clinking of glasses and the murmur of conversation.

I move to the glass bowl of punch, picking up a cup and turning to smile at the server. 'Punch, please. Do fill my glass to the brim.' I hear a tut behind me. I straighten up and pull my shoulders back, turning to face the men. They've already walked away, indicating in my direction.

'Can I offer you something to eat?' the server asks. He points at the grand array of serving plates. They're all perfectly positioned on a table that's adorned with ornate porcelain plates and silver utensils. This is luxury.

I shake my head, but he isn't looking at me.

'There's an assortment of small appetisers and hors d'oeuvres on offer. Perhaps crackers with cheese and slices of cured meat.' His speech is polished. He smiles. He's proud of his delivery. He pauses to walk to a plate and point, before moving to another. 'As well as larger dishes. Roast beef, salmon.' He looks at me then. There's not a hint of affection or concern. He cares neither if I eat five full platters nor starve myself to death.

'Thank you, but I'm really not—'

'Perhaps a little something from the selection of sweet treats. Cakes, pastries…'

He glances for a response. I shake my head, apologising. My

stomach rumbles in protest. 'Just the punch,' I say. I smile. I hear his tut this time – he's offended – as he spots another guest and walks to her. A smile and then he attempts to convince her to try his food.

I shake my head, not quite sure why I said no. I'm hungry, there's free food and I'm trying to ignore the tempting aromas surrounding me. It's as if to eat would be a sensory overload too many. I can't trust myself to walk, to drink punch and to eat. I move with purpose and determination, then recall that I don't know another soul here. The room is filled with young, well-dressed people, laughing and chatting as they don't question their surroundings. It all feels excessive: excessively flamboyant, excessively loud, excessively articulated. I watch as they wolf the food and drink on offer. Perhaps I could be more like them, but the effort feels tedious and unnecessary. This isn't the adventure I crave. Yet, I can't shake a growing unease that accompanies the scene. I'm as guilty as they are. The extremeness of it all, the lack of restraint and moderation, it's as if this society is losing its balance, on the verge of spiralling into a frenzy of indulgence and extravagance. What are the consequences of such unrestrained behaviour? How is that shaping their values and priorities? What impact is that having on the very fabric of our society? I won't find my answers here. Times and social expectations are changing, though. My stomach grumbles in protest as I stand still, perspiring in a too-tight dress.

My eyes are drawn back to the large platters of food on the table. My mouth waters at the sight of the juicy roast beef and the perfectly cooked salmon. With a confident smile and unwavering gaze, I gulp down my drink, in a way that's entirely not ladylike. I savour the sweet taste on my tongue, then walk further into the room. Where are you, Mrs Lapointe?

Movement from the corner of my eye. I turn. I see a curious couple. He's leaning against a pillar deep in conversation with a truly elegant woman. His presence feels dwarfed by hers, even though she's clearly trying to make herself appear smaller. His dark hair's slicked back in a modern style, and his eyes seem to both study and devour his companion. She looks uncomfortable, while he exudes an air of entitlement.

He glances at me and I panic. I wave confidently. I don't even know why. I see his confusion and fast recovery as he waves back and feigns recognition. The entire encounter is over in a blink. He's impeccably dressed in a suit that hugs his lean frame. I can tell by the way he stands, or rather inclines, that he displays confidence. It's not earned confidence from his appearance or height, though, so it must have been bought with money. Excessive amounts of it. The woman he's devouring takes her chance and seemingly ducks into the shadows. I watch him look to the floor at the exact spot where she was standing, as if she's disappeared into thin air. His face contorts and he squints as he swivels, searching for her.

'That's Henry Hills. Mrs Winthrop's younger brother.'

I turn and Mrs Lapointe is here. 'Better late than not at all,' I say, but then pause. She's the vision of refined elegance in a floor-length silk gown with a high collar and fitted bodice that's adorned with intricate lace detailing.

'Was that in your chest of clothes?' I ask and she nods.

'It's a little loose here.' She pulls at the material in the pit of her arm. 'I must have been larger five years ago.'

'You're wasting away.' I pinch at her waist. She looks considerably paler than she did this morning. Still, her hair's elegantly coiffed, and a feathered hairpiece perches gracefully atop her head. Elbow-length gloves made of delicate lace complete her ensemble, adding a touch of sophistication to her appearance.

'Stunning,' I say and her cheeks blush red.

'What do you think?' She nods towards Henry, and I laugh. I try to study his face and demeanour objectively. The lighting is flattering, emphasising his bone structure, larger-than-average eyes and pimple-covered skin – though his condescending expression overshadows any physical features.

'Do you want to eat? Are you starving?' I gesture towards the server and food.

'Come,' she whispers, looking concerned. She pulls my hand and strides towards him. 'Let me introduce you. He's desperate for a wife, and we need money.'

'What?'

I'm about to shake my hand free and run for the ballroom doors when I hear, 'Mr Hills. So wonderful to see you again.'

I bang into Mrs Lapointe, causing her to stumble forward into Mr Hills. In an instant, he's not leaning on the pillar, and he attempts to catch her. It's an odd embrace as she's both taller and wider than him. That's quite something as my friend's leanness could be considered an asset. Mrs Lapointe appears to melt into a giggle in his embrace. It's entirely fake but Mr Hills laps it up. His desperation for female attention is palpable. I roll my eyes, marvelling at how someone could be so obnoxious and self-absorbed, but then realise that he's staring at me.

'Henry Hills, this is my closest, oldest and very dear friend,' Mrs Lapointe says. 'Annie Edson Taylor.'

'Hello,' I say. She's attempting humour; I'm slightly older than her. I laugh. I'm the ageing aunt respectable mothers would hate.

'Charmed to make your acquaintance,' he says. His eyebrows are too thick and too bushy. I'm convinced I could flick at them and they'd wiggle away.

'Mrs Taylor was once on a stagecoach that was held up by *the* Jesse James and his gang.' I turn as Mrs Lapointe waves and walks off into the crowd.

'Who is this *lady*?' That's the original woman. She's back. She pulls her furs around her shoulders and stands at her full height beside me. 'Has her hair ever been brushed?' She must have reconsidered or recalculated the financial gain from being with Mr Hills. She's not happy that I've distracted her prey. It seems that he has something the women here desire. But it's certainly not his personality.

'Really?' Mr Hills says. 'And you lived to tell the tale?'

For a second, I must look confused.

He sighs. 'Jesse James?' He looks concerned. 'Are you unwell?'

I shake my head. I smile, pushing up my dress sleeves in readiness for story time. 'I lived, and I kept my eight-hundred dollars, too.'

Mr Hills laughs, and that spurs me on.

'How old are you?' says his original prey.

I turn to her. Her mouth is pinched and I'm waiting for her to waggle a finger in my direction. 'Forty-three,' I say, my eyes daring her to question the fact.

She laughs. Mr Hills waves her away. He's dismissing her. He clearly likes what he sees, or he's detected something in my persona and considers it an indication that I desire him. His arrogance is astonishing. Does it matter? This could provide entertainment to distract from the fact that these shoes are strangling my toes.

'You don't believe me?' I ask, looking at him through my eyelashes. I used to flirt with my Samuel in that way, but now I possibly look like I've got a squint or am hovering on hysterical.

'I think you're a talented storyteller,' he says. I pause. Not sure if that's a comment on my encounter with Jessie James or on my age.

'I had almost a thousand dollars hidden in the hem of my skirts,' I say. 'It went undetected because the gang had no desire to explore me further.' I speak with animated gestures, punctuating my words with hand movements.

'Mrs Taylor.' He says my name as if it were sugar on his tongue. It sounds sickly and makes my stomach flip in a bad way. He stretches out a hand and I do the same. Our palms are a similar size. Despite his unimposing stature, he carries himself with an overblown sense of self-importance. 'Annie.' A nod and a wide smile. 'I'm thrilled to make your acquaintance. You really are funny for a woman.'

Rolling my eyes dramatically I say, 'Thank you.' The words are soaked in sarcasm. 'And you are rather full of yourself for a man.'

Funny, unusual, difficult – that desire to label women bothers me. My wild hair will be confusing him, though. Men like Mr Hills fear women like me; they can't predict our next moves. They like us tamed and docile. Society demands it. Still, I'll never fear life in the way that he does, and I'll never be restrained. My grasp of impermanence makes me terrifying.

He bats away my words as he doubles over with laughter. Perhaps not terrifying, then. This man really does consider me hilarious. 'I'm intrigued as to why you would believe Mr James to not wish to know you…' he looks around, before leaning in, '…intimately.'

I point my right index finger at my face and paint a circle in the air that is wider than my hair. I maintain eye contact with him as I do. This man is the pot to my kettle.

He roars with laughter, and I wait for that to stop. 'I would like to know you better,' he says. He's still holding my left hand.

'You would?' I ask, letting out an exasperated sigh. He nods.

I assume this is where women are expected to swoon. My fluttering is deep in my abdomen. It feels more like a stomach bug or the impact of too much punch than anything remotely positive. He'll know that my palms are sweaty, but I imagine he'll consider it an attraction.

'Tell me about the stagecoach.'

'It was making its way through rugged terrain when, quite suddenly, it was stopped by a group of armed men on horseback.'

I feel his thumb making circles on my palm. It causes me to pause. To look at our hands and then to his face. He shows no emotion. I'm holding my breath as if that'll stop me from vomiting on his polished boots. He perhaps interprets that as a nervous desire. He nods for me to continue.

'The door to the stagecoach was flung open and a man stepped aboard.' I fling my arms out wide. Mr Hills' entire body moves with the force of my movement and with his hand still being in mine. Everyone takes a step back.

'Mr James?' Mr Hills draws himself up to his full five feet and two inches. He rubs at his shoulder socket. The yank hurt him.

I nod a yes. 'He was tall, with piercing blue eyes and the wildest mane of hair I'd ever seen.' A small crowd has gathered nearer about me. Mr Hills has noticed this, too. He stretches his neck and pushes back his slender shoulders. A cock amongst hens.

'I heard he was handsome,' one of the women says, but I don't turn to look at her. My eyes are stuck on this odd man, whose every action seems to demand attention. The fact that he's reached out and is attempting to hold my hand again must be a curious sight for others. Are we equals? Is his ugliness matched by my old age? Who is the more desperate?

'Did he speak to you?' a different woman asks.

'At first he stared at me,' I say. I nod to Mr Hills. Like you are doing now. 'There was kindness in his eyes, though.'

'Perhaps you reminded him of his mother,' one of the women says. The others laugh.

'I am no one's mother,' I say, squaring my shoulders. The harshness in my voice shocks me.

'Yet,' Mr Hills says.

I bat his hand away. I don't mean to, but that thought. Five, four, three, two, one—

'Then what happened?' one of the women asks.

'I told him, "Blow me away. I'd as soon be without brains than without money."'

'Then what happened?' Mr Hills asks, his voice breathy. Is this exciting him?

'Jesse James spoke to me.' A pause for dramatic effect. 'Said, "We're just after the strongbox under the driver's seat. You won't come to no harm."'

A collective gasp.

'Astonishing.' That's Mr Hills.

'What did you do?'

'Nothing.' I spin slowly, making eye contact with each of the listeners. 'I nodded, my heart racing. Watched the strongbox being handed over. Watched a group of men, with bandanas covering their faces and guns in their hands, ride off into the sunset.'

The laughter and applause are like music to my ears. I bow flamboyantly.

'And he never asked you to hand over your fortune?'

'Guess I looked poor,' I say. 'Or maybe he recognised that we shared the same intentions.'

'The same intentions?' Mr Hills asks, his eyes dancing, his pimple-covered face glowing.

'Yes.' A smirk plays at the corner of my lips. 'We both had nothing left to lose.'

1234 Center Avenue,
Bay City.
January 1st 1901

Dear Mrs Taylor,

I hope this letter finds you in good health and high spirits.

I must confess, meeting you at the party last night has been the highlight of 1901, thus far. Your wit and charm captivated me in a way that I have rarely experienced. As I was well-nigh the host of the gathering, I was delighted to be gifted the opportunity to participate in such a charming and stimulating tête-à-tête with you.

I would, thus, be somewhat pleased if you would accompany me to a dinner engagement. I believe our ponderings could be yet more enjoyable in a more intimate location.

I assume this proposition meets with your approval, and I anticipate confirmation – by return post – that you will grant me the pleasure of your company once again.

I eagerly await your response.

Yours sincerely,
Henry Hills

Bay City Boarding House,

Bay City.

January 2nd 1901

Dear Mr Hills,

Thank you for your words and your invitation.

Unfortunately, I decline your offer. I appreciate your interest, but I deem our interaction to have been rather dull, and consider it best left with the memory of your sister's gathering.

Wishing you all the best,

Mrs Annie Edson Taylor

Annie

3rd January 1901

When I was a child, I stopped speaking for three months. Not for any specific reason. Now I've been summoned to the parlour. Told to sit in an armchair like a badly behaved infant. And I'm considering muteness again.

'Well?'

I sigh. Being an adult is full of dull demands. 'Surely it's not that bad?' I ask, crossing one leg over the other and pointing towards her ledger.

'Could you be the illegitimate child of a rich man?' Mrs Lapointe says, but she isn't smiling. She isn't being comical. Things are clearly worse than I'd considered. This situation is entirely my fault.

'My father died and I was sent to Charlotteville, Schoharie County,' I say, and she emits a low growl. I hesitate. Perhaps her question was rhetorical? 'To a seminary for boys and girls,' I add. I pause, waiting for reaction. I shift in the armchair, uncrossing my leg and leaning in closer to her. 'He's long dead. No chance of financial assistance.' I chuckle to myself; she's focusing entirely on the ledger and not responding to my words. Why am I laughing?

Mrs Lapointe looks over the spectacles that are perched halfway down her nose. A single glare stifles my amusement instantly. Then she's back lifting pages, turning them carefully, running her index finger down the rows of numbers. Her movement is elegant. The entries are handwritten with precision. The calligraphy is consistent; Mrs Lapointe takes pride in her work. She releases a weary sigh.

'What can be done?' I shuffle uncomfortably. I'm in trouble. Still, I can't help but feel relieved that she now knows what I've been undertaking.

She looks over her shoulder towards the parlour door, checking who might be earwigging. 'Money is needed,' she says, and I nod. I understand; she doesn't want any of our boarders to overhear. 'And it's needed quickly.' She jabs her finger at the ledger.

I squint through my eyelashes to see where she's jabbing, but it doesn't help. My eyes aren't what they once were. Age and the parlour being dimly lit don't help matters, either. The atmosphere is as blurry as this conversation. Though the script is methodical, occasionally, a note appears in the margins – perhaps a reminder, or a brief commentary – but I can't quite make it out in this light.

'Perchance you could consider Henry Hills and his—'

I shake my head. 'I'd rather wrestle a moose and then politely ask said moose to step on my foot, rather than endure another moment with Mr Hills.'

'Even if it means evicting *your* boarders?'

It's the *your* that bites. I fold my arms across my chest defiantly, refusing to budge an inch on this. Minutes pass. Neither of us speaks. She looks at the ceiling, I look at her. Then, 'My roommate – Jennie Taylor – soon became my closest friend.' The subject's wholly irrelevant to our predicament. I see confusion splash across her face, before she glances at me.

'A relation of your Mr Taylor?' she asks but returns to the figures before I can respond.

My stomach churns at the thought of my husband's sister. After Samuel died, I lost contact with his side of the family. I moved from place to place, never leaving a forwarding address. Never staying long enough to make friends. My grief was burden enough and I had no capacity for attachment. I even vowed I'd never let anyone close again. Sorrow was weight carried.

That changed two years ago when I arrived on Mrs Lapointe's doorstep. She'd inherited this boarding house from her mother-in-law and had worked her behind off to keep it afloat. A blink of an eye and those two years had gone. Perhaps time passes differently in the later stages of life. A guest at first, I soon earned my keep by helping her out. Two ancient women running a business is accepted in Bay City, but only because we're both widows.

'It's simple,' Mrs Lapointe says. 'Our outgoings don't match our incomings.' She's concentrating and her brow is furrowed.

'I'm sorry,' I say flatly. 'You must understand why I couldn't turn the women away. I didn't consider that even more would arrive…'

She nods again; she isn't angry or unsympathetic towards the boarders. It's rather that she's only just grasped that over the last two years, young and vulnerable women have arrived here with just enough to pay for a couple of days. That would be fine business, but though I call them boarders, I've been convincing them to stay until they heal sufficiently to continue their journey, recuperating at their leisure and without paying. Is there a word for that? To cover the deficit, I've been using my money – a monthly allowance begrudgingly given from relatives – but that has now dried up and I've still not been turning women away. Mrs Lapointe had no idea and now, understandably, she's unhappy with me.

'Some days I wake and feel eighteen years old,' I say. I'm rambling, attempting to distract her. 'For a moment, before I creak, ache and struggle to sit up. Then I remember I'm sixty-two.' I laugh nervously. My stomach wibbles, and that makes me laugh even more.

'Ageing is near impossible to put into words,' she says. She observes me as if to find them. 'I'm convinced my body and mind have parted company and are living two different existences.'

I nod. 'I told that Henry Hills I was forty-three and he believed me,' I say. 'Men find younger women more palatable. They have a purpose that we no longer offer.'

'Will you reconsider walking out with him?' I hear the spark of hope in the rise at the end of her sentence. It's her best solution to this problem I've caused.

'No,' I say. 'I'm happiest not letting go of my past. I still enjoy its companionship.' I sigh contentedly, closing my eyes for a moment and thinking about my husband. 'It's been a nomadic life since Samuel passed, travelling around to find work. This is the longest I've stayed anywhere for decades.'

'And look at the messiness you've caused.' She smiles, though. A gentle smile; she's thawing. She nods, too, closing the ledger and placing her hands atop it. 'I was sixteen when I married. A widow by the time I was fifty… I will forever be grateful for the many years we had together.'

Mrs Lapointe was a stout woman when we met. Now she's vanishing before my eyes. She turned sixty recently, but still she's beautiful with her grey hair pulled back into a severe bun and rosy cheeks on pale skin. All that gives her a no-nonsense air but, really, she's as soft as butter and the kindest soul. Now, though, she places her hands together as if in prayer and looks to the ceiling, before resting her fingers on her jade mourning brooch.

'Life,' I say, as if that's explanation enough, and she stares at me. A new tactic, perhaps. Thinking if she glares long enough, I'll suddenly agree to be courted by Mr Hills.

An awkward minute. Another sigh from her; it's familiar, even soothing. Her need to understand me has been increasing in frequency recently. Perhaps she hears time running away from us.

I watch her open the ledger again, running her index finger back down the rows of numbers. Possibly she hopes they'll have altered in the past few minutes. I hope that, too. She rechecks her sums, lips moving but no sound escaping.

'Any miraculous solution?' I ask.

She shrugs her shoulders. I can see her sadness. 'We should make all our current boarders pay.'

'No.' I shake my head vigorously and she bobs hers slightly in support.

That's it. One word. End of conversation. Her eyes are sharp and intelligent, hinting at the life she's lived and the things she's seen.

'We'll find a better solution together,' I say.

I really do believe we can fix this. The world's changing, with women like us pushing against the boundaries of what's expected. We're not just surviving; we're setting the stage for young girls like Olive – who is staying here with her mother – to thrive, to dream bigger than we ever could. Life's easier and better when us women work together. That's what's made me stay in this boarding house for so long. Two years ago I was passing through Bay City, now I help other women who are passing through. Transient souls with no place to stay; make them feel safe, give them the protection they crave in their core.

'Would a cup of tea help?' I smile. My well-rehearsed response.

Mrs Lapointe shakes her head but still the corners of her lips curl upwards slightly. She's accepting what I've done. She closes the ledger.

'I hoped business would pick up,' I say.

'Our number of guests is not the problem.' She grins, shaking the book at me. Her strong hands – fingers calloused from years of hard work – grip the tattered ledger. I glance at my palms, weathered and rough. 'We're not getting any younger.'

I tut. 'A few good years remaining; still time to leave our mark,' I say.

'No hiding from ageing, Mrs Taylor,' she says. 'Our faces tell the stories of our lives. The laughter, the tears, the countless hours spent working to persist.'

I tap my index finger on my right cheek. 'Still room on here for my best and most adventurous story yet.'

She hesitates, her right eyebrow raised and waiting. 'What are you planning?'

Some might want women of a certain age to fade into the shadows, to wait there to die, but that's not me. I've survived this long for a reason, and I'll be damned if I don't figure it out before I exit this world.

'Now … about that cup of tea, and I think there are some leftover butter tarts,' I say.

Annie's Diary

3rd January 1901

The cup of tea and butter tart turned unexpectedly poignant. Minnie, one of the women who's passing through here, had made them. She'd told me that baking made her heart hurt less. I liked that and was telling Mrs Lapointe.

This boarding house collects abandoned womenfolk. It appears that we're pulled by the invisible threads of shared sorrows to find solace in the company of others like us.

I imagine Samuel's arm around my shoulder and a gentle kiss being planted on the top of my head. His love for me was boundless. It was without condition of behaviour or reaction. I have been loved entirely. How fortunate am I?

Annie

4th January 1901

'Have you been here all night?' I ask, stepping into the parlour.

Mrs Lapointe hasn't moved or changed her clothes since yesterday. I left her curved like a comma in her favourite armchair, with the ledger on her lap. Can't say I slept much, either.

She shakes her head. 'I didn't feel too grand.' She stretches upright in her seat, but then folds into a cough.

'Maybe we just need a list,' I say, hesitating in the doorway.

'Can't seem to shake it…' She points at her chest. Though her face is lined with worry right now, I've seen it light up with laughter on many occasions during our time living together. She adjusts the neck of her dress and wiggles to sit upright. 'A list?' she asks. She smiles, and her face transforms; her softness is beautiful.

I keep my features composed, refusing to let my concern show. 'A plan of possible opportunities really.'

'Look at this place.' Mrs Lapointe flings her arms out, and the ledger hits the floor. She's clearly forgotten it was on her lap.

I do as she instructs, striding around the room purposefully with a determined gait. Shoulders back, head held high, I nod and gesture.

Left then right. Left then right. She giggles, and the sound fuels me. I curl my fingers slightly, forming the shape of a telescope and pressing my hand against my right eye.

'It's not the grandest of rooms,' I say.

The first thing anyone walking into this parlour would notice is the worn floorboards. I'm sure each creak whispers tales of years gone by. 'The once vibrant hue here…' I stomp my foot. 'Might have dulled, might even be marred with chips and scratches, but there's life in them still.'

'And the smell…' Her fingers nip the bridge of her nose.

I sniff the air in an exaggerated manner and then let out a contented sigh, as if savouring the aroma. 'Yes … a damp scent does permeate the air in here,' I say. 'It's not oppressive, though … more reminiscent of rainy afternoons and memories that dance in the shadows.'

Mrs Lapointe claps her hands together. The sound lacks energy, though. This place is a home currently, and us transient souls welcome the current. Dusty windows filter in weak streams of sunlight, and mismatched armchairs find themselves in random spots around the parlour. The wallpaper – a once lively pattern – is now slightly peeled and faded. Maybe not the best first impression, but we make up for that in our energetic hospitality. Our boarders don't stay for the decoration.

'I'll give the room a good brush later,' I say, knowing it'll make little difference.

Mrs Lapointe smiles and then bends to retrieve the ledger from the floor. Her brow furrows.

'Are you in pain?' I ask, rushing forward, bending—

'I can do it!'

I freeze on the spot. A cold shiver runs down my spine. I rub my hands together for warmth and comfort.

'Sorry,' she says, shooting me a look.

I wave my hand to shoo away her concern.

'We need paying boarders.'

I bob my head; I know. 'We could advertise in the local newspaper, try to draw in travellers.'

Mrs Lapointe nods, her eyes brightening. 'That's a good idea. We could offer a special rate for a week's stay. Maybe include a meal or two for free.'

'Let me write this down.' I grab my writing slope from the corner of the room. Lifting the hinged lid, the glorious scent of parchment meets me. My fingertips stroke the velvet-lined interior before grabbing the pen and inkwell.

'Once a teacher, always a teacher,' she says, watching as I sit in the armchair closest to her.

I miss the busy days teaching. Curious minds, the questions, the goodness. Teaching was a demanding job, and I was good at it. If only I'd been capable of staying in the same place for long enough.

'Don't welcome any women, unless they have the means to pay for our hospitality?' Mrs Lapointe says, smiling. 'Also, best embellish the truth in the advertisement, a little.' She scans the room, looking entirely doubtful. 'Say it's homely.'

'Don't worry,' I say, and I mean it. I'll be creative. 'We'll weather this storm and make our fortunes.'

Mrs Lapointe reaches out her hand, places it over mine, and squeezes. It's unspoken, but still a thank you.

'What's the worst that can happen?' she asks.

I shrug. 'No guests, we die of starvation – and no one finds our bodies for months,' I say.

She lets out a hearty laugh, throwing her head back with joy. The sound is infectious.

~

Stay Close to the Excitement at 'Bay City Boarding House'
Your Affordable Home Away from Home!

Travellers and thrill-seekers! *Experience the charm of Bay City at Mrs Lapointe's modest yet homely lodgings. Our clean, cosy rooms provide a warm welcome after a day of exploring.*

Hearty Meals: *enjoy home-cooked breakfasts to start your day right.*

Convenient Location: *perfectly situated to explore Bay City.*

Affordable Rates: *enjoy some of the best prices around. Rooms for less than 50 cents a night.*

Join Us: *a warm bed, hearty breakfast and homely atmosphere await you!*

Book Today!

For Reservations and Enquiries, contact: Mrs Lapointe, Bay City Boarding House, Bay City.

~

Matilda

18th January 1901

First impressions?

I pull the advertisement out of me pocket. Ripped it from a newspaper in the diner two days ago. Had to do it shifty while the guy was in the restroom. I don't attempt to shelter the paper from the rain, though. Instead, I look from the words and back at the building in front of me, then back at the words again.

Maybe, once upon a time, it was a pretty sight – all grand and inviting,

But now? Windows slant a bit, porch is sagging. Is that a mouse?

Think they missed a few things off the description. *Ugly, rundown, and only for desperate folk who can't be affording anything else*. Maybe we're at the wrong place?

I scan the wet advertisement again. *A warm bed, a hearty breakfast, and a homely atmosphere await you!* Dim gaslight flickers through the grimy windows and casts deformed shadows over the wooden planks outside. *Modest yet homely lodgings?* Everything's uneven, creaky and in need of a firm brush.

'I think this might be untruthful advertising,' I say out loud. Not that I'm expecting me companion to respond. I wrap me shawl around us both. Protecting me baby from the heavy downpour and attempting to keep her warm. If we had anyplace else…

The steps creak under me weight, but at least the porch offers some shelter. It's past both of our bedtimes. Nora's only ten months old and we've been travelling all day. She's too heavy on me right hip. One single bag's thrown over me left shoulder. A different pain shoots from there and up me neck. Bag contains only what I could grab, but still it's too heavy. Everything's 'too something' now; I'm too sweaty under me skirts, me clothes too drenched from the rain, the backs of me knees aching too much.

'Looks like we're stuck here, Nora.' I adjust to place her rear on the porch, but me daughter's entire body stiffens. She squawks, too, in protest, and I pull her back onto me hip.

'Just for a minute, little one,' I say, and she squawks again. Louder this time. 'Shush.' I jiggle me hip. I smile. I like that she already knows what she doesn't want. No way she's letting me place her on the wet planks and away from what little warmth her mama's giving her. Don't blame her.

Nora nuzzles nearer. Wants to be as close as possible. She's a constant reminder of me purpose. I'm needed. Having a reason not to give up keeps me focused. She's me world and I'm hers. A gentle pat on her hindquarters soothes her and she releases a tiny gurgle. Already, she's me compass and I'm her home. I'd happily curl up on this top step and sleep for days, but I won't. I'll keep her away from him until me dying breath; Nora being safe's all that matters.

I look back into the darkness and rain. Forever vigilant he might be lurking. 'We're okay, little one,' I say. 'We'll be safe here.' Perhaps I'm trying to convince meself.

Bay City Boarding House. I stroke me fingers over the sign. Paint peeling from years of harsh American winters. I knew the price was too good to be true. I take a deep breath. Check over me shoulder again. Look up and look down. Still no one watching. Feels like the stars are playing peek-a-boo though, showing up in the gaps and then hiding behind them clouds. It's something special, even with the cold rain touching me face. I rap on the door with me knuckles. The sound echoes through the empty street. It's late, maybe eleven o'clock at night. All the occupants will be sleeping inside, too. I've no choice, though. Me daughter needs shelter. Deep breath in. I knock again.

The door creaks open.

'Do you know what time it is?' A woman. Her voice has a growl in its corners. She's dressed in an ivory-coloured cotton nightgown with delicate lace trimmings around the high collar and cuffs. It's fancy. Her grey hair's escaping from a bun at the nape of her neck. She fiddles to tuck them loose hairs, then rubs at her eyes. I've woken her.

'Miss Hamilton.' I wave the soggy newspaper cutting at her. I've written, she was expecting me earlier today. 'I'm late.'

And I'm apparently incapable of being either an adult or explaining meself.

She points a plump finger at Nora. 'You didn't say anything about a child.'

I pull me daughter closer. Put me shawl over her. 'Mrs Lapointe?' I ask. Me heart's pounding in me chest.

She nods and her face softens. 'You got money?' She pulls her draped shawl across her nightgown, shielding herself from the evening chill. It's a deep burgundy.

'That hue's pretty next to your hair,' I say.

Don't mean to confuse her. See it on her face, though. Her lips curl at the compliment, but not quite into a smile. Door's open just enough for her to fill the doorframe and to stop me from entering. She's not yet decided if she'll let us in.

'Anyone else with you?'

She's looking over me shoulder and out into the darkness.

'No.' I look down at Mrs Lapointe's feet. They're in well-worn slippers. No doubt threadbare from years of tending to the needs of her guests. There's an honesty about her, or perhaps me lateness has caught her off-guard and she's revealing more than she usually would. I like her immediately, though, almost as much as I wish she could see inside me head and understand that I'd not be here if I had any other option.

Seconds pass with neither of us talking. I glance up and she's looking from me to Nora. Me daughter's pulled me shawl from her, all curious and not wanting to miss out on meeting some new folk. She's still nuzzled into me neck, but she unclasps and then clasps her hand. A tiny wave.

'Hello, you.' Mrs Lapointe's eyes meet Nora's and her face transforms. She reaches over. Strokes me daughter's face. There's gentleness in her touch. Can I trust her?

'She's ten months and no bother.' I jiggle Nora on me hip. Praying she won't start squawking again.

'This is a nice establishment. I cater for a nice clientele.' The door behind her opens a little more. The hallway's gloomy. The stink of stale tobacco and damp escape.

'I can't do this,' I murmur. Me eyes are full of tears. Fighting a battle with meself and this overwhelming urge to flee. Everything's overwhelming. Everything's threatening to engulf me in a suffocating fog. She doesn't hear me, though.

'No loose morals and no—'

Nora needs to be safe. Nora needs to be safe.

'Me husband died last year. In a war.' Me voice is barely over a whisper, fearful that any louder might betray the desperation in me heart. A war? What war? Why am I talking about a war? 'Nora's lost her daddy, but she isn't no bother.'

Mrs Lapointe hesitates. A beat. I hold me breath.

'And you've money to pay for staying here?' she asks, and I nod.

She steps back inside, opening the door wide and allowing us entry. I cross the threshold. Me footsteps echo in the dimly lit hallway. Wallpaper's peeling, floorboards creak under me feet, yet there's a warmth to this place. I know better than to presume we're safe though. Me eyes jump about. Checking. It's a routine; a necessity, too. Always looking. In the shadows and every hidden corner. A flickering light from a single oil lamp casts outlines on a ragged rug; its once vibrant colours are now faded with time.

Scents of stale air, tobacco and dampness mingle with the stench of Nora's diaper and me. Perhaps that's acceptance, of sorts, but I've no idea which of us is worse. I shiver. Me clothes, soaked from the rain, cling to me quivering body. That's when Nora squirms in me arms, her face scrunching up as she lets out a soft cry.

'I'm sorry, I just ... I need a moment.' Me voice is a whisper. It trembles slightly as I struggle to grasp at composure. There are too many possible dangers. Don't know where to look first. I don't know where best to stand in the room. 'Can we ... can we please leave?'

'Leave?' She's confused.

'Don't feel safe here,' I whisper. Me eyes dart nervously around the room. Searching for the best way to be escaping.

Her gaze softens. Maybe she sees me distress.

'Now, now. This way.'

She guides us into a small parlour. A few mismatched armchairs have been moved to huddle around a dying fire. She gestures for me to sit on one of them.

'Let's get you both warm and dry,' she says. Her voice is somehow both strict and compassionate. 'Sit.'

I hesitate and she waits. A safe distance between us. I settle into the chair nearest the door. Bag touches me feet. Mrs Lapointe leaves the room and I rub me shoulder. The relief. Nora's now wide awake and stiff as an upright plank on me knee. I bounce me thighs and she giggles. A new game. I kiss her neck and she wriggles and giggles with the tickle.

Mrs Lapointe returns with fresh linens and a basin of warm water.

'You doing well?'

'I'm fine now,' I say. 'Sorry for fussing.' I force a shaky smile despite the knot of fear squeezing in me.

'Shall we?' She nods towards Nora before laying out a piece of muslin cloth. It's worn but clean. The dim room barely glows from the faint light of a single candle.

Removing her wet clothes, I hold little Nora over the basin. She wiggles and fidgets. I soothe me daughter. Whisper little comforts to her. Mrs Lapointe dunks the cloth in warm water and wipes away the mess.

'Taking care of her must be difficult on your own,' she says, and I nod. 'She's beautiful,' she says and any barriers between us crumble.

Nora giggles in delight. A shared sense of camaraderie and some unspoken understanding. Maybe she's a mama, too.

'Mrs Lapointe?'

I turn to the doorway. A different woman stands there. She's wearing an ivory nightgown, too; I've woken someone else. Not the best introduction. She's old like Mrs Lapointe; wrinkles etch into her skin. Perhaps her hair was vibrant once but now it's a faded grey and frizzy. Wild. Like a Medusa without snakes.

'I'm sorry. Didn't mean to be waking everyone.' Me voice is tinged with guilt and shame. Now I'm crying even though I don't want to be crying. Can't control me emotions. Is this fear or relief?

'It's not a problem,' she says. The unsteady light from her oil lamp dances on her features. She looks mad. 'Better you wake us than spend the night out there alone. I'd be furious if you did that.' She's smiling now. Maybe something's flicked in her head and she's changed how she was feeling about us. I like how she looks now. Hope that she's as kind as she seems.

'She has money to pay, Mrs Taylor,' Mrs Lapointe says, as I wrap Nora in a clean cloth. 'Didn't expect there to be a baby, though.'

'You read our advertisement?' Mrs Taylor asks me.

I nod me head and she claps her hands with delight. Twirls and bounces on the spot. It's unexpected. I jump from me belly, but her joy's contagious. We're all laughing along.

'Shush.' Mrs Lapointe points to the ceiling. 'The women need their sleep.'

'Women?' I ask.

'Women like you,' Mrs Taylor says. 'We've all had our fair share of tragedy.' She moves closer to us.

Mrs Lapointe lowers her head and whispers, 'Amen.'

Nora giggles again. I hold me breath, but there's no need. The two women laugh at me daughter's timing. Mrs Taylor winks at me. This woman has the disposition of someone unfamiliar. She's not normal and doesn't want to be. I don't want to, but I love her already. I grab Mama's gold cross on a chain and fiddle with it between me trembling fingers.

Mrs Lapointe spots it straightaway.

'Me husband, God rest his soul, would like that his little Nora's being raised amongst God-fearing folk.' Me voice is barely audible.

Mrs Lapointe blinks rapidly, her expression solemn. 'How long's it been?'

I nearly say three years, the first number that jumps in me head. Then I remember Nora's age and that the maths won't work out.

'He never got to meet her.' Vague but still with a punch of heart.

I look at Nora, and she cries on cue. Me daughter knows our script.

'Poor lamb.' Mrs Lapointe reaches out her arms and Nora plays along. She's already at ease here; is it wrong to be envying a baby? She lets herself be held, even cuddles into the stranger.

I watch them, already friends, as our host walks around her parlour and hums a tune to me daughter. I wish I were more like Nora. She navigates this interaction with ease. How she's being doesn't match me own sense of isolation and fear. Those feelings make me quiver from me belly to me lips. Can't focus on that, though. I think about how the fading floral wallpaper holds the whispers of many long-forgotten stories instead. Each groan from a floorboard tells its tale of the weary travellers and desperate souls who sheltered here. Are their hopes and dreams interwoven in this place? Will mine and me Nora's be, too? I want to add me story to the ones that remain, but I can't. Not yet. Instead, I watch me daughter at home and safe with the ghosts of those lost souls. She'd know if this were a bad place, wouldn't she?

'And you even brought the advertisement with you.' Mrs Taylor points at the wet piece of paper on top of me bag, then turns to Mrs Lapointe. 'See. The listing worked.' She's beaming with delight. The wind rattles the windowpanes in response. The flickering flames in the hearth add a comforting light on the furniture. All the women, all the fixtures and all the furniture in this room are mismatched and muted with age, but they still work together. I want to belong here, too.

Mrs Lapointe shawls Nora in a clean blanket and the warmth from the fire seeps into me cold bones. She hands her back to me with a nod. 'Let me show you both to your room,' she says and, for the first time since I fled me old life, I feel a flash of hope.

'For you, it'll be two dollars a week. No male visitors and curfew's nine o'clock.' She coos at Nora and points to the door. 'Let's not dilly-dally,' she says, looking over her shoulder as she leaves the room.

I pick up our bag. All our worldly belongings. I've enough to pay for two weeks.

'That it?' Mrs Taylor glances around the room for the rest of our stuff.

'Always ready to be leaving quick,' I say, forcing a shaky smile. Mrs Taylor nods her agreement, but her eyes are quick. She knows.

'And your … dead husband?'

'I wish he was dead. Does that count? We'll move every time he finds us.' I don't voice the horror of it all, but me body knows. I'm rooted to the spot and there's a quiver at the end of the words.

'Are you well?' she says, taking a step towards me.

I hold up me shaking palm. Can't have her any closer. Can't be touched. 'Just need to breathe.' Me hands are trembling as I attempt to steady me ragged breaths. Me chest's that tight I think it might crack open.

'I'm Mrs Taylor.' She holds out a hand for me to shake.

'Miss Hamilton. Tilda, to me friends,' I say, but I don't reach out me hand in return.

Annie's Diary

18th January 1901

It's an anniversary I wish I could not recall. Little Nora arriving just now feels punishing. Or perhaps I'm the cruel one. There was a moment when I hoped Mrs Lapointe would turn her away, back into the rain.

That's not what we do, though. Not what I do. We collect the lost here.

Still, another year has passed without my son ageing. I won't voice that pain. I can't speak his name out loud. It's as if to call him by his name would bring that sorrow barging into the room. Unwelcome energy that would drag all positivity and joy from those present. I can talk about Samuel – in so much that Mrs Lapointe knows of my husband's existence – but I cannot tell her about my boy.

That denial is where my shame resides. It haunts me, just as he does, too. Still, to speak the words and to tell someone about him would be to acknowledge the loss all over again. I would be giving information that could be dropped into conversation without warning. That could knock me from my feet.

Thus, in concealing both his existence and my truth, my son remains in an intangible place. David is both mine and he does not exist. I deny him, and in that he has died a million deaths that only I can grieve. It's not that I don't want to remember him; rather that I can't ever forget.

Annie

23rd January 1901

I push my fingernail into a slit between the planks of the tabletop. The kitchen hums with the quiet activity of its inhabitants, the aroma of brewed coffee mingles with the scent of a hearty stew simmering. I like these mornings best – an informal gathering with the women.

'Here you go.' Sarah places a cup of coffee next to me.

Mismatched pots and pans hang from hooks above the stove, their well-worn surfaces testament to years of faithful service. On the wooden table, chipped cups and mismatched crockery await use. Each piece bears its own tale of past meals shared and conversations exchanged from others passing through. We are all temporarily here. Our humble surroundings are honest. There's no pretending to be anything other than who we really are – abandoned women with no place to plant our roots. Still, there's a sense of warmth and camaraderie in the air, as if the very walls of the room embrace and welcome who we are. Outside, the wind howls, sending flurries of snow dancing against the windowpanes, but inside, we're cocooned in a haven of comfort and companionship. On mornings like this, I want to stay here forever.

Olive clears her throat. I look up. She's a petite teenager with curls cascading down her back and framing a heart-shaped face that's dotted with freckles.

'Mrs Lapointe told Mother that you're going to close down,' she says. She rubs her fingertips against her sleeve.

'Shush,' her mother, Sarah, says, nipping at Olive's bicep and sitting down next to her.

I shake my head, partly out of annoyance that Mrs Lapointe's been sharing our woes with the women boarding here. They've enough on their minds without worrying about us abandoning them too. There are four of us sitting around the table, waiting for the stew to be cooked. Each of us has our own burden to bear, but we're bound together by the shared journey that's brought us here. I wrap my hands around the steaming mug of coffee.

To my left is Edith, who stares at me expectedly, her face etched with lines of weariness earned through years of hard work in the fields. 'Closing down.' She says the words as if to help absorb them. Still, her eyes hold a quiet strength, a resilience born of countless struggles and setbacks. I can read the weight of her worries drawn in the furrow of her brow, but there's a glimmer of hope too. I recognise it. A belief that perhaps here, in this new land, she can find the peace she's been seeking.

Olive widens her eyes, urging Edith to comment. Olive and Sarah have been staying here two weeks so far. They've only been able to pay for three days, but Mrs Lapointe won't have any of them back out on the streets.

'I didn't make it up.'

'Olive!' Her mother says her name quickly and in a thin voice. Sarah's gaze is sharp and defiant, despite the weariness that lurks beneath the surface. She's just past thirty and has already faced more than her fair share of hardship. Within an hour of turning up on the doorstep, she'd told me all she'd been through and how she'd refused to be broken by any of it. She said it all in a hurry. The words gushed like they were falling. There's a fire within her — a determination to carve out a better life for herself and her daughter — and I admire her fierce spirit. She had Olive when she was sixteen, and they're more like bickering siblings than mother and daughter.

'Did you hear me?' Olive says. Her wide eyes are filled with a mixture of fear and curiosity. It's fair to say that she's been thrust into this journey against her will, torn from the familiar comforts of home and shoved into the unknown. But despite her trepidation, there's a spark of resilience within her – a determination to face whatever challenges lie ahead with courage and grace. We're kindred spirits, but I won't be telling her that.

I breathe in through my mouth, feeling the air rushing past my teeth. 'Listen here, folks,' I say, my voice ringing with conviction. 'We've faced our fair share of trials, but by the stars above, we're not going down without a fight.'

Edith raises an eyebrow, a hint of scepticism in her expression. 'And just what fight d'you suggest we pick?'

I meet her gaze head-on, unwavering, before lifting my cup to take a sip of coffee. 'The fight for our freedom. The fight to carve out a future that's ours and not dictated by anyone else.' Edith's calloused hands fidget with the hem of her apron. It's a habit born from years of practical work and a slight nervousness in social settings.

Sarah snorts derisively. 'And how d'you propose we do that, Mrs Taylor? Last I checked, we're just a ragtag bunch of women with nothing but the shirts on our backs.'

A smirk plays at the corners of my lips. Coffee cup back on its saucer, I recline in my chair and cross my arms defiantly. 'Oh, ye of little faith, Sarah. Haven't you heard? Fortune favours the bold.'

'But what can we do?' Olive says, her voice tentative. She twirls a lock of her chestnut curls around her finger absentmindedly, a habitual gesture that reflects her thoughtful nature. 'We're just ... lost.'

I shake my head and I'm sure a fiery glint ignites in my eyes. 'Lost, maybe. But not defeated. We're pioneers, carving our place in a world that's only just realising the power of a determined woman.' I pause. 'We'll find our way. Together. A revolution.' I punch the air and the three women laugh in unison. 'We'll forge a path through the darkness, one step at a time, until we stand tall in the light of our own making.' I'm on my feet, punctuating the words with hand movements.

The room falls silent. Sarah gently tucks a loose strand of hair behind her ear. I think I might be able to measure the weight of my words hanging heavy in the air. Still I watch them. I look from face to face. No one speaks.

A cough. We turn to the open doorway.

'Tilda, come in, come in.' I spin my empty chair towards the newcomer. It's the first time she's been brave enough to venture into one of our communal areas. 'Come sit with us. This is Olive, Sarah, Edith… They're boarders, like you.' I point at each of the women. Matilda nods, but she's not moving from the doorway and her eyes stay fixed on her shoes. She's been wearing the same outfit for five days now. I think she might be holding her breath.

'You've got a baby.' It's a statement from Olive.

Tilda exhales, allowing the air to pass out through her nostrils, and she nods her head again.

'Think she might be the most beautiful baby I've ever seen,' Olive says, and I watch as Tilda's entire face brightens. She lifts her eyes to Olive, holds her head high, and her smile's so wide it alters her entire face.

'You're just in time.' I can't help but interject with a mischievous grin. 'We're about to discuss our grand plans to take on the world. You've come to join our very own female riot, haven't you?'

Tilda's cheeks flush pink, but a glimmer of curiosity sparkles in her eyes. I think we all might be holding our collective breath as she tentatively steps further into the room. I gesture for her to take a seat at the table.

'Come, sit with us. You're among friends here,' I say, my tone light but I can't hide my excitement. She was bolder when she knocked on the boarding house door. Her determination was set on keeping Nora safe. I imagine that's exhausted her. Now, that task removed, she's a scared stray who's been observing her surroundings for five days now. I watch as her gaze flickers between each of us, uncertainty giving way to a tentative smile. As she sits on the edge of the chair, her posture straightens and, for the briefest moment, the weight of her worries seems to sink to the floor. Could it be that they're replaced by a sense of belonging among kindred spirits? That's perhaps too much to wish for just yet.

'And don't worry,' I add with a wink, 'we'll make sure to include your little one in all our schemes. After all, even revolutions need a touch of sweetness now and then.'

Tilda lets out a hearty giggle, her tired eyes brightening with amusement, as she settles into her seat.

Annie

23rd January 1901

Hours later, and the other rooms in this boarding house are calm and empty. Not the kitchen, though. As the sun began its descent, the women gathered here once more. This time they've got bowls of food in front of them. The room vibrates with talk, candles, and female voices. The rich aroma of beef, onions, and carrots fills the space, mingling with the warmth of the crackling fireplace. We're safe in here.

'Will you tell us another one of your tales, Mrs Taylor?' Olive's voice breaks the lively chatter. She pokes her finger in melted candle wax and flicks it at Sarah, who dodges with a laugh.

I chuckle. 'A tale?' I repeat, feigning surprise. 'Why, of course.' I look at Matilda. 'But I must warn you. Once I start spinning a yarn, there's no telling where it might lead.'

Sarah leans back in her chair, a knowing smirk playing at the corners of her lips. 'She's the best storyteller around, Tilda. You won't want to miss this.'

'Oh, don't oversell me,' I say with a grin, standing up from my seat. 'How about the story of a servant who outsmarted a band of thieves with nothing but her wits and a humble jar?' I suggest, my voice dropping to a conspiratorial whisper.

Edith raises an eyebrow, curiosity gleaming in her tired eyes as she takes a bite of her stew. 'And who might this clever lass be?'

I twirl on the spot and then curtsy before them. I'm sure my eyes must gleam with mischief. 'None other than Morgiana, the heroine of a tale as old as time itself. They say she outwitted forty thieves and saved her master's life without popping a bead of perspiration.' I swipe at my forehead with my hand, pretending to wipe away sweat.

'Sounds like a tall tale if you ask me. What could a mere servant possibly know about outsmarting hardened criminals?' Edith exhales as if she doesn't have time for my nonsense.

I chuckle. 'Never underestimate a woman,' I say. 'Morgiana may have been a simple girl, but she had a sharp mind and a fiery spirit. She knew how to use what she had to get what she wanted, whether it was a clever disguise or a well-timed distraction.'

Tilda leans in, her eyes wide with wonder as she absentmindedly stirs her bowl of stew. 'But how did she do it? How did Morgiana outsmart the thieves?'

I take a step towards her, crouching to the floor. I hope she can see the twinkle of amusement in my eyes. 'Ah, now, that's the question, isn't it?' I pause, and Tilda nods enthusiastically. 'But I'm afraid I've a date with Mrs Lapointe and her blasted ledger.'

Their groans of protest combine. I laugh. 'You'll have to wait for another day to hear the full tale.' I hold up my palm to silence further protestations. 'Suffice it to say, Morgiana's story is one of cunning, bravery, and a healthy dose of wit. Just like ours, wouldn't you say?'

'Oh, come on, give us a little more!' Olive pleads, tossing a piece of bread crust at me, which I deftly catch and toss back. It hits her square on the nose. The room erupts in laughter.

Unexpectedly, Edith starts humming a tune. We all turn to her. I recognise it instantly – 'In the Good Old Summertime' – and soon the whole room joins in. Sarah stands and pulls Olive to her feet, and they dance. Their movements are entirely uncoordinated, but they're light and carefree.

'Look at them go!' Edith breaks off singing, her face bright with a rare smile.

'Keep your back straight, Sarah, and let your feet glide,' I instruct, standing to demonstrate a graceful waltz. Olive mimics my movements, her face lighting up with joy as she follows my lead.

Tilda joins the circle shyly, her eyes sparkling with delight as Olive twirls her around.

'That's it, Tilda! One, two, three, one, two, three,' I chant, ensuring everyone keeps the rhythm.

Urgent footsteps echo along the hallway. I exchange a puzzled glance with the ladies, and they freeze mid-dance as Mrs Lapointe rushes into the room. She's breathless, her face flushed.

'Have you heard the news?' She coughs violently, her frail frame trembling with the effort as she struggles to catch her breath.

My heart quickens with anticipation. 'What news?'

'It's Queen Victoria,' she announces, her voice trembling with emotion. Her breathing's laboured, each intake of air a struggle, and the rasping wheeze constant. 'She's passed away.'

A gasp escapes my lips, and I feel Tilda's hand reach out to grasp mine. The news spreads like wildfire through the room, stirring a whirlwind of disbelief and sorrow among us all.

Mrs Lapointe seems to crumple into herself. 'This is momentous,' she murmurs, her face sliding into sadness. 'She was a remarkable monarch.'

I nod in solemn agreement. 'Her passing marks the end of an era,' I say. The weight of the news settles heavily upon my shoulders. 'The world is changing before our very eyes.'

Mrs Lapointe sighs, her gaze distant. 'A symbol of strength for women everywhere, ruling with grace in a man's world. It's hard to imagine what comes next.'

I squeeze her hand gently. 'We've lost more than a queen; we've lost a beacon of possibility. But we can't let that light fade.' I pause, watching as the women consider my words. Sarah bobs her head in agreement. 'We'll carry it forward in our own ways, showing the world that women can lead, endure, and inspire.'

'Do you think we can? Be as strong as she was?' Matilda's eyes are filled with a mix of sorrow and determination.

I look at her, then at the other women gathered around the table. 'We already are. We face struggles and rise above them every day. We might not wear crowns or sit on thrones…' I pat my head as if to check there's still no crown there. 'But our resilience, our courage – it's what keeps us going.'

'Belief in ourselves and each other,' Olive says. She straightens up and I clap my hands together.

Sarah wipes a tear from her cheek and nods. 'If Queen Victoria could rule an empire, we can surely find ways to keep this boarding house alive and well.'

'Exactly,' I say, feeling a renewed sense of purpose. 'Her legacy lives on in us, in every woman who refuses to be defeated by circumstance.'

Edith stands a bit taller, the weariness in her eyes replaced with a spark of resolve. 'For our future, and for those who come after us.' She raises her cup of water to the ceiling.

The wind howls outside, but within these walls, a fire burns brightly – one that Queen Victoria herself would have admired.

Bay City Boarding House,
Bay City.
January 24th 1901

Dear Mother,

I pray this letter finds you well.

I recently arrived at a temporary shelter with two kind women, Mrs Lapointe and Mrs Taylor. They took to Nora immediately and welcomed us into their home. Their strength gave me the courage to write to you.

I see now how much family means. I want to mend things between us, woman to woman, mother to mother.

I ask for your understanding and forgiveness. Most of all, I need safety from the man who hurt me. Having Nora made me realise how much I need you. I want her to feel the love and safety that only you can give.

Please, Mother, let us come home. Let us mend our family and heal together.

With love and hope, your daughter,
Matilda

Annie

1st February 1901

I walk into the parlour, a glass of water in one hand, a book in the other. The familiar scents of Mrs Lapointe's morning porridge, butter tarts and the promise of another evening stew waft through the boarding house. Perhaps that's what home smells like now.

'More butter tarts later,' I say. Patting my stomach with my book.

The floorboards whisper beneath my weight. Today, the oil lamp casts a warm glow across those well-loved armchairs. By my definition, it's homely; it's cosy, too. Olive was truly excited, telling me about selling butter tarts to our neighbours. I've sampled three already. Everything looks and feels positive today. With my book and a glass of water, I head for the comfiest chair – unusually not occupied by Mrs Lapointe.

'Hello?' I spin on the spot, scanning the room.

I didn't imagine the noise. The howl is more like a wounded animal than a human. Can't see anyone, though. My movement is stealth. I place my water and book on the table. I'm holding my breath, but my hand forms into a fist. I'm ready to pounce. A sob. Then another, and another. Cautiously, I take a couple of steps in the direction of the sound. Slowly, slowly. Kneeling on the sofa, I peer over its back. Tilda. She's weeping. I study her. She's hunched on the floor behind the chair. Her head is bowed and her elbows rest on her knees. Glossy tendrils of hair frame her face.

'Why are you hiding down there?'

She freezes – as stiff as a statue at my words – but then her slender shoulders begin to shake.

'And what are you wearing?' She's clothed in a calico dress that's at least four sizes too big, the faded material swamping her.

'Found it … in … the lost property … box,' she stutters between sobs.

'We can do better than that,' I say. Mrs Lapointe has chests of wonderful clothes, but that's perhaps a discussion for a different time. Now, Tilda's appearing younger, and smaller, too.

'Do you want a drink?' I pass her my glass of water. She gulps it down.

'Tilda.' My voice is soft, but she refuses to look up. She places the empty glass next to her on the floor. 'Where's Nora?'

I stand from the sofa. My steps echo as I move to sit down beside her on the floor; my black woollen skirt snags on a protruding nail. Every movement is amplified. I think we're both holding our breaths now.

'Where is she?' My voice remains firm and steady, a mask of strength concealing the fear bubbling from my abdomen and shooting up my torso. Perspiration prickles and drips down my neck. Something feels wrong. I need to know her baby is well.

She wipes her eyes with the back of her hand, her cheeks flushing. A mix of embarrassment and frustration, perhaps. She looks up at me. She blinks. 'Mrs Lapointe's taken her for a walk.'

'Thank God in the heavens.' The tension releases from my shoulders like a weight lifted. My body slumps back against the wall.

'Did you think…' A pause.

Did I think Nora had died? That something horrific had happened to the baby? Yes, I did think that. I don't voice that, though. Instead, I'm staring and trying to figure out why she's hiding. I imagine Matilda is confused by my reaction, too. She doesn't know my history; none of the women here do. Outside the wind gathers in the trees. We hear the branches rattling at the window's glass as if knocking to come inside. I dig my fingernails into my palms. Five, four, three, two—

I breathe in, then out. Again, and again. 'So why are we hiding down here?'

'Did the post come today?' Tilda's voice is somehow heavy. She stares at me, her mouth slightly open and her eyes – dark, tear-filled and with impossibly long lashes – plead for a positive response. I want to lie and say yes. I'm overwhelmed with a need to take away her pain. Can a voice be weighed down by unshed tears and disappointment?

Instead, I shake my head, my heart aching for her. I understand, but more important is how much I already care. 'No, dear, no letter for you.'

Her face crumples, the rejection hitting her once more. 'Wrote to me mother eight days ago. Begged her to let us come home.' She fidgets with the lost property dress. 'But … she's not … she's not replied.'

I reach over and she pulls her hand away. Still, I grasp it. Cover it with both of mine. She's trembling. I count to ten and hear a shift in how she's breathing. The weight of my hands calms her slightly. 'Don't dwell on what you can't control.'

She looks at me; her eyes are red and puffy. I think she's been crying here for hours. 'I … I don't want to be no burden.'

A wave of affection hits me. She's so very young and yet truly brave. Her shame's compounded. She shouldn't be weighed down by worry about burdening others with her grief. How does it feel, not to have to present a false front? To be a truthful version of yourself? To know that others love you despite your seeming flaws? She won't know those answers. I want to show her.

'What's bothering you?'

'Two dollars a week.'

'To stay here?' I ask, and she nods. I hesitate. 'Is that a problem?'

'Only had enough to be paying for two weeks.' Her entire body's trembling now.

'And that two weeks is nearly over?' I ask and she nods again. She sobs again, too.

'I don't want to be a burden.' The second time she's said that.

'You're not,' I say, but I've paused while observing her and thinking how she's repeated herself. I've hesitated. She spots it, pulls her hand out from between mine, and nods. *Go on*, she's saying. I see that flicker of courage I know she possesses. Still, I watch as she pinches the fabric of someone else's dress into ridges.

'Perhaps you might feel better about living here if you had a role. Some chores to keep you occupied and to earn your room and board?'

'Really?' She wipes her nose on her hand. I begin to protest, patting my sleeves for a handkerchief, but stop myself as a smile tugs at the corner of her mouth. 'I could help with the cleaning ... and maybe with the cooking?'

'That sounds perfect.' I reach over and give her hand a comforting squeeze. I'm grateful for the break in the sad atmosphere. 'It's what Edith, Olive and Sarah do. They pay to stay here by helping. Mrs Lapointe appreciates that, and it'll make you feel more a part of things.'

'Hello?' On cue, it's Mrs Lapointe. I stand, reaching my hand down for Tilda's. She stands, too, and we move from behind the sofa.

'Are we playing hide-and-seek?' Mrs Lapointe asks from the doorway.

I laugh but the sound isn't convincing. Holding Tilda's hand, I guide us both to sit on the sofa. Mrs Lapointe walks towards us. Her figure's slightly hunched and her movements are slow and laboured. She's exhausted herself walking with Nora. Despite her attempts to hide it, the pallor of illness clings to her like a shroud now. With each step, it casts a shadow over her once vibrant demeanour. There's hesitation as we both observe Mrs Lapointe collapsing into her armchair. Tilda and I exchange a nod, a downward glance, too. She sees what I see.

'I'll make a start with the cleaning up from breakfast. Thank you. I love you,' Tilda says, the words rushing out, and she blushes instantly. She didn't mean to declare her love. I can't help but smile at her excitement.

'And what are you two plotting?' Mrs Lapointe asks. Her voice is hoarse with fatigue. She wipes her nose on her sleeve, as if to pull out her handkerchief would be too laborious.

'Not your sleeve.' I raise my palm to protest and Tilda giggles. Still, Mrs Lapointe's symptoms grow increasingly pronounced with each day – the slight tremor in her hands, the hollow look in her eyes. There's a flicker of determination there, too, though, a spark of resilience that refuses to be extinguished. She pulls her white handkerchief from her sleeve and waves it weakly in surrender.

'I'll brush the floor in here … and then make your beds?' Matilda looks from me to Mrs Lapointe. She's practically bouncing on the spot. She's ready. She wants a change right now. She wants to contribute immediately.

Mrs Lapointe raises an eyebrow – *another one*? – and I nod. I mouth, *I'm sorry,* but she bats the words away. She already cares for Matilda, and Nora, too. After losing her own family to illness and hardship, Mrs Lapointe vowed to create a haven here for those in need. She's got a compassionate heart, giving others a chance to rebuild their lives. That support gave me the strength to keep fighting, to keep hoping. I want that for Tilda, too. Still, Mrs Lapointe's more aware than I am that without financial stability, this sanctuary cannot survive. I really must discuss this with her further, though. Money's already tight and two extra mouths to feed is a concern. I'll figure out a way to pay for Matilda and Nora. It's important that they feel safe.

'That sounds perfect.' I reach over to give Tilda's hand a comforting squeeze. 'You're very welcome here.' Her relief dances on the breath she exhales.

'Wonderful news. Little Nora is the ideal houseguest,' Mrs Lapointe says. She smiles and Tilda claps with excitement.

Perhaps my eyes ask *Where is Nora?*

'In her cot,' is the response.

I turn to see Edith, Olive, and Sarah standing in the doorway. Sarah's waving a piece of paper so enthusiastically that it's on the verge of flying away from her.

'What have you got there?' I ask. I'm smiling. Sarah's infectious excitement travelled across the room and covered me instantly.

'A new list of potential jobs for us women,' Sarah says, her face a mix of curiosity and determination as she steps into the parlour. She carries herself with grace; her posture has become increasingly upright and confident during her time here. 'We included you, too, Tilda.'

I turn and see Tilda's beaming smile, and fight back tears. 'Tell me your plan,' I say, with a nod of acknowledgement and a breath to ground my emotions.

'I can help with the sewing! I've been practising my stitching, and I'm sure I could learn quickly,' Olive, ever eager to contribute, chimes in. She plonks herself on the floor, chin cupped in her hands.

Sarah smiles proudly at her daughter's enthusiasm. 'And I could assist with more baking,' she offers. Her hair falls in soft waves around her face, framing expressive hazel eyes that reflect both kindness and wisdom beyond her years. 'We could sell other homemade goods like bread, pies, and preserves to the visitors. Folk appreciate a taste of home when they're travelling.'

'Olive and I could offer our sewing services to the local community,' Mrs Lapointe says. Her fingers trace the delicate lace edging of her handkerchief, but she's looking at Olive, who smiles with delight.

Edith nods thoughtfully. Her features might be weathered from years of outdoor labour, but she's got strong cheekbones and a determined jawline. I think many would consider her handsome. 'I could help with the laundry services,' she suggests. 'We want guests to stay for an extended period, and they'll need someone to wash their clothes.'

A way to balance the books without compromising on these women's – on all of our – safety and ambition. I'm proud of these women.

'And they'll be paying actual dollars to stay here,' I add, glancing at Mrs Lapointe. She laughs and waves her hand at me, as if batting away my silliness.

As our boarders continue to share their ideas, they move into the parlour and form a messy semi-circle on the floor with Olive. Sarah's gaze drifts to the lace curtains billowing gently in the breeze. She nibbles at the skin around her thumbnail. She's got something to say; she hesitates.

'What is it?' I ask and I'm convinced there's a collective intake of breath.

A pause, a beat. 'But we won't stay here forever,' she says softly. 'We've been here for some time now, and we're becoming…'

'Too safe?'

Sarah nods and I shift forward in my seat, leaning to place a reassuring hand on her shoulder.

'I think we've healed enough,' she says gently.

'To take the next leg of your journey?' I say.

Sarah bobs her head in agreement, her expression a mixture of determination and apprehension. 'It's time.' She pats my hand with her own. 'It's just daunting… Starting over again.'

Olive shuffles her rear across the floorboards to be closer to her mother. She reaches out to squeeze Sarah's spare hand. Her eyes are the brightest shade of blue, sparkling with youthful exuberance. 'We'll make it work, Mom. We always do,' she says with a reassuring smile. 'But can we stay here a few more weeks to help them out?'

'I hate that you're leaving when I've only just found you all… I have cleaning to do.' Tilda jumps from the sofa. 'Need to get to it before me Nora wakes from her nap.' She swipes her fingers at her tears discreetly, but we all see.

I watch her leave, though, shoulders straighter than they've been since she arrived here. There's a hint of purpose emerging already. I grip the sofa as I stand. My knees creak in protest. The branches tap the panes in response. Perhaps they're communicating in a code I've not yet figured out. Still, Bay City air creeps in through the drafty windows. Some days, the comforting familiarity of this boarding house wraps around me like a well-worn shawl. I know Olive, Sarah and Edith feel the same. I want that for Matilda and Nora, too.

'We'll stay a little longer,' Sarah says.

A stabbing pain in my belly and I double over, pushing the area with my sweaty palm. What? Why? But I know the answer. I used to scowl at the thought of female friendships. I feared they demanded a mastery of a language I didn't understand. That I wasn't quite woman enough. I was entirely wrong. I'm being wrapped in affection. I hate that I feel love for these women. That's not what I do. That's not part of my plan. I keep people at a distance. That's how I cope. To let them close, to love them – that's the path to pain. That's not what I want.

'You're strong. Stronger than you know,' I say. Loud and in the direction of the doorway. Perhaps the words are for Tilda, possibly they're for me.

'Amen to that,' Mrs Lapointe says.

Annie

2nd February 1901

The following evening, as the sun dips below the horizon, the boarding house's hall is filled with the hesitant shuffles and mismatched steps of my would-be dancers.

'Be turtles, ladies,' I say. 'Think like turtles.'

A tinny rendition of a Strauss waltz crackles from the gramophone in the corner, its brass horn gleaming in the low light. Sarah focuses with a mix of determination and amusement, whereas Olive and Matilda giggle nervously as they struggle to keep up. Edith left today. Slipped away before breakfast. We all know, but none of us have mentioned it.

'Ladies, if your feet were any slower, we'd be moving backwards,' I quip, tapping my foot impatiently to the beat. 'Sarah, lift your chin. You're not a turtle retreating into its shell. Be a dancing turtle. And Olive, for heaven's sake, those feet belong to you. Control them.'

Olive blushes but grins, her eyes sparkling with the challenge. 'Yes, Mrs Taylor,' she replies, trying harder to match the rhythm.

'Tilda, a waltz is not a race. Slow and steady. Imagine you're gliding, not running from a bear,' I say, my tone sharp but playful.

Matilda stifles a laugh. 'I'll try, Mrs Taylor. But you've never seen a bear waltz.'

I smirk. 'You'd be surprised. I've seen strange things in my time. Now, from the top. One, two, three. One, two, three. Sarah, focus. Turtle. Turtle. Olive, keep those feet in line. Tilda, glide!'

As they move through the steps, any initial awkwardness begins to melt away. Laughter fills the room as Sarah stumbles, nearly taking Olive down with her.

'This was your job?' Tilda says. 'A dance teacher?'

'The best job I've had,' I say.

'Sarah, if you're going to fall, at least make it look graceful.' I help her back to her feet. 'Remember, I've danced through worse stumbles than this. Imagine doing a quadrille on a riverboat with Jesse James himself watching.'

The girls erupt in giggles, their faces glowing with enjoyment despite their clumsy attempts. In this moment, the world outside seems distant and unimportant. Here, now, in this room, we're simply women finding joy and strength in each other's company.

Mrs Lapointe walks down the stairs. 'Mrs Taylor, you've got these ladies looking like they might actually know what they're doing.' A hint of a smile plays on her lips. A sudden cough shakes her, and she grips the wooden bannister, pausing to catch her breath.

'Flattery will get you everywhere, Mrs Lapointe,' I reply with a wink. 'But I'll settle for getting them through this waltz without stepping on each other's toes.'

She chuckles softly, her laughter trailing into another cough. I walk over to her, concern etching my features. I grip her arm to help her descend the last few stairs. 'Would you care to join us and show these young ones how it's done? I remember you telling me about the dances you used to attend with your late husband.'

She smiles, her eyes brightening for a moment. 'Oh, those were the days. But I'm afraid my dancing shoes are well past their prime.' She takes a deep breath, the effort visible. 'I'm not as sprightly as I used to be.'

'Nonsense,' I say, taking her hand. I'm keen for us all to be moving and keeping warm. The temperature's dropped to freezing outside. 'Just one turn around the hall? For old times' sake?'

She hesitates, then shakes her head with a sad smile. 'Another time, dear. But thank you. It's lovely to see you all enjoying yourselves.'

I nod, giving her hand a reassuring squeeze. 'We'll hold you to that, Mrs Lapointe. Rest here, and watch our performance instead.'

Tilda and Olive pull an armchair from the parlour into the hallway and, as Mrs Lapointe settles into it, I turn back to the girls. 'All right, ladies, let's make her proud. One more time from the top. And remember, it's not just about the steps. It's about the spirit.' A pause, and then I swing my arms out theatrically. 'Let's dance!'

The music starts once more, its melody filling the hallway with elegance and charm. As we move through the waltz, I feel a spark of hope. Amidst the laughter and the missteps, there's a glimpse of the simplicity and joy they long for. For me, it mingles with the bittersweet reminder of time's relentless march.

As a child, thanks to my highly connected mother, I'd split my time between summer on a farm and winter in the town. Dancing joined those two worlds. Still, my father died when I was nine, and my mother when I was fifteen, leaving me to navigate the world alone. After my mother's death, I went to live with my aunt in the city. It was a transitory stop. The losses, the adventures, and the unyielding spirit that kept me moving forward defined me. I think of Samuel and the waltzes we shared before the war claimed him, of the countless towns I've drifted through, teaching others how to step in time, too. Now, though, perhaps I've found a different rhythm in this small community.

Well, I think, watching the women stumble through another waltz, if I can teach a farmer's daughter to dance in a cow pasture, I sure can teach this eclectic gathering to glide across our hallway.

Annie's Diary

3rd February 1901

For months now I've listened to boarders revealing their stories and I'm always hit with waves of awe and admiration. They're participating in the present. They're voicing their pain in the hope that they'll be both heard and healed. This new world, with its electric lights and the marvels of the wireless telegraph, changes so swiftly around us.

I won't reveal the darker side of me to the women who seek solace here. It's my duty, my role, to uplift and inspire, to weave tales that captivate and enchant. I'm a teacher, a performer; older, wiser. Yet, hidden from sight, and with each aspect of their life that's revealed, the shackles of my grief nip tighter. The freedoms they speak of, the societal changes they witness, serve only to remind me of the world my David will never see.

Truth is, I'll die and all trace of David's, of my son's, existence will pass with me.

My death will be his final death.

Annie

18th February 1901

There is something entirely comforting about the weight of a book as it sits pages down, with its cover face-up in my lap. This one's blue cover is worn, the pages softened by countless hands before mine. I found it amongst Mrs Lapointe's small collection of books last year and was surprised she had a collection of fairy tales amongst her novels. I asked where she'd acquired it but she said she had no idea, said that perhaps a former traveller had left it as they passed through. I look down, tracing the gold embossed title on the creased spine. *The Blue Fairy Book*.

'You've been reading that one for weeks now.'

I nod. I read Tilda three different stories from it last week. 'I like to dip in and out.'

Currently, she's cross-legged on the rug. Snow's prevented us from going out today. She's stopped asking about the post each day; seems she's entirely at home here now. Nora's flat on the floor in front of her, lying on her back and grabbing at her own tiny feet. Matilda hides behind her hands and then pops out. With each peeking, Nora's squeal of delight echoes through the parlour. The sound is catching, and I can't help but smile each time.

'Will you read us a story?' Tilda says, looking at me. 'Please. I'm too slow at reading. It's too hard for me.'

I shake my head, but I can't resist her eyes. They somehow hold both sorrow and joy. 'Which story?' I lean back in the armchair and smile.

'Any.' She lifts Nora onto her feet. Nora grips Matilda's fingers and giggles. 'Mother never read to me… It's a treat when you do.'

I hesitate, waiting to see if she'll react to speaking about her mother. She doesn't. I flip over the book and thumb through the pages.

'Come on, Mrs Taylor, don't keep your audience waiting.' Mrs Lapointe stands in the open doorway.

'Any requests?'

She shrugs, moving slowly. Her steps are like tiny, painful gasps.

'Let me help.' I stand quickly, but her scowl makes me freeze. My expression remains firm and steady, a mask of strength that conceals fear. I want us to talk about what's ailing her.

'I'm fine.' Her voice is fierce. End of topic. I move to a different armchair, letting her sit in the one nearest to the doorway.

'Are you ill?' Tilda asks, and Mrs Lapointe bats away the words with her hand. Tilda looks at me and I shrug; we're helpless, watching our friend's health decline.

'The one with the thieves?' Mrs Lapointe says. I see the relief as she slumps into the chair. She rubs at her neck.

I nod. I reach over to squeeze her hand, but she refuses eye contact. '*The Forty Thieves* it is.'

I find the story and clear my throat. 'In a town in Persia, there lived two brothers, one named Cassim, the other Ali Baba.' I follow the words with my finger.

'No, no,' Tilda says loudly, and Nora squawks in response. 'Start with the bit where they hide.' She's remembered the story from last week.

'You can't just skip to halfway through a story. Where's the fun in that?' I look over to Mrs Lapointe. She smiles and then flaps a hand to shoo my words away. 'Tough audience,' I say, shaking my head, and returning to the book. I move my finger through the words. 'Okay, so not this bit.' I clear my throat again, secretly enjoying the drama of the moment. I read in my head until I reach the requested opening point. 'So,' I say, 'to kill Ali Baba, the thieves buy nineteen mules, and thirty-eight leather jars. All empty except one, which is full of oil.' I pause for a moment, scanning my audience's faces to check they're following. They nod. 'Then the captain puts all of his thieving men in jars.'

'I can't even imagine what a leather jar might look like,' Tilda says.

'A jar,' I say. 'They're men in big jars. Like barrels.'

I look down at Tilda. She's clasping her hands together with a delighted grin. She radiates happiness, her mouth open a little in concentration. Nora sits in her lap. She's listening, too. 'But why barrels?'

'Reliable, solid and unexpected? Or rather, expected for oil?' I shrug. I don't know the answer, but sometimes it's the simplest explanations that work best. 'Are you sure you want me to go on? You've heard this story already.'

'Please keep reading,' Matilda says.

I return to the book.

'The captain stopped his mules in front of Ali Baba's house and told Ali Baba, "I am selling this oil at tomorrow's market. It is late and I require somewhere to stay."'

'So, the jars must be vast if they're big enough to have men inside them?' Tilda stands and positions her hand to measure where a jar might reach on her. 'Up to here maybe?' She points at her shoulder.

'I imagine they were scrunched inside. Can't have been comfortable,' I say and Tilda nods as she sits down. Nora giggles.

'Have we missed the part with Morgiana?' she asks. I shake my head and laugh. The reading is entirely chaotic.

I skip forward a few more lines. 'Though Ali Baba asked his servant Morgiana to prepare supper for his guest, she needed oil. As she approached the first jar, the robber inside spoke, "Is it time?"'

Tilda gasps and Nora's harsh cry breaks the spell. A foul odour hits my nostrils, too. I gag a little.

'I think she might need changing,' Matilda says.

Mrs Lapointe steadies herself on the armchair as she stands. 'I'll get some water.' She scoops Nora into her arms and wobbles to the doorway.

'But Morgiana went to the jar,' Tilda prompts, keen to get back to the story.

I don't mean to let out a hearty laugh or throw my head back with joy. 'We need to work on your storytelling,' I say. 'Don't spoil the ending when you've just started your tale.'

She grins mischievously. 'That's the good bit, though.'

'You really want me to skip all the interesting set-up and get right to the action, don't you?'

She nods enthusiastically and I laugh. 'An impatient little adventurer.' I pause. 'What if I changed it slightly? Gave Morgiana a central role?'

Tilda looks around the room, palms tracing the tabletop. She's smiling.

'What are you looking for?'

'A pencil,' she says. 'I want to write down what you say. In case I forget your story.'

'Listen closely and you'll retell it in a way that fits with your journey,' I say, and she bounces slightly in her seat. 'It should be a decision. We each decide which parts of our story we reveal.'

'Carry on.'

'Legend has it, their greatest treasure lay hidden in a cave, guarded by a secret phrase known only to the captain himself. "Open Sesame," he'd utter, and the mouth of the cave would swing wide, revealing mountains of gold and jewels beyond imagination.' I fling my arms out as I utter the command.

Matilda gasps.

'One day, fate intervened in the form of a servant named Morgiana.'

An audible gulp from Tilda. I can't help but chuckle softly in response.

'As luck would have it, Morgiana had stumbled upon the thieves' secret, overhearing the captain's magical phrase. With bravery in her heart and a plan in her mind, she thwarted the thieves' schemes, using her wits to outsmart them at every turn.'

'She used wits? Didn't you say it was a jar?'

I laugh again, but there's emotion that runs deeper than Tilda's mere words. It's the resilience in her steady gaze, the determination in her tone. Already, to me, she's more than just a lost soul seeking refuge, she's a survivor, and we're bound together by an unbreakable bond we've yet to identify. I hate that I'm already attached. This wasn't part of my plan. I shake my head to displace that thought.

'With courage burning in her heart and motivation only she could voice, Morgiana devised a plan to outwit the thieves and claim the treasure for herself.'

'For herself? All of it?' Tilda's confused by my heroine's motivation.

I shrug. 'Do all quests need to be selfless acts?'

'But...'

'But she sought more from life,' I say, picking up the story's pace. 'And so, armed with nothing but her wits and a humble jar, she set her mind to the task. She knew that sometimes the simplest of tools can wield the greatest power.'

Mrs Lapointe re-enters the room. Her expression is softened by a tender smile as she cradles a sleeping Nora against her chest.

'Is all well?' I whisper and she nods.

She moves with a gentle sway, rocking Nora in her embrace as if she's the most precious treasure in the world. Nora's small form nestles against Mrs Lapointe's shoulder, her rhythmic breathing a soothing melody that fills the room with a sense of tranquillity.

'She's happy here.' Tilda places her palm over her heart. 'We both are.'

Mrs Lapointe's eyes sparkle as she whispers to Nora, her words a tender lullaby that's already transported the child into a peaceful slumber.

'Tell me more,' Matilda says, eyes back on me, and Mrs Lapointe nods in encouragement.

'As she ventured into the depths of the thieves' den, Morgiana relied on the jar as her silent ally. With careful precision, she concealed herself within its depths, blending seamlessly with the stolen goods it held. It became her shield, her sanctuary amidst the chaos of the thieves' lair.'

'How can you tell all of this story from in here?' Matilda taps her forehead.

I shrug and continue. 'Through twists and turns, traps and snares, Morgiana navigated the treacherous maze of the thieves' hideout, her jar never once betraying her presence. She listened intently to their whispered schemes, observed their every move, all the while biding her time for the perfect moment to strike.'

'This Morgiana sounds like a man,' Mrs Lapointe whispers, but I ignore her.

'And strike she did, with a cunning born of desperation and determination. When the thieves least expected it, Morgiana emerged from her jar sanctuary, her eyes blazing with fierce resolve.'

'How, though?' Matilda asks. She's sitting on her knees now. Her back remains straight, and her hands bounce on her thighs.

'How what?'

'How did she, a woman, outmanoeuvre them? The men.' She tilts her head slightly, but her gaze is focused fully on my face. It's slightly unnerving.

I pause to think. How could she use a jar to outmanoeuvre men? 'Okay, spool back… She contorted her body to fit within the confined space and then maintained her balance as the jar shifted and rolled along the uneven terrain of the thieves' hideout.'

'It must have scared her,' Matilda says, and I shrug my shoulders. Would that be her first thought if the hero of our story were a man?

'With each twist and turn,' I continue, 'Morgiana adjusted her position within the jar. She shifted her weight to maintain stability and prevent herself from being jostled about.'

'I'd have been terrified,' Matilda continues. I hate that she's centring on fear. If I were in that jar would my focal point be fear, too? I'd hope not. I'd hope it would be on survival and my end ambition.

'She anticipated the movement of the jar, bracing herself against sudden shifts in direction,' I say, keen to steer the conversation back to my tale.

Tilda nods her head eagerly, likewise keen for me to continue.

'Despite the challenges posed by the narrow passages and treacherous obstacles, Morgiana remained resolute in her determination to navigate the maze-like layout of the thieves' hideout. With each twist and turn conquered, she drew closer to her goal, her faith in her own abilities unwavering.'

'Can't imagine how that'd feel,' Tilda says to herself, and I pause, waiting for her to return to the conversation. 'What next?'

'As the thieves gathered in their den, plotting their next heist, Morgiana slipped into the shadows, her jar in tow. Then, as the night wore on and the thieves revelled in their ill-gotten gains, Morgiana remained hidden, her breath shallow with anticipation. She listened intently to their whispered schemes, biding her time for the perfect moment to strike.'

'Perfect moment to strike,' she repeats.

'Then, when the thieves least expected it, Morgiana emerged from her jar sanctuary, her eyes blazing with fierce resolve.'

Tilda claps her hands together with the purest glee.

'And so, dear Tilda,' I say. 'What is the moral of this story?'

She shakes her head vigorously. 'Tell me. Please.' She leans forward eagerly, her eyes sparkling.

I laugh. 'That true greatness lies not in the grandeur of our tools, but in the strength of our resolve and the cunning of our minds.'

'I've no idea what that even means,' she says.

I chuckle. 'Well, that's fine. Sometimes stories are like desserts; you don't need to understand them fully to enjoy their taste.'

Mrs Lapointe lets out a soft laugh. 'Exactly, my dear. Life's mysteries are what make it interesting. Imagine how boring it would be if we understood everything right away.'

Matilda tilts her head, her face scrunching in thought. 'So, the story is like … a sweet mystery?'

I nod. 'Exactly, and you never know, one day it may or may not all make sense. Regardless, it's the journey that counts.' Tilda's expression is infectious. My grin is wide. 'Just make sure that you write and tell me all about those sweet mysteries you have,' I tell her and a playful smile stretches across Tilda's face.

'I promise. I will,' she says.

Annie

19th February 1901

The next morning, they're all already gathered around the kitchen table when I enter.

'Good morning, boarders!' I sing, as if I'm the sunrise itself and ready to brighten their day.

There are nods and grunts, as spoons full of porridge are shovelled into mouths. The sun has barely risen, but still it casts a gentle glow through the window and fills the room with a warm, comforting light. The aroma of oats and a hint of cinnamon makes our kitchen feel even more welcoming.

Sarah eats quickly and moves her dish to the sink. She grabs a broom and starts sweeping the floor around us. Olive and Tilda chat although they eat while Mrs Lapointe, looking a bit more rested than last night, stirs her porridge thoughtfully.

'What's the hurry?' I say, waving my hand at Sarah.

'No rest for the wicked,' she says, pointing her broom at me and then at Mrs Lapointe. She clutches her lower back and releases a mock groan, but there's a sparkle in her eye. 'Feels like spring's on its way.'

'I'll clean the kitchen when we've all finished,' Olive says, then grins.

'That's the spirit,' I reply, my gaze shifting to Matilda. 'And Tilda, if you could handle the laundry later today, that'd be a great help.'

She nods, her expression serious. 'I'll make sure everything's clean.'

Mrs Lapointe sets her spoon down, looking around at us with a soft smile. 'You're all doing a wonderful job. This place feels like a real home, thanks to you.'

As I gaze around the kitchen, I can't help but laugh at the daily dance we do without running water. Every drop's a treasure fetched from the well and heated on the stove. Washing dishes? It's an event requiring careful preparation and plenty of elbow grease. These little challenges are our routine, but they also make me dream bigger. One day, even our humble boarding house might bask in the luxury of water from a faucet, turning these chores into a breeze. No more lugging heavy buckets or scalding our hands. Progress is out there, and I can almost feel it knocking on our door.

I unfold the latest newspaper, eager for a bit of news from the wider world. Seems like there's something new to marvel at every day now. Rapid changes happening, even if we have no electricity and still rely on gas lamps and candles.

'Listen to this,' I say, jabbing the newspaper. Olive and Tilda, ever curious, lean in to see what's caught my interest. 'The Pan-American Exposition in Buffalo,' I begin, my voice animated, 'is a grand fair showcasing the achievements of the Western Hemisphere.' I pause. 'Can you imagine? They've got electric lights illuminating the entire fairground, making it look like a city of light. It's all about progress and unity among the nations of North and South America.'

'Sounds marvellous. What else does it say?' Sarah asks, moving closer with her broom in hand.

My eyes scan the article. 'It's got everything from the latest agricultural machinery to exotic exhibits from far-off lands. There's even a replica of the Alhambra Palace in Spain and a four-hundred-foot Electric Tower!' I jab my finger at the article. 'It's meant to "show off our technological advancements and foster economic cooperation".'

Olive stands and moves next to me. She leans over my shoulder, her eyes wide with delight, pointing at the photograph next to the words. 'Electric lights? Like the ones me and Mom saw in the city?'

I nod, remembering my brief stay in Buffalo, where I first witnessed the dazzling glow of electric streetlamps. 'Exactly. The whole fairground will be lit up like that. It's a "marvel of modern engineering, and is set to draw thousands of visitors".' I read the article's words excitedly.

'Do you think we'll see changes in our small town?' Mrs Lapointe looks concerned.

I fold the newspaper's corner thoughtfully. 'It's possible. Innovations have a way of trickling down, even to places like Bay City. Improved agricultural techniques could mean better yields for our farmers.'

'New machinery might make local manufacturing more efficient,' Sarah says, knowledgeable, and I pause, nodding at her. There's much about her I don't know.

'And the spirit of progress, well, that's contagious. It inspires people to dream bigger,' I say.

My eyes flick back to the article. 'And listen to this: "The exposition's location in Buffalo offers easy access to the natural wonder of Niagara Falls, just a short train ride away. Visitors can experience the grandeur of the Falls, an awe-inspiring symbol of nature's power and beauty, while marvelling at human ingenuity on display at the fair."'

I pause, letting the words sink in. Niagara Falls is said to be one of the most spectacular natural wonders of the world. I've even heard that when the mighty Niagara River plummets over the cliffs, it creates a thunderous roar and a mist that can be felt from many miles away.

Sarah resumes her sweeping, a contemplative look on her face. 'Seems like a grand thing, that exposition. The grandest yet.'

I smile, feeling a flicker of excitement. 'Maybe so. For now, though, we can dream of electric lights and towering marvels. And imagine standing by Niagara, feeling the mist on our faces while thinking about all the progress on display just a short distance away.'

My mind buzzes. The combination of human achievement and the raw power of Niagara Falls, the juxtaposition of progress and nature, thrills me to my core. The idea that I could witness such marvels, that I could be a part of something grander than the everyday, sets my heart racing.

Fact is, our world is moving rapidly. I know that worries some folk my age, but it excites me. It makes my stomach flip. Electricity is transforming cities, bringing light and power to homes and factories. Public transport, like the streetcars in Buffalo, is making travel more accessible. Education is becoming more widespread, too. Tilda and Olive are fortunate to have basic schooling. Not every girl their age gets such a chance. I have lived through the Civil War and witnessed the world shift in unimaginable ways already. Still, there are battles to be fought, not with guns and cannons, but with determination and courage.

'I've never been to a fairground,' Olive says.

Annie

21st February 1901

Last week the snow was heavy and wet, today there's sunshine. Its smile is icy, though. Still, the air crackles with the promise of adventure as Olive rushes ahead onto the fairgrounds. The bright colours and lively sounds swirl around us like an icy dream.

'Goodness, will you look at that!' Olive exclaims, her eyes widening as a juggler deftly tosses flaming torches into the air.

I grin; excitement bubbles up inside me. Coins from Mrs Lapointe jingle in my pocket. She and Nora are back at the boarding house – the weather offered as an explanation – but she wanted to treat the women for their hard work. 'This is what life should feel like,' I say, linking arms with Olive and pulling her towards the centre of the fair.

I turn to check that Matilda and Sarah are close behind us. Their faces are alight with anticipation, too. The fair is a feast for the senses – children's laughter mixing with the calliope's merry tune, the scent of caramel apples mingling with the earthy smell of hay.

'Look, Mrs Taylor!' Olive points to where a man in a striped suit balances on a unicycle. His movements are smooth and graceful despite the precarious nature of his act.

'That's impressive,' I say.

We make our way through the bustling crowd towards a stall that's drawing a significant amount of attention. A banner above it reads, *Meet the Man Who Survived the Niagara Rapids*! The queue is long, filled with people eager to catch a glimpse of the daredevil. Families with children on their shoulders, married couples linking arms, and groups of men all strain to get a better view.

'Can you believe it?' I say, craning my neck. I want to catch a glimpse of the man, too. 'Surviving those rapids is no small feat.'

'All these people determined to meet the man,' Olive says, waving her hand at the crowd.

A young boy climbs a nearby tree, high enough to see over the heads of the mass. 'Do you think he really went through the rapids, Pa?' he shouts, his eyes sparkling with wonder.

'Sure sounds like it, son,' his father replies, hoisting himself onto a thick branch and climbing for a better view.

Two women beside us are stretching upwards on tiptoes and trying unsuccessfully to peer over the heads in front of them. One of them clutches a parasol, using it to balance herself. 'I can't believe he survived,' she says, her voice filled with awe.

'I heard he was under the water for nearly an hour,' the other replies, her eyes never leaving the crowd ahead of her.

The gathering shifts to the right slightly and I catch a glimpse of the stunter himself. He sits atop a small platform. I think he might be recounting his harrowing experience, though his voice fails to carry over the noise of his audience. He gestures animatedly, nonetheless. Perhaps he's describing the ferocity of the rapids and his near-miraculous escape, but only to those lucky enough to hear. The crowd shifts again and I can't see him anymore.

'Just imagine,' I say, almost to myself, 'the courage it takes to face those waters.'

Olive nudges me. 'Can we get closer to hear?'

I scan the gathering for a gap to burrow our way nearer. 'Women can perform stunts in this day and age.' I turn to the voice: a woman with her back to me, addressing a small group of male admirers.

'And you are?' says one.

'Name's Martha Wagenfuhrer.'

I can't move nearer to her, but I'm convinced my ears have doubled in size.

'People still think we're just for show, but let me tell you…' She pauses and the men appear to hang on her words. My guess is that she's beautiful. She sounds it, and intelligent, too? 'Women can be just as daring, if not more so, than men. It's not about strength; it's about bravery and skill.'

I try to catch a glimpse of her, but the crowd's too thick and she isn't turning in my direction. The notion of female stunters intrigues me, though. Could I ever be that bold?

'Come on, Mrs Taylor, there's something you need to see.' Tilda tugs at my sleeve. She drags me away from Olive, towards another part of the fair where a crowd has gathered around a small arena. The sign reads, *Test Your Mettle – Daredevil Challenges for the Brave!*

Tilda grins. 'Let's try something daring ourselves.'

We watch as people take turns attempting various stunts – walking a short tightrope, jumping through a hoop, and balancing on a wobbling board. It's thrilling to watch, and I feel a flutter of excitement.

'You first,' Matilda says, nudging me towards the tightrope.

It's strung about five feet above the ground, and though it isn't high enough to cause serious injury if I fall, it's high enough to make my heart race. The rope stretches taut between two sturdy wooden posts. It sways slightly with the icy breeze. I hesitate, but then I hover my foot above the tightrope. My too-small boots pinch my toes and rub against my heels. Each step will be a test of balance and pain tolerance. I take a deep breath and place one foot carefully on the rope. I feel its rough texture beneath the thin sole. The world around me quietens as I focus intently on the cord beneath my feet. I extend my arms for balance. My heart pounds in my chest.

Tentatively, I take a step. The rope wobbles, and every muscle in my body tenses in response. I concentrate on keeping my steps steady, ignoring the discomfort in my cramped boots. The crowd's cheers and chatter grow loud again. I stop. I wobble right. Counter left. I take another deep breath. The noise fades into the background again, replaced by the sound of my heartbeat thudding in my ears.

Step by step, I inch my way across the rope. The air is somehow cooler up here, and the ground far away. I exist in my own climate and in my own world. A few more steps. The rush of accomplishment simmers inside me. My legs tremble slightly, but I push forward. I'm determined; I'll reach the end.

When I finally step onto the solid platform at the other side, my knees quiver like blancmange. I turn to Tilda, who beams with pride. Her applause is the loudest in the crowd. My heart races, but I grin widely. This is what it feels like to be triumphant. It spreads across my face.

'Your turn,' I say, breathless with exhilaration, as I climb down from the platform.

She shakes her head vigorously. 'I like me feet on the floor.' She stretches her foot to a pointed position. It's a graceful yet firm movement; she shows promise as a dancer.

Olive appears. 'Tilda, you're always so sensible!' she teases, nudging her playfully. Should I repeat my stunt for Olive to witness, too? I like this feeling. Every part of my body tingles.

'Wonder what folk think of us four women out here without an escort!' Tilda says, looking around as though she is searching for someone. I've no idea who.

Olive laughs, a carefree sound. 'Isn't it thrilling? To be out here on our own, making our own choices.'

'It's 1901,' I declare, putting my hands on my hips. 'Time you started living like it. The future's bright, and it's yours for the taking.'

Olive nods vigorously, linking arms with Tilda and pulling her along. 'Come on, let's see what other trouble we can get into!'

'Mrs Taylor!' Sarah rushes through the crowd, her face flushed with excitement. 'They're starting the big show in the main tent.' She grabs my arm.

'We must get good seats. Hurry!' Olive bounces on her toes, her enthusiasm infectious.

We weave through the throngs of people, dodging children

clutching cotton candy. The sounds of laughter and carnival barkers fill the air, blending into a joyful loudness. My heart still pounds from my little stunt. There's anticipation and the desire for more, as we approach the big top.

'Quicker,' Olive says, and she rushes past the ringmaster.

We find our seats near the front – close enough to feel the heat of the lights and the energy of the performers. We're just in time, as the show has begun and acrobats soar through the air. Their bodies bending in ways that seem impossible. The crowd gasps and claps, and I cheer louder than anyone else.

'This is incredible,' Olive whispers, her eyes large with awe.

Tilda nods, her usual reserve replaced by a look of pure joy. 'Never seen nothing like it before.'

The ringmaster strides to the centre, his red coat and top hat gleaming under the bright lights. He raises a hand, commanding attention, and the murmurs of the crowd fade into an expectant hush.

'Ladies and gentlemen.' His booming voice could wake the dead. 'Prepare to witness feats of daring and bravery like never before. Presenting, the stunters!'

A dashing man with a cape steps into the ring. His eyes flash with confidence as he takes a running start. The crowd collectively holds its breath as he approaches a flaming hoop suspended in mid-air. In one, fluid motion, he leaps through the ring of fire, his cape billowing dramatically behind him. He lands with a graceful flourish, his arms outstretched, and the audience erupts into applause.

'Show-off,' I mutter, earning a giggle from Matilda.

The heat from the flames lingers in the air, mixing with the scent of sawdust and perspiration. I can feel the energy of the crowd, a pulsating wave of excitement that courses through the tent. A woman with fiery red hair appears next. She stands tall and fearless on the back of a galloping horse, her posture impeccably poised. She lifts one leg behind her, extending her arms out in a perfect arabesque, like a ballerina on a stage. The crowd gasps, mesmerised by her. Her presence commands immediate attention. The horse moves with powerful strides; its hooves pound against the ground in a rhythmic beat.

'Now that's impressive,' I whisper, leaning closer to Matilda.

'Bet you couldn't do that on Butcher Bill's mule,' Olive says, grinning.

The woman waves to the crowd. A confident smile plays on her lips. Her movements are fluid, with each gesture exuding grace and strength. I like her assurance. The crowd's cheers swell. I'm encircled by a roaring approval of her daring display. She shifts her weight and – in a breathtaking move – leaps from the horse's back, performing a series of flips mid-air. The fabric of her costume glitters under the lights, creating a cascade of sparkling trails. She lands with effortless poise, as if gravity itself cannot hold her down.

Olive gasps. 'Did you see that?'

'I can't even jump off the porch without twisting something,' Matilda says.

The collective admiration for the stunter's bravery is palpable, and the crowd explodes into applause, deafening in its enthusiasm. I can feel the vibrations of it through the wooden benches. Climbing back on, she circles the ring with her horse's mane flying like a banner of freedom. I'm awestruck by her fearless display. Each daring stunt she performs seems to defy the very limits of human capability. A testament to what courage and skill can achieve.

'I think I need to lie down,' Olive says, fanning herself with her hand. 'Watching all this excitement is exhausting.'

I laugh. Olive's older than her years.

As the performer takes her final bow to more booming applause. I clap until my hands ache, caught up in the magic and thrill of the stunt.

Annie

23rd February 1901

I don't want to consider why there's a trunk full of Sarah's and Olive's possessions in the hallway. So, instead, I focus on the clinking of utensils and the vibrant chatter of youth that fills the kitchen. Tilda and Olive work side by side chopping vegetables and fruits.

'Careful with those carrots, Tilda. You're butchering them worse than a Sunday roast,' Olive teases, her eyes twinkling mischievously.

Tilda shoots her a playful glare. They're the very best of friends already.

'Mom, did you see that recipe in the paper? The one for cherry pie? I thought we could make it together for dessert tonight.'

'Sounds like a wonderful idea, sweetheart. I'll make the extra pastry. Check Mrs Lapointe's pantry for cherries,' Sarah says.

'I can do that.' Matilda puts down her knife and strides to the pantry. 'Preserved or canned cherries?'

'Either,' Sarah says. She's rubbing flour and butter together. 'I think the recipe suggested using canned cherries or a substitute fruit during the colder months.'

I wipe my hands on my apron. 'What's all this fuss about cherry pie?'

Sarah smiles. 'Olive, Tilda and I are planning to make one for dessert tonight.' She then turns to see if Tilda's still in the pantry. 'A leaving pie,' she whispers.

I nod solemnly. I don't mention how I kicked their packed trunk in the hallway earlier. 'I'll lend a hand with the eating.'

Mrs Lapointe bounces Nora on her knee. 'Looks like we've got a baking party on our hands,' she says, and chuckles at Nora's giggles.

I watch as Tilda steps out of the pantry. She observes the scene. With a hand on the door, her eyes fix on the interactions, surveying, and a soft smile plays on her lips at the warmth and camaraderie. Her friends leaving will break her heart all over again.

I lean against the kitchen counter. 'Did any of you say that you've visited Niagara Falls before?'

'Niagara Falls?' Olive repeats, momentarily distracted from her chopping. Her left hand reaches for the pendant hanging from her neck. She does that often; a comforting gesture perhaps. 'Too scary.'

A smirk plays at the corners of my lips. 'The grand spectacle of nature herself. Imagine the thrill of riding the rapids, the roar of the water as it crashes against the rocks. It's a shame we're missing out on such a spectacle here in Bay City.'

Sarah's moved to the sink. Quietly stacking her used utensils in the bowl of water, then she looks at me with curiosity as water drips from her hands to the floor. 'What do you mean? What spectacle?'

I pause for a moment, considering my words carefully. I've been thinking about this over the last four days. 'There's this daredevil spirit in me.' I tap at my chest with my palm. 'It's itching for adventure. It's unleashed again.'

'You desire a day trip to the Falls?' Mrs Lapointe asks.

I shake my head. 'Not quite. I read in the newspaper…' I pause, and Mrs Lapointe bobs her head for me to continue. 'It was an article praising daredevils who'd ridden out the whirlpool rapids at Niagara Falls.'

Mrs Lapointe's eyes widen slightly with horror. 'The whirlpool rapids? Isn't that incredibly dangerous? I haven't even been in a boat before, let alone been near water!'

I bob my head in agreement. 'Daredevils navigate the treacherous waters of the Niagara River, where the current is fierce and the rocks are unforgiving.'

'Why, though?' Olive's simplicity makes me smile.

'Because it's a thrilling and risky venture, but one that's seen as a test of skill and bravery… Not quite as deadly as going over the Falls themselves.' I pause. All eyes are on me. I tap my right foot rhythmically. 'Since our fairground outing, I've been toying with the idea of a little stunt myself … one involving the mighty Niagara Falls.'

Tilda looks up, her face brightening with a sudden idea. 'Morgiana would do it. She'd show the men how it's done, wouldn't she, Mrs Taylor? Don't you think Morgiana would do it?'

I pause, letting the idea sink in. 'You know, Tilda, I think you're right. Morgiana would.'

She leans in, intrigued. 'So, you're thinking about the Falls, not the rapids?'

'Perhaps,' I say.

Sarah's eyes broaden in disbelief. 'You cannot be serious!'

'The Falls are treacherous, Mrs Taylor,' Mrs Lapointe says.

I roll my eyes dramatically in response, batting away their words with my hand. Not embarrassed, more bothered. I wasn't asking their opinion and – in terms of self-preservation – I'm keen to dismiss any views that don't align with my own. Truth is, I'd relish the challenge. It's like I walked that tightrope, and something was awakened within.

'Perhaps they are,' I say. 'But where's the fun in living life on the safe side?' I pause. 'Besides…' I smile. 'A little risk adds spice to the journey, wouldn't you say?'

As Olive and Sarah exchange a glance that perhaps questions my sanity, another surge of excitement loops my belly. Going one better than those whirlpool stunters – I could do that? Perhaps it's just a fleeting thought, but now the thrill of the idea lingers in the air, along with the savoury scents of what's cooking.

'Has anyone attempted to go over the Falls? Not in the whirlpools,'

Sarah asks. Her gentle smile widens into a warm grin. 'This is another one of your tales, isn't it?' Her eyes crinkle at the corners with genuine warmth and sincerity.

'Hundreds have attempted. Some intentional, some accidental.' I pause and Sarah waves an arm for me to continue. 'I read about it in the paper. Folks have tried to prove their mettle or met their end by sheer misfortune.'

Sarah laughs, but I don't see which part of that statement is funny. She doesn't believe I'll go over the Falls.

'And how many were successful?' Mrs Lapointe asks. Her arms cross over her chest. She doesn't consider my idea a good one.

'From my research and reading?' I stand up straight, pulling my shoulders back. I hold my palms up in surrender. 'None.'

'What?' Mrs Lapointe shouts.

I can't help but laugh at their reactions. They clearly don't understand. 'I'll be the first person to survive.'

'What makes you so sure?' Mrs Lapointe asks.

I point at my face and smile. 'I've got strength of resolve and a cunning mind.'

There's a mix of gasps, murmurs and headshaking.

'Like Morgiana,' Tilda repeats. I look at her and she's beaming. She's excited for me, or perhaps she also considers this a tale I'm telling.

'Almost…' I grin at her enthusiasm. 'She'd probably be the first to join me in this adventure, singing sea shanties all the way down.'

She chuckles, her eyes bright with laughter. 'She'd be shouting, "Land ho!" as you plummet toward the Falls.'

The image of Morgiana's fearless spirit adds an extra layer of thrill to our lively conversation. I move to the kitchen window, staring out at the icy landscape beyond. Going over Niagara Falls. Madness, some might say. But not me. At this point, the idea is more of an aspiration rather than a certainty. Perhaps I'm not yet sure how I'll survive – maybe it's a test, a way to find out if I'm destined to keep living through what kills others. And what a magnificent way to find out.

'I'll find a way to survive,' I say, matter-of-factly.

With my back to the women. I don't see their reactions. Instead, I'm contemplating Mrs Lapointe's question. What makes me think I'll succeed where others have failed? A simple notion, really – I refuse to be bound by the limitations others place on me. When I'm ready; when the time is right, I'll conquer the Falls. Not yet, though.

'I'll happily be a dime-museum curiosity, if it helps us all out of poverty,' I say, turning back to the women.

'I reckon we've already made a fair sum,' Mrs Lapointe says.

'Really?' Sarah moves over to her. 'How much?'

My idea is being dismissed. They consider me ludicrous. They think I'm inventing a new tale to entertain them. They've moved on. I like that they have.

'Between our cooking and cleaning services, embroidery work, and selling homemade goods, we've managed to bring in a respectable sum.' Mrs Lapointe's expression grows contemplative, her brow furrowing slightly as she ponders the topic at hand. 'Folk have been generous in their patronage. Our reputation for quality work's spreading.' She nods slowly. 'I'd say we've earned enough to keep us floating. For now.'

Olive and Tilda clap in unison, then embrace, Olive's curls tickling Tilda's face.

The rootless life I led before settling here was filled with adventures and near-misses. I like thinking about those days, especially when I crossed paths with the infamous Jesse James. It was a wild, transient existence, and it's made me who I am. Now, I'm here, daring to dream again, even if it's just about going over Niagara Falls. I chuckle softly. I bet there's a rebellious twinkle in my eye. The fact that no one's yet managed to survive going over the Falls is a constraint I won't be wearing. I'm already thinking about how I'll do it.

Annie

23rd February 1901

'Ladies, gather round,' Sarah calls from the hall, clapping her hands to get everyone's attention.

I'm not yet fully awake from dreaming about fire. I uncurl from the armchair, stretching my legs and arms in front of me like a cat who's just remembered it's the queen of the house.

Sarah enters the room, her hands still dusted with flour.

'What's this about?' I say, observing her. She carries a mysterious air about her.

'A surprise for you all.' She smiles and gestures towards the doorway, where Olive and Tilda appear with a large object that's covered with a sheet. They're struggling to manoeuvre it into the room. Olive's excitement is palpable.

Mrs Lapointe, Sarah and I watch with bated breath as the young women push the object into the corner of the parlour. With a flourish, Sarah pulls off the sheet.

Olive's eyes shine with delight. 'A piano!' She sweeps into a deep, theatrical bow, a mischievous grin playing on her lips as if to say, *And that, ladies, is how it's done.*

I walk to it; the wood is scuffed, and a few keys are missing, but it still holds a certain charm.

'From someone I met at Butcher Bill's,' Sarah says, a smile spreading across her face. 'They were kind enough to part with it for a few coins. Olive and I thought it would be a perfect gift to leave behind for all of you.'

Tilda's face lights up with a mixture of surprise, joy and a flicker of confusion, too. 'It's wonderful! But aren't you staying a few more weeks?'

Sarah glances at Olive, then back at Tilda. 'We're moving on, dear. This piano is our gift to you, to remember us. We wanted to leave something special behind for all of you.'

Tilda's smile falters slightly, her brows knitting together. 'When?'

'Tonight.'

Olive steps forward and hugs Tilda, who nods slowly, fighting to accept the news.

'I'll miss you both so much.'

Sarah runs her fingers over the keys, and though a few notes are off, a melody begins to form. She looks up at the group, her smile widening. 'It may be a bit out of tune, but it still works. Who's ready for a dance?'

Without hesitation, Olive pulls Tilda into the centre of the room. 'Come on, Tilda, let's show them how it's done!'

Sarah begins to play a lively, rhythmic tune in 4/4 time. The melody's cheerful, with a bouncy bassline and a bright, staccato right hand. It's the kind of piece that invites spontaneous dancing. I can't help but tap my foot to the beat, counting *one, two, three, four* in my head.

The two girls begin to dance, their laughter filling the room. We all clap along and tap our feet. Even Mrs Lapointe can't help but smile and sway to the rhythm.

'Let's keep those steps light and remember to follow the beat. One, two, three, four,' I instruct, clapping my hands in time with the music.

As they dance, the room seems to transform. The old parlour, with its worn furniture and faded wallpaper, is filled with energy and joy. Tilda looks every bit the carefree young girl she should be. Being around Olive, her age-mate and confidante, has given her a chance to reclaim her stolen youth. They twirl and spin, their faces glowing with happiness. This is pure joy and camaraderie.

As the music ends, Sarah stands, her eyes bright with excitement. 'We've been through so much, but look at us now. We're not just surviving; we're living.'

I nod, my heart swelling with pride and affection for these women who have become my family. 'Here's to the future, then,' I say, raising an imaginary glass. 'May it be filled with more moments like this for you all.'

Annie's Diary

27th February 1901

Riding over Niagara Falls? Better than those daredevils riding the whirlpool rapids. It'll make me famous.

Has Morgiana always influenced me? Am I alone in being trapped? Are all of us lost women trapped with our own barrels? Is it an invisible vessel that connects us all? Are we not all buffeted by waters and by powerful forces way beyond our control? Are we not always on the verge of being tipped over the edge into an abyss?

Still, now, we congregate here in a boarding house in Bay City. Persisting. Waiting.

Four days on, and I keep returning to Mrs Lapointe's question. It prods and prods at my soul. I think I have a more suitable answer now, though. One that fits better. So, I'll ask myself again – what makes me think I'll succeed where every single other soul has perished? And my answer – David. David makes me think that.

Today's thoughts of him somehow both interconnect and exist alone. I fear others might consider my inability to voice David's name unforgivable. Yet I would argue that that is what keeps me alive and able to function. I dwell on the notion that our bodies serve as powerful instruments for exploring the limits of our human experience. And perhaps, through a physical act, I might eventually confront this grief and find solace?

After Samuel died, I once considered taking a gun to my head. One bullet. One attempt. That I'd simply let God decide my fate. Just as He did with my son and my husband. But I didn't. And here I am, always surviving, always persisting. I'm still here and, surely, I must make that count for something.

Annie

4th March 1901

I see her before she sees me. Tilda sits at a small desk in the parlour. I watch from the open doorway, as her slender fingers deftly embroider intricate patterns onto a pillow. The soft glow of the oil lamp casts gentle shadows across her features as she works, her concentration unwavering as she attempts to poke thread through her needle's eye.

'Botheration!' She pricks her finger and throws the pillow onto the desk.

'You're talented with a needle.'

She jumps. A beat. She glances up, a faint blush tinting her cheeks. 'Thank you, Mrs Taylor. It's just something I've picked up along the way.'

A few strides to her and I pick up the heart-shaped cushion; the embroidery is exquisite. A heart shape has been sewn into the material using red thread.

'Did you do that?' I ask, turning for a response. She nods. 'It's beautiful.' I lift it closer to me and examine the needlework. 'I'd no idea you were such a talent.'

'It's for you.' Her words are whispered. Begrudging almost. 'Not finished yet.'

'For me?'

She bobs her head. 'To say thank you.' She sighs. 'Wanted to give you something from Nora and me.'

I gulp down the emotion that's threatening to escape. It's the most perfect gift. It's the most beautiful gift I've received in years.

'You've certainly made this parlour look more inviting with your handiwork.' I gesture to the embroidered tablecloth draped over the nearby piano.

Tilda releases a little lump of air, like laughter but not. A sense of pride is evident in her expression. 'Just wanted to do me part to help around here.'

I nod appreciatively, placing the pillow back on the desk, but she's not looking at me anymore. She's back to attempting to thread her needle.

'Are you well?' I ask her.

She freezes. She sighs, then looks at me. Her eyes reflect her sadness. 'I guess,' she says. 'It's just strange without Olive and Sarah here.'

'They left rather abruptly, didn't they? Determined about something.' The grief of losing a recently made friend is unexpected. It's Tilda's first experience of it; Edith left but they'd not really connected. Not like she did with Olive. I doubt she'll let herself close to another boarder.

'Arrive broken, leave determined,' she says, and I nod. That's my role here: rounding up lost women, knowing they'll leave. After a moment's pause, Matilda asks, 'Did you find the note I left for Sarah? I put it under her pillow.'

I pull the folded piece of paper from my sleeve. I step to the desk and place it beside her embroidery.

Thank you for showing me how to be a good mama. You have given me hope. No matter where life takes me, I will never forget you or Olive. Your friend, Tilda x

'Think she read it before leaving?'

I'm not sure she did, but Matilda doesn't need to know that. I bob my head weakly, a faint smile playing on my lips. 'A touching gesture Sarah appreciated.' A pause. 'You'll miss them terribly, won't you?'

Tilda's gaze falls and I see a tear drop onto her material. 'They were like family.' Her voice is barely above a whisper. 'But they gave me hope, too.'

'How so?'

'Seeing them together, Olive and Sarah… Made me realise not all mother-daughter bonds are neglectful,' she says softly, her tone tinged with longing. 'Maybe one day I can have a relationship like that with me Nora.'

'If I had a dollar for every time someone underestimated me, I'd be richer than old man Rockefeller himself,' I say. 'Don't underestimate yourself, Tilda. You and that little girl of yours have an unbreakable bond.'

'Wish I'd your belief.'

'Neither you nor I need a knight in shining armour to rescue us.' My voice rings with conviction. 'If they won't open the door, we must kick it down ourselves.'

Her hesitant smile is accompanied by a shy tuck of her golden hair behind her ear. It's a habitual gesture she does when she feels uncovered.

'You're strong and determined, just like them and just like me,' I say but she shakes her head to protest. 'You are! And I'll be here to help you every step of the way.'

Matilda looks up, gratitude shining in her eyes. I place a comforting hand on her shoulder and give it a squeeze. 'Why don't we make some tea and talk some more?'

Part II: Unfurling Rapids

'I was pregnant and barely fourteen. Mrs Taylor was more than just working in the boarding house; she was a guiding light in a world I believed was vicious and unforgiving. She taught me how to sew and how to tell stories. Made sure my voice was heard. Gave me hope. God bless her.'

Evelyn Sinclair

Annie

2nd August 1901

I walk fast, boots scraping the cobbles, lungs filling and emptying. 'This way. Quicker,' I say.

I adjust my hat, the wide brim casting a welcome shade over my face as I navigate the bustling grounds of the Pan-American Exposition. This marvel of modern innovation and cultural exchange sprawls across acres of landscaped gardens and grand pavilions. The air hums with both excitement and the mingled scents of exotic foods, freshly baked bread, and the sharp tang of newly printed pamphlets.

'Wait,' Tilda says, taking in the sights with awe. One hand grips the skirt of her dress as she hurries to keep up. It's a simple but neat lavender frock that Mrs Lapointe insisted she wear, and contrasts with the more elaborate gowns around us. Her other hand fidgets with the lace collar, clearly unused to such finery.

'This place is extraordinary,' I say, my voice carrying a mix of wonder and determination.

Tilda looks at me, wide-eyed. 'It's like nothing I've ever seen. Can't believe we're here.'

'Believe it, Tilda. The world's changing, and we're part of it,' I say, squeezing her hand and pulling her along with me.

We weave through the crowds, passing families, vendors, and performers. A juggler tosses colourful balls into the air, while a group of musicians play a lively tune that sets the crowd tapping their feet. The laughter of children mixes with the murmur of conversations in a dozen languages. The vibrancy of the exposition contrasts sharply with the dull and shabby boarding house of late.

We move towards the Electricity Building, a towering structure adorned with gleaming lights and banners proclaiming the wonders of modern technology. The building itself is a marvel, with its white neoclassical facade and domed roof. It is covered in thousands of incandescent light bulbs that glow even in daylight. Inside, the latest innovations in electric lighting, heating, and appliances are on display. They're illuminating the future of modern living. As we approach, a lively discussion catches my ear. A group of men and women stand near a demonstration booth, where a man in a crisp suit explains the benefits of electric appliances. I nudge Matilda, and we sidle closer to listen.

'With these innovations,' the man says, gesturing to a shining electric stove, 'household chores will be revolutionised. Less time spent on cooking and cleaning means more time for education, for personal growth.'

A woman in the crowd, wearing a practical but stylish hat, raises her voice. 'And what about our roles at home? Will these machines truly free us, or just change the nature of our work?'

The crowd murmurs, a combination of agreement and dissent. Some nod in understanding, while others exchange doubtful glances. A familiar fire ignites in my chest. I step forward. 'These innovations are indeed remarkable, but true liberation for everyone comes from education and equality, not just convenience.'

The speaker turns to me, looking slightly taken aback by my interjection. 'You make a valid point, Madam. The technology we showcase here is just one part of the puzzle. Social change must accompany technological advancement.'

Tilda grabs my hand again, her eyes shining with pride. 'Well said, Mrs Taylor.'

We move on, the hum of the exposition filling the air with a sense of wonder. We pass the Transportation Building, where the latest in automobiles and even a prototype airplane are displayed. The automobiles – sleek and shiny – promise a future of faster travel. A steam-powered vehicle catches the eye of many onlookers; its polished brass fittings gleaming in the sunlight. The sharp scent of gasoline mixes with the earthy smell of the nearby gardens, creating an oddly invigorating atmosphere. It's a testament to human ingenuity and the relentless march of progress.

'Did you see the automobiles?' I ask, pointing to a sleek, horseless carriage. 'They say one day they'll be as common as horses.'

Tilda giggles, her eyes wide with amazement. 'I'd love to ride in one someday.'

Our attention is caught by a sudden cheer from a nearby stage. We turn to see a crowd gathering around a platform where a man is giving an impassioned speech about the future of transportation. His words soar with the promise of progress and innovation, and the crowd's combined face is alight with hope and curiosity. The cacophony of the exposition surrounds us — vendors calling out their wares, the distant strains of a brass band playing a lively tune, and the excited chatter of families exploring the exhibits. Summer is in full swing. The cool evening breeze carries the faint aroma of popcorn and roasted nuts from nearby stalls.

'Is that … is it the Niagara Falls Pavilion?' I say, and Tilda hurries ahead.

A huge, meticulously detailed replica of the Falls stands proudly. The sound of rushing water is cleverly mimicked by hidden machinery. Tourists marvel at it, exclaiming over its likeness to the real thing.

'Look at that, Tilda. The grandeur of Niagara Falls, right here for everyone to see,' I say.

She nods, her expression thoughtful. 'And to think, you could be the talk of the town for conquering the real thing.'

I smile, my excitement bubbling over. 'Imagine, the real Niagara

Falls, formed thousands of years ago. The mighty river carving its path, rushing and roaring over the cliffs.' I move, flapping my hand along the replica of the river to demonstrate. 'It's fast and high because the water flows from Lake Erie into the Niagara River, picking up speed as it travels. By the time it reaches the Falls...' I point to where that is, 'it's a powerful force, dropping 158 feet here. At the Horseshoe Falls.'

Matilda looks at me, eyes wide. 'That's incredible. But what about the other Falls?'

'The American and Bridal Veil Falls have rocky bases,' I explain, 'but the Horseshoe Falls have none.'

'You've really studied this,' she says, pointing at the model. Her voice is filled with admiration.

'I still am,' I reply, and then grin. 'If I'm going to be the first to conquer the Falls, I need to know every detail.'

Just then, a man steps in front of us, holding a banner that reads, *Meet the Great Stunter, Carlisle Graham!*

Excitement pulses through me. 'He's here!' I exclaim, and Tilda's eyes light up with anticipation. I grab the banner-holding man's arm. 'Where is Mr Graham?' My voice is sterner than necessary.

He looks confused and I point to his banner.

'Gone home,' he says, and then continues walking through the crowds.

I raise an eyebrow and turn to Tilda. 'Graham survived the rapids, not the Falls.'

Matilda laughs, her eyes broad and curious. She absorbs every snippet of detail overheard and given. Her understated intelligence emerging.

The sun begins to set, casting a golden glow over the exposition grounds. The lights of the pavilions twinkle like stars, and the energy of the place infuses both hope and determination.

'I'd quite like to live here,' I say.

'Me, too.'

I take one last look at the grand buildings and bustling crowds, a smirk playing on my lips. 'And to think, some people believe women should only ever stay at home. What fools!'

Tilda giggles. 'We stay at home too much.'

We link arms and keep walking, past a booth selling postcards and pamphlets. Matilda pauses, picking up a card with a picture of Niagara Falls. 'For Mrs Lapointe.'

'She'll appreciate that,' I say. 'And we'll have plenty of stories to tell when we get back.'

As we walk, I can't help but feel another surge of excitement at the changing world. And the thought of conquering the Falls fills me with a boldness that matches the spirit of the exposition around us. The bustling, vibrant world here has filled us with a sense of possibility and adventure. This is just the beginning.

23 Queen's Road,
St. John's, Newfoundland,
Dominion of Newfoundland.
August 5th 1901

My niece Matilda,

I hope this letter finds you well. It has been several months since our paths last crossed, and, of late, I must admit that I have found myself thinking about you often. With a little persuasion, your mother revealed to me that you have made a home for yourself and little Nora in a boarding house in Bay City. I hear the place is entirely unsuitable. Though, I must say that I am rather curious to see for myself the life you have built since we parted ways last year. For, while our past together was far from idyllic, I cannot help but feel a certain longing to see you entirely again. Perhaps it is time that we re-entered each other's lives? What says you? Yes? Your mother would like that, too. We are, after all, one big joyful family.

No doubt I shall be in your area soon, and I can but assume that you will be willing to receive me. Until then, take care.

Yours sincerely,
Uncle William

Annie

10th August 1901

It's a Saturday and it's my first time in Battery Park. The meadow stretches, a vast canvas of emerald hues in front of us, interrupted occasionally by the graceful dance of butterflies. Birds flit about, too; their songs mock our tense wait.

'This moss-coloured dress fits in with the scenery too perfectly,' I say. It's cinched at the waist and flows down to my ankles. A small hat, adorned with lace and a single white feather, sits atop my hair.

'Too perfectly?' Tilda asks.

'I resemble a walking pasture.'

In contrast, she's wearing a simpler, pastel-pink dress. Its hem brushes the tips of her brown boots. Her hat's plain, casting a shadow over her eyes, and she's carrying a closed parasol, its fabric's a deep shade of burgundy.

'Stop fidgeting,' I say.

'I'm dressed like someone else.'

She is. We both are. Quite literally. None of these items belong to us. Each is borrowed from Mrs Lapointe's chest. Clothes worn when she was married and wearing colours, or they're from her dead mother-in-law, who apparently had more money than days to wear all her dresses. Still, Tilda's an elegant, slender silhouette – or she would be if she stopped swinging the parasol in circles like the blades of a windmill.

'Tilda.' It's almost a growl. Mrs Lapointe had presented it to her before we left, saying that all ladies needed a parasol. 'You'll remove someone's eye…'

She laughs, twirling it faster until she drops it.

'He's late,' I mutter, feeling the weight of the lace collar around my neck.

Tilda doesn't respond, but stoops to pick up the parasol. Her gaze is fixed on the pathway ahead, where families stroll, lovers whisper, and children chase after balls.

'Why are we even here?' I ask.

'I told you, Mrs Taylor,' she says, straightening up. 'We're meeting George here so he can introduce us to some folks from the Pan-American Exposition. He thinks they might be able to help with your stunt.'

My question was rhetorical, but still I nod, trying to keep my irritation at bay. 'Right, the Pan-Am people. And you met George at Butcher Bill's.'

'He mentioned something about the stunter who might offer advice,' she adds, twirling the parasol more gently now.

'He'd better be more exciting than watching paint dry.'

Just then, a figure emerges on the path ahead. The sun gleams off the polished buttons of his well-tailored coat. He waves.

Tilda catches my gaze and nudges my arm. 'Told you he'd come.'

A book – a novel, judging by its red cover – is stuffed into the pocket of his jacket. The pocket's material is now stretched and uneven. His waistcoat clings to him, hinting at his unusually lean frame. Above it, a crisp white shirt peeks out, buttoned right to the top and complemented by a neatly tied cravat.

'He looks nervous,' I say.

She nods, taking a deep breath.

He lifts a long, skinny arm in another awkward wave, fingers trembling ever so slightly.

'We should probably wave back,' I say. She does.

'Don't recall him being that tall,' she whispers.

'Like a giraffe.'

She sputters, lifting her hand to her mouth to hide the smile.

He's almost reached us. The man's trousers seem to stretch on forever, hinting at his staggering height. His shoes, also polished to a shine, tap on the pathway, and a modest bowler hat sits atop his head. It somehow serves to emphasise his elongated features – sharp with pronounced cheekbones.

'Remember the sign,' I say.

'I drop me parasol.' She waves it so I can see.

As he closes the distance in two final strides, his towering figure becomes even more pronounced. When he reaches us, he bends, extending his gangly arm. My head's in line with his chest. I must crane my neck uncomfortably to meet his eyes, and the sun casts a halo around his looming silhouette. I look at his outstretched hand; his fingers seem to dance in a bid to find Tilda's hand.

'George Whitman,' he says, stooping closer to our level. 'Of the Bay City Whitmans.'

'Matilda Hamilton. You know that.' She points to herself and giggles. 'And this is Mrs Taylor.'

'Charmed to meet you,' Mr Whitman says, straightening up. He looks around the park, seemingly searching for something. 'Shall we walk?' I nod, and together we set off back the way he came.

'Mrs Taylor,' he begins hesitantly, turning to see me, 'I heard about your interest in the Pan-American Exposition. I thought perhaps you'd like to meet some of the organisers today. They're always looking for local stories to feature.'

Tilda beams. 'That would be wonderful, Mr Whitman.'

'And Miss Hamilton mentioned a stunter?' I say.

Mr Whitman chuckles nervously. 'Yes, Carlisle Graham. He's planning a barrel plunge over Niagara Falls. I thought you might like to meet him, too.'

'Perhaps *he'd* like to meet *me*.' I raise an eyebrow. 'I'll show him how it's done.'

'I'm sure you will.'

Mr Whitman leads us over the grass and to a gathering of people near a grand gazebo. The structure is adorned with banners and bunting, its columns wrapped in patriotic colours. The crowd is a mix of well-dressed men and women, their conversations a hum of excitement and anticipation.

'Mrs Taylor,' he says, gesturing to a group of individuals, 'I'd like to introduce you to some key figures who can help with your Niagara stunt.'

A distinguished-looking man steps forward, extending his hand. 'Pleasure to meet you, Mrs Taylor. I'm Thomas Greene, editor of the *Buffalo Courier*. I've heard about your daring plan.'

'Pleasure to meet you, Mr Greene,' I say, shaking his hand firmly. 'I appreciate your interest.'

'This is Clara Dawson,' Mr Whitman continues, indicating a woman with an air of authority about her. 'She's a prominent advocate for women's rights.'

'Mrs Dawson,' I say, stretching out my hand. Her grip matches mine in confidence.

'Mrs Taylor, your bravery is inspiring,' she says. 'Your stunt could be a powerful statement about what women can achieve.'

'That's my hope,' I reply, feeling a swell of determination. 'I haven't finalised anything yet, but I will soon. It's all in here for now.' I tap my forehead.

As we move through the introductions, shaking hands, I notice Tilda's rapt gaze. She's absorbing every detail, her curiosity evident.

'Mr Graham sends his apologies,' Mr Greene adds. 'He was unable to make it today. Now, come, let's have tea. We can discuss your plans and how the exposition might feature in them.'

Annie's Diary

10th August 1901

Today, walking home from Battery Park, I considered that since I lost David and Samuel, I've moved constantly. Literally, metaphorically, both. Studying, teaching, working, physically chasing. I fear standing still as much as I dread silence. That's when my mind fills with shouts. Loud, demanding, consuming.

George Whitman of the Bay City Whitmans carried a book today, and it made me deliberate how I struggle to read new stories. I search my memory, but everything I've read of late I've read before. I know those tales already. No surprises. Nothing unexpected. Repetitive like walking. Everything new I read takes an age. As if each page is a first step – unsteady and hesitant.

Now, though, externally at least, it appears that I've settled into a home. Almost three years in one place – and there's a shift in my heart as a result. In moving around, I've avoided connection. I've become difficult. Here I've resisted connecting, but it has persisted. It's Tilda, it's Nora – this maternal love is suffocating. Still, those I love here have no clue as to what chaos endures inside me. Mrs Lapointe is ill, and I'm involving Tilda in all that I do. Am I not exposed and vulnerable now?

I've no recall of what it feels to be at peace. I can't remember what it is to have stillness and space inside my head. To rest. To pause. To experience a break in fighting. Have I not already spent a lifetime waiting for pain to pass?

I thought about that as I walked home today. Each step a beat. Perhaps I even dread what might happen to my mind if I remove all the chatter. What would fill that empty space instead? Demons? Swirling wisps of blackness? Seems this dance teacher waltzes with hysteria daily; this is the maddest I've ever felt.

Keeping busy suppresses thoughts from pushing into reality. It keeps God from penetrating too. The chatter is too loud for David's or Samuel's voices, for His voice to be heard either. I prefer that. It's easier this way. Today I walked in a park. Other days I walk through crowds, in the market or both. Always, I wonder how many of us might be hiding our grief. I wonder how many untold stories are rotting them from the inside out, or how many consider themselves entirely alone with that pain.

Today I imagined a world where those suffering wear sunflower-coloured scarves or hats to communicate that we're grieving. A simple sharing of pain that required no additional words. I long to shout and for it to be heard, to let my voice echo against the roaring cascade of Niagara Falls. A primal release of all the pent-up emotions swirling within me. To feel the power of my words reverberate through the misty air, carried away by the rushing waters. Surely that would be a cathartic release unlike any other?

If only for a moment, I would be truly free amidst the thunderous roar.

Matilda

11th August 1901

Mrs Lapointe sits at the kitchen table, the heart of the boarding house she inherited from her late mother-in-law. They say this place was once a bustling haven for travellers; now it's as tired as she is. She said she felt better today. Even promised to help peel potatoes, but they lie untouched. The knife beside the pile remains idle. Her eyes, once lively and filled with determination, now seem distant. Her usually rosy cheeks are pale, and there's no tight bun, instead her hair's wild, more like Mrs Taylor's. It's a painful reminder that she isn't better. She's worse. Much worse.

'Is everything fine?' I ask.

Her smile is weak. She refuses to look at me. 'Yes, dear,' she says, but her voice lacks any friendliness and strength. She squeezes a handkerchief, balled up in her hand. Stepping closer to her, the weight in me chest grows.

She looks up, eyes locking with mine. 'Stay over there.' It's a shout. Holds up her palm to stop me. The handkerchief falls into her lap. Speckled with blood. We both freeze.

'I'll be well, dear.'

I'm not daft, though. Sunlight pours in through a sheer curtain, creating dancing patterns on the well-worn floorboards. I like them. Every crevice and nick in those boards holds stories: late-night whisperings, savoury meals prepared, dancing twirls. The wood-burning stove – with its pots and pans gleaming from recent use – is proof of the many meals she's prepared. From times before she got ill.

'How's everything with you?' she asks. She wants a change in topic. 'Anything to share?'

'Yesterday was an interesting day. We met George Whitman and folk from the Pan-American Exposition.'

'The expo?' she asks, her entire face lighting up.

'They might help Mrs Taylor with her stunt,' I say.

'That's wonderful, dear,' she says, but there's worry in her eyes. 'Just be careful.'

Nora toddles into the kitchen. Small hands clutching a stuffed toy. She looks up with bright eyes and a smile that lifts me heart.

'Hello, little one,' I say, bending down to pick her up. 'Have you been having fun?'

She giggles and nods, her tiny arms wrapping around me neck. Stuffed toy forgotten, it falls to the floor.

The door bursts open and Mrs Taylor storms in, along with a gust of cold air. Her cheeks are rosy. Her hair wilder than three birds' nests combined. She's all fingers, trying to unbutton the woollen jacket she found in Mrs Lapointe's clothes chest. It's fastened up to her neck and refusing to budge. A navy-blue walking skirt with an ivory-coloured blouse peek out underneath. She squirms in someone else's clothes.

'I adore them,' I say, pointing at the tiny mother-of-pearl buttons on the jacket. They gleam. 'And that hat.' It's wide-brimmed. Decorated with a white feather and a ribbon bow cascading down her back. I like how it's almost perched atop her wild hair. Like a fancy bird on its nest.

Held carefully in her right hand are bags. They're bursting with fresh produce: greens are peeking out from one and fresh bread from another. A different bag's got oranges in it.

'I've just been telling Mrs Lapointe about George Whitman,' I say and Mrs Taylor nods. The weight of them bags is causing her to shift from foot to foot. 'Can we afford that?' I ask, moving to help her with her load.

'Gifts,' she says, as if that's response enough.

It's the wooden box that piques me curiosity. Old, and tied with rough twine. The fingers of Mrs Taylor's left hand are white from clutching it. Must be heavy.

'What have you brought now?' Mrs Lapointe asks, pointing at the box.

'You're out of bed!' Mrs Taylor grins at her. There's no hiding the mischievous glint in her eyes. She places the bags and box on the table with a slight thud.

'I hate being a burden,' Mrs Lapointe admits. Her pride's warring with the reality of her deteriorating health. Mrs Taylor takes a step to her and Mrs Lapointe almost yelps, then coughs. We all wait.

'Stay over there,' she says eventually.

'You're not a burden.' Mrs Taylor bats away her friend's words. 'And these? Oh, just a few essentials from the market.' She gives the box a gentle pat. 'And maybe a little surprise.'

She moves towards the counter, where her fingers wrap around the wooden handle of the knife that sits next to Mrs Lapointe's untouched potatoes. She slices through the coarse twine. 'We have mice.'

A shiver runs down me spine.

'Two of them were having a party in the pantry yesterday.' Mrs Taylor smiles. Her eyes twinkle.

'It's not funny,' I say, me disgust there in me voice.

'Oh, Tilda, worry not… For in this very box, I believe I've procured our salvation.' She hesitates. Think I might be holding me breath. 'I ran into Butcher Bill at the market.'

Mrs Lapointe, glancing between us, looks bewildered, too.

'When I mentioned to Bill our little … mouse predicament, he said he had just the solution.'

She reaches into the box. Lifts out a cat.

'Mrs Taylor!' I exclaim.

Its plush coat is a deep blue-grey hue, each hair shimmers with a silvery sheen. The cat is thickset, and its weight makes her change her grip a little.

'Look at him!'

'Meet Lagara,' she says.

Its round face boasts large, coppery-orange eyes. They're wide with curiosity yet also carry age-old wisdom. Its cheeks are full. Its nose short and broad. Its sturdy chin aligns perfectly with the tip of that nose in profile. He's handsome. Mrs Taylor cradles Lagara like a newborn baby, and the cat struggles. Its tail swishes from side to side.

'Butcher Bill claims this one's the best mouser in all of Bay City,' she says, a hint of pride in her voice.

In a swift movement, Lagara sinks its teeth into her hand. Yelping in surprise, she releases it. The cat bolts. Its short, thick legs carry it under the kitchen table quickly.

I stare at the table where the cat now hides.

'Think I might go back to bed,' Mrs Lapointe says.

Annie

12th August 1901

I freeze; did I wake her? I push the door to Mrs Lapointe's bedroom again; its worn hinges creak. Morning sun filters in through the faded curtains and casts a muted light across the wallpaper. The colour and pattern are both faded. The scent of chamomile hangs in the air; my latest attempt to mask the stale undertone of sickness.

I stare at the foot of her bed – a solid wooden frame with a headboard adorned in intricate crosses – hoping for movement. The bed sits as a centrepiece in the room; its sheets, though well-worn, are meticulously smoothed. I take a single step forward.

'Mrs Taylor?' Her voice is a fragile thread, but its warmth is unwavering. The pillows are plumped with care and cradle Mrs Lapointe's frail form. This bed's a small island of order amid our chaos.

'No sitting here.' She pats the bed beside her lightly, her movement slow like honey. 'Stay by the door.'

I shake my head, smiling. 'I was near you yesterday. In the kitchen, with Lagara the cat.'

No response. She seems to have gotten worse since she came down to the kitchen. As though that used up all her energy and she can't now get it back. I settle onto the wooden chair between the doorway and her bed, reaching over to squeeze her hand.

'No touching,' she says. 'You need to protect yourself.'

I lean forward with my elbows resting on my knees. 'You'll be well again soon,' I say. I hate myself instantly. I know better than to offer empty comfort, just for the sake of it. She isn't going to get better, and my words won't give her comfort. I know that. 'I'm sorry.' Me repeatedly telling Mrs Lapointe how sorry I am isn't helping her, either.

'I'm not afraid,' she insists. Her voice is steady.

We both know the spectre of death looms ever closer with each passing day. Still, accepting that I don't have the power to fix her is a struggle. No doubt my gaze is full of concern and affection, and my dear friend will be hating me for that too.

'I should warn Tilda,' I say.

'Why?'

'In case she thinks you'll be well…'

Religious relics grace the walls; faded depictions of saints observe from above. Their serene faces offer quiet assurance and might even remind others that strength can be found even in the shadow of illness. I don't believe that, though. A simple crucifix hangs beside them, suspended by a single nail.

'I've tricked her into liking me,' I say. 'I tricked you, too. Hid the truth. Now I'm waiting for the wind to change…'

'I'm dying,' Mrs Lapointe says. 'That means I've limited time, yet here you are still yapping in riddles.' Her lips curve into a soft smile, the wrinkles around her eyes deepening. 'There's still some fire left in this old soul, though.' She taps her index finger against her chest. 'So if you could get to the point.'

Today her skin appears thin, almost translucent. Her gaunt cheeks and pronounced features contrast with her meticulous hair, which, despite her frailty, is swept into a severe bun. It exudes a quiet dignity amidst her suffering. Tilda must have been in here, trying to trick the illness. God, I hope she protected herself. Still, the escaped strands have a silvered sheen that catches the morning light in an imperfect halo. My friend is beautiful.

Perspiration-covered palms. That's how I am around her now. 'Because I'm preoccupied with not telling my secrets…' I gulp. 'She'd not like me anymore if she knew the truth.'

'Your secrets?' The words are forced out on a breath. 'We all have them.' I miss her laughter. I miss my friend.

Shame compounds. 'I never wanted to burden you, and now I don't want to burden Tilda,' I say. I twirl my hand in a circle about my face. 'The truth is, I'm drowning in grief and loss.'

A pause. 'Do you think I didn't realise?' my friend says. 'I know you, Mrs Taylor.' She releases a tiny sigh. 'I know you're carrying everyone else's struggles on those shoulders of yours.' I don't look at her. 'I just don't know exactly what's made your heart hurt.' A pause while she catches her breath. 'I'd argue our connection's built on mutual trust, respect, and understanding.' She coughs violently, her frail frame trembling with the effort as she struggles to catch her breath. 'I'm sorry,' she murmurs, her voice barely above a whisper as she fights to maintain her composure. 'You not sharing every aspect of your past doesn't make me love you less.'

My heart aches as I look upon Mrs Lapointe. Sorrow deepens; her rosy cheeks have faded to a delicate pallor.

'The less authentic I am, the less connected I feel to myself.' I'm crying. I wipe the tears onto my sleeve and push my tongue to the top of my mouth. I hate shedding tears. 'To let others near. To love again … that's opening myself up for loss. I didn't want to love again. Promised myself I'd not…'

A gentle chuckle escapes her lips, followed by a raspy cough that tugs at her chest. 'It's faith and love that's carried me through the last decade. When money was scarce and life uncertain, my faith held me steady and my ability to love guided me.'

'It's difficult keeping it together,' I say. 'Nora, Tilda, you… I've not felt this happy for years. I hate you all for making me happy. This is where I belong, but I'm furious about it.'

'Furious with me?'

'Yes, with all three of you.'

We're both smiling. My heart tightens, and I nod, unable to tear my eyes from the woman who has become a cornerstone in my life. Knowing that everything I hold dear hangs by a fragile thread, again, and there's nothing I can do but keep searching for solutions. 'Furious that you three have shown me how to love again.' I shudder as I voice my fear. 'I don't want you to die.'

Annie's Diary

12th August 1901

'I don't want you to die.' The stupidity of my words. Why did I say that? Do I believe she desires that fate herself? Ageing, dishonesty, death – my head is full.

Consequently, pen in hand, I attempt to articulate my life right now – the tangled mess of thoughts that swirl within me and in the physical world. I can't help but wonder about the version of myself I once knew; a version unencumbered by concerns of beauty or perception. It was a time when I felt content in the role Samuel and David gifted me, a role that brought me the purest happiness I've ever known. Yet, it was fleeting, never to be repeated. I ponder, were the tragedies and traumas that followed a consequence of allowing myself to want and need for the first time in my pathetic life? Would I trade one for the other? Yes, in a heartbeat. For my narrative is undeniably richer because of the brief time they were my world.

Was I entirely honest then though? Are we ever? Do we not always retain an aspect of ourselves that others never see? Preservation of self, perhaps. I don't really know what it is I'm seeking to resolve.

But could it be that Mrs Lapointe is correct? Can connection be built on mutual trust, respect, and understanding, rather than solely on sharing every aspect of one's personal history? Still, certainly my desire to be fully known and accepted for who I am reflects a universal human longing for authenticity and vulnerability in relationships.

I don't, in all honestly, know what it is that I'm attempting to express. I'm neither here nor there today. Instead I'm replaying how my friend may soon meet Death.

In recent days, the nagging presence of beauty and how others perceive me has become a constant companion. Perhaps it's because Tilda is young and beautiful, perhaps it's because she's close to the age I was when I met Samuel. Regardless, I find myself scrubbing at the spots on my hands as if hoping to erase them and transport myself back to being a wife and mother. At least once a week I wear black, donning high-necked garments to hide the signs of ageing that seem to be overtaking me. Am I transforming into a turkey, ready to be plucked at Thanksgiving?

I feel older today. Sagging jowls, lines marking weight gain, loose skin, breasts without shape. Unable to sleep, my hands run over this new territory, sad at how this newfangled me's an empty vessel. Perhaps I attempt to map my body through my fingertips. No part of me is familiar, though. Impermanence is whispered; the fragility of life is constant. I'm crippled by this fear that to love is to lose. That to live is to die. It's inevitable. To age a privilege. And yet, I try in vain to hide the effects of time, dabbing cold cream on my face as if it holds the power to turn back the clock. How absurd it seems now, to hope that such efforts could erase the years entirely and allow me to find David and Samuel again. To live this life differently. But no matter how hard I try, I cannot trick God.

I've no fear of physical death though. To die without meaning and legacy – that's where my fear resides. To die without the answer to, 'Why not me?' would be cruel. That I've survived this life for nothing. To die in poverty and to be buried in a pauper's grave with no one mourning my passing? To die without my name ever being spoken again? That's where horror resides.

Am I trapped in a barrel?

Still. I find solace in the women we've taken in. They are my hope. They will speak my name when I am gone, ensuring I am not forgotten. This is my legacy. This is why I teach, why I care. In them, I live on.

Matilda

12th August 1901

'Bloody cat,' I say.

It's been one day and the creature seems more interested in meowing at mice than killing them. Think it might be making friends. Mrs Taylor hasn't been downstairs all day. That's not like her. She's usually the sunshine around here. Bedroom door's open and her room's dimly lit. I think the cat needs feeding and I don't know what it's allowed.

'Mrs Taylor?'

There's no answer. I've looked every place else I can think of, so I take a step inside. Bed, chest of drawers, rocking chair, writing slope. There's a piece of paper. Looks like it's been covered in words. Been crumpled into a ball, though. I pick it up, unravel it carefully, and read it.

> *It was a time when I felt content in the role Samuel and David gifted me, a role that brought me the purest happiness I've ever known.*

That's when I see Mrs Taylor. Huddled beside the chest of drawers, facing the wall and with her back to me. Her shoulders are trembling, like she's trying to make her sobs little, but still they're filling this room. I can almost taste the sourness of her tears. They coat me tongue. I hesitate. Should I approach? Should I give her privacy?

A step closer. Should I cough? Should I say her name again? Don't want to frighten her.

A lit oil lamp's on the floor beside her. She holds two photographs: one in each hand. Another step closer. A baby perhaps, and a man in uniform; photographs so faded that their faces are barely visible. Room's colder than usual, too, and it clings to me skin now. I don't like this.

Mrs Taylor bristles: she knows I'm here.

'No,' she whispers. 'Don't look at me.'

She doesn't turn to face me. I see her tucking the photos under her skirt. Out of sight. She pats her cheeks with the back of her hands. Pat, pat, pat. Still, I don't speak. Maybe I'm holding me breath. Mrs Taylor doesn't turn to face me. She's on her knees, searching for something on the floor. Her movements are quick and I'm as still as a statue.

'Tilda.' Her voice sounds strained. 'Do you have any idea what true, deep pain feels like?' She turns to face me. Her eyes look different – more like a wounded animal's as it retreats into its den than the bold woman I know.

Whatever I thought was going on here wasn't this. But I nod; I really do have an idea of that kind of pain.

She exhales. Something unspoken and raw dances between us. I stand still. Terrified to move an inch. I'm trying not to breathe. I'm listening to the silence. She crouches, unmoving. We're connected: the shared burden of pain. We're separated: unspoken secrets. Don't really know each other. She understands all of that, too.

She's breathing weirdly. Heavy and panty. 'A pain so deep that you don't want to find the words to express it?' she asks.

I nod again; I really do.

I think about what happened to make me with child. Once, then another after that. Dead babies. I hesitate, then Nora. This is me chance to be heard, and I'm deciding not to take it. Some secrets need burying deep. Works for me. Only way to stop me brain from breaking.

'I … I can't tell you.' Me words are stammered. Tears trickle down me cheeks and I let them. Can't look at her. Don't want to see her disappointment.

'You shouldn't observe me like this,' she says.

Mrs Taylor stands and moves to her rocking chair. Her actions are slow, like each one pains her. I think truly sad people can spot sorrow in others. Like we see ourselves but different. I've always known she was hiding her sadness. Today though her grief's even heavier. Ages her from the inside out. She leans back in her chair, eyes on the flicker of the light. Not on me. Her hands rest on her lap; it looks like she's squeezing them.

'Sometimes, the pain becomes so intense that it morphs into a physical presence,' she says. 'Like a monster lurking in the shadows.' I glance at the corner of the room. What do I expect to see?

'Waiting to eat you up,' I say.

Mrs Taylor looks at me. She hesitates; long enough for the church bells to ring and a dog to bark. 'You want to scream. To let it all out.' She smiles a thin smile. Our eyes remain locked. 'But you can't, because that's not what us women do.'

I nod me head again. 'I can't.' I won't remove me eyes from her. First time seeing her like this. I'm frightened to blink, case this version of Mrs Taylor disappears. That I'll spend the rest of me life wondering if this happened. Even though she looks older than I've ever seen her look, she seems more me age than her own right now, too. How's that even possible? Like I've travelled back in time and I'm talking to the young Annie who I'd have as me friend. Slowly, I lower meself to the floor and sit cross-legged, shoving me shaking hands under me thighs.

'So, you keep it all bottled up inside, locked away. In here.' Her words tremble and I vibrate with them, like they're contagious. 'Terrified what others will do if you show them all of your broken pieces.'

I think that might be what's happening to her now. She's showing me she's broken. Me thighs quiver like I'm cold. I ache for her; ache for meself, too. Me secret pain – the broken bits I vowed I'd never share with no one – it gnaws at me insides. It's the monster in the corner of every room. Bottled up so tight I can't breathe. All of them things are it. Fear he'll find Nora, fear she'll like him best, fear she'll hate me for keeping them apart. Fear he'll take her away; me world would end if he did that.

I can't think about those broken bits, though. They're too mighty. They'll form into a living thing that'll swallow me whole. Instead, I spend me days standing guard. On the lookout for something I can't voice. Maybe Mrs Taylor would understand that not voicing, but does she understand what it is to fear another living soul? There's an irony that as me love for me daughter grows and grows, me fear multiplies, too. Perhaps it would end if I stopped loving the very bones of Nora, but I won't. She's the reason I breathe.

'Who's David?'

'No,' she says.

I nod. I understand. 'How do you… How do you keep going?' I ask, me voice barely over a whisper. 'When the pain and fear's eating you whole.'

'The hardest part is when you're still in love.'

She closes her eyes. I wait. When they open, they're full of something that makes me sob. Sorrow? Determination? Both? She's lost someone in a different way to me.

'You find a way to channel it. To turn it into something else … something that can't hurt you anymore. It's not easy, but it's the only way to survive,' she says, and her voice changes, deeper, stronger.

I see the switch happen. Subtle and instant, but still it's like a drape drops. Show's over. That's how she lives – protecting herself. How she survives. Like Morgiana passing through the labyrinth of deceit and secrecy. That's what I do, too, but, again, different.

'Find your answer to "Why not me?", Tilda.'

Mrs Taylor stands, steadies herself on the rickety rocking chair. She wibbles slightly at first. Another shaky step and she makes her way to the window. Her movements are slow and deliberate. Atmosphere's somehow stoic and calm though.

'Why'd you do that?' I ask. 'Pretend like none of this has happened.'

She shakes her head. 'I'm just being silly,' she says. 'This kind of talking won't find us solutions.' She pulls the net curtains back, watching the last light of day before it gives way to darkness.

'Will Mrs Lapointe be well?'

'Survival, Tilda, is something women fight for every single day.' She places her hand on the windowpane. 'We wake up. We face the world, with all its challenges and heartache ... and then we push through.'

I fiddle with the frayed edge on the cuff of me blouse. 'But it's not enough, is it? To just be surviving.'

I wait as she considers me words. A minute passes and she turns to me. A small smile tugs at the corners of her lips. 'You're right. It's what we do after we survive that truly matters. How we find a way to make the most of the life we have,' she says. 'Even when it's...'

'Difficult?'

Mrs Taylor laughs. The sound's like magic. A drop of rain after midday sun.

I laugh, too. It isn't because I find her words funny. It's a relief. The lightness is welcomed, and I can't help but think about Nora and the life I want to give her. I want me and her to be like Sarah and Olive. I need what I never had with me mother.

'We owe it to our past,' she says. 'Don't we?'

'I owe it to me future.'

I look back to where she was sitting on me floor. Where are the photographs? I want to ask her about the man in the uniform and about the baby, too, but I don't. I rush to hug Mrs Taylor. She pulls away and holds me hands. Reaches them out in front of us, and I watch as her smile grows stronger.

'Yes, we both do,' she says. 'We can help each other.'

'Cat needs feeding,' I say.

Annie

28th August 1901

I'd noted a difference in Mrs Lapointe these last two weeks. Last night was the worst she's been though. The coughing made her entire body rattle and shake. I hate that I wanted silence, that I prayed for her to sleep. Now, with daylight not yet breaking, I'm worried she might not wake up. I fall back onto my bed. The darkness feels alive, wrapping around me and making the silence even more profound.

The door creaks, shifting open slowly. Tilda holds Nora on her right hip and a candle in her left hand. She offers me a weary smile, her eyes searching mine.

'Has Mrs Lapointe settled?' Her voice is soft and laced with concern.

I hesitate for a moment, exhaling. 'She has.' My voice is nothing more than a whisper. I pause to find the right words. I don't want to scare her, but she needs to understand. She's not a child. I sit up straight. 'But… I'm growing increasingly worried about her. I hear her coughing every night, and she seems constantly fatigued.'

'I hear her, too.' Nora rests her head on her mama's shoulder, her thumb finding her mouth. She's tired.

'Last night was bad … she was in pain. The medicine helped, but it's dulling her.'

'At least she can sleep now.' Matilda hands me the candle and walks to the window. She pulls back the thin covering, her face bathed in the pre-dawn light reflecting deep concern. The light disappears. 'She needs a doctor again.'

I nod, a heaviness weighing on my heart. 'I'll arrange for one tomorrow.'

There's a pause, filled only with Nora's soft sucking of her thumb. The occasional sliver of moonlight peeks through the window and dances across the floorboards, giving the space an ethereal air. I move to the chair beside the window and opposite Tilda, lifting the book from it. My fingers trace the gold-embossed title: *The Blue Fairy Book.* I place it on a nearby table; its pages whisper as they rustle together. That's where I found my idea. It was resting in plain sight all along.

Settling into the chair, I face Tilda. Nora's even more peaceful now, her eyes closed, lulled by the rhythm of her mother's heartbeat.

A low series of coughs from the nearby bedroom. We freeze. We wait; they stop.

'I was reading *The Forty Thieves* again.' I nod towards the book.

Matilda's face lights up. 'Without me? Do you want to read it to us again now?'

I shake my head. 'Morgiana's story gave me an idea.' My voice is hushed, but I'm speaking quickly, like I'm sharing an urgent secret. 'I've been thinking about it since the meeting with George Whitman.'

Matilda bobs her head enthusiastically, urging me to continue.

'Mr Whitman said Carlisle Graham was planning a barrel plunge over Niagara Falls. And I said, "I suppose I'll have to show him how it's done properly." I meant going over the Falls.' I pause. 'And back when I first mentioned going over the Falls. We were all in the kitchen. Olive and Sarah, too. And you said I was like Morgiana. Do you remember?' She shrugs. 'But it's been in here.' I tap my forehead. 'Like a lodger that won't leave.'

'Mrs Taylor,' she says, swaying on the spot. The pace of her movements has quickened. 'Tell me.'

I lean forward with my elbows resting on my knees. 'Imagine, if you will, an oil jar. Well, not a jar … a pickle barrel. One large enough to jam a person inside.'

She looks at me, puzzled. 'Why on Earth would I imagine someone jammed into a barrel?'

'To survive going over the Falls.'

I see her face shift. I see her look of genuine shock. 'Mrs Taylor.' She breathes out the words.

'Fame and fortune or instant death,' I say. My heart is giving long, dragging thuds.

'Are you pretending?' Her voice is laced with disbelief. 'I was expecting a kayak or a raft.'

I shake my head, resolute. This is not a joke. 'Think about it.' I hold up my palm to stop her arguments. I shift in the chair, sitting with my back straight and shoulders squared. 'It makes perfect sense.'

Tilda raises an eyebrow, scrutinising me, a half-smile on her lips. 'They lock women away for suggesting less.' She giggles softly. She still considers this a joke.

I inhale and hold my breath, rubbing my fingers across my forehead. 'Tilda, just listen,' I say, and she bobs her head cautiously. 'A barrel floats on water, right?'

'Well … yes…'

Her hesitation spurs me on. 'It gets tossed about, especially in turbulent waters, but it never sinks.'

'If it's watertight,' she says.

I nod at that. 'But you accept that a well-made barrel would go over the Falls and come out the other side intact and floating?'

Nora moves in Tilda's arms. She shushes her to calm her and then looks up. 'I accept that … assuming it misses sharp and jagged rocks. Or doesn't get sucked into a whirlpool and forced under the water. Or get washed down the river to God knows where.'

'So you accept that a barrel could … in theory … traverse the Falls safely.'

She shrugs her shoulders but says, 'In theory, yes.'

'So…' I extend the word as if trying to buy time. 'Now consider this.'

She bobs her head for me to continue.

'If I jam myself inside that barrel, I won't be thrown around. If the barrel survives, then so does the person inside. Sure, I might get a little seasick, but the barrel will eventually reach the calm waters and that's where they'll scoop me out.'

'Like a pickle,' Matilda says, frowning.

'Yes, yes.' I laugh, but she doesn't.

Still, she's not removed her eyes from me, but there's a growing expression of understanding on her face. A spark of excitement. A tiny spark, but I see it.

'But wait…'

I nod again, urging her to ask whatever questions she might have.

'Well … aren't you—'

'Don't you dare say it, Matilda Hamilton.'

'It's just, it's the kind of thing a young man might do.' She slumps back in her chair.

'I'm neither too old nor the wrong sex.'

We stay in silence for a moment. I let her ponder it all. She's not looking at me, but I'm observing her. I see her excitement. I see it all fall into place.

'The Lady of the Falls.' Her voice is loud. Nora whimpers and stirs. Tilda shushes close to her daughter's ear.

'See, I'm not a crazy old goose.' It's a whisper. 'But there are just a few problems.'

'Other than certain death?' She's grinning, and now I am, too. I shake my head.

'First, I don't have a barrel; it would have to be specially made.' I hold up one finger. 'I've already drawn up some dimensions and ideas.' I point to the paper on my writing slope. 'But that won't be inexpensive.'

'You can't just nip to the market and buy a special barrel for going over Niagara Falls?'

I like her humour, and snort. 'It'll need to be very strong and watertight, with some kind of padding inside.'

'You've thought this through.'

I nod; of course I have. Constantly, and for weeks already. 'It's ongoing. And I'll need someone to get the word out, make me famous, and help us gain financially,' I say.

Matilda frowns. 'It always comes back to money.'

'I think I can do it,' I say, standing from my seat and bowing dramatically.

Annie's Diary

7th September 1901

As we boarded the train in Buffalo, a subtle shift enveloped me; an intangible anticipation lingering in the air. At first, I marvelled at its sleek and modern design – compared to the horsedrawn carriages of my youth – but now the rhythmic chug of the locomotive marks the beginning of a journey. Buffalo to Niagara Falls; Tilda, Nora and me. A journey that will extend beyond the mere physical distance between destinations. Each passing moment blurs outside the window; a fleeting reminder of the transient nature of time.

Lost in the gentle sway of the carriage, my thoughts meander like the tracks beneath us. Tilda hasn't spoken for the last hour. She's in awe. This journey is more than a mere passage; it symbolises the twists and turns of life's voyage. With each mile traversed, I embrace the uncertainties ahead, knowing that all bends hold the promise of new beginnings.

Annie

7th September 1901

Since stepping into the train station, this afternoon's passed in a dreamlike exploration. Matilda and I have been walking back and forth along the dirt path, taking in the view of Niagara Falls. Sometimes in silence, sometimes in single file, now side by side. Nora sleeps in her pram and our shoes crunch a rhythm against the gravel beneath them. I adjust the bonnet on my head. Most of my hair's escaped, refusing to be tamed under the head covering. The air's more biting than I'd anticipated. The wind whips around us, but I don't mind.

This path runs parallel to the Niagara River, with the water churning and frothing as it rushes towards the Falls. There's a viewing deck that we can't access with the pram, so I've not ventured along it. In the distance, the spray from the Falls rises like a giant misty cloud.

'It's beautiful here,' I say. 'Otherworldly, even.'

We've passed couples strolling arm in arm, well-dressed ladies shopping, and businessmen in top hats and tails. Folk flock here and we fit right in; Mrs Lapointe's chest of clothes continues to gift us appropriate apparel. Tilda's been telling me about the invitation she received to a party.

'His name's Mr Henry Hills,' Tilda says, refusing to change the topic. Her cheeks are ruddy and the glow's making her look even more beautiful.

'I wasn't interested in him gone January and I'm definitely not interested now.'

'In courting?'

'In Henry Hills.'

'You never take me ideas seriously.' She's sulking. 'Mrs Taylor. Please.'

'No.' I've no real excuse other than I've no desire to attend. My time is better spent making lists of plans for my trip to the Falls and writing letters to folk for help – financial and practical. I walk on, pushing Nora's pram a little quicker. Matilda accelerates her pace to keep up.

'The barrel is my plan.'

She laughs and I turn, scowling at her.

It's cold, and I shiver. I move my tongue over my dry lips. I tug at my jacket – actually, Mrs Lapointe's – trying to keep the chill at bay. Matilda's wearing a dress that clings to her curves, cut too low for propriety, and too thin for the biting cold. Seems youth doesn't feel the chill. I've forgotten how that must feel. Even my teeth knock against each other with the cold.

Still, the air's thick with the smell of coal and industry. Here the buildings are old and dilapidated, some made of wood and others of brick. Signs advertising hotels, saloons, and shops hang haphazardly from their facades. Times are hard and needs must. I can't help but wrinkle my nose. I focus on the floor and my feet. They're crammed into Mrs Lapointe's mother-in-law's boots. They're a size too small.

'Seagulls,' I say. I smile. I look up to see that soaring and mewing.

'Gulls,' Tilda replies. 'Seagulls don't exist.'

I grin; I like her mind. She hides her wit and intelligence. Dismissed too quickly by others, but not by me. 'Look.' I nod for Tilda to take the pram. I quickstep away and down to the viewing deck.

'Mrs Taylor,' she calls, and I wave in response.

Its wooden construction takes me too close to the edge. Is it odd that the thought of tumbling over unnerves me? Niagara Falls stretches below; a mesmerising display of force and beauty. The noise is thunderous. Birds glide above and beneath, their cries muted by the sound of the Falls. This is the closest I've ever been to nature like this, in all its glory and power. Its deep rumble harmonises with the planet's heartbeat. Its noise overpowers. I look down. The water's cascade sparkles in hues of blue and white. It takes on a silvery glow under the sun's brilliance.

'Mrs Taylor,' Tilda shouts again. I don't turn around. I pretend I can't hear her.

'I vowed I'd not let anyone else close to me,' I say, knowing the Falls is listening and Tilda won't be able to hear. Caring for others comes with the risk of a disintegration of self. Still, I love Tilda, Nora and Mrs Lapointe like they're my own flesh and blood. They're all I've got. I can't lose them – I realise that now. My definition of unconditional is to love despite knowing it'll end in pain.

'Look, Father.' A small boy brushes past me, stopping at the wooden construction. My hand reaches out instinctively.

'Not too close to the edge,' I say, but he isn't listening. Instead, he jumps up and down on the spot as he points. He stares at the water in awe.

'What do you see?' I crouch to his level and follow the direction of his finger. Endless torrents of water crash down with a booming echo. They launch a mist into the air, and as the sunlight kisses that vapour it transforms into gleaming rainbows. Magnificent, hopeful arches.

'Beautiful,' I say. 'Truly beautiful.' He rushes back in the direction he came but I don't turn away from this view. Nothing else matters here. The Falls commands my attention. They demand my entire focus. All my senses are screaming. All of them have something to say.

Still, my knees creak and quiver under my skirt. I clutch the railing as I straighten up.

'I need a barrel,' I say and the Falls roar in agreement.

The wind shifts the mist, giving me a cool, invigorating splash. A sudden cold shock. I giggle. I'm alive. I'm truly breathing. From here, nature's vastness is undeniable. It puts into perspective my tiny place within its grandeur.

'I'm going to do it. I'm going to go over there in a barrel and I'm going to survive.' I nod my head to the Falls. Fame, foolishness and financial gain are going to dance hand in hand this time.

The barrier on this viewing deck prevents me from stepping closer. It stops me from falling. Still though, the draw of this water is magnetic. My hair's responding to the call, too. It's wilder, it's even more chaotic. It's blowing out from my bonnet in all directions. I pull it into a bunch, taming with a knot at the base of my neck.

'You're a decision I've already made,' I say.

The Iroquois believed the roar was the voice of the spirit of the waters. The mist rises, it envelops, it becomes me. Or, perhaps, I become it. I turn and there are souvenir carts and food stalls near Tilda. With their vibrant colours and tempting smells, they all stand insignificant against this backdrop. They're artificial. They're fake. This is nature's raw power. Still, business is good. Crowds gather, and that's without a daredevil performing.

I look around. Those visiting are enthralled, too. Gentlemen in tailored suits – their hats held to their chests – stand beside women in long flowing dresses. Parasols are angled to shield their clothes and hair from the mist. Young ones, some with bows tied neatly in their hair, point; I like that their faces are all lit with wonder. Nearby, an older man with a silver beard and spectacles, sketches the scene in a worn leatherbound journal. We're all hypnotised, though. The noise demands that we pay the Falls attention. I turn back to them, too.

'Even more crowds will gather to witness a daredevil woman risking her life,' I say. Can I almost hear the cheers and excitement? I nod; I can. I'd be watched. I'd be seen. No longer invisible. People would speak my name again and again.

I pause. Hoping for a response. I used to teach children about Lelawala, Princess of Niagara. There was a dance that accompanied the story. Her canoe was caught by the rough waves and hurtled toward the Falls. As it pitched over and she fell to her death, Heno, the God of Thunder caught her in his arms. He carried her to his home in the Falls, just beneath the thundering veil of water. A memory stirred, a story I'd forgotten until this very moment.

A misty veil obscures Lower Niagara below, concealing the base of the drop and making the fall over the edge seem insignificant. It doesn't feel impossible, yet all those lives lost attempting it. Surely that's evidence that it is? I shake that thought away.

'Long way down?' A voice behind me, but I don't turn to respond.

This force of nature fills me with wonder and possibility. It's urging me or perhaps its thunder is giving me the power I need to stay focused. The barrel will be the key to my success.

I release the knot in my hair and pull my bonnet from my head. I shake my hair free. I close my eyes. It's out of control. It's free. Am I? 'You're in the mist. You're in my hair. You're showing me what I can be,' I say, my voice barely audible against the cacophony. 'You're the spirit that resides here.'

I shift my head to the right. To the left. I listen. The continuous roar fills my ears and drowns any other voice. The sound calls to me. As I think this, the wooden planks beneath my boots shake in confirmation. My eyes jump open, and my fingers grip the railing for support. Excitement flutters in my stomach. I can do this. I really can. I'll survive the Falls. I'll be the first woman ever to achieve that. The first *person*, period. In a barrel. Me – Annie Edson Taylor.

I close my eyes again, and I imagine David and Samuel in the mist. Being cared for by the spirit of Lelawala residing there; they're all guiding and protecting me. Morgiana is, too. I smile. I have much to gain. For me, for my friends. Maybe I can even buy some land in Texas again, and put down roots. It would be good to go back there one day. Matilda, Nora, Mrs Lapointe, too.

The smell of roasted peanuts drifts up my nostrils. I'm not alone. A stranger stands on my left, crunching his food from the fair. He grips a paper cone of peanuts, half of them eaten. He picks at a side molar, attempting to free a lodged peanut skin. A different tourist approaches on my right, breaking pieces of cotton candy from a wooden stick as she walks. She stands close enough for her skirt to overlap with mine, yet she doesn't look my way.

'This view always makes me cry,' she says, dabbing at her eyes.

I nod, I bite my lip. The two strangers stare ahead, mesmerised by the power of the Falls. One observes the water and twirls the sugar strands into solid balls, before popping them into her mouth, the other is fixated and nervously crunching peanuts. I wonder what they are contemplating. I bet they're not planning a trip in a barrel. I smile, I nod. My palms are clammy. My plan is decided – to build a barrel, to conquer the impossible, to no longer be poor, to help my friends, to make history, and to prove that I am more than just an invisible, ageing woman on the edge of a precipice. Failure is not an option here. My death would leave my friends in a worst situation.

'I'm going to embrace my age, and redefine what it means to be a strong, determined woman,' I shout to the Falls.

'That's nice.' The candy-cotton-eating woman offers an encouraging smile.

The peanut-eating guy laughs.

I turn and walk back to Tilda and Nora. 'Did I ever tell you about Lelawala, Princess of Niagara?'

Part III: Barrel Dreams

'I remember Mrs Taylor's storytelling making that boarding house a sanctuary, but it were her presence that made it feel like a home. I'm not exaggerating and don't want to tell you all my secrets, but that woman saved my life and enjoyed a butter tart. I owe her everything I have and more.'

Minnie Montgomery

23 Queen's Road,
St. John's, Newfoundland,
Dominion of Newfoundland.
October 13th 1901

Dear Matilda,

I have little doubt that my other letter arrived with you, yet still you have resolved to pay no attention to me. I am deeply hurt by your continued silence. Despite our strained past, I had hoped that the bond of family would prevail, and you would welcome the opportunity to reunite. It is disheartening to see that you have chosen to ignore my letters. Your naivety was once sweet, but I can see that now it misguides you. Nevertheless, I will not let this inhibit our reunion.

I find myself increasingly eager to meet with little Nora again. As family, it is only right that I become acquainted with the child who shares our bloodline. Rest assured, Matilda, I will not be dissuaded from my goal of reuniting with you both and intimately.

With that in mind, it is important that you understand the gravity of our situation. Family ties are not easily severed, and neither are the responsibilities that come with them. I expect you to reconsider your stance and receive me with open arms when I arrive. Your reluctance thus far has been disappointing, but I trust that will not persist. The clock is ticking. My arrival is imminent.

I implore you to think about what is best for both you and for little Nora. The world can be a cruel place for those without the support of family, and I would hate for either of you to suffer unnecessarily.

Consider my words carefully and remember that there is much at stake for us all.

Yours and with anticipation,
Uncle William

Annie

16th October 1901

'Well that was easier than I expected,' I say. I look at my piece of paper, then back up at the travelling fair's sign. My senses rattle to the sound of laughter and the distant roar of the Falls. This is the right place.

The air's thick with expectation and the sickly smell of cotton candy. It's as if the whole area's been spun from sugar that's now beginning to melt. Still, I'm drawn to the amusement park this balmy evening. I'm seeking out a specific man. His name's come to me in whispers. I'm told he's the man who makes dreams come true. I'm running out of time, many letters asking for help have been unanswered and I've depleted all other ideas and contacts. This must work.

As I step closer to the cotton-candy stall, a man with weathered hands deftly spins sugar into delicate wisps. His apron's dusted with a sugary haze and his warm smile beckons passersby. 'Do you know a Mr F. Russell?' I ask.

He points his wooden stick to the right. 'Russ,' he shouts. 'Old woman wants you.'

I shake my head as I walk away. An earlier downpour has left scattered puddles, and now the light plays on the water – dancing and flickering. They form soggy stones that lead to a wooden construction. Mr Russell is leaning against a booth. His strong jawline's framed by a well-groomed beard, and his eyes are black like coal beneath a stylishly tipped hat. Our gaze meets. His tailored suit speaks of his attention to detail, and he has an air of confidence that comes from either good breeding or success. I'm assuming the latter.

The heels of my too-tight boots tap rhythmically on the wooden planks near him. 'Are you Mr F. Russell?' My voice is bold and unapologetic. I sound more male than female.

He looks me up and then down, and I watch his eyes calculating my worth. He must reckon I prove no threat and possibly could have money, as he smiles warmly. 'Indeed, I am. And who might you be?'

I offer a firm handshake, gripping tightly and looking directly into his eyes. 'Annie,' I reply. 'Annie Edson Taylor.' I hesitate and then add, 'Mrs.'

I've no idea why I add my marital status, but Mr Russell chuckles from his abdomen.

'I've come to inquire about your work with stunters,' I say, batting away the air that carries his laughter.

A knowing grin plays at the corner of his lips. 'You've been listening to rumours?' A statement that curls into a question. I nod. 'Well, Annie Taylor…'

I note that he doesn't say Mrs. He's standing close enough for me to smell alcohol on his breath.

I roll up the sleeves on my dress in readiness for hard work. 'I want to be a daredevil, Mr Russell.' I say the words without emotion. So much so that he doesn't respond. He's frozen in the moment and waiting for a punchline. He's staring, too, and my throat tightens. No doubt he's attempting to formulate a suitable response.

Planting my feet firmly on the ground, hands on hips, my gaze is stern. 'I want to feel the rush of performing a death-defying feat. To hear the gasps of the audience … and to know I've done something extraordinary.' The words rush out like water.

He regards me with an odd expression. A mix of admiration,

scepticism and disgust; there's no hiding that his eyes linger on the wrinkles decorating my face. I'd bet money on him wondering if I truly understood the physical demands of the profession.

'Aren't you a bit…' he hesitates, perhaps trying to be polite, 'mature … to be considering such a dangerous career?'

My body bristles at his doubt and my fingers form into a fist. Still, I reply with my best smile. 'Age is just a number, Mr Russell. I've more spirit and vitality than many half as old.' I pause to let him respond, but he doesn't. Have I shocked him? 'Please don't underestimate me. I've travelled here by train and have a limited time to convince you.'

He stands up straight. Do I detect a twinkle of respect in his eyes as he brushes the sleeve of his jacket? 'How about we explore this here fair together, and you explain why you think you've got what it takes to be a daredevil?'

I nod at that, and Mr Russell loops an arm for me. He's daring me already.

'So,' I say, hooking my arm inside his and stepping into the colourful maze of the amusement park. 'I've got an idea, but I need a barrel that's made of Kentucky oak, about five feet in height and weighing around one-hundred and sixty pounds.'

'A barrel?' He stops, unlooping his arm and reaching for my hands. He holds them. The energy of the fairground pulses through the soles of my boots and to our fingertips. Anticipation hangs in the air between us.

'To confront the sheer drop of the Horseshoe Falls itself,' I say. The words rush out – harsh and unregretful.

'Not just the rapids leading up to the Falls?' he asks, and I shake my head.

'That's been achieved too often now.' I bat the air as if pushing away his suggestion. 'None have survived the full plunge… So, to take the barrel stunt one big step further … I intend to tumble over the precipice of the Falls itself.'

'In a barrel?'

'In a barrel.'

'That's suicide.' He thumps his fist into his palm to emphasise the point. He's shaking his head vigorously, too. 'I don't want any part of that.'

'I read a story about hiding in barrels.'

'I'm sorry?'

'If I can stay wedged inside and it is upright, then I'll float.'

A pause. I think he might be about to speak but he hesitates instead.

'Those Indian maidens tried to conquer Niagara in birch canoes,' I say, words gushing out and filling the silence. I will convince him to work with me. 'Insanity. Going over the Falls in a Kentucky oak barrel is a much better idea.'

'You know that no man's survived this before?'

Perhaps he prides himself on being logical. I nod again, and with a little more vigour. 'No woman has, either.' My smile is so very wide and full that he'll perhaps consider me hysterical. 'I'll be the first person ever to survive going over the Falls.' My head feels like it might burst. 'I want to do this by October the twenty-third,' I say.

'Why the urgency?'

'The day before my birthday.'

'You'll be…'

I hesitate, but only for a second. 'Forty-three,' I say. 'Worst case, I die, and you still make money. But I plan on surviving … and that'll make us both rich.'

'Both of us?'

'I need a manager,' I say.

He takes a step away from me, holding up both palms in protest. 'I'm a mere circus promoter. A ringmaster, too.' He's smiling. We both know he's more than that.

'I've taken the liberty of preparing a bill of sale.' I reach into my handbag and pull out a piece of parchment. I hold it out to him, and he hesitates before taking it.

He runs his index finger over the words, perhaps he's checking that they won't disappear.

'It's a guarantee, Mr Russell,' I say. 'A bill of sale for everything I own in the world. Even my bedlinen.' I laugh at that. Mr Russell doesn't react. He's still studying the list of my belongings. 'You fund this stunt and, if I die during it, you get everything I own … as well as all funds we make from the stunt itself.'

I hold my nerve. I wait. Mr Russell sighs loudly. 'I knew you'd be trouble, from the moment I set eyes on you, Mrs Taylor,' he says, then he laughs from his abdomen again.

'Seven days.'

'That's when you're proposing to complete the stunt?'

I nod and he whistles.

'Needs to be while the Pan-American Exposition in Buffalo's still open.'

He bobs his head to himself. Another pause, and then he loops his arm back through mine. 'I said to myself, that first minute I saw you… Said this chance meeting would change the course of both our lives. Do you know Carlisle Graham?'

'Do you know the barrel man who braved the Niagara rapids?' I ask, surprised.

Mr Russell grins widely. 'He once told me that he wanted to go over the Falls himself, but never found the right barrel. I told him he was a coward. Now, you, Mrs Taylor, seem to have more guts than any man I've ever met.'

'Thank you,' I say, my voice filled with pride.

'And you'll need all that courage,' he continues. 'The circus is full of folk with incredible stories. There's Magnus, the strongman who once lifted a horse above his head in front of the Sultan of Zanzibar. And Lolly, the bearded lady who charmed the King of Siam into dancing with her.'

I laugh, unable to contain my fascination. 'You certainly have a flair for the dramatic.'

'And then there's me,' he says, a twinkle in his eye. 'I started as a juggler in a backstreet circus in Paris. One night, I was kidnapped by a rival troupe and had to escape by tightrope walking over the Seine with nothing but a balancing pole. When I reached the other side, I knew that I was destined for more than juggling.'

'Your tales are as grand and colourful as the fair itself.'

We pass acrobats practising their flips and spins. 'These folks,' he says, gesturing towards them, 'they risk life and limb every day for the thrill of the performance and the roar of the crowd. You'll fit right in.'

'I can see why they say you're the man who makes dreams come true.'

'Welcome to the circus, Mrs Taylor,' he says, tipping his hat with a flourish. 'Let's make history together.'

'Let's, indeed,' I agree, feeling a surge of determination and excitement. The fairground shimmers with the promise of adventure.

Going Over the Falls - Mrs Taylor's Notes and Requirements

- *<u>Material</u>: the barrel needs to be constructed from sturdy and reliable materials, such as Kentucky oak (and definitely not birch), to withstand the force of the water and the impact of the fall.*
- *<u>Size</u>: the barrel must be large enough for me to fit inside comfortably, with some space for cushioning materials to protect from the impact. It needs to accommodate my height and width, while still being agile enough to navigate the Falls.*
- *<u>Watertight</u>: the barrel must be watertight to prevent water from entering and filling during the descent, which could lead to drowning or increasing the impact force.*
- *<u>Air Supply</u>: it's crucial to ensure a sufficient air supply within the barrel for me to breathe during the stunt. The cooper must provide a secure method of ventilation or air supply that won't compromise the barrel's watertight integrity.*
- *<u>Harness</u>: to prevent my bouncing around inside the barrel during the fall, I require a harness or some form of internal strapping to secure me in place.*
- *<u>Opening and Closing Mechanism</u>: the barrel needs a secure and reliable opening and closing mechanism, like a hatch or a lid, which can be easily opened from the inside or outside to allow for a quick*

escape after the stunt. However, the other factors are perhaps more important.

- *<u>Cushioning</u>: to further protect from the impact, the cooper must incorporate cushioning materials, such as pillows, blankets, or straw, into the barrel's design.*

Possible dimensions

- *Ten hoops of Kentucky oak riveted every 4 inches.*
- *Head – 12 inches*
- *Middle – 34 inches*
- *Foot – 15 inches*
- *Overall height – 4 ½ foot.*
- *Overall weight – around 160 lbs.*

Annie

17th October 1901

Still excited from yesterday's meeting with Mr Russell, and with my feet tingling from sitting cross-legged on the worn wooden floor of the parlour, I count the pieces of templates already cut. The dim light filters through the lace curtains, casting a pleasant glow over the room and illuminating the cardboard sections around me. It's a sturdy material, though nowhere near as durable as the Kentucky oak of a real barrel. For now though, it'll have to suffice. Ten hoops, riveted every four inches – each one with loops of string carefully cinched tight around the cardboard to mimic the strength of the original construction.

With a ruler in hand, I meticulously mark out the final length and width, double-checking my calculations against the measurements of the original barrel. The head, the middle – both cut already. I measured and remeasured, determined to get them perfect. Now, the foot.

'This has to work.' The sound of my voice echoes faintly in the too-quiet room. 'It must.'

I tap my pencil against my chin, then pop it on the floor and pick up the scissors. The sharp edges of the blades slice along the pencil outline and through the cardboard with ease. My mind races with all the reckonings and dimensions, hoping that every piece fits together just right. Each portion needs to be precise, every angle exact; my makeshift creation needs to mirror the dimensions of the real thing as closely as possible. This is the final piece – the foot of the barrel. One cut left.

'Done.' I stretch my legs in front of me, wiggling my toes inside my boots. 'Now more hole punching.'

Using the scissors, I make holes along the foot's edge. The tip of my tongue protrudes, and I bite down as I concentrate. 'All done.'

Pulling to slacken the ball of string, I begin to lace the cardboard pieces together. Lengths of sturdy twine weave through the many holes I've carefully pierced along the perimeters. I knot every five holes and each of those knots pulls tight with a satisfying tug. The makeshift barrel slowly takes shape beneath my fingers. Rough around the edges, temporary and crude, but it's mine – a testament to my determination and resolve.

Finally, with the last knot secured, I lift the cardboard barrel and set it on the floor before me. It's rough and ready, but sturdy enough for my purposes. I shift onto my knees and, with a sense of anticipation fluttering in my chest, I lift and then lower the cardboard barrel over me. The cardboard creaks softly, but I fit. The dimensions are just as I'd imagined. Head, middle, foot — each section snug against my body, the overall height rising above me. It cocoons me in a space both confining and liberating all at once.

Closing my eyes, I imagine the roar of the Falls, the rush of wind against my face as I bob along. Gripping the cardboard edges of the barrel, I lean forward, feeling the increasingly familiar sensation of anticipation and fear mingling in the pit of my stomach.

'Here goes nothing,' I say, my voice barely more than a breath as I tie string around myself.

With one final tug on the knots, I settle back against the cardboard walls. I allow myself to linger in this too-quiet space; the weight of my dreams presses against the confines of the cardboard barrel. The dim light of the parlour fades into darkness around me. There's a tangible sense of weightlessness within the cramped confines. It's a surreal moment. Me in a cardboard barrel, amidst the humble surroundings of my improvised workshop, yet knowing I'm on the brink of something monumental. A surge courses through my veins; my knees tremble, my jaw chatters. I imagine the roar of the Falls, the thunderous rush of water against wood and rock. I can almost feel the spray on my face. I close my eyes, take a deep breath—

'Mrs Taylor?'

'In here.'

'Where?'

'In the barrel.'

'Where on earth have you been these last three days?' Tilda's voice cuts through the hush of the parlour, her tone laced with curiosity. 'Mrs Lapointe said you were visiting friends.'

I glance up from the cardboard barrel, and she's looking down. I shake my head; that's not where I've been. 'Back to Niagara Falls,' I say and then grin. 'I found us a manager.'

Matilda's eyes widen in surprise, her mouth forming a silent 'O' of realisation. 'You went back to the Falls on your own?' Her disbelief is evident in her tone.

I nod enthusiastically. 'I'm sorry,' I say, hearing that my voice is shaded with determination. 'But I figure if we're going to make a splash, we might as well start at the top. And who better to help us navigate the waters than someone who knows them like the back of their hand?'

With a sly smile, I lean back against the cardboard barrel, a sense of satisfaction washing over me.

'Tilda,' I say, my voice popping with enthusiasm, 'I found someone willing to take a chance on me.'

'You did? Who?' She leans forward eagerly. It's like she's looking to see if there's room for her to climb into the barrel with me.

I chuckle softly, relishing this opportunity to share my news. 'A man by the name of Mr Russell,' I say, with a note of admiration creeping into my voice. 'He's the ringmaster of a travelling circus and, let me tell you, Tilda, I've heard he's quite the character.'

'And what did this Mr Russell have to say?'

My heart races with excitement at the memory of our conversation.

'He's interested,' I admit, unable to keep the smile from my face. 'Interested enough to give me a shot, at least.'

Matilda's eyes are wild with excitement, her smile mirroring my own. 'That's wonderful. I knew you could do it.'

I shake my head, hoping that'll detach the nagging thought of the bill of sale tucked safely away in Mr Russell's pocket. Matilda won't comprehend the lengths I'm willing to go to for this chance at success. It's a secret I'll keep for now.

'I must ask…' She gestures to the cardboard barrel. 'What are you doing?' Her incredulous expression only fuels my excitement further. With a smirk, I tap the cardboard walls and they wobble.

'It's time to shake things up and to make our own luck.'

'But with cardboard?' Tilda says, and I hear the concern. Perhaps she's worried I've lost my mind.

I wave her apprehension away with a dismissive flick of my wrist. 'Cardboard, string, whatever scraps I can find,' I say. 'I might not have riches or resources these days, but I've got grit and determination in spades. And mark my words, Tilda – I'm going to turn this little stunt of mine into our ticket to the big time.'

With a mischievous grin, I gesture grandly to the makeshift barrel. 'This may not be the most glamorous start to my journey, but it's a start nonetheless.'

Matilda's laughter bubbles into my improvised cask. It's infectious and warm. 'And if anyone can turn cardboard into gold, it's you, Mrs Taylor.'

Annie

18th October 1901

The scent of freshly cut wood and a hint of oil fills my nostrils as I step into the workshop. I carefully manoeuvre yesterday's four-and-a-half-foot cardboard barrel inside. Sawdust coats the floor, and the sound of hammers, chisels, and the occasional creak of a workbench echo through the air.

'Hello?' I say, but no one replies. I place the improvised vessel on the floor next to me. Various tools hang from hooks on the walls, while planks of wood and barrels in various stages of completion are scattered about. I approach a burly man with a grizzled beard; he's carefully shaping a stave.

'Excuse me, sir,' I say, clearing my throat to get his attention. 'Are you the cooper?'

He looks up. I guess my appearance in his workshop is surprising. His eyes fill with curiosity, and I watch as he hesitates to take in my appearance: an old woman, wild hair, accompanied by a makeshift cardboard barrel as if it's my chaperone. He doesn't attempt to alter his expression; he hasn't expected someone like me to walk into his workshop.

'Who wants to know?' He returns his attention to his stave.

'I'm Annie Edson Taylor. I wrote and asked you to visit the boarding house, here in Bay City.' I offer a firm handshake, gripping tightly and looking directly into his eyes. 'You didn't visit.' He pulls his hand away and then shrugs his shoulders dismissively.

'I've an unusual request…' My voice is steady and determined, despite the many beads of perspiration fully formed on my brow.

The cooper wipes his hands on his apron, not hiding his quizzical expression. 'Go on,' he urges.

'First, I need you to promise not to tell anyone.'

He raises an eyebrow then turns away. I assume that's him not agreeing to my demand.

'I need you to build me a barrel.' He doesn't turn back. 'But not just any barrel,' I say, pausing for effect. 'I need a barrel exactly like that but strong enough to withstand the force of the Niagara Falls.'

I point at my makeshift construction. His eyes widen. Still, he examines me like I'm deranged and then he looks past me to the barrel. He's expecting a punchline. Seconds pass.

'You can't be serious, ma'am.' I nod and his nose turns up in disdain. 'That's a suicide mission, especially for a woman of your … age.'

I cross my arms defiantly. 'I'm forty-three.' Why do I lie?

He clutches his belly as he laughs. It wibbles. 'Of course you are. And that…' He points at the cardboard. 'That's not goin' to get wet in water.'

I bristle at his mocking but need to press on. 'I've made that replica.' I wave my hand towards it. 'To save you time. The design's based on my studying of the currents, and I can climb inside … if you like.'

He draws in a sharp breath, but steps closer to my contraption. His eyes narrow as he examines my handiwork.

'I also have notes and requirements. Based on weeks of research into the river, and much advice.' I unfold my list and lean towards him. He takes the parchment and I watch as he reads it.

'You're not just ridin' in the rapids like that Carlisle Graham?' he asks.

I shake my head. 'Been done too many times now.'

'Actually goin' over them Niagara Falls?' he says.

I nod enthusiastically. 'Horseshoe Falls. The Canadian Falls.'

The edges of his mouth curl. 'My God, woman. I will not, and you better not, do it.'

'I will though. I'm entirely serious.' I clutch my hands together, knuckles whitening. I can't let him see that I'm shaking. 'I need a barrel made of Kentucky oak, large enough for me to fit inside comfortably, and with cushioning to protect me from the impact. It needs to be watertight and have a secure opening and closing mechanism.'

He shakes his head at that. 'It's suicide.'

'I also need a harness or some form of strapping to keep me in place during the er … descent.' My heart hammers in my chest.

The cooper glances around his workshop as if searching for an escape from our conversation. I wait. My eyes stay on him as he returns to examining my cardboard barrel. Seconds pass, maybe even a minute or two.

'Need for ventilation or some kind of air supply's the worry,' he says, his tone slowly shifting from disbelief to concern.

'Indeed.' I nod, keen to keep him engaged. I'm not sure if I'm still breathing. Is he going to make it for me?

He scratches his beard, his brow furrowing. 'Ma'am, I can't in good conscience encourage you to go through with this. Far too dangerous… I won't be responsible for your demise.'

I meet his gaze, unwavering. 'I've made up my mind.'

'Men have died attemptin' it.'

'And?' I scowl. I'm daring him to break eye contact first. He does. He blinks. He looks to the sawdust-covered floor.

'I know the risks. I won't be swayed,' I say. 'My manager, Mr Russell, said you were the best in Bay City. He'll cover the cost of the barrel in exchange for a share of the profits I hope to gain after the stunt.'

'Russ sent you?' He hesitates, as if considering adding more, but he decides against it.

A sleek black cat emerges from a hiding spot. With the grace and dignity of a queen surveying her realm, she prowls towards me. I like how her tail swishes languidly in the air.

'Hello, you.' I bend and place my fingers for her to sniff. The cat rubs its nose against my hand, then nudges for a stroke. I oblige and she purrs contentedly, a soft rumble that is barely audible. Still, I smile.

'You're lovely,' I say. I watch as she moves with delicate precision. She presses her body against my skirts, then retreats, only to return. Each movement's calculated, almost as if she's performing a dance as old as time itself.

'If you won't build it, I'll find someone who will,' I say, my eyes still on the cat. 'But I heard you're the best and that's what I need … if I'm to stand a chance against the Falls.' I wait. No response. I look to the cooper, and he hesitates. His eyes dart between me and his tools. Finally, he sighs and extends his hand.

'You'll need to be vertical throughout,' he says, shaking my hand vigorously. 'A strap at the waist. That'll keep you upright even when unconscious.'

'Okay,' I say. He's still gripping my hand. I don't think he even realises.

'And that…' He waves our combined hand towards the cardboard barrel. 'That's not right.' A pause. I wait. 'Needs a blacksmith's anvil, needs to be bolted and strapped with iron to the bottom.'

'To keep me upright?'

He nods energetically. 'A barrel over them Niagara Falls.' He hesitates. 'Might be doable, if you stay central and only attempt the Horseshoe.'

I bob my head in agreement. 'Will you do it?' I think I'm holding my breath.

'All right, Mrs Taylor. I'll build you the best barrel I can from an old pickle one.'

A pause and I wave my hand for him to continue.

'But I hope you know what you're gettin' yourself into. Your chances of survival … they're slim.'

I shrug that bit off, clasping my hands together with a delighted grin. I could kiss the man, but instead I thrust my hand out to shake his. He bats it away and laughs, turning back to his stave. Mission accomplished – I have a cooper. A mixture of excitement and trepidation bubbles in my stomach.

'Oh, and I need it within three days. Preferably two,' I say.

Going Over the Falls - Mrs Taylor's Plan of Action

- ~~*Find a manager.*~~
- ~~*Build a barrel.*~~
- *Talk to a successful stunter.*
- *Hire boatsmen.*
- *Travel to lodgings.*

Annie

18th October 1901

Later, I hear polite chatter in the hallway as Tilda guides my guest into the parlour.

'Mrs Taylor,' he says. 'Call me Carlisle.'

Finally, Carlisle Graham, the man who survived several journeys through the treacherous rapids at Niagara Falls. He towers over me, stooping as he holds out his hand for me to shake. His eyes seem weathered, maybe by the years spent amid those roaring rapids. What was I expecting? They lack Mr Russell's mischief and joy.

'Call me Annie.' I shake his hand; his grip is weak. 'Come, sit with me.'

He seems to be overheating in his wool, tailored suit, his high-collared shirt and waistcoat. Each garment is stained and a little damp-looking. This man's as thin as a whisper carried on the breeze of yesteryear. His clothes appear to belong to a man shorter in height and wider in body. Still, he moves to the armchair and takes off his flat cap and his hand stutters. He's looking for a place to rest it.

'Let me,' Tilda says, taking the cap and walking towards the door. 'Would you enjoy a pot of tea?'

'That would be wonderful,' he says. He has a quiet air about him. A nervous quake that doesn't quite communicate the stunts he's conquered.

'Please, sit.' I point to the armchair next to mine. 'I'm thrilled that Mr Russell convinced you to visit.'

'It's a pleasure to finally meet you.' His voice is tinged with a hint of gravel. He's a smoker without his pipe.

'Mr Russell has informed you about my plans?'

He nods solemnly, perching on the edge of the armchair.

'I've heard so much about your remarkable feats in the rapids… I hoped you'd have advice for me?'

A pause. His expression hardens, a flicker of contemplation crosses his features. 'My dear…' His thick, black moustache twitches slightly as he speaks. 'The path you've chosen is fraught with peril. Courage alone is not enough to conquer the Niagara Falls. One must also possess a healthy respect for its power.'

I nod, waiting for more, hoping for a gem of guidance, but instead he observes the parlour. Is he searching these walls for my motivation?

'Mr Graham?'

He turns his attention back to me. His movement is slow and stiff; a hint that he isn't as sprightly as he once was. He leans in closer, pointing to his ear, as if trying to catch my words in it.

'Forgive me. I find myself hard of hearing,' he says. 'A souvenir from my days riding those rapids.'

I nod sympathetically. Had I considered the toll that such daring adventures could take on a person's body?

'You're tall,' I say.

'One-hundred and eighty-three centimetres.' He sits a little straighter as if to evidence his claim.

'And you squeezed yourself into a sturdy barrel to ride the rapids?' I think about my cardboard barrel. He'd not fit in it.

He smiles weakly. There's no sparkle in his eyes. They're not reflecting the thrill that must have coursed through his veins during the stunts. 'I did. With the lid securely fastened, too. I made that first perilous trip through the great gorge rapids and the whirlpool.'

'How long did it take?'

'A harrowing thirty minutes of tumultuous waters.' Another pause. I'm struggling to link this man to the stunter Mr Russell spoke about. 'Felt like I was in there for three days. Left me physically drained and disoriented, but I emerged victorious.' Does his voice carry an echo of past elation? I think I detect it hanging on the curls of the ends of his words. Still, I want to stick a key in the man and wind him up. His lack of enthusiasm is a little draining.

'Testament to your resilience and determination,' I say. I want to reach over and squeeze his hand. Maybe that would encourage him to pick up pace a little. I don't, though.

Perhaps this all links to the stark difference between what Carlisle Graham achieved and what I propose to do. His daring feats involved navigating the rapids near Niagara Falls in a barrel. This meant he rode the cascading waters leading up to the Falls, facing the wild currents and obstacles in his specially designed barrel. While his exploits demonstrated incredible courage and skill, we both know that they lacked the additional daring I propose. His focus was on surviving the turbulent waters leading up to the Falls, whereas I intend to plunge over the precipice of the Falls itself. This man didn't directly confront the sheer drop, and that's why my proposed stunt is even more daring. My heart races with a mix of excitement and apprehension.

'Riding the rapids was thrill enough for me.' His brow furrows. 'For the four times I made that perilous journey…' Solemnity creeps over him. The lines etched upon his face betray the toll exacted by years of valiant exploits and near-death escapades. Stunting's broken him, whereas I'm gambling on it saving me. 'And each time, I emerged victorious…'

'A testament to the strength of human spirit,' I say, clapping my hands together and attempting to urge him on. 'Surely true courage isn't in the absence of fear, but instead in the willingness to face it head-on.'

'Perhaps.'

'I've been studying the currents,' I say, and he nods for me to continue. 'I think I know where to be set adrift to avoid the talus.'

He leans in a little closer. His interest is piqued. 'Do you plan to be towed out?'

'From the American side and then over the Horseshoe. Best survivability is there,' I say.

'No talus at the base of those Falls.'

I nod. 'Unlike the American and Bridal Veil Falls,' I say.

He bobs his head in agreement.

'There's less water flowing over the American Falls due to Goat Island's shape. It's narrow to wider, so makes the water flow slower,' I say.

He smiles. 'You know your stuff.'

I bat my hand in the air, as if to dismiss his irritating comment. 'My life depends on me knowing my *stuff*.'

He laughs. He must consider that a joke.

I shake my head. 'By my calculations, it would be difficult to go over the American Falls without sticking to the shoreline or launching very near Goat Island.'

'Because the flowing water would want to pull you toward the Canadian side of the river?' I bob my head enthusiastically, but he holds up a palm to silence me. 'I should perhaps advise you against this stunt,' he says.

I shake my head. 'And I'd advise against that.'

'I won't insult you then,' he says. He pats at his trouser legs and then the front of his jacket, a look of confusion sweeping across his face. 'I thought you might like this,' he says. 'For luck or for ambition. Your choice.' He rummages in the inside pocket of his suit jacket, before pulling out a photograph and handing it to me.

I smile. Carlisle Graham stands confidently next to his legendary seven-foot-tall cask. He's wearing tight breeches and sporting a huge black moustache. He embodies the spirit of adventure and daring. His stance is sturdy, his expression resolute, as if challenging the very forces of nature that he once dared to defy. He's unrecognisable now. I can't help but wish I'd met that version of him.

'I see how you climbed inside it.' I point at the barrel on the photograph.

'Why, Annie?'

I look up. It takes me a moment to realise what he's asking. I shrug, a flicker of uncertainty might flash across my features as I consider how to respond. I'm bored of telling folk what they want to hear or justifying my decision to make them feel better – that it's something I feel compelled to do, or that I want to make my mark on history, or to prove that women are capable of daring deeds just as much as men. None of that matters anymore.

'I thought a change in career would be nice,' I say.

Mr Graham chuckles softly. 'They called me "Nero of Niagara".' He laughs; he likes that name. 'Many have since died copying.'

'Even the boldest of dreams carry a weight of consequence,' I say.

He nods solemnly, his gaze distant. A loud sigh. 'In truth, after my success in the rapids, I entertained the notion of riding the Falls. But as fate would have it, earlier this year…' I nod for him to continue. 'On July fourteenth, I found myself caught in a whirlpool vortex for what felt like an eternity.'

My eyes widen in alarm. 'Goodness, Mr Graham, that sounds harrowing.'

'It was.' I note a trace of regret. 'And it made me realise the folly of attempting such a stunt. The Falls are unforgiving, and no amount of bravery can guarantee survival in the face of their might.'

A pause. He's observing me. I swallow hard, the weight of his words sinking in. 'So you believe I shouldn't go through with it?'

Mr Graham bobs his head slowly, his expression grave. 'Niagara Falls is known as "Suicide's Paradise" for good reason. No one survives the drop.' He twirls the ends of his moustache. 'I cannot in good conscience encourage such recklessness, Mrs Taylor. Your life is too precious to gamble away for the sake of glory.'

His words punch my stomach. They appear to be a plea for me to heed the warnings whispered by the ghosts of his past adventures. Conflicting emotions are unleashed and swirl like rapids within me.

'A nice pot of tea.' Tilda comes into the room, Her eyes averted from us as she walks. Has she been listening to our conversation at the door? I glare at her, but she refuses my eye contact.

'Wonderful,' Mr Graham says.

'Will you come?' I ask. Matilda freezes on the spot next to Mr Graham, the tray with a teapot, cups and saucers outstretched in front of her.

'Me?' he says.

'To the Canadian shore. I'd like you to be there when they release me from the barrel.'

Annie

19th October 1901

The two men seem like giants in the cramped workshop. The next undertaking on my list is to discern whether William Holleran and a Fred Trusdale should be my rivermen. I inhale deeply. Rows of shelves laden with tools – chisels, hammers, and saws – line the walls, each bearing the marks of frequent use. I focus on the worktable. It's covered in countless creations, stained with rings of dark-wood polish and flecks of paint.

'When you're ready,' Holleran says. I look up and he's gazing down at me. An old brass lantern hangs from the ceiling, casting a golden glow over him. He's waiting for an explanation.

I draw another deep breath, locking eyes with one man and then the other. 'I want to start by thanking you for agreeing to talk with me, but I need to be brutally honest.' My voice reverberates in the workshop's stillness.

I shift on the creaky chair they've provided. The weave of the fabric prickles through my dress. Mr Holleran's kind face reminds me of seasoned oak. Mr Trusdale's usually stern demeanour softens in this intimate setting. They're standing as still as tall statues.

I cross one leg over the other with authority. 'I want to hire you both because you're affordable and … quite frankly, no one else will help. They all seemed to think my plan suicide … and they wouldn't accept me being a woman.'

Holleran chuckles, his warm eyes crinkling at the corners. He brushes a hand through his greying hair and smiles at me. 'Honestly, Mrs Taylor, I don't care about the rumours around Bay City or the naysayers.'

'Rumours?'

'That you're hysterical,' Trusdale says and Holleran whacks his arm.

'I'd be thrilled to be a part of your venture. You're on to something grand, and I'm confident you'll succeed,' Holleran says.

I narrow my eyes; his optimism isn't enough. 'Mr Holleran,' I say, measuring my words, 'while I appreciate your faith in me, I need more than just belief. I need pragmatism. Honesty.' He opens his mouth to speak but I hold up my palm and he smiles broadly. 'If I needed your approval, I'd be in a rather sorry state, wouldn't I?' He nods. 'So, if there's a flaw in my plan, or a danger I'm blind to, I expect you both to speak up. Understand? My life may very well depend on your candour.'

Holleran's smile doesn't falter. 'I promise, Mrs Taylor, to be nothing but honest.'

I nod, relieved but still apprehensive, adjusting my posture by straightening my back. 'I've been studying the currents and I've met with Carlisle Graham…'

They bob their heads in unison for me to continue.

'My best chance of survival is if you row me out to hit the Canadian rapids. I need to go over the Horseshoe Falls.' I look to the men and they're communicating silently. One raises an eyebrow, the other shrugs. 'I don't want to see the route beforehand, but I do need to aim for the Canadian shore.'

'You've considered the talus?'

I bob my head. 'I know there's no guarantee, when you cut me loose, but if we could aim for Canada.'

'That's perhaps the easiest part of the stunt,' Holleran says, and I raise an eyebrow.

'Then perhaps *you'd* best explain the potential dangers I might face?'

He takes a deep breath, glancing at Mr Trusdale for a moment, as if gathering silent support, then reaches into his pocket, pulling out a piece of paper that's clearly been refolded multiple times. As he opens it, I can see the neat lines of handwritten text: a list of potential hazards. His fingers trace the first line; a brief hesitation in his actions betraying the weight of the information.

'Drowning,' Holleran begins, his voice steady yet carrying a hint of gravitas. 'It's not just about the barrel remaining intact. Even the sturdiest of casks could pose risks.' He taps the paper, emphasising each word. 'Water's a relentless force. If there's even the smallest gap or crack, it'll push its way in. Especially given the tumultuous nature of the Falls.'

'The pressure and sheer volume of water might overwhelm the barrel's interior in seconds,' Trusdale adds. His voice is deep and rough from years of beer and tobacco. It rumbles through the room, adding a different sort of gravity to the discussion.

'Okay,' I say, drumming my fingers rhythmically on my thigh.

Holleran looks up and then back at the list. His fingers slide down the paper, pausing at the next line. There's a subtle shift in his demeanour.

'Traumatic impact,' he says, lifting his gaze to meet mine. 'The descent isn't just a simple fall. It's a tumultuous journey with the sheer force of thousands of gallons of water pressing and churning around.' He hesitates and I nod for him to continue. 'Even if you've cushioned the inside of the barrel, there's a serious threat to consider.'

'Which is?'

'The abrupt drop, combined with the crushing force of the water, can wreak havoc on the human body. Think of it almost like a carriage crash … but with the added weight and unpredictability of the Falls.'

I swallow hard; the imagery he paints is both vivid and unsettling.

'It could lead to severe internal injuries,' he continues, his voice gentle yet firm. 'Broken bones, potential damage to internal organs, even with the best padding inside. The human body isn't made for such brutal forces.'

'At least you're honest.' I try to smile.

Holleran again glances back down at the list, frowning before taking another deep breath.

'There's more?'

He nods. 'Next, we have the risk of crushing injuries.' He shifts his stance, seemingly gathering himself to deliver more overwhelming details. 'The path of the Falls isn't just a clear drop from top to bottom. It's littered with rocks, debris, and other obstacles – some visible, but many lurking beneath the tumultuous waters.'

I hesitate. The majestic Falls, with every jagged edge and hidden boulder, pose a greater threat than I imagined.

'If the barrel – regardless of its sturdiness – were to directly hit any of these obstacles at the force and speed of the descent, the consequences could be catastrophic.' He holds his hands together, mimicking the barrel, then suddenly forces them apart, illustrating the potential destruction. 'It could break apart upon impact. And with that, the risk of crushing injuries becomes terrifyingly real.'

'The human body inside would suffer from grievous wounds, or even…' Trusdale adds.

Is this a major concern? Beneath my confident facade, my heart beats with the rhythm of a turncoat.

'There are no rocks in the middle part of the Falls,' Holleran says.

'If there's an anvil attached to the bottom,' Trusdale adds, thinking back to the design I shared with them. They're talking to each other, as if I'm already in the barrel.

'Then we release it to make sure it goes over the lip where it is safe,' intercepts Holleran.

'If the tide pulls her off course…'

'So,' I wave my hands in the air. They both turn to look at me. 'Let's make sure that's not the case.'

Holleran's eyes darken a fraction as he returns to the list and reads the next item. 'Asphyxiation,' he murmurs, the word hanging heavy in the air. Seeing my puzzled expression, he adds, 'The barrel isn't just a protective shell; it's also a confined space. Even if water doesn't breach its interior, the air supply inside can become dangerously limited if it gets trapped underwater or against a submerged obstacle.'

I feel the weight of his words. The thought of being trapped, my breathing becoming more desperate, shallower, is harrowing.

'Imagine it as like being inside a locked room with no ventilation. The walls of the barrel, meant to protect, could inadvertently become a prison.'

I let out a long sigh, then, 'Is that … it?'

'Er … no, that's number four.'

'Of how many?'

He looks up. 'Eight.'

I swallow. 'Then you best go on.'

Holleran's brow furrows as he navigates to the next point, his fingers tracing the words on the paper. 'Hypothermia.' The word carries an icy edge. 'The waters of Niagara Falls are not just tumultuous; they are chillingly cold.'

He hesitates, looking from the paper to me with a steady gaze. Perhaps he's emphasising the gravity of each point. 'Debris is a concern. The waters of the Falls aren't pristine; logs, broken branches, and other refuse can strike the barrel with unexpected force.' His brow furrows with concern. 'A direct hit might injure you, even inside.' Pausing, he taps on the next point. 'Entrapment's a daunting risk, too. The waters have deep crevices and boulders jutting out. The barrel could get wedged, making rescue a harrowing task.'

He meets my gaze squarely. 'And we cannot underestimate the human body's response. The overwhelming stress and trauma from this ordeal could lead to shock. It's a sudden drop in blood flow, which … believe me, can be as life-threatening as any physical injury you might sustain.'

I try to hide my alarm. I thought I'd taken all the risks into account, but I was mistaken. So incredibly incorrect. Gratitude for Mr Holleran's attention to detail washes over me.

'One last thing,' he says, 'but one of the most important.'

I nod for him to continue.

'One of the most treacherous aspects is the lack of quick rescue,' he says. His eyes lock with mine. 'The area around the Falls isn't just a stretch of clear water. It's a labyrinth of swirling currents, rocks, and pockets of deceptive calm.' As he talks, his hands move, as if he's painting the scene in the air. 'If, God forbid, something was to go awry, rescuers could face immense challenges in reaching you promptly.' His fingers clench. 'That means prolonged exposure to all the risks we've discussed.'

There is a silence while I digest the list in its entirety. Then I nod, solemnly.

'Thank you, Mr Holleran.'

'You're a brave woman, Mrs Taylor. You have my word that I'll do all in my power to help you… I repeat, you have my word.'

'Again, thank you.' I hold his gaze. He means what he says. I trust him.

Mr Trusdale takes a step forward, the weight of his responsibility evident in his stance. 'I'll be atop the Falls in the boat,' he says, his steel-grey eyes finding mine. 'It'll be my duty to cut that rope and set you on your way.'

'We'll make sure there's another boat waiting to retrieve you at the bottom. They'll get you out in Canada,' Holleran says.

'I promise you I won't make that cut unless I'm certain it's safe.' Trusdale takes a deep, raspy breath. 'But the river's unpredictable. If the boat, with me in it, gets caught by those merciless currents and we're being dragged to the edge… I'll be cutting that rope and setting you free.'

'To save yourself?' I ask, and he nods in reply.

His bluntness, stark against Holleran's softer approach, underlines the sheer volatility of what I'm doing. The room feels colder, the risks never more apparent.

'Thank you for your honesty.'

'You should probably test it out first,' Trusdale says.

'The barrel?'

'Do you have a cat?'

Holleran opens a drawer, revealing a half-drunk bottle of amber whisky and three small glasses. He wipes them on a rag that looks filthy, and pours the liquid, then passes a glass each to me and Mr Trusdale.

'To successful endeavours,' Holleran says, holding his glass aloft.

I smile and we clink. I watch at they both down the whisky. Holleran's eyes meet mine and I do the same. The harsh alcohol burns, but I resist the urge to cough. A grin flashes across Holleran's face.

'I'm tougher than I look.'

He nods enthusiastically. 'We're all counting on that being true.'

Matilda

19th October 1901

Bay City's autumnal air is crisp and nips at me cheeks. Makes me skin tingle. Feels like it's pulled taut. The marketplace beckons. I'm going to make Mrs Lapointe a nice dinner before Nora, Mrs Taylor and I leave for Niagara Falls. Mr Russell's arranged a carriage and then lodgings for us all. I'm not convinced I want to watch the stunt, but Mrs Taylor's asked for me support.

'Best be quick,' I say to both Nora and meself as I look over the produce.

Every time I'm out and about in Bay City feels like the first time – the sights, the sounds, the smells that dance in the air. Comforting in its constancy, ever-changing in its details. I love living here. Nora's wrapped in a shawl. She's all snuggly. She likes perching on me hip and waving at anyone who smiles at her. She's too heavy to be carried like this, but it's the easiest way to navigate this market. The pram's too bulky and letting her walk would add too much time to the trip, and I'm running late. A spike of pain shoots through me hip. Nora's already nineteen months old. Nineteen months of loving her. Never expected I would. Don't think I really considered meself capable of this depth of emotion. That I could love something that was part of him. But I do. More than anything else I can name.

All me senses are overwhelmed here. Customers haggle for the best prices. The calls of vendors peddling their wares are loudest. Everywhere I turn, there's a burst of colour: the vibrant hues of fresh produce, the subtle shades of handwoven textiles, the glistening of metal trinkets catching the sun's rays. And then there's that smell. Me belly grumbles in response. Nora's tiny hand clutches me coat. Her curious eyes take in the world around her.

'Lots to see, little one,' I say. It's that inquisitiveness that bursts pride out through me belly. Already, she's the best of me tied up with the best of her.

Some stalls are closing for the afternoon, though. Men putting away crates, boys sitting with pocketknives and peeling fruit while they chatter. One of the vendors lifts his produce into a cart.

'Time for Mama to make a deal,' I whisper. 'Look adorable, Nora.' I jiggle her, partly to ease the stab of pain in me hip, but she giggles. That sound fuels me. Makes me want more and better for us both. I can't help but smile; me daughter's joy is infectious.

'How much for a pound of these?' I ask, gesturing to the pile of muddy potatoes loose in the cart.

A slight pause while the vendor observes me and Nora. 'Five cents, Miss.'

'Five cents?' I scoff, pretending to be shocked. 'I'll give you two.'

The vendor shakes his head, chuckling. 'Three, and we have a deal.'

'Fine.' I hand over the coins, placing Nora on her feet on the floor and filling me basket with the potatoes. She looks around, and then back up at me. I can't help but wonder if she thinks about running away. 'No,' I tell her, wiggling me middle finger. Losing her would break me heart.

'No,' she says, her bottom lip thinking about wibbling. She tilts her head. Hesitates, but then she smiles. She reaches out and grabs the material of me skirts.

'And now let's get home before dusk.' I scoop her back on to me hip. 'It'll be faster if I carry you.' Don't want to keep Mrs Taylor waiting. Ten strides forward and I make me way through the crowd of shoppers.

Suddenly, I freeze. I quiver. As still as a statue in an earthquake. The hairs on the back of me neck react. A wave of warmth rushes from me belly, up me throat and out in a stutter. It's sudden. Quick. Panic. A smell? A sound? A shape? A movement? I don't know why, but I do know that it's behind me. Me heart races. Pounds against me ribcage. I accelerate me pace, trying to shake the feeling. Can't turn around. Won't. The sensation persists. I need to get back to the boarding house.

I hurry down the street. Nora bounces on me hip, the shopping basket tucked under me arm. Focusing on me breath and the slaps of me steps on cobbles. Round the corner. I see them.

A group of men huddle together in a dark alley; their voices are low and hushed. I slow me pace. Me heart thumps in me chest. Something about what I'm seeing sends a shiver through me body. Makes me teeth chatter; me knees feel unsteady. I stick as close to the wall as possible. Hoping I blend into it. Me steps are tentative. A few more strides and I'll pass them. I stop. Hold me breath.

I recognise him.

Uncle William; his shape unmistakable, his laughter booming. I duck behind a stack of crates. Hoping to remain unseen. I place a finger over me lips and Nora mimics me, in tune with me reactions. She knows to stay quiet. I strain to hear their conversation, but me heart's pounding in me ears.

'… Take the child away from her.' That familiar, that menacing voice. Me uncle growls. 'She's unfit to be a mother and does not deserve to keep her.'

Nora wriggles. I'm squashing her. 'Shush,' I whisper, before she can squeak. She snuggles closer. Puts her head on me shoulder. Needs me comfort, too.

I peek over the crates and spot one of the men –- a burly figure with the palest skin I've ever seen – nod. 'We'll make sure of it,' he replies. His voice is raspy and cold. 'Just tell us when and where. We'll handle the rest.'

I hold me breath. It vibrates inside me body. Me jaw rattles. Spreads like a spiky rash. Within seconds me entire body's shaking. They're plotting to take Nora away from me. I gulp. Try to push down the rising emotions. Drowning again. This isn't the time to be falling apart. The thought of losing her, though, me precious little girl. She's me reason to stay living.

'I will be in contact,' Uncle William says.

I duck lower. Try to shrink into the ground. I hear heavy footsteps on cobbles as the group disperses. I wait, me heart hammering in me chest. Is it too early to slip away unnoticed?

Minutes pass before I peek over the crates again. 'All clear,' I say. I wobble as I stand, lifting the basket and adjusting Nora on me hip. I ache from the bending and the quivering.

'Let's get home,' I say, me voice unrecognisable. Looking left, looking right, I practically spin as I walk.

'Matilda, my dear niece.' The voice a sneer.

I whirl around. Startled. Me cheeks are flushed. Uncle William. He cracks his knuckles. His eyes bore into me. They're cold and conniving. In shock, I drop the basket of potatoes, watching as one rolls to the toe of his boot. I tighten me grip on Nora, shielding her from evil.

'What do you want?' Me voice trembles despite me efforts to appear bold and confident.

He smirks. Palms facing me in surrender, he takes a step closer and I take a step back. 'Isn't it obvious? I want my family. You and Nora belong with me.'

I swallow hard. Vomit rises in me throat as memories of what he did to me jump into me head.

'No,' I shout. 'Stay away.' I'm waiting for his pounce. Nora reaches up and wraps her arms around me neck. She's clinging.

'Matilda, Matilda, Matilda.' He waves his hands in further submission, glancing around, but I'm not falling for that. He won't trick me again. I know what he's capable of. He approaches with hesitant steps.

'We don't want anything to do with you.' Me words are growled. Uncle William flinches. The venom in me voice unnerves him. He can hurt me all he wants, but he's not getting near me daughter. I'll protect her with me last breath. 'Stay away from us.'

Nora laughs. I smile; an instinctive response me little girl.

His smirk widens. He's spotted weakness. Two steps towards us and he leans in. 'I like that you feel you have a choice, Matilda. But you don't.'

He reaches over to touch Nora's cheek, and I jerk me hip away from him. The movement's violent. A stab of pain for me. His fingers will not touch me little girl.

'Lift your skirt,' he says. 'Here. Now. Lift your skirt and bend over.'

'No.' It's a whisper. I need to protect Nora. I need to get out of here.

'You will come back with me now and willingly.' A pause and he sneers. 'Or find out just how far I will go to reclaim what is rightfully mine. You will never ignore me again,' he says. 'You are mine.'

I stare at him. Watching his every movement. Ready to protect Nora.

'It is rude not to reply to letters,' he says. 'My daughter needs me in her life.'

His daughter? I shake me head vigorously. Fury rushes through me. Not his daughter; never his. She's all mine.

He grins with smug satisfaction, reaching out to take Nora from me.

'No,' I say. It's a growl.

'My daughter is coming home.' He steps closer.

Me arms tighten around Nora. I will protect her, no matter the cost. With a primal scream, I launch meself at him. Me foot connects with his shin in a swift, powerful kick. He staggers backwards, caught off guard by the sudden assault. It's now or never.

Ignoring the pain shooting down me thigh, I turn. I sprint down the narrow alleyway. Me daughter rides me hip like she's on a little horse. Me heart pounds with every step. I push meself to go faster. Farther away from the danger that lurks behind us. I won't look back. Only focusing on putting as much distance between us as possible. Nora's cries grow louder. She's spurring me on. Even as exhaustion threatens to overwhelm me. We disappear into the crowd. Only then do I stop. Me entire body trembles. I wrap me arms around Nora. Clutch her and she whimpers. I pull her as close as possible. She squirms in response, though. Tries to twist free to look at me. Observing. Finding her own answers. Darkness threatens to engulf our lives and I reckon me little girl knows. I must protect her. The seeds of terror were planted within years ago. Me Uncle Willian did that, in the darkness. Its branches are grown and they're waving now. From the inside. Desperately trying to find their way out.

'We can't stay here any longer.' The words are for meself. 'We can't go back to the boarding house.'

I know what I need to do. It's time to run again. Even if it means leaving behind the only place and the only people who've felt like home.

Annie

20th October 1901

Perhaps Mr Russell didn't consider what time I would arrive. He's not here to greet me. My stomach flips as I step through the flapping canvas, eyes attempting to adjust to the dim light within the circus tent. Matilda and Nora are supposed to be here with me. I told them the time I was travelling, even waited an hour. I shake my head. Can't be worrying about that right now. The air's thick with the smell of sawdust and popcorn, a heady mix that both tickles my senses and stirs the excitement already bubbling inside.

'Mr Russell?' I say, but there's no reply.

Instead, I'm hit by colours and sounds. My eyes travel around the perimeter of the tent. Brightly painted banners stretch between poles depicting fantastical scenes of daring feats and exotic creatures. Lanterns hang from wooden beams overhead, flickering and dancing with anticipation. In one corner, a small stage has been set up; its boards look worn smooth with use. On it a group of musicians huddle together, tuning their instruments and exchanging jokes in hushed tones. Nearby, a cluster of performers practise their routines. It's their laughter that mingles with the strains of music. No one even turns to look at me. They're each in their own world. I think I might want to be in those worlds, too.

I step inside, making my way to the centre of the tent. It's dominated by a collection of stalls and booths, each one offering a different form of entertainment. Still, no one pays me any attention. They're all too busy setting up their wares. There's games of chance and skill, their prizes gleam enticingly. A fortune teller sits at a table covered in velvet cloth, her crystal ball catches the light and casts rainbow patterns across the floor.

A makeshift carnival or, simply, a travelling one? Here, anything is possible. I stride further into the fray.

'Mr Russ—'

A duo of a strongman and bearded lady arrest my attention. I've seen them before. They're to the right of the fortune teller. The strongman, with his bulging muscles and imposing stature, lifts weights with ease. Beside him, the bearded lady stands tall and proud, her flowing blonde beard a testament to her strength and resilience. With a smile on her lips, she applauds, then cheers her strongman friend.

'Mr Russell?' I shout.

I spin on the spot. Behind me there's a sign, Little Egypt. Next to it a woman mesmerises two men with a hootchie-kootchie dance. She's exotic. She moves with grace and allure. Perhaps her movements weave a spell over me, as I can't tear my gaze away from her. Close to her and still in the tent's centre, a man with skin as dark as ebony regales other carnival folk with stories of his homeland in Africa, while a woman adorned with intricate jewellery speaks of her travels through the markets of Marrakech. I'm eager to hear tales of far-off lands, too. Later, perhaps. We are all travellers here. Perhaps I don't want to belong, but I do.

A tap on my shoulder. Turning around and expecting Mr Russell, I'm met with the warm smile of the bearded lady.

'Well, hello there, darling,' she says, her voice as melodious as a songbird's. Her eyes twinkle with mischief. 'Couldn't help but notice you standing here, looking like you're all ready for a grand adventure.'

She taps the toe of her boot on the wooden box. Old and tied with rough twine.

'Name's Lorraine, but most folks around here call me Lolly.'

Her energy's infectious and I can't help but smile back at her. 'Nice to meet you.' I extend my hand. 'Annie Taylor.'

Lolly clasps my hand in hers and wiggles it enthusiastically. Her grip's surprisingly strong, despite her delicate appearance. 'Annie, eh? Well, ain't that a lovely name.' She says that with a wink. 'Tell us, what brings a bright-eyed lass like you to our humble carnival?'

Her voice is loud enough to bring the tent to a hush. That catches me off-guard. A breath in and I smile on its release. 'I suppose … a new career,' I say. 'Life's been feeling a bit dull lately, and I thought maybe a visit to the carnival might inject a bit of magic back into it.'

Lolly chuckles softly, a sound like wind chimes in the breeze. 'Ah, I know that feeling all too well, dearie,' she says. 'But fear not, for you've come to the right place.' She curtseys dramatically and her fellow entertainers cheer. 'Here at carnival, we specialise in turning the ordinary into the extraordinary.'

A sudden commotion draws our attention to the entrance of the tent. Through a throng of people, a man emerges, commanding the attention of everyone around him. He's tall, broad-shouldered, with a neatly trimmed beard and piercing black eyes that sparkle with excitement. His clothes are adorned with colourful sequins and feathers, giving him an air of flamboyance and grandeur. He moves with the confidence of a lion tamer and the grace of an acrobat. He nods over at me, and I wave back.

'Mr Russell, you have a visitor,' my bearded friend says, though she's confused that we already know each other.

'Ladies and gentlemen, gather round, gather round!' His voice booms with enthusiasm. 'We have a stranger in our midst.' He makes his way towards me, and the circus folk erupt into cheers, hands slapping on surfaces and applause. Their excitement is palpable. He beams at the crowd, soaking in their adoration like a seasoned showman. They all admire him.

'Now, who do we have here?' Mr Russell says, his eyes alight on me.

He winks and I chuckle. 'Why, if it isn't our fearless stuntwoman, Mrs Taylor!'

A surge of excitement bubbles in my stomach, a mix of pride and exhilaration.

Before I can respond, Mr Russell steps forward. 'That's right, folks! Our Annie here is about to make history by going over Niagara Falls in a barrel.'

'A barrel?' Lolly says. I nod and she claps her hands in delight.

'She'll be the first person to survive going over the Falls,' Mr Russell says. 'Let's give her a round of applause!'

The crowd erupts into cheers and clapping once more, their excitement reaching a fever pitch as they rally behind me. I spin on the spot, absorbing their energy. I'm surrounded by the jubilant faces of my newfound friends and supporters.

'This reminds me of the time I crossed the Sahara on a camel,' Mr Russell announces. 'The sun was blazing, and the sand stretched as far as the eye could see. We had no water, but a troupe of acrobats and I entertained a Berber tribe in exchange for our survival. We performed under the stars, our bodies glistening with sweat and determination. It was a sight to behold!'

The circus folk listen intently, their eyes wide with fascination.

'Name's Magnus,' the strongman introduces himself, stepping forward to join Lolly and Mr Russell; an imposing figure, his muscles rippling beneath the fabric of his leotard.

'You'd not fit in my barrel,' I say, and he laughs. It's a booming sound that reverberates through the tent like a thunderclap.

As I shake his hand, I feel the rough calluses of his palm against mine. His grip's firm, yet surprisingly gentle; like he's a kind giant with a heart of gold.

'You'd not catch me near them Falls, lass,' Magnus booms, his voice carrying over the din of the crowd.

'Lolly, my dear, you have the gift of gab like no other,' Mr Russell says, throwing his arm around her shoulder. I'm not sure but I think Magnus might growl. 'Keep rallying the crowd with your infectious energy, and let's make sure Annie is the queen of the carnival tonight!'

He claps her on the shoulder then turns to the strongman. 'And you, Mighty Magnus, my stalwart friend, I need you to lend your strength and support to Annie in any way you can. Whether it's helping her with her training or simply offering words of encouragement.'

'Consider me your servant,' Magnus says, bowing as much as his expanded muscles will allow, and I smile.

'And as for you, Annie Taylor.' Mr Russell turns to me with a warm grin. 'Did I ever tell you about the time I faced down a Bengal tiger in the jungles of India?' His eyes sparkle with excitement. 'We were performing for a Maharaja, and during the act, the tiger escaped. With nothing but a whip and my wits, I managed to calm the beast and return it to its cage. The crowd erupted in cheers—'

'I need to send a telegram to Tilda,' I say, before he can continue.

He nods. 'No problem at all. You're part of the carnival family now. You'll stay with us for a couple of nights, soak in the camaraderie and excitement, and then we'll make sure you're settled in lodgings near the Falls…'

'Ready for my big moment,' I say. It's a whisper.

'Did you bring your cat?' he asks, and I point to the wooden box on the floor.

'Your cat?' Lolly says.

'Lagara.' I say the name as if that's explanation enough.

'We'll take care of you like one of our own,' Lolly says, reaching her hand to mine. 'Come…'

'About the lodgings,' I shout over my shoulder to Mr Russell. 'Don't forget the wrench and saw, or I won't be able to get out of the barrel.'

The Western Union Telegraph Company October 20th 1901
From: Annie Edson Taylor
To: Matilda Hamilton, Bay City Boarding House

URGENT. STOP.
MRS TAYLOR NEEDS YOU IN NIAGARA FALLS. STOP.
ARRIVE OCTOBER 23. STOP.
FOR THE STUNT. STOP.
PLEASE CONFIRM RECEIPT. STOP.
STOP.

Annie

20th October 1901

My first night with these circus folk and I'm hiding in Lolly's cosy wagon. I breathe in deeply, and the heavy scents of incense and lavender envelop me like a warm embrace. It's a stark contrast to the bustling chaos of the carnival outside. I needed a moment of relief from the whirlwind of activity. Mr Russell's been running around like a headless chicken, pulling me behind him like I somehow know the way. I don't. The stunt's happening in a few days and I've no space in my head for his nerves, too.

Instead, I've retreated in here. The interior's dimly lit by flickering candles, casting dancing shadows on the walls. They're adorned with colourful tapestries and velvet drapes. Mismatched furniture dots the tiny space and I'm already convinced that each piece bears the marks of countless journeys and adventures. Lolly sits on the chair opposite me, her attire a riot of colour and texture. The hem of her flowing skirt, made from a richly patterned fabric I've never seen before, brushes against the worn wooden floor of the wagon with a swish each time she moves. A fitted blouse hugs her curves, its sleeves billowing slightly at the wrists. I like that what she wears reflects her vibrant personality and the eclectic nature of carnival life. What I wear reflects propriety, dead people's tastes and expectation. Soon that won't be right for Annie Taylor the stunter.

'Sweetheart…'

She pauses and I take my eyes from her clothing to look up at her. She's beautiful. Sturdy yet feminine, with a muscular build that speaks of years spent on the road. I nod for her to continue.

'I've got to ask. Why in the world are you risking life and limb with this stunt?' She reaches over and lifts a steaming kettle from the nearby stove.

'It's a tangled web, Lolly,' I say. 'A web of dreams and disappointments, of highs and lows. You see, back in San Antonio, I thought I had it all figured out.' I pause, as she stands to grab two cups from their hooks. 'I was teaching at a high school, dancing and physical culture, rubbing elbows with the principal, even. But then…'

'… then life happened?' Lolly says, nodding sympathetically. Her blonde hair cascades in loose waves around her shoulders, framing her face and her warm smile.

I sigh. 'You could say that. There was this clergyman, you see…'

A slight pause as she pours two cups of tea from the steaming kettle. The sound of the boiling water being poured mingles with the soft strains of music drifting in from outside.

'A man broke your heart and so you're risking your life?'

I'm pleased to see a flicker of disappointment. She doesn't want a love story and I've not got one to offer.

'Good heavens, no,' I say. I laugh. 'I had a tidy sum tucked away. Seventeen-hundred dollars, to be exact. Thought I was set for life. But then, in the blink of an eye –' I clap my hands together and she jumps in her seat, 'it was all gone. Boom and bust, they call it. And it wasn't his fault, poor soul.'

Lolly clicks her tongue. She passes me a cup of tea. 'Ain't that the way of the world? Boomtowns and busts, riches to rags in the blink of an eye.'

I bob my head in agreement. 'Exactly. And then there was the small

Texas ranch I owned. Thought it was my ticket to stability, to finally getting on my feet. But it slipped through my fingers like grains of sand.' I rub my fingers together to demonstrate.

Lolly places a comforting hand on my shoulder. 'It's a hard road you've travelled.' Her reaction is one of quiet understanding, her eyes meeting mine with a depth of empathy that speaks volumes.

I chuckle and she looks confused. I want to say that she doesn't know the half of it, but I don't. Instead, I smile. 'It's been a bumpy one, that's for sure. I used to mix with the cultured and refined…' I take a sip of tea.

'And now you're drinking tea with a bearded lady, about to go over the Falls in a barrel.'

Laughter rushes out of me before I can swallow the mouthful of tea and I spit it into Lolly's beard. 'I'm so sorry,' I say, reaching over to touch her facial hair. She recoils. There's fear. How many times has she been touched without permission? How often is she mocked? I lower my hand, reaching over to squeeze hers. 'You're a diamond,' I say.

She smiles. 'Money may come and go, but your spirit? That's worth more than all the gold in the world,' she says. She fiddles with the glass beads around her neck. In varying shades of blue and green, each bead catches the light and shimmers like drops of water. Her hands are fascinating, too. They're adorned with rings of diamond, gold and turquoise, glinting softly in the candlelight. This woman was born into money.

'Isn't it horrible to be poor?' I ask. 'I can't live decently, and I will not scrub. I'd rather face death than live like I have been.'

Lolly shrugs her shoulders. I attempt to read her expression, but she resists sharing my financial woes. The life she's living now is preferred to whatever existence she's escaped.

'When I make up my mind to do a thing, that's all there is to it,' I say, hearing the frustration and determination in my words, but there's resolute conviction, too, which leaves no room for doubt.

'So hold fast to that fire burning within you,' Lolly says. 'Let it guide you through the darkest of nights and the fiercest of storms.'

There's an undeniable elegance to this woman, and a regal bearing that sets her apart from the crowd. I raise my teacup and she does the same. We clink. Then sip our tea in silence, the gentle flicker of candlelight dancing across her beard.

Part IV: Daring Plunge

'Unique. That's the word I'd use to describe her. I've not met another soul like Mrs Taylor. I swear I can still hear her laughter. Brought warmth and joy to my gloomiest days. She was the boldest and bravest person I'll ever know. Quick-witted, too. Did you know she was friends with Jesse James?'

Rose Baker

FELINE SURVIVES NIAGARA FALLS STUNT

NIAGARA FALLS, NY - OCTOBER 22, 1901

Conflicting reports have emerged regarding the feline's fate, but we can confirm that, yesterday afternoon, a daring stunt at Niagara Falls took an exhilarating turn. Mrs Annie Edson Taylor, an intrepid adventurer with dreams of conquering the Horseshoe Fall of Niagara to seek fame and fortune, decided to send a grey cat in a barrel as a test of the apparatus. Miraculously, despite the treacherous journey, reports have confirmed that the cat emerged from the adventure unscathed, sparking jubilant celebrations among onlookers.

Mrs Taylor, whose belief in the possibility of surviving a journey over Niagara Falls in a barrel remains unwavering, expressed her joy and relief at the cat's miraculous survival. She articulated her admiration for the cat, which she rented from a Bay City butcher named Bill several weeks ago, boasting of the feline's prowess as a mouser in her hometown. She recounted how the cat – which she had affectionately named Lagara – had been an integral part of the test, proving the resilience of the barrel and offering hope for her future endeavour.

This heartwarming incident has captured the imagination of the public, with many celebrating the cat's remarkable feat and the triumph of courage over adversity. As the news of Lagara's survival spreads, questions about the safety of such stunts have been replaced by admiration for the indomitable spirit of both Mrs Taylor and her feline companion. Her scheduled stunt will occur tomorrow.

Annie's Diary

22nd October 1901

Yesterday's experiment went to plan. Still, if I live past tomorrow, Butcher Bill might kill me for risking Lagara! For here we are, the night before my stunt. The night before I live or die. Perhaps writing this on paper is part of my final preparation for that.

I draw strength from the possibility that in pushing the boundaries of what my body can endure, I might also push the limitations of my emotional and mental capacities one final time. Perhaps, through this, I'll step closer to Samuel and David. Closer to understanding death. Closer to understanding life, too. If I die, Mr Russell will gain financially. If I live Tilda, Mrs Lapointe and Nora will gain even more – and I cling to the anticipation that my life will be given a hopeful purpose. That would be a very pleasant consequence.

Thus, my controlling and final thought is that I've nothing to lose tomorrow. What scares me most is that I'm thinking such thoughts when I've got a family for the first time in decades. Perhaps I was never meant to be surrounded by others. Perhaps I'm stronger alone. Truth undeniable is that Mrs Lapointe is dying, and although I know that I have the capacity to love Tilda and Nora, Tilda considers herself entirely alone with her pain and is yet to trust me fully. Perhaps she never will. We are alike, that girl and I. Self-annihilation and grief dance together.

I lost my identity when my son and husband died, but because of that, this new identity was created; one that is defiant and bold, that plunges into adventure headfirst. I must accept responsibility for that. Perhaps I considered emotion a weakness that dictated a need for distraction, but in doing so I've lived the fullest of lives. This was a choice. The way I survived was a decision.

I have no regrets.

Now, I've breathed for almost forty years as this creature. And what will happen when an intrepid woman becomes the first to conquer the Falls? In a barrel, even! I hold my hands in surrender and wait to see.

Still, there are two possible outcomes for tomorrow – I'll live or I'll die going over the brink of Horseshoe Falls. Folk persist in asking why, and I must admit that I persist in liking their reaction when I respond nonchalantly with, 'I thought a change in career would be nice.'

Annie

23rd October 1901

The barrel's walls encircle me, close and confining. The curved wooden planks are rough against my fingertips. We're still in the rowing boat and it's yet to be sealed fully and so, above, the world is reduced to a small circular patch of sky. It's a shade of blue that's so vast and endless it appears almost surreal.

From down here, it's like peering through a hatch to another world. Every so often, a face eclipses that expanse of sky and curious eyes stare down for a moment before darting away. The air inside the barrel is stifling, carrying with it the earthy scent of damp wood. This is seclusion. This is being removed from the outside world.

'Wind's picked up.'

That's Holleran. He and Trusdale are as close as brothers. Grew up on the same street, and their voices mimic each other too.

'Where are we?' I ask.

I'm clutching the heart-shaped pillow Tilda made for me and the men are in the process of shifting the lid to seal me in. I'm struggling to hear much but the sound of the rushing water and the howling wind's creating a cacophony of noise. I'm sheltered from the elements here though.

'Upper river,' one of the men says. 'Still rowing.' There's something else but the voices are muffled.

'Everything fine?' I ask.

There's a pause. I imagine they're looking at each other. Maybe one of them's mouthing or signalling something.

'What are you saying?' I'm shouting. I don't need to be patient or polite, given my current circumstances: cramped in a barrel, knees already aching, heart trying to pound its way out of my chest. My ears strain to absorb all and every sound. How can I already crave familiarity? I'm greedy for snippets, for noises to be signs that it's all going to be fine. The distant rumble of the waterfall – its incessant pounding – rebounds against the wood. A relentless drum. The cocoon of the barrel offers an odd sort of comfort, though. A semblance of safety within the very instrument that might soon become my coffin. I trace my fingers along the coarse grain of the staves. What am I doing? Have I slipped into madness?

Time passes. Merely minutes perhaps. The world continues to churn. The wind howls outside. Its moaning crescendo is a haunting soundtrack. Hurry up, hurry up, hurry up. Gusts rattle the barrel; a sudden motion that mirrors the turmoil inside my belly. I cling to the straps that will eventually keep me upright, as if that'll stop the topple now. The shouts of men are still muffled. Have they moved further away? This thick oak encasement contorts their words.

The men are moving me in a rowing boat. They'll knock me into the water at some point soon. I'll be at the mercy of the rapids then. I don't know why they've not done so yet. Is this it? Will it happen now? Should it have happened already?

Wait. Am I going in the water? They haven't secured the lid yet. Have they forgotten? I'll drown. 'Hey, hey.' I pound my fist on the barrel's curve. Is it being tipped? Is that grinding sound a pebbled shore?

'Hello? Hello,' I shout.

No reply. Instead, jolts in movement increase the pounding in my heart. A chill rushes through me, not from the cold October air seeping through the small opening. This is fear. Raw and constricting. What am I doing? The barrel wobbles in response.

'You're at the shore, Mrs Taylor. A tiny plaything at the mercy of this raging river.'

'Is that Holleran?' I ask. The world outside remains only a whirl of wind, roaring Falls and water. 'What's happening?'

'Too risky, Annie.' That's Mr Russell. He's shouting over the tempest. 'No choice but to bring you back in.'

Fear coils in my belly. Will I be given another opportunity? Is that it? All the courageous talk and nothing to show for it again.

I grip the inner rim of the barrel tighter and shake my head.

'We can't steady the boat to release the barrel,' one of them says.

'Who is that?'

'Holleran, Mrs Taylor. Wind's too strong.'

'River's flowing too deep and quick,' Mr Russell says.

'No choice but to ground it.' That might be the other one. 'There's an inlet here.' He sounds out of breath. 'Hard steering in that wind with just this oar,' he says. The words are stuttered and wheezy.

I wonder what all the spectators are making of this. Despite the blustery weather, Mr Russell has proven himself an excellent manager. Tourists and locals have flocked to the Falls today; I couldn't believe my eyes when I saw so many dotted around. Hair whipping around their faces and the roar of the water in their ears. Some even waved as I climbed in the vessel. It was like they knew me. The report about Lagara piqued their interest. The fact that a random, old woman had chosen today to get in a barrel and roll in it over the Falls, well that had made those spectators brave the elements and stay to witness the event. The barrel's lid is removed fully. Too bright. I shield my eyes with my hand.

'Too much of a risk, Mrs Taylor,' Holleran says.

They've decided. I'm not sure if I should offer them more money. Maybe this is their money-making idea – get me in the barrel and force me to pay additional amounts.

'My risk, not yours,' I say. 'I'm not paying you extra—'

'This isn't about the money. If we take you out there…' I imagine he is pointing in the direction of the brink. 'You'll be tethered to the boat. It'll be the lot of us going over the edge.'

The unspoken is that they don't think any of us would survive that, and they're either not being paid enough or stupid enough to risk their lives.

'I'm not giving up.' I sound defeated. I sigh. I'm helpless. I'm in a horizontal, wooden barrel and trying my best not to stamp my feet in protest.

'Didn't suggest you would,' Mr Russell says.

'But launching the barrel in this weather's near impossible,' Holleran insists.

I snort. I don't mean to. I don't want to hear that my idea's impossible. If this is some elaborate scheme to stop me from going over Horseshoe Falls, then I'm not going to make it easy for them. I get it – no one's survived before – but that doesn't mean I won't.

I imagine my face is like thunder. 'I'm not getting out of this barrel unless you tell me when I can try again.'

'Forecast's better for tomorrow.' That's Mr Russell. He's calm and unbothered.

'I'm not going to keep putting it off,' I say.

There's a pause. I think I can hear them talking to each other. 'I believe in you, Mrs Taylor. But you need to trust me. I'm confident that you'll succeed, but surely you can hold off for one more day … if it means sparing our lives, too?' One of the voices rises to a shout. That's Holleran.

I can't really disagree or argue with that reasoning. I'm not irrational, and I'm certainly not wanting to appear hysterical.

'Abort,' I say, and I imagine those out of my view smiling at that. Like I have any power or control here. I loosen the straps that are too tight around my body. 'And help me out of this bloody barrel. Is Matilda here yet?'

NIAGARA FALLS STUNT POSTPONED DUE TO WIND

NIAGARA FALLS, NY - OCTOBER 23, 1901

The much-anticipated stunt of Mrs Annie Edson Taylor, who had planned to go over Niagara Falls in a barrel, was postponed today due to high winds.

Former teacher, Mrs Taylor, 43, was already inside the barrel when the decision was made to call off the feat. Some speculate that nerves may have played a role in her inability to go through with the stunt, as Mrs Taylor has been vocal about her desire to gain fame and fortune from the act. However, she later refused interview and has remained tight-lipped about the incident.

The postponement has disappointed many who were eagerly waiting to witness this historic event. A man in Chippawa reported observing the boatmen travelling back to Port Day with the barrel. He rode on the back of a trolley car on the Canadian side and gave details that the stunt had been abandoned. The news then spread rapidly and served to disperse the gathered crowd on the Canadian shore. Conversely, those patiently waiting on Goat and Three Sisters Islands received no word, thus remained until dark before finally giving up hope of witnessing the stunt.

A Mr Russell, stunt manager, told reporters that a second attempt is scheduled for tomorrow afternoon. He stated that Mrs Taylor, known for being intelligent and venturesome, has previously topped the Alps, participated in dangerous swimming experiences, and discovered feral, unknown countries.

The public remains eager to see Mrs Taylor go over the Falls in a barrel. Will she be the first to survive the daredevil attempt, achieving what numerous men have failed? Weather permitting, we will all know tomorrow.

with me index finger. Cold. Doesn't move. I grip her wrist. Can't feel any pulse. I wave me hand in front of her eyes. No blinking.

'No,' I whisper, wiping a tear from me cheek with me fingers. 'Not now. Not when I must go.'

I shouldn't be in here. Shouldn't be breathing her air. Shouldn't have come back. A few steps to the window and I open it, pushing me head outside into the darkness. I'm scared, but the wind's cool on me cheeks.

Thoughts spin in me head. 'What do I do now?' I ask the darkness. I need Mrs Lapointe to wake up. Me body stiffens with the weight of the moment. Mrs Taylor said Mrs Lapointe was the anchor of this place. That her strength was holding us all together. She said that without her, the future would be uncertain. Like a storm without a lighthouse. I need Mrs Taylor to come home. To fix this mess. But I've got to keep Nora safe from Uncle William.

Walking to the door and a sparkle catches me eye. I glance at the small statue of the Virgin Mary on Mrs Lapointe's bedside table. She found comfort in her faith. Last Rites were performed when she took her first turn for the worse, but what happens now? I need to let her church know. Least I can do for her.

'I hope you're at peace,' I say. 'Hope you're free from the discomfort and suffering.' I think about the coughing – hacking, painful – that's plagued her weeks. She's at peace now. But she died alone.

'Should have been here for you,' I say. Snot drips from me nose, tears flow from me eyes.

I undo me necklace, turning to place Mama's cross in me friend's hand. Closing her fingers around it. Don't know who to pray to. 'Thank you for looking after us when no one else would.'

Rotating, I knock a prayer book to the floor. As I bend to place it back on the bedside cabinet, I spot the envelope. It's under the Virgin Mary. I glance back at Mrs Lapointe's face.

'I promise you. I'll be better. I'll keep Nora safe,' I say.

Lifting the statue, I see what's written on the envelope. *Tilda.*

My dearest Tilda,

You've not returned home in time, and I must leave for the stunt. I've been pacing the boards downstairs. Maybe you changed your mind and you're worried about my chances of survival. Perhaps you've decided to protect little Nora from my death. Know that none of that matters now. Plans don't always unravel as we wish, and you will have valid reasons.

There are things I need to tell you, my friend. I'd planned on telling you during our journey to Niagara. Instead, I've had a few unexpected hours to fuss and to worry about how much of me you don't know. But it is important that you do – you and Nora are truly significant to me.

I've spent a lifetime fending for myself and I struggle to share. Those untold stories rot from the inside out, though and, perhaps, this letter will allow you to speak your truth, too; to voice the seemingly impossible. Here I am, about to face the very definition of impossible. No one has survived what I'm about to attempt. It appears unachievable.

Still, with closer contemplation, that doesn't make the task hopeless. That doesn't mean that no one ever will, but rather that it's not happened yet. I'll survive. Fact is that I've already exceeded my life expectancy, so what do I have to lose? You, Nora, Mrs Lapointe… Perhaps this is indeed the realisation that I've let others close enough to fear what life will be without you all. Nonetheless, it's time now, and before I leave – be it for a few days or for this lifetime – to tell you a story that connects us all. One that I mentioned in passing to you at the Falls. I've shared Morgiana with you already – you can now recite her tale with the ease of drinking a cup of lukewarm tea – but this one won't slip as easily from your tongue. It resonates through time though and it pulls us all to Niagara Falls. May you whisper her name, your name, Morgiana's and mine together.

Because they called her Lelawala, the Princess of Niagara. Do you recall my speaking her name? Perhaps, though, you haven't heard how she lost her husband and her hope at a young age? Perhaps there is something that joins those who suffer trauma at the time where adolescence meets adulthood. Before we are fully formed, tragedy carves itself into our beings. We find ourselves drawn to water, though. Little dots of iron pulled to our magnificent magnet. Drawn to any substance that both listens and understands.

Lelawala couldn't find her way through the sorrow upon sorrow that was her lot in life, but one day she stepped into her birch canoe and paddled out into the current, singing a death song softly to herself. She believed that it was her time; it was the right decision for her. In that moment and in those unique circumstances, she accepted her life.

Can you understand the power of that acceptance? The peace it would bring?

There is a moment in all our lives where we weigh the cost against the gain. And when we have nothing to lose and much to acquire, the decision is an easy one. I've been singing my death song since my David died. My son.

I married Samuel David Taylor when I was eighteen; it was 1856. We had our son, David, in 1861. He lived only a few days, though. I both became, and ceased being, a mother before understanding the magnitude of either. Two years later, my husband lost his life in Gettysburg – July 6, 1863. A war widow and a childless mother, I was left with no immediate family. I was given a personal allowance, but not love. Daily since then, and until meeting you, I haven't cared if each day was my last. Liberating, because it means I have lived my life without fear and to the fullest.

So, you see, I've always understood Lelawala's story. Her canoe – note that I've avoided a birch barrel for my stunt – was caught by the rough rapids and hurtled toward the Falls. As it pitched over and she fell to her death, Heno, the god of thunder caught her in his arms. He carried her to his home in the Falls, just beneath the thundering veil of water. From there, he and his sons ministered to Lelawala, and she stayed with them until her heart healed. Then the younger son spoke words of love to her and – much to Heno's delight – they married. Soon, a son was born, and he followed his grandfather Heno everywhere, learning what it meant to be a god of thunder. Can you see how Lelawala was rewarded for her bravery? She was gifted a life that she had never – in her darkest despair – envisaged or hoped for. Is it wrong to voice that I hope for that, too? To be rid of this current death song I sing.

Lelawala's home beneath the Falls was a magical place, with the roar of the water as their constant lullaby. Heno and his sons were kind and wise, and she was grateful for their love and care. Yet even in that idyllic setting, she could not shake the ache in her heart. She longed to see her people once more, to feel the warmth of their embrace and to share with them the joy of her new life.

As I write this to you, I acknowledge the joy that you, Nora and Mrs Lapointe have given to me. Since meeting you, you have become my people.

Lelawala's chance came in an unexpected and unwelcomed way. A great snake came down the mighty river and poisoned the waters of her people. They grew sick and were dying. Heno told her that the snake would return to devour the weak until all her people were gone. She begged him to let her return for one hour, to warn her people of the danger.

The god himself lifted her through the Falls and set her down among her people to give warning about the evil snake that was causing such pestilence among them. She directed them to move to higher ground until the danger had passed, and they agreed. Then Heno came and took her back to her husband and to their home beneath the Falls.

In a few days, the giant serpent returned to the village, seeking the bodies of those who had died from the poison it had spread. When the snake realised that the people had deserted the village, it hissed in rage and turned upstream to search for them. But Heno heard the voice of the serpent and rose through the mist of the Falls. He threw a great thunderbolt at the creature and killed it in one mighty blast. The giant body of the creature floated downstream and lodged just above the cataract, creating a large semi-circle that deflected huge amounts of water into the Falls. It was at the place just above the god's home though.

Aghast by this disastrous turn of events, Heno swept in through the Falls and did his best to stop the substantial influx of water, but it was too late. Seeing that his home would soon be destroyed, Heno called for Lelawala and his sons to leave with him. With her husband and child, Lelawala followed Heno through the water of the Falls and up into the sky and he made them a new home. From this place, she still watches over the people of Earth, while Heno thunders in the clouds as he once thundered in the vapours of the great Falls.

Even now, as she looks out over the cascading waters and hears the distant rumble of thunder, Lelawala is filled with gratitude for the love and protection that Heno and his sons provided her. It's that love and gratitude that exists in the mist. It answers her question. A question that every one of us who have experienced pain and suffering must ask: why not me?

No matter what happens next, I know in my heart that I must do this. This feat will answer that question for me, too.

Still, the pull of the Falls is beyond words. Within its water my answers – my hope and breath – exist. Like Lelawala, I've nothing to lose and much to gain. Moreover, we can't deny that we need money, and the fame that this stunt will attract will give us the security that we all crave. Regardless of whether I survive this stunt, the outcome – the financial gain – remains the same. If I don't survive, Mr Russell will claim all that I own.

I've exhausted my mind scratching these thoughts to paper, and this letter rambles into nonsense. For all that you truly need to know is that to go over the Falls in a barrel is my destiny. Whether or not I survive is in the hands of God – be that Mrs Lapointe's saviour, or my Heno and Lelawala. Yet, know that as the mist rises to envelop me, I'll be home, in her embrace of the mighty Niagara Falls. I will survive this – in whatever form that takes.

You and I have suffered. This life has dealt us trauma that many would crumble beneath. I know that we have secrets so horrific that we fear speaking them aloud. Yet still, the water has brought us each other. There's no coincidence in that. You're my people and I'll do all in my power to keep you safe.

I'm trusting that I will be guided back to you and that our future will be a joyful one, but, please, love Nora with the strength and power of two mothers.

Your devoted Mrs Taylor

Matilda

24th October 1901

Still in the boarding house. The light from me oil lamp's making shadows dance along the walls. They're mocking the darkness of me gloom. With Nora cradled in me lap, her little form's warm against me chest and I'm hunched over on the cold, hard floor. Almost at the door. Couldn't quite leave. Mrs Taylor's letter's on the floorboards beside me. Read several times already. Me tears fall silently. I feel the weight of every word, every unspoken promise. What do I do now? What if Mrs Taylor dies? Why didn't I tell her about Uncle William? Who do I need to tell about Mrs Lapointe? I don't want to abandon her.

Two bags sit beside me. One more than when I arrived here. The contents are a jumble of hastily packed belongings. Life reduced to the necessities. The kindness of strangers, though. That's what's in those bags. Strangers who became me family. And now I've lost everything all over again. What do I do?

I can't hear me own sobs over the pounding of me heart. Each beat's a painful reminder. There's nothing but uncertainty out that front door. How's it come to this? How's me better life crumbled so swiftly? Again.

I'm here again. No home. Begging for help. No one to turn to. Abandoned in this hallway.

The bang on the door makes me leap to me feet. I pull Nora to me chest. She's too tired to wake, though. Can't see who's banging. Too dark. Danger. No other way out. Danger. Must protect me daughter.

'It's Henry Hills,' comes a voice. 'Please, let me in.'

I release a breath. Relief that isn't who I dreaded. I go to the door and open it and Mr Hills rushes in.

'Why are you standing there looking like a startled goose?' he says, and he looks a little wild. Unkempt, his dark hair wet. It's not raining. I think it might be perspiration.

'Why are you here in the middle of the night?' I ask. 'That's not proper.'

He holds up a palm to shush me. 'Is *the* Mrs Annie Edson Taylor in the barrel over Niagara. *My* Annie?'

'No,' I say, me voice cutting through his nonsense like a butter knife. She's not *his*.

He slumps to the floor beside me. He's dramatic. He swipes at his forehead with the back of his hand. 'Phew. I read about her in the newspaper and thought it couldn't be. My Annie would never be reckless and—'

'In the newspaper?'

He nods. 'Saw the article about her postponed stunt and—'

'Postponed?'

He looks up at me and raises an eyebrow. Me repeating his words is making him curious. 'So, she, Annie, wasn't about to do it?' he asks. 'Her name is an unusual one… Perhaps mistaken identity, and not the woman I courted?'

'You absolutely didn't court her,' I mutter, me words laced with bitterness.

He crosses his arms across his chest in protest. 'I planned on marrying her,' he says, pride and regret in his tone.

I have no time to challenge this, though. 'The stunt at Niagara was postponed?' I ask.

He tuts. Considers me dumb. 'Yes, Miss Hamilton.'

'So, Mrs Taylor's still alive?' A flicker of hope ignites within me.

'If indeed it is her?'

'It is,' I say firmly.

He doesn't hesitate. 'I have a carriage waiting outside, and there is a train departing within the hour.' He looks at his pocket watch. 'This is our only chance to make it to the stunt in time. We must leave now.'

I look towards the stairs. Mrs Lapointe's dead in her bed upstairs. Can't discard her, but I need to leave here.

'Miss Hamilton, we must hurry.' He's striding to the door, his voice filled with urgency. 'The train will not wait.'

I glance down at Nora, still sleeping soundly in me arms. A wave of hesitation washes over me. Leaving means abandoning Mrs Lapointe, but we're in danger here. Uncle William could come for us at any minute. I've put everyone at risk. I'm a coward. I've failed Mrs Lapointe. Left her to face her final moments alone. Never repaid her kindness. Never thanked her.

'Miss Hamilton?'

'She died alone,' I say, me voice choked with emotion. I sob. The weight of me guilt threatens to crush me. 'I couldn't save her.'

'Who?' His voice is raised as he's gripping the front door. Impatient. Doesn't have time for me silliness. He's stepping out.

'Mrs Lapointe.' I point to the ceiling.

'Dead?'

I nod.

'She is still here?'

I nod again. 'Up there. Came home tonight to pack and found her dead.'

Henry shakes his head. 'We have to leave now.'

'But…'

He exhales loudly. 'You can't help Mrs Lapointe, but Annie needs us both.'

'What do I need to do though? She's had her Last Rites.'

'I'll write to her church from the carriage. Make sure she receives all that is proper. I'll cover every cost.' His words rush out on a breath. He nods to me two bags. 'Right now, though, we need to focus on getting to Niagara Falls. For Annie. Your choice…'

I wipe the tip of me nose with the back of me hand. I bob me head unconvincingly, then bend to try and pick up the two bags without waking Nora. Henry walks to his carriage with no turning back.

Annie

24th October 1901

The day after the failed attempt, I'm trying not to vomit on my skirts. Happy Birthday to me.

I'm still waiting, hoping for the opportune moment to climb into the barrel again. The uncertainty makes my insides flip and flop. The mist from the Falls hangs heavy, casting an eerie veil over the rugged shoreline. Tall trees sway gently, whispering secrets of the ancient landscape. Nearby, a group of men huddle together, their breath visible in the frigid air as they smoke their pipes. The faint aroma of tobacco mingles with the damp surroundings. Gulls squawk overhead. Despite the cold, there's an air of anticipation and excitement. We're all awaiting my momentous attempt to conquer the mighty Niagara.

The instructions have been explained several times. We're near Buffalo Avenue in Niagara Falls, with two rowing boats waiting. One holds my barrel. Both will travel to Grass Island, where I'll enter the barrel, and Mr Russell will be rowed back here. Now, he paces briskly along the shoreline, his footsteps crunching against the rocky terrain. He stumbles over outcrops and boulders, the newspaper gripped tightly in his hand, adding to the constant roar and mist in the air.

'Mr Russell,' I shout, the biting chill seeping through my layers of clothing, settling into the woollen weave of my crimson shawl. It sends shivers down my spine. 'Mr Russell.' Louder this time. He turns towards me, pausing as if checking if I want to speak, then nodding for me to continue. 'I've been thinking…'

'You have to speak up.' He points his newspaper towards the Falls.

'I don't want to continue with this deception about my age.' I'm shouting. My hands grip the fabric of my skirt tightly, my knuckles white with tension. The huddle of men hears, too, and they each freeze like stone statues, pipes paused mid-suck.

'Your age?'

'I'm not forty-three.' I indicate towards his baton.

Mr Russell glances at the newspaper and shrugs. 'You told me that was your age.'

'I lied.'

He pauses, scanning the horizon with furrowed brows, eyes darting back and forth amidst the mist and spray of the Falls. 'Changing it now would only confuse people.'

'I understand that,' I say, 'but I can't keep pretending to be someone I'm not. I'm sixty-three today. It's my birthday, and I want to be seen as such.'

His horror is evident. 'Are you sure?'

'Of course I am.'

He shakes his head, panic flickering across his face. 'Being forty-three will give you extra time to enjoy your fame.'

'That isn't how ageing works, dear Mr Russell,' I say, shaking my head in bewilderment, but he waves away my words. 'And I've never topped the Alps, participated in dangerous swimming experiences, or discovered feral, unknown countries.'

He turns away, stomping back along the shoreline.

'I've achieved other things, though – survived a house fire in Chattanooga, an earthquake in South Carolina. Are they not adequate accomplishments for your public?'

He ignores me, but then he turns, striding purposefully in my direction. 'Why does it matter? You'll still be the first person ever to survive going over the Horseshoe Falls in a barrel. That's what people care about.'

'It's charming how you think talking down to me will change my mind,' I say. 'It matters because I want to challenge the notion that women need to make up stories to be perceived as interesting, or visible. I'm a remarkable woman already.' I shift uncomfortably, crossing and uncrossing my legs beneath me. 'Today I'll show the world that women, whatever their age, can be more daring and adventurous than men.'

With a frustrated sigh, he clenches his fingers around the newspaper, his jaw tensing as he crumples it in his hand. 'This stunt is risky enough as it is,' he says. 'We don't need to complicate things further by changing your age.'

'Thank you for your perspective. It's a rare insight into irrelevance. You're not seeing the bigger picture,' I shout, stretching my arms out to allow Lelawala a step closer. 'When I succeed, it won't just be a victory for me. It'll be a victory for all women, before me, after me and yet to be born.'

'You're being silly, and you're refusing to hear me.' He resumes his pacing, his movements agitated and restless, running his free hand through his hair in exasperation. 'Folk are more likely to help a younger woman than … an old lady.'

'I'm sixty-three today.' I nod in support of myself, with a steely resolve in my eyes. 'I'll be the person giving the help.'

'I can't hear you,' he shouts, waving the newspaper at the water. It's noisy, and I'm not loud enough.

'I'm sixty-three today.' It's the loudest I can shout. There's laughter from the huddle of men.

Holleran claps and cheers. 'Many happy returns of the day, Mrs Taylor.'

'We'll show them what a real daredevil looks like … wrinkles and all.' I wave at Holleran.

'Bloody seagulls,' Mr Russell says, kicking out at one that's flown into his path. 'Noisy and pointless.'

'Gulls,' I correct. 'No such thing as seagulls.'

He shakes his head, disappointed. 'Let's talk further after the stunt, Mrs Taylor. Holleran…' he shouts. Holleran turns from the group of smoking men and waves.

'Is it time?' I ask.

'It is,' Mr Russell says. He turns back to the water's edge and, with a swift motion, hurls the crumpled newspaper into the churning waters. His expression is a mixture of defiance and resolve.

I'm not sure he hears the exasperated sigh I release.

Annie

24th October 1901

We've made it to Grass Island. I'm sitting on a rock beside the shoreline. Waiting.

'Fair weather's expected all afternoon,' Mr Russell says. He's shouting to a photographer who's leaning in closer to hear. 'With moderate temperatures.' They both look to the sky and nod.

'Still good to go?' says a reporter. Mr Russell has carefully chosen such individuals and given them the opportunity for a select amount of time with me. I like that he's constantly got an eye on the dollar, but this island's small and rocky and I'm not in the mood for trivial conversation.

'Aim is four o'clock,' he says, and both the reporter and his photographer look at their pocket watches. 'Just over an hour to go.'

The rowboat carrying my barrel is near to shore, its hull threatens to scrape against the rocks. They've covered the barrel with a blanket, as if it's napping to reserve its energy before the stunt. Holleran and Trusdale huddle together, Mr Russell kicks at small rocks with the tip of his boots. We're about three-quarters of a mile upstream from the raging Horseshoe Falls and I'm picking up information about the stunt's schedule in drips. I'm sure Mr Russell considers that a way to control my mood, to keep my spirits high. In reality, it's making me more anxious. Am I getting in that barrel today or not? Is the rescue boat already waiting for me at the bottom?

'This crescent is calmer,' I say. No one responds, but still the Niagara River flexes its strength a little more gently in this sheltered inlet. Gulls squawk in support, though. The towering, leaf-cloaked trees manage to buffer and embrace the rocky outcrop, nudging it into the water.

'Ethereal,' I say, but still nothing. They're all lost in their own heads.

In the last hour, a police officer, Eagan, rowed out here. He commanded we stop the stunt. Mr Russell convinced him that the crowds were already too big to be let down. He left, but I'm worried he'll be back with his colleagues. Now my barrel sits tethered inside the rowing boat. They both bob in the river. As promised, a former pickle barrel rebuilt to my specifications.

'Gives a whole new meaning to being in a pickle,' I say, but no one replies. To be fair, I said the same yesterday. Is this repeating what it means to be superstitious? A sturdy plank extends to the rowing boat; a trembling bridge over the roiling grey water. That precarious pathway awaits me, and I wait for Mr Russell to tell me to make my daring transit from solid ground to the barrel.

'My wooden vessel for the impending journey over the thunderous Falls,' I say to no one.

I exhale. Perhaps I've been holding my breath. I don't even know anymore.

'Please, Mrs Taylor, can I get a picture of you in the costume you've got for your trip over there?' The photographer points in the direction of the Horseshoe Falls. He's at least half my age and appears to be bouncing on the spot with excitement.

'Young man, it would be unbecoming of a woman of my refinement and years to parade before a holiday crowd in abbreviated skirts.'

The photographer blushes and the reporter scribbles notes onto paper.

'Can you hear them?' It's Mr Russell, holding a hand to his ear as if to amplify his range.

'The gulls?' I say and I nod. I can.

He shakes his head. 'Listen.'

I hold my own hand to my ear, and the noise hits me. First, the water and then a roaring cacophony of thousands of spectators above on the viewing deck. I see them, then, too. Their excited cries ride on the brisk October air.

'Mrs Taylor. Mrs Taylor.'

They're shouting my name. It's become part of the roar of the Falls. More than that, there's a fervour. It's like nothing I've ever known. Mr Russell did say that spectators would access various observing points from both the American and Canadian sides of the Falls. On the American side, attractions such as Prospect Point and Goat Island offer direct views, while on the Canadian side, Queen Victoria Park affords scenic vistas of the Niagara River and Horseshoe Falls. He told me all of that. He said crowds would gather on both sides, but I don't think I ever considered that they would. I certainly never predicted that they'd chant my name.

'I see hands waving,' Mr Russell says.

'From the crowd?' I shield my eyes from the autumnal sun and look in the direction he's pointing. My eyesight's too poor to see far.

'There's some swinging of hats, too,' he says. 'Spirited encouragement. Bet it's a frenzy, a thunderous testament to human curiosity, up there.' He's excited. 'I should be with them.'

I spin on the spot, looking in all directions.

'Are there people watching from all sides?'

'From every available space,' he says. His words flutter. 'Not just up on the viewing deck but crowding on the shore and banks, too.'

He wasn't this excited yesterday. The article about the postponement has served us well. Even more people are curious today.

'Are there folk at Goat and Three Sisters islands again?' I ask and Mr Russell nods.

'It's madness,' I say, laughing. I'm defining madness when there's not another human on Earth who has survived to tell this story. If this stunt doesn't make me unique and remarkable, then what will?

'It's louder than the roar of the Falls you're about to challenge,' Mr Russell says. 'This isn't a free show, though. I need to get up there and collect money. Lolly and Magnus will be working the crowds well. Must get to as many as possible.'

I nod. 'So, we're truly doing this?'

'We are,' Mr Russell says. I cock my head and take in the sight of this well-mannered and well-dressed man. Is he nervous? I think he is. If I die, there's talk of him being charged with manslaughter. I'm not sure how that works. He walks towards his rowing boat, but then turns back.

'You've still got the bill of sale?' I ask.

He pats his breast pocket. 'See you on the other side, Mrs Taylor.'

I'm actually doing this; those words spin in my head. I'll be taken to Upper Niagara and the barrel will be untethered when I'm in the middle. From there I'll plunge over the Horseshoe Falls and plummet 158 feet into the boiling cauldron of Lower Niagara. That's our plan. Holleran and Trusdale stand from their huddle and walk to me.

'You need to stay over there and make the others turn away, too,' I say to Trusdale. 'For the sake of my decency.' He tips his bowler hat to me and shouts to the others.

The arrangement is the same as yesterday. Only Holleran will help me into the barrel. I take off my hat and hand it to him. My hair's pulled into a tight bun. Restricted and practical. I peel off my heavy woollen coat, and the cold air latches onto my abbreviated skirts. No hem to hide money in this time. The divided pieces flap against my legs; the crisp breeze trying to sneak up the folds. I wave my pillow from Tilda and place it on the floor.

'For in the barrel,' I say. I did all this yesterday. Same order, same words.

Drawing in a deep breath through my nostrils, the scent of autumn leaves and wet earth mingles with the distant mustiness of the river. It's invigorating, it's grounding. Inhaling courage, exhaling fear, I approach the plank. Mr Holleran steps into the water and holds out his hand to guide me.

'My ark amidst the deluge to come,' I say, taking his hand.

Mr Holleran's usual kindness is replaced by a mask of stern professionalism. The ten hoops of Kentucky oak loom before me. The barrel is waiting in the rowing boat; it will swallow me whole.

'If it's God's or Heno's will, then my life will be spared,' I say. 'If not? Then let's pray that my death is quick.'

'No talk of death, Mrs Taylor,' he says. 'You'll be the first person ever to…' His trailing words are unconvincing.

With a final glance in the direction of the distant and waiting crowd, I gather my divided skirts to climb into the barrel. It's an awkward dance; there's less material than usual but still the bulky fabric hinders more than aiding my movements. I catch a wry smile flickering across Holleran's face as I grapple with the unruly garment.

'Slowly does it, Mrs Taylor,' he warns. 'And grab the material tighter.'

Heeding his advice, I bunch up the black skirts. The coarse fabric in my fists, I hoist myself up. Black stockings and tan slippers on show. My foot searches for purchase in the barrel's narrow foothold. My legs buckle as a sliver of fear nips at my courage; a reminder of the dark confines I'm willingly entering. It's a tomb. It's a cradle. It's my ticket over the Falls.

Once seated, the reality of the confined space crashes down on me again. The barrel contours my body. The oak presses into my back and my hips. There's an anvil on the outside, at the base. A weighty promise of stability against the fury of the Falls. I must stay upright. My heart flutters like a trapped bird.

'Annie.' Mr Holleran's never called me by my first name before. He's standing in the rowing boat and his face hovers over me. It's a mask of concern and something akin to admiration. He fixes the cushions at the front and back of my body. His fingers work deftly. He bends and leans in to tighten the straps of my harness, checking, and rechecking. 'Tug at the waist strap,' he says. I do what he instructs. I trust him entirely. He's ensuring my safety as best he can.

Additional cushions are pressed around my neck and head; extra padding to safeguard me from the violent tumble. 'Think about Lagara,' he whispers. A reminder of the test run that went well a couple of days ago. I hope Butcher Bill didn't expect me to return his cat. The feline's got legendary status now. The two of us will make a fortune.

'Wonder if he used one of his nine lives,' I say.

'Here.' He thrusts my heart-shaped pillow into the barrel. I clutch it to my nose, breathing in the lavender scent. Tilda and Nora are with me. I like that they are. I wish I knew if they were safe though. 'Do you remember what to do if you need more air?' His voice is filled with concern.

'I remember.' I reassure him by placing a hand on one of the corks for emphasis. Inside the barrel, there's a small air tube that runs to a bicycle pump on the outside. The tube is securely sealed around a hole to prevent water ingress. If I need more air, I can signal to him through the cork hole, and he will pump fresh air in. The corks are there as an emergency measure; I can pull one out to create a small air hole and then quickly seal it again after receiving the air.

'I'm ready.'

'You sure?' he asks. He looks at me with kind, knowing eyes. 'You can still change your mind.'

I shake my head and he dips his bowler hat to me.

'Not goodbye,' I say. '*Au revoir*.' With a deep breath that fills my lungs with the crisp October air, I give the signal. The top is pulled across entirely, and I'm plunged into darkness. The muffled sounds of the outside world fade, replaced by the pounding of my heart. I pull out a cork and it works fine.

'Ready?' Mr Holleran shouts.

'As I'll ever be,' I say, as the cork is pushed back in.

He pumps in air. I grip the tube; my remaining link to the surface. Pump after pump of precious air is forced into my wooden sanctuary. Each gust is a promise of survival.

'Godspeed, Mrs Taylor.' Mr Holleran's voice filters through the barrel. His words are a low hum that vibrates through the oak staves. 'Me and Trusdale are with you. See you back at your lodgings.'

Tears sting my eyes, a mix of fear and gratitude. I blink them away, focusing on the rhythm of my breath, the feel of the barrel around me and the distant, ever-present roar of the Falls. Still, even in this tight, restrictive womb, I'm convinced that the sounds of the crowd and gulls seep through. The anxious shouts, the fervent prayers, the squawks, the electrifying excitement – it's all for me, Annie Edson Taylor.

Still tethered to the boat, he pushes the barrel. I feel it plop into the water and the anvil does its job. I'm vertical.

Annie

24th October 1901

My breathing's heavy. It doesn't feel right. I can't have been in here long. Minutes, if that. It must be the air from the bicycle pump. I need different air. Need it now. I grab the little tube over my head, working my fingers along it. One. Two. Three. A cork. I pull it towards me. Fresh air rushes through the gap. A piece of my strap breaks loose and falls to the bottom of the barrel with a tiny splash.

'No. Can't be,' I say.

I stretch my tiptoes down, moving side to side slowly. Water. There's water coating the bottom.

'Water,' I scream, pounding my fist on the interior. 'Water's coming in. From the bottom of the barrel.'

The vessel jerks. It must be being pulled. 'How much?' Mr Holleran's voice strains through the wood. He must have yanked the rope back to the rowing boat. I'm safer now. Breathe. Breathe.

I swish my tiptoes back and forth again. 'A couple of inches.' The barrel creaks and groans around me, protesting at being held captive.

'That'll be from where the anvil was joined,' he says. He doesn't sound alarmed. 'A couple of inches isn't anything to worry about. The stunt will be over in ten minutes.'

'Over in ten minutes.' I whisper the words. My heart might burst.

'I'll keep you near the boat for two minutes. Observe the water until then,' Mr Holleran says. I nod, though he can't see me. The barrel bobs and bounces in response.

'Did Princess Lelawala think her heart would burst, too?' I'm talking to myself. I like how the words sound in the barrel.

I focus on her courage, her resilience in the face of seemingly insurmountable odds. No one can know how she felt in that moment. How scared she was in the rapids. Despite the dangers lurking beneath the surface, Lelawala embraced the unknown with awe and wonder. She plunged headlong into the churning waters, and in that moment of surrender, she found not death but life – a second chance to experience the beauty and majesty of the world around her.

The roar of the water reverberates through the barrel. It's a demanding symphony, echoing in my ears and rattling my bones. 'How did Butcher Bill's cat emerge unscathed from these tumultuous waters?'

I shake my head slowly. My mind's decided that now – while I'm trapped in this barrel – is the time to contemplate how a cat survived, when so many others perished in these relentless waters. Why am I smiling? Nine lives or a second chance at life? Do I believe in reprieves from the merciless grip of fate?

Is that hope stirring within my stomach? I ask myself. I chuckle softly. Dare I grasp the belief that perhaps, against all odds, I too will emerge unscathed from this maelstrom?

'Mrs Taylor, are you fine?' Mr Holleran again. Do you require assistance?'

'I am fine,' I shout.

'How much water now?'

'About a pail,' I shout back.

The world around me shakes and shifts with each ripple. The river has no rhythm to lull me into a trance-like state. There are rises, then falls. It's theatrical. It demands attention. My own mortality is in this barrel with me.

'Is there a similar fate to Lelawala awaiting me on the other side?'

I don't know who I'm asking. God or Heno; will I recognise whoever replies? A rebirth, a renewal, a second chance at life. Those thoughts fill me with comfort. A glimmer of hope amidst this actual darkness.

'Even in the face of death, there's the possibility of something more. A palpable reminder of the precariousness of life,' I say.

My jaw rattles. That comfort's fleeting. This is fear.

'What would my husband, Samuel, think about all of this? If he had lived, would I be here?' The words shake at their edges. My voice is unrecognisable. Still, I need the sound of my voice in this barrel to overthrow the intensity of my dread.

The roar of the Falls booms in my ears. Its relentless symphony reverberates through every fibre of my being.

'Do I hear the echoes of cannon fire? Does the ground tremble beneath the weight of countless marching feet?'

Those distant fields of Gettysburg, stained with blood and sorrow. I think I hear them. I do. Right now. I hear the cries of the wounded vibrating within the wooden walls around me. The sacrifices made by too many in the name of freedom and justice.

I shake my head. It's not 1863. The chaos and confusion of battle won't ever be comparable to this stunt of mine. Men fought and died for causes they believed in. Their lives snuffed out in an instant by the brutal realities of war. A battlefield, littered with the shattered remnants of lives cut short. The cost of conflict and the fragility of human life. Their purpose. My being in a barrel is a choice.

My Samuel was there. He was. He will always be there. Amidst the devastation and despair, standing shoulder to shoulder with his comrades as they braved the horrors of war. Didn't he make the ultimate sacrifice, his life snuffed out in an instant by the brutal realities of conflict?

Would he be proud of this choice I've made?

I shake my head. No. He'd have expected me to fulfil a domestic role, to prioritise family and propriety over this. Perhaps I'd have wanted that, too. I'd have been ordinary with him. Instead, I'm a stunter at sixty-three. The notion of a woman engaging in daring and dangerous feats is unconventional. Even scandalous. Yet here I am – challenging the propriety and expectations of someone my age and sex. Which path do I wish I were on?

I know what he'd say. 'You should be protected and sheltered from harm rather than actively seeking out danger, Annie.'

Would he say that?

I can't remember his voice anymore.

Answers elude me. I teeter on the precipice of my own abyss. I'm lost amidst the tumult of emotions and the roar of the Falls.

'Much more water?' Mr Holleran's voice again. He's shouting.

I stretch down my tiptoes again, moving from side to side. 'A little more. Not enough to call it off, if that's what you're about to suggest.'

'I'll slacken the rope. Not much further to stay tethered and then it's all down to you, Mrs Taylor.'

I push the cork back in.

Matilda

24th October 1901

'Miss Hamilton. Matilda. Matilda Hamilton.'

I stop me pacing back and forth on the wooden planks, turning to the squeaky voice. He's too short to be seen in a crowd, so instead, the shouting bounces off capes and bowler hats.

'Mr Hills?' I say and Nora giggles. She's on me right hip. Fascinated by the crowds around us.

'There you are.' A break in the swarm and Henry Hills waddles through the surge towards me. He carries his pride with him as if he has reason for it; his face as red and moist as steamed beetroot. He bends to catch his breath. One hand resting on his knee and the other waving his bowler hat in the air.

Seconds pass. I wait, stepping from boot to boot. Desperate to push on. 'Okay,' he says. His voice is still breathy. Think he might need to sit down, but I'm not suggesting that. No time for that or for this.

'So…'

I wave me hand for him to quicken. Nora waves, too.

'What I've gathered is that she began almost a mile from the brink.' He points a tubby finger feebly. Possibly to where the crowds are pushing forward. Niagara Falls is beyond them. 'The towboat's captained by two men and already they've travelled – with the barrel – to Grass Island. It's there that she seemingly climbed into the barrel.'

I shake me head. 'I can't believe…' I've said that at least six times since Mr Hills arrived at the boarding house. He's told at least thirteen people that he's 'been courting' the stunter. Mrs Taylor would be horrified to be claimed in that way.

'It's happening,' I mutter, moving Nora from me right to me left hip. She's too heavy for this. A carriage, a train, another carriage. Our two bags in Mr Hills' lodgings. I'll leave from here later. After I've said me goodbyes. No idea where we'll go next. Perspiration gathers at the base of me neck. It's possible that I'm talking to meself, that I'm commentating as a way of accepting the news: Mrs Taylor's about to go over the Horseshoe Falls. In a wooden barrel. In a rebuilt pickle barrel. She's actually doing it. She's a ridiculous goose of a woman. How'd we ever figure this was a good idea? Odds of her survival are zero. First Mrs Lapointe, now Mrs Taylor. Today might be the worst day of me life.

'They said…' Mr Hills is upright again now. He's brushing down his jacket and trousers. Trying to rid himself of any specks of poor people. He turns and points back towards the crowd. Face twisting into a grimace. 'That she's … that she's speeding into the Canadian current.'

I hear a mix of bewilderment and amusement in his voice. I hate him. Want to punch his face until he cries for his sister. Mr Hills is a man with a big ego; that makes him a dangerous one. I scan the crowd for Uncle William. Faces blend and morph into his. Think I might vomit. I pull Nora closer to me, kissing the top of her head. She wriggles out of the embrace.

Mr Hills' laughter breaks me panic. Perhaps he said something amusing; Doubt it, though. He's finding this entire situation comical. A woman going over the Horseshoe Falls in a barrel, but even better – a woman he's claiming to be linked to romantically. Mrs Taylor might die, and he'll be dining out on her story for years to come. Might even attract a wife in the process. Mrs Taylor's suddenly become his new currency, even though he's rich already. His money talks a language that's louder than a handsome face, above average height and intelligent observation.

'A female stunt devil.' He laughs from his belly at that. I whack his arm – as if to say *show some respect, you slithering worm* – and he's caught off-guard.

'Feisty and pretty,' he says. Looks me up and down as if I'm a piece of meat on one of his fancy platters. His hand moves to his crotch and me eyes can't help but follow. A single stroke and he's aroused. He looks at Nora and shakes his head. Wishes she wasn't here.

'Annie declared she'd be the first person to survive the Falls,' Mr Hills says, loud enough for those around us to turn. All eyes on him; he loves that. 'Of course, I laughed. Who wouldn't? I thought she spoke in jest.'

'The joke's on you,' I say.

'To attempt the Cataract means death,' he says, not hearing me. There's a murmur of agreement around us. He smiles and nods to the strangers.

I'm having to clench me lips closed to stop me words. Me friend's about to die and he's making this about him? Instead, I pull me arm around Nora and push against the backs of the crowd stepping towards the viewing deck.

'Folk get caught in the suction of the rapids and swept over the brink.' He's behind me again. 'I told her we could marry, but this fiasco will mean I may have to reconsider my options.'

He pauses, perhaps wanting a response. Perhaps he thinks I'll barter or take this opportunity to declare me love for him. None of them scenarios are happening.

'It's not as if she's even beautiful,' he says.

The fingers in me right hand form into the tightest fist. I take a step closer to the ridiculously short man. 'Would you like to say that again?'

Spit from me words lands on his cheek, and he reaches up, dabbing at it with his fingers, then places them in his mouth.

'Vile worm,' I say.

His quizzical expression twists into a laugh. 'I didn't want her hand in marriage. She's no match for me.' He doesn't meet me eyes. He's looking at his feet. He clocks me formed fist. 'I pitied her—'

Nora reaches over to grab his jacket. She's exploring the world. Wide-eyed curiosity. But he flinches. Man's scared of a little girl. I shake me head at him.

The crowd groans in unison. They're static. Impatient, too. Wind whips bonnets and bowler hats, as people grab their headwear and fasten their coats. They pull their clothes tight to their bodies, attempting to stop heat from escaping. Still, they move on a wave, pushing into the backs of those in front. Mr Hills wobbles unsteadily with each push from behind. His sea legs are rickety. Everyone's keen to be witnessing the spectacle. They want to watch Mrs Taylor die.

'Heard she's a teacher,' says a voice to the right, but buried in the crowd. The gossip ripples like a stream and causes me entire body to shiver then shake. A teacher's someone normal and normal folk don't get in barrels, let alone go over Horseshoe Falls in them.

Is she hysterical? is unspoken but still it dances in the air, and I hear.

There are hundreds watching Niagara Falls. If a piece of land has a view, then it's crowded with folk. This is their chance to witness history happening. They'll be talk of 'some woman they saw die' and 'the woman who went over Niagara Falls in a barrel' for years to come. Will they even remember her name? Everything – the seeing and the recounting – will be from a distance; like that somehow makes it fine. Like it isn't real.

They'll not think that there could be folk who love Annie Edson Taylor. After all, if you were loved or if you were normal, then why would you be going to the brink in a barrel? They're noisy, though, this crowd. They're whipped by the sharp wind and drowning in the mighty roar, yet still they're eating cotton candy or roasted peanuts from the footstalls. Seems that we're in a carnival and me Mrs Taylor's the main act.

'I wish she'd agreed to marry me … and that Mrs Taylor and I were sitting in lawn chairs in Hamilton,' Mr Hills says. The liar's almost singing. He wants to be the hero. Maybe the victim. Probably both. This man's mama has really made him believe the world spins around his tiny rear. I know, for a fact, that he doesn't wish that and so I don't grace him with further response. Instead, I focus on the roar of the Falls and leave him to practise his storytelling on this excitable crowd.

Seems the wind's blowing in from the southeast, and the people at the front can see that from the way the mist from the Falls is gusting. Bet they all think it beautiful. Cold but beautiful. I think it's deadly; I don't want Mrs Taylor to die.

'Any minute now,' someone says. The crowd pushes forward again. I've managed to gain a row. Gulls soar and squawk above us; are they here watching her, too? Almost at the front of the viewing deck. Mr Hills shuffles and worms to behind me. He's touching me back with his hand; if that hand gets any lower, I won't be responsible for how I react.

'Can't believe this sixty-three-year-old, former schoolteacher, is going to be set adrift. She'll be at the mercy of the Falls,' someone says.

'Sixty-what?' Mr Hills shouts.

'What kind of crazy woman would do this? She must know these waters have never spared a human life.' That's a different voice.

'Hysterical women.' Another man.

A ripple of laughter emerges; they like that one.

I'm sure Mr Hills is nodding in agreement. Building a case for how he's been tricked by the wicked, and possibly hysterical, Annie Edson Taylor.

'What's her name again?' someone else asks. There's a rumble of whispers, but no one seems to have the answer.

Mr Hills is next to me now. Wormed his way through the crowd. He swivels his upper body at his waist. 'But she's forty-three?'

'No,' I say. Protecting Nora, I elbow into the row in front. A tut and an 'Oi' but I ignore them both. Two more rows to go.

'Now, now, now, there's no such thing as a free lunch.' We all twist to that voice. Crowd moving as one. It's like we've no choice. His voice is commanding, and the crowd parts for him too. A strong jawline, a dapper suit, a spruce beard. He looks at me with steady eyes; his are black like coal. Is this Mrs Taylor's manager? He tips his head and then winks. He's taking his opportunity to make money from her. Probably his only chance, jumps into me head; I hate that it does. He waves at Nora and she waves back. Me daughter's a friendly little one.

Mr Russell shakes his hat at the crowd. 'Ladies. Gentlemen. Let's see your generosity for Mrs Annie Edson Taylor.'

A man and woman lean closer to him, dropping their coins with a rattle into the hat.

'Come to think of it,' Mr Hills says. I turn to him. See that he's rooted in the same spot facing forward. He's not turned to face Mr Russell, clearly more interested in the spectacle than in Annie's safety or success. 'Sixty-three is pretty obvious.'

Me stomach's churning. 'Think I'm going to vomit,' I say. It's loud enough for the men to the right and to the left to quickly step sideways, mumbling panicked apologies to their neighbours.

'Excuse me, excuse me,' Mr Hills says. He's pushing aside the crowds in front, a bowler hat guiding the way. 'My girl's going to vomit.'

The crowd parts, and then we're at the wooden railings, looking down. Wind is stronger here. Spray from the water makes everything wet. Me hair will be dripping soon. I pull Nora's blanket over her, but she bats it away. Shaking her head and shoulders. Left then right. Closer to nature and nothing's protecting us from the roar. It covers me; it terrifies me. The spray catches her off-guard. She's startled. Wide eyes and a moment of uncertainty. Fingers to her face, she pats her skin. Giggles.

Beneath, the water throws itself down like it's furious. Vanishes into a thick cloud of mist; so thick I can barely make out what's what. It's like trying to see through a foggy window, everything blending and shifting. With every inhale, the damp air fills me lungs. Tiny water beads form on me face and lashes. Everything looks a bit dreamy. Tiny droplets are on Nora's lashes too; she's beautiful. The Falls don't just make a sound, they create a deep, echoing rumble that fills me chest and makes me heart race.

'It's going to be fine,' I tell Nora.

Then, from that haze, a tiny thing appears – a rowing boat. Bobbing along like it doesn't have a care in the world. It looks near foolish against that fierce rush of water, disappearing and reappearing in the mist. I squint harder. Trying to catch a glimpse of who might be in it.

'This is suicide,' Mr Hills says, and though I hate that he's right, I nod in agreement. It really is.

'Once grasped, these waters don't let go.' It's a voice behind us.

'No man's survived a plunge over Niagara Falls and now a woman thinks she can…' A different voice. There's laughter too.

'Things folk do for fame and dollars?' Mr Hills says. He's bobbing his head. Bonding with those around us.

'She's got nothing to lose,' I say. I look at the scale of what she's doing. Can't see how she can expect to survive this. No other human has and it's not like her life's been touched with fortune.

'Am I nothing to lose?' Mr Hills sounds like a spoilt child. He is one. I don't turn to look at him, so I doubt he sees me expression of disgust.

'Who could survive plummeting one hundred and fifty-eight feet in a four-foot tall, wooden barrel?' someone else says. A man. The crowd behind them laughs. *If.* They like this. I really don't.

Why does every male spectator feel the need to voice their opinion? How are they all experts?

'We know her,' Mr Hills says. His thin lips stretch into a smile. He's waving his bowler hat over the edge of the railing. Is he trying to make it seem like he's waving at Mrs Taylor? This man's a goose. She's sealed in a barrel and, so, not able to wave back. Mr Hills needs to feel important; it's his fuel.

'She's got cushions in there, too,' I say. I don't add that I made her a pillow. 'And a leather harness to stop her from rattling about.'

Mr Hills almost scowls at me. 'She's going to die,' he says, wanting everyone to think that he's the expert and not me – another hysterical woman – who might know more about Mrs Taylor's plans than he does.

'Her name's Annie Edson Taylor,' he says.

Is that all he's got?

Someone cheers and stupid Mr Hills thinks they're cheering him. They aren't though. They're cheering that it's almost time. Mrs Taylor's manager is still rattling his hat and telling everyone about his daredevil client.

I grip the railing with one hand and see me knuckles change colour. In me free arm, Nora giggles while Mr Hills places his stubby little hand over mine, no doubt ready to exploit any sign of vulnerability. Any hint of weakness and he'll swoop in. I wrench me hand away and wipe it on me skirts. His touch makes me skin crawl.

'I read the cat survived.' The words are shouted.

'Definitely didn't die.' That's someone else.

The crowd cheers in support. They're celebrating Lagara, a cat who may or may not have died. This is weird. I flinch. Heat rushes from me stomach up to me throat.

'Annie,' Mr Hills whispers, as if she can hear him. 'Don't do this.' He's performing. His words and tone don't match. 'Stop her.'

Any minute now and his hand will be on his forehead as he swoons into a faint. He isn't fooling me. I can hear the excitement in his words.

The Horseshoe Falls stretches out in the distance. It's a natural wonder unlike anything they can grasp or understand. The water plummets over the edge of the cliff with a force that's overwhelming. Its mist fills the air, creating a rainbow of colours as the sun catches the droplets. There's part of me that thinks this view miraculous. Yet here I am, standing on the edge of this majestic place as Mrs Taylor attempts something every single person surrounding me deems impossible.

Save her, Lelawala, Princess of Niagara. It's a silent prayer.

I close me eyes and let the energy of the Falls cover me. The constant roar of the water's a reminder of the power of nature. I suck in a deep breath.

'Look,' someone to me left shouts.

Eyes open, I turn to see a man on me right waving his hat over the railing. I recognise that mix of excitement and concern on the stranger's face. The man gives me a smile and a nod. Mrs Taylor's ready. It's happening.

Nora beams at me, giving me comfort and purpose.

'We'll be fine, little one,' I say. I kiss the top of her head.

Me eyes fix on the mighty Horseshoe Falls. Its waters cascade with a ferocity that sends shivers down me spine. Amidst that powerful display, there's the barrel. It's looking so small and fragile against the backdrop of all that roaring water. It bobbles uncertainly. Thrusts to-and-fro by the whims of the currents. Every ripple and wave pushes it closer to that looming brink. The sunlight catches its surface, making it glisten for a fleeting moment, before it's engulfed again.

Around me, the murmurs of the crowd grow. There's a mix of anticipation and concern, but all I can hear is the pounding of me own heart echoing the thunderous falls. I strain me eyes. Trying to discern any sign of hope for that lone barrel, as it edges, ever so slowly, towards the abyss. Wondering if Mrs Taylor's been practising holding her breath, if she's been building her strength secretly. Has she been gaining knowledge about the currents of the river, too? Did I ever really believe she'd attempt this impossible, this horrendous thing? Thoughts tumble and jumble together.

I can't take me eyes of the barrel, and the crowd inhales. For a moment there's nothing but the bobbing barrel, the rush of the water and the sound of me own pounding heart.

'Save Mrs Taylor,' I whisper, air rushing out on the word.

Annie

24th October 1901

This isn't the best birthday I've ever had. The cold air seeps through the cork. It's near darkness in here. The scant light that does poke through the crevices casts only faint, mottled patterns against the walls. I'm huddled in this barrel, cramped. The sensation of being tossed about by the powerful currents already makes my stomach churn. I've not even had the signal yet. I've not yet been cast adrift.

'Still time to stop this,' I say. To whom? Am I expecting a reply? That someone will intervene and make this stunt end?

With every jolt and spin, waves of dizziness wash over me. I'm disoriented already, trying not to vomit. The relentless motion of the water amplifies the confines. It's claustrophobic. The staves are closing in around me. Is this how I die?

I clench my jaw and close my eyes. Do I want to stop the stunt? It's my last chance. Act now if I do.

I can't block out the sensation. I'm being tossed about like a ragdoll in the raging river. I'm still tethered to the boat, though, I think.

'We've not started yet, Annie,' I say.

Speaking to myself in the third person. How long has madness danced with me? Could everyone else see that waltz? Do they all consider me insane? Am I?

With every sway and bob of the barrel, there's increased weightlessness in my stomach. It's an unsettling mix of nausea and exhilaration. An odd sensation; being upright yet tossed by the liquid expanse outside. Is this womblike or deathlike? Perhaps the two are the same.

I'm in a barrel. I'm actually in a barrel. I'm on the edge – metaphorically and literally. What is this life of mine? All decisions have led me here. The world has shrunk around me, pressing close in this wooden embrace. The air's thick, stuffy, every breath laden with the musty scent of damp wood. Eyes still closed, I press my palms against the barrel's insides, feeling the coarse grain of the wood, the slight vibrations from the water it displaces.

'Should I stop this stunt?' I ask. No one replies.

There's a deep, muffled sound – the murmur of the outside world translated through layers of wood and water – but it's distant and surreal.

'Hello?' I say. 'Is it too windy? Are you calling it off again?' My voice is breathy. I hear my fear.

No reply. I attempt to listen to a world I'm no longer in. This thick, wooden case provides some sense of protection, but it ensnares me, too. They leave me at the mercy of the water's whims. Every tilt and shift a stark reminder of the unpredictable world outside, of the life, love, and trauma I've left behind.

'No going back,' I say.

Was there sanity in my decision? My heart pounds in my chest, echoing the roar of the waterfall. Both grow louder and more powerful. The odours of damp wood and iron fill my nostrils. I clutch my pillow to my chest, seeking solace in its familiar softness. Will I see Tilda, Nora, or Mrs Lapointe again?

There's a rap on the barrel. It's an oar hitting the top. My body jolts instinctively, a sharp twitch. My muscles tense. Every nerve in my body's awake. I can see in the dark, hear conversations a mile away, smell roasted peanuts from vendors on the viewing deck, taste them too. All of that and yet none of it. My breath's caught in my throat. My heart races.

That's the agreed signal. They're cutting me loose from the rowing boat.

'Here we go.' Without meaning to, I've whispered the words. The thunderous roar of the Falls swells around me. I nod my head in response. 'You can do this. You will do this.'

My body moulds to the barrel's shape; each hurried breath, each frantic heartbeat echoes in this confined space.

'No one has ever survived before.'

Panic, Annie. Panic now. Why am I not panicking? Why am I not clawing at the rim to dig myself out of this coffin?

Annie

24th October 1901

'Can't back out now.'

Wind whispers through the tiny fissures. It carries the raw symphony of the Falls; a feral harmony that waits for me to add a bar or two. A final breath? Last words? Both? I worry my heart might suffocate me.

I shake my head. 'No. In a day or two I'll be home with Mrs Lapointe, Matilda, and Nora.' I smile. I nod. I will. A new life for us all.

With every crest and trough of the water, I ride this wild beast. As I move, the roar of the Falls grows louder, drowning out all other sounds. Louder. Still louder. Is nature itself challenging me to defy its power? The barrel bobs and tilts on the water's surface. It's a wild dance and I'm both a prisoner and partner. I clutch the leather harness tighter.

In the darkened belly of this barrel, there's nowhere to hide from the reality of pain. Not the physical kind – which awaits me in the fury of the Falls – but the invisible, relentless grief that has burrowed its way deep into my marrow; now it fills this air, too. Unspoken words and suppressed emotion add an unfamiliar stench. I've nowhere to hide anymore. No escaping.

'David.' It's a whisper. My son's name fills the small space around me. This grief anew. More searing than any I might face at the bottom of the Falls. 'Can you hear me?' I call out.

Can ghosts perceive my sound? How adrift am I? How close am I to spectators? Will they consider me reaching out to them? Desperate. Perhaps they'll worry I've changed my mind. They'll call for help.

I hold my breath, straining to listen. If they reply, it travels as a murmur of sound. It's distorted through the oak walls. No matter though. I don't care to speak to them. I communicate with Niagara herself, to the spirit of this relentless river that's swallowed too many before me. To the brave souls who've succumbed to her strength, to the women whose whispers I can hear in the furious hiss of the rapids. All of us, trapped in barrels.

'Sisters.'

Lelawala, Morgiana, Matilda, Mrs Lapointe, Nora, the lost women desperate for a safe place to rest… I breathe out. My voice is a raw whisper inside this potential coffin. I think of their courage, their despair, their determination. All of us are linked by this powerful place, by this overwhelming force of nature, by the need to be heard. Do we collect grief and congregate in silence around it?

My knees quiver, my jaw vibrates. Still, there's no backing out. If the Falls are my end, then so be it. They can take my life, but not my choice to be here. If I'm to be claimed by the water, then I join the chorus of women who came before me and those who are yet to try. We are all part of this water's song. We sing in unison, even if our melodies differ.

With each breath, I ready myself.

A drop. Sudden. My head whips against the unforgiving wood. Dizzy. Disorientated. Was that rocks? A sickening lurch. The barrel rolls. Left. Right. Tipped onto my side. The Falls roar louder and louder.

'I'm Annie Edson Taylor, the first to survive the mighty Niagara in a barrel,' I say. 'Today, the river will not consume me.'

I breathe in fear, I exhale fear. It sticks in my throat. Cough. Cough. Eyes watering.

'See you soon, David. Samuel.' There's strange comfort in that.

My voice is barely a gasp against the roar outside. I'm no longer in control. I'm at the mercy of the Falls. Eyes closed, I hold my breath. Not as a woman going to her death, but as a woman claiming her destiny, etching her name in the annals of the Niagara. I'm adding my voice to its mighty roar.

'I'm being heard.'

Is that calmness? Am I done? That drop, was that it? I smile. I nod. The current must be pulling me closer to the edge by now. Is the barrel still? Have I stopped? It's pleasant. The barrel rises and falls with the waves of the Niagara River. There's a rhythm. The deafening roar, though. I hold my breath, steeling myself for the plunge or for a rescue. Waiting. Waiting some more.

Seconds pass like minutes.

'Was that it?'

No. I'm spinning. Spinning. Faster. Faster. Like I'm a dasher. I'm in a churn and someone's churning with all their might. Pushing me this way. That way. Thrusting me up and down.

Judgment Day has come.

I grip the harness tighter still. My knuckles are white with the effort. They lock in position. They ache. The leather digs into my palms, reminding me of the lines etched into my face – each one a testament to years of pent-up pain. My husband and son have gone, buried in a family plot alongside my father, mother, and brother. Am I loved? Tears fill my eyes. Why can I scarcely remember those times? Where do those memories live now? That void in me is grief-shaped. I survived a devil of a time. But I chose how I survived. I've lived. I've truly lived.

'Will I survive this?'

The barrel is tossed. My face scrunches into a grimace. Eyes closed tightly. I grip the harness even more. Pain in my fingers. I lurch to the right. Perhaps that was a reef? Was that it? Am I veering left? I need to be central. Panic. Am I heading for the rocks? Panic.

'Make it stop,' I whisper.

The barrel rights itself. I exhale. Still. Calm. A pause.

'Was that it?'

No. Still more to come. I move the pillow from my head to under my knees. Scrunching myself to the bottom of the barrel. Waiting. Holding my breath. Still waiting. Water at my waist. Water coming in from the bottom. The anvil hitting rocks must have cracked the barrel some more. Will the sides of the barrel stove in? Churning. Churning. Head whipping. Left. Right. Forward. Make it stop. I'll drown.

Now.

The drop is sudden. Like a streak of lightning.

I scream. The sound's inside my head. It rattles my entire body. From the inside. From the top of my head to my toes. Shock.

I'm weightless. Floppy. Lifeless. Suspended in the air. The barrel and me.

My breath catches in my throat.

Plummet. Fall. Drop.

'Help.' The word's guttural.

My heart races. Faster than the falling water. This is how I die.

Impact. The barrel strikes the water with a jarring force. I'm shaken like a rag doll by a giant invisible hand. The sheer strength threatens to wrench my limbs from their sockets. My skull cracks against the oak and a sharp flash of pain lances through me. The violent jolt reverberates through every sinew and muscle of my body. Bones rattle. Teeth clatter together. Stomach lurches. Head spins.

Silence. All is still. Is mute. The barrel is upright.

The wind is knocked from my lungs; I gasp for air. Excruciating. Progressing through my body, like a thousand needles piercing my skin all at once. The world buckles. This is torture. The harness bites into my flesh. Iron fills my mouth.

Water. Too much water. Water pours in torrents from the top of the barrel. Cracks in the barrel. Down on head and shoulders. Too much water. Wakes my senses. Am I going to drown and be lost forever? Am I under falling water? It rushes in around me. The barrel is broken. Help! Help! I can't speak.

The barrel whirls. It whips. It's thrown violently. Everything is noise; I'm within it. Spiralling. A maelstrom of disarray. I'm flung around the barrel's belly. My skull cracks against the oak staves once, twice, more. With each contact a white-hot cut of agony pierces my senses. The world lurches. Tilts. Spirals. Blood, warm and wet, trickles into my eyes. I can't see. It blinds me.

I'm dying.

More water. Too much water. It forces itself into the barrel. Cracks. Fractures. It's finding a way in. Desperate. Drowning. Drowning. Darkness tugs at the edges of my senses. My breath's a ragged echo in the barrel's hollow belly. Claustrophobic. Encasing me. I'm dying. A blur of water, spray, and noise. My pillow? Where's my pillow? Wet. Full of water. I lift it to my face; my only tether to the life I once knew. Throbbing head. The intensity sickens. I clench my teeth. Agony.

Must fight against the encroaching darkness; it moves closer. I'm losing.

Swallowed.

Whole.

Still.

Has it stopped?

I want to live.

Annie

24th October 1901

'Why ain't she responding?' A man's voice. Muffled and hard to hear. The corks are removed. 'You think...'

'Of course. T'was suicide. She knew it.'

'Mrs Taylor. Annie. Mrs Taylor.'

'You think she's—'

I must strain to hear the ends of the words.

'Mrs Taylor is not dying today,' a voice interrupts. It's gravel-tipped. Familiar. Carlisle Graham. A smoker without his pipe. His voice is different to the other ones. It's veined with a forced optimism. The thud-thud-thud of their efforts to get me out of here punctuates his words. My head throbs. I want to shush them all.

The barrel bobs, rhythmically swaying in tune with the gentle ebbs of the Niagara. Though my eyes remain shut, the world swirls in a dizzying dance behind my eyelids. Consciousness teases at the edges. A thin covering separates me from the muffled sounds that bleed into the barrel. The voices are low, hushed, coloured by fear. I wish the throbbing would stop.

'Did you see?' A man's voice. 'Barrel popped out of the water to fall back in, then slammed into some rocks for good measure.'

The dull echo of wood against wood reverberates around me. A series of thuds quicken my pulse, each one louder and more urgent than the last. 'Careful with it,' that same gravelly voice warns. I like that Carlisle Graham shatters the oppressive silence. Did they remember the saw and wrench? Is that what I'm hearing?

A searing creak. The barrel's lid being pried open is a groan of surrender. Fresh air against my skin is a soothing balm. It's a reprieve from the stifling darkness.

'Annie,' Mr Graham's voice calls. It's closer now. He clicks his tongue. 'Come on, Annie. You're safe now.'

'She's dead,' a man says. Then there's a whack sound and, 'Oi.'

I can sense people. They're waiting for a sign. They're searching for confirmation of my survival. I reckon their breaths are held; I'm sure their hearts pound in sync with mine. They all think I'm dead; they expect me to be dead. They've braced themselves to see a mangled body. They've gambled on my bravery or stupidity.

It's time to show them their bet has paid off.

Summoning the last of my strength, I crack open my eyes to the slanting sunlight. I allow the blurred outlines of my rescuers to seep into my vision. 'Help me up, Mr Graham,' I manage to rasp out. My voice is a mere ghost of itself.

I hear the gasps. Shock echoes around me. I blink into the sunlight. I see a crowd of onlookers, their faces a mixture of disbelief and awe.

'My God,' someone says, 'the woman's alive.'

'Welcome to Canada, Mrs Taylor,' Carlisle Graham says. 'You're bleeding and soaked through. Stay still.'

His hand on my head feels like a weight too much. I shake my head to move his hand, the pain intensifying.

'Looks like a cut. Maybe three inches. Behind your ear,' he says, leaning in. Sour pipe smoke coats his breath. 'Are you in pain?'

I squint up at him. I wrinkle my nose at the smell. Of course I am, you idiot. I can't quite figure out how to get all the words from inside my head to have any sound. The pain between my shoulders feels like a million tiny knives are attacking.

'She's soaked through. Get her out of there.' I don't recognise that voice.

'Best we get you checked out,' Mr Graham says.

Perhaps my facial expression is response enough. He nods.

'Can you stand?'

I try to say yes but there's no sound.

'You're a tough old bird.' His voice is a whisper. His words are for my ears only. I look to admonish him, but he's smiling. A broad, toothy smile underneath his bushy moustache. I see a spark of something in his eyes too. Admiration?

Carlisle Graham turns to the crowd around. 'Come on, you lot, let's get brave Mrs Taylor to safety.' He's all business. 'You did it, Mrs Taylor. You actually did it.' He's twiddling with the ends of his moustache, but his eyes are sparkling. His hands thrust towards me. I stare at them, hesitating. Any thought of my skirts and decency are soon gone; I'm sitting in water. I need to be out of this barrel.

I'm helped to upright, then a plank is thrust towards the barrel. Every noise and each movement are amplified. It's a rough bridge to solid ground. It scrapes against the wooden hull, setting my teeth on edge. Sounds and smells are sharper. The roar of the Falls is louder, too. Is it cheering? Is it claiming me as its own? They – the men – help me out of the barrel. I'm pulled. I'm their doll. I stand on shaky legs.

'Well done, Mrs Taylor.'

I look at him, confused. Should I recognise this one? Why do all the men look the same in their bowler hats?

'John Ross.' He points at himself. 'I opened the barrel – helped by Harry Williams.' He points to a different man, just off to the right. That one waves. 'He's proprietor of Lafayette Hotel. We caught you in the Maid of the Mist eddy. Held you there until it could be reached by means of a hook and pole. And that's Mark Wonder, the Italian.'

A different man. He stands next to Mr Ross. I'm dizzy trying to catch all that he's saying. I know it's important. I know I'll want these details later, but now—

'He got in the river, attached the pole to the rings on the barrel. And him over there … that's Kid Brady, the riverman.' More pointing. Their faces blend. Kid's in the *Maid of the Mist* – the rescue boat – still clutching a long pole. He waves it triumphantly. Cheering as he does. He must have hooked the barrel. I stare at him.

'Goddess of the water,' he says, waving the pole towards the Falls. He laughs.

'Thank you.' That's all I've got, and it feels inadequate.

'Are you fine?' That's Carlisle Graham.

I shake my head slowly. 'No one ought ever to do that again,' I say, my voice hoarse with emotion.

'You've done what no other woman or man in the world had the ability to do,' Carlisle Graham says. 'You're a braver soul than me.' His grip on my arm sends pain shooting through me.

Annie

24th October 1901

I stagger as I step from the boat onto a plank. It's surrounded by men in bowler hats or caps. Some are in the water, others are struggling to remain upright on the rocky shore. There is no preserving of my decency. Six, maybe seven, men help me across the wooden beam. They blend into one, though. Carlisle Graham is my focus. He walks in the shallow water. He grips my hand as I shuffle along the plank. He still towers above me.

'Alive with just a cut,' he says. 'You made it look easy, Annie.'

I shake my head. My clothes squelch and my body aches. Still, the taste of the river's mist lingers on my lips. Wet and shivering, being held upright by a man who survived the rapids, I look at the raging waters.

'Alive,' I whisper.

The air is heavy with the scent of churned earth and damp foliage, and I can't help but smile. Why not me? Why have I survived all these years when my son and husband didn't? This is why. I was destined for this. For greatness. The relentless current of the river flows onward, and so, too, will I.

'I'd prefer to walk into the mouth of a cannon than to ever do that again,' I say.

'Mrs Taylor, Mrs Taylor.' It's a man, with paper and a pen. 'Canada welcomes you.'

I smile. 'I'm very grateful to be here.'

'We need to get her to her rooming house. There's a doctor waiting.' That's Carlisle Graham. Stern and focused.

'Mrs Taylor, Mrs Taylor…' It's the same reporter. 'What advice would you give others?'

Others? I look to Carlisle Graham and then I look all around. Cheers, waves, thousands of spectators. They all saw me defeat the Falls. I have witnesses. So many witnesses. I raise my hand and wave. The response is a roar. It travels in a wave across the crowds.

I turn to the reporter. 'Advice?' I say, not hiding my bewilderment that he'd ask such a ridiculous question. He nods enthusiastically; he's oblivious.

'Don't do it,' I say.

'Pardon?'

'Are you deaf, boy?' I say. 'My advice is simple – don't.'

The world sways around me, the rocks feeling unsteady beneath my feet. Carlisle Graham places a blanket around my shoulders. His concerned expression is a blur against the backdrop of my queasy vision.

'You did it. Your plan worked. You're alive,' he says. 'This is going to make headlines, bring in crowds, and earn you a fortune.'

'I did it.' I wobble, my ragdoll body floppy.

'Mrs Taylor, are you fine?' His voice breaks through the haze of nausea.

I nod weakly, trying to steady my breathing. 'I'll be fine, just need a moment to catch my breath.' My words come out in a strained whisper.

He nods, his gaze scanning my face. 'We need to get you to the carriage,' he insists, his arm wrapping securely around my waist. 'A quick journey over Honeymoon Bridge and we'll get you to your lodgings. Russ will meet us there.'

As I take a shaky step forward, the reality of what I've accomplished begins to sink in. I survived the mighty Niagara Falls. I defied the odds, and now, standing on the shore with a crowd cheering for me, a surge of triumph mixes with profound exhaustion.

'You're a heroine, Mrs Taylor,' a voice calls out from the crowd. The words echo in my mind. Heroine? I never set out to be a hero. I wanted to prove something – to the world, to myself.

Every step is a battle against the overwhelming fatigue. Carlisle's grip on my arm is both supportive and grounding. I glance at him, seeing the determination in his eyes. He believes in me. They all do.

'QUEEN OF THE MIST' TRIUMPHS OVER NIAGARA FALLS IN BARRELL

NIAGARA FALLS, NY - OCTOBER 24, 1901

Mrs Annie Edson Taylor, 43, has become the first person in our history to survive a trip over Niagara Falls in a barrel. Her daring feat took place less than two hours ago, to the amazement of thousands of spectators who had gathered to witness the historic event.

The barrel, which had been designed by Mrs Taylor herself, was made of Kentucky oak and reinforced with metal hoops. Inside, Mrs Taylor was surrounded by cushions to help absorb the shock of the fall. The barrel was then sealed and set adrift in the Niagara River, shooting out from the Cataract, plunging over the Falls and into the churning Canadian waters below. Luck or design, this woman's life was spared.

After the barrel was recovered downstream, a dazed but triumphant Queen of the Mist emerged, alive and well. Mrs Taylor is already being tended to in a rooming house nearby. Doctor Clarke stated that his patient was suffering from 'brain fever', but that a full recovery is 'expected'. The former teacher's bravery and determination have captured the hearts and imaginations of many, and she is already being hailed as a true American heroine. She lives to tell her tale.

Part V: Beyond the Brink

'I arrived on the doorstep with only the clothes on my back and money for one night's bed. Mrs Taylor provided free shelter for a month. No questions asked, no prying, just care. Generous, bold and patient, that Mrs Taylor was one of a kind. She spoke her mind and she saved mine.'

Margaret Chen

ANNIE EDSON TAYLOR A DISTINGUISHED FIGURE OF THE DAY

NIAGARA FALLS GAZETTE - OCTOBER 25, 1901

Dear sirs,

After her daring and successful attempt to go over the Falls in a barrel, Annie Edson Taylor's name must become a household word in the Niagara Falls community. Surely her accomplishment should gain her much attention and admiration, with many regarding her as a distinguished figure of our times. Is there not an award she, and I – her manager – can be given?

I argue that Mrs Taylor's bravery and skill should win her fame not only in the local community but across the country as well. Let her bask in the limelight of her accomplishment, but surely both she and I need to be admired as symbols of courage and perseverance in the face of great danger? Her example will undoubtedly inspire future generations to push the boundaries of what is possible and to strive for greatness in all that they do. If that were to happen, I can guarantee my commitment to managing and guiding the many aftercomers. Thus, why not begin that revering of us now?

Yours sincerely,
Mr F. Russell.

Annie's Diary

27th October 1901

News of Mrs Lapointe's passing has left me in a haze of contemplation. I survived the Falls, whereas my dear friend died alone. I went over Niagara Falls in a barrel, defying death and the odds. I thought it would make me invincible, but I am not. Her lonely end has jolted me awake, reminding me of life's fleeting nature. A reminder that we have little control.

Mrs Lapointe – who lived a quiet, steadfast life – is gone. She always had a kind word, a gentle touch, and faced her own struggles with a quiet strength. Did she feel peace in her last moments? Was she afraid? Did she know how much she meant to those around her? Did she know she was loved?

The questions swirl in my mind – unanswerable and heavy. The instability of life is like the thin ice on a winter pond: beautiful and dangerous, capable of breaking at any moment. People come and go. None of us are here to stay.

I know how life works – every moment is borrowed, every breath a gift.

Annie

28th October 1901

I've only been back in the Bay City boarding house half an hour when the door creaks open. Then, a slither of a hat, a rolled newspaper, a gloved hand, green sleeve of a dress enters.

'Mrs Taylor.' It's a squeal really.

Good job I'm already awake and propped up in bed. Tilda rushes into the room, pulling off her gloves. The single window provides a meagre amount of natural light, but it's enough. I close my book and place my hand on it.

'I've been waiting to see you. They said you'd been staying somewhere else?' I say.

She bats my words away with her glove. 'You're back.' She's only slightly out of breath, but her face is pale and her eyes wide. 'You're on the front of the *Bay City Courier*. Three different articles about you.'

She throws the newspaper onto the bed and I glimpse the first heading.

Mrs Taylor the First Human Being to Go Over Niagara Falls and Live.

'Look at your big, beautiful face.' She stabs her finger at the huge portrait of me in the centre of the front page. 'They're calling you Queen of the Mist.' Each jab of the newspaper feels like a thousand needles are being poked into my earlobe.

I'd been staying in the rooming house since the stunt. Being observed, as if my survival made me either miraculous or a freak. They thought I might have 'brain fever' and kept all visitors from me. That remains undecided, but Dr Clarke agreed that I could return home. Once I heard about Mrs Lapointe's death, they couldn't really stop me. I needed to be here. Wanted to be here. Apparently, any lasting damage will be visible within the next few days. I'm not entirely convinced that's comforting.

'Shush,' I whisper, putting a finger to my lips. She needs to use a soft voice. 'More like *Old Woman in a Barrel*.'

She hesitates. 'Can't believe you did it.' Her words rush out breathy and quieter, not fully formed, though. 'We were there, Henry Hills, Nora and me. We saw it all.' She kisses me on the top of my head, resting her chin there for a moment. She plonks herself down on the bed next to me, brushing at the creases in her dress. The rickety bedframe shifts, and I wobble slightly. All her movements shoot pain through me.

'What are you talking about?' I ask, confusion filling me. I push my pillow to the base of my spine, attempting to sit up straighter, even though my entire body still wants to bend into a barrel shape. It's like my form's changed. I can't get comfortable. All of me aches. My mattress is thin and lumpy; it's only slightly more comfortable than the floor. I pull the threadbare quilt up to my shoulders.

'I was packing,' Tilda explains. 'It was the middle of the night, and Mr Hills turned up here. He'd read about…' She pauses, looking at me. 'I didn't know what to do. The newspaper reported the abandoned attempt and…'

'It's fine,' I say, then something of her words pierce through the haze of exhaustion and soreness that envelops me. 'Why were you packing, Tilda? Where were you going?'

'Doesn't matter now. I'm staying. Going to stand up for meself.'

I'm confused but know better than to prod at secrets. Instead, I look at the newest addition to my room. A small wooden dresser with chipped edges. It stands against one wall and its drawers are slightly ajar, revealing the too few items of clothing that I own. Everything I have is in there. There's no hiding how little there is to show for my sixty-three years. No pictures on the walls, no knick-knacks, no sentimental objects on display. It's a room stripped down to the essentials: a space for sleeping and little else. I've been surviving to exist for too long. The only sign of life is a small vase of wilted flowers on the windowsill, but those petals droop from neglect.

'I saw what you did, Mrs Taylor. How you faced Niagara, something so powerful and frightening. You didn't run, you didn't hide. If you can do that, I can face him. I won't let him control me life anymore.' Her voice is steadier now. '

I nod, understanding beginning to dawn. She's tired of running, tired of living in fear. She's ready to confront her past and fight for her future.

'Mr Hills was pretty upset, to say the least,' Matilda says. 'Took all I had not to slap his face. Think he was disappointed you survived.' She laughs. 'Kept saying how he couldn't believe you were in a barrel. That you were clearly hysterical. That it was too dangerous for a woman, let along an old one.'

I snort at that. 'I imagine there are many who think the same, but the proof is there.' I point at the newspaper.

'I was worried.'

'You didn't need to fret.'

She closes her eyes, tears visible on the lashes. 'I thought you'd die too…' She hesitates a little too long. 'Like Mrs Lapointe.'

I reach over, a bolt of pain shooting from my shoulder to my fingers, and squeeze her hand. 'I'm a tough old bird.'

'You did it, Mrs Taylor,' she says, her eyes wide and her tears falling down her cheeks. 'You actually survived. The huge crowd watched, cheering you on. I was worried sick about you…'

My head's pounding, and my body aches all over. 'You saw everything? You came…'

Matilda nods. 'The towboat captain cut the rope and you went over the Falls. The barrel bounced around like crazy. Thought it was going to smash on the rocks, but it held together. And then…' Hesitation, she gulps, brushing away tears with her fingertips. 'You disappeared into the mist. Thought you were gone… I thought you were dead.'

I think she's struggling to comprehend that I'm not. I'd not considered what someone who cared about me might feel during the stunt. I can't shake a sense of detachment from the event. It's like I'm hearing about someone else's experience, not my own.

Matilda squeezes my hand. 'After twenty minutes, your barrel emerged from the mist. It was battered and torn, but you were inside. Alive and conscious and clever. We all cheered when we heard you were alive… I cheered loudest.'

A smile tugs at the corners of my mouth.

'And now everyone knows your name.' Her words burst with admiration. 'You're a heroine. A legend.'

I shake my head softly, still trying to comprehend everything that's happened. 'I did it,' I whisper. 'I really did it.'

'At least you don't need to worry about Mr Hills anymore.'

'Was I worrying about him?' I shift uncomfortably, wincing at the twinges of pain that shoot through my body with every shift.

'He doesn't believe you're forty-three.'

'He found out my true age?' A wave of shame washes over me. Not because I'm old, but because I lied. I had a chance to instigate a change in society's view of older women and instead I pretended to be younger.

Tilda nods again. 'Initially, he kept saying that he wished you'd agreed to marry him instead of getting in the barrel. Something about how you should be sitting in lawn chairs in Hamilton instead of risking your life…'

I can't help but laugh. It starts as a giggle then rumbles into a guttural release from deep within.

'Typical Mr Hills behaviour,' I say. 'Always a day late and a dollar short.'

Tilda nods in agreement. She doesn't react. Her emotions seem unnatural. Perhaps I scared her? Music plays from downstairs but I don't recognise its tune.

'Thank you for arranging everything for Mrs Lapointe.'

She shrugs, but avoids making eye contact with me, instead she picks at the skin around her thumb. It's bleeding. There are dark circles under her eyes and her face looks thinner, too.

'And then, after you're already sealed in the barrel and over the Falls, Mr Hills got all frantic. Yelling at the top of his lungs, "Annie, don't do it,"' Matilda says, mimicking his voice. 'I'm convinced he thought that'd make a difference. Like you'd even hear him, and I'm all, "She's already doing it, you goose." But he just stands there, looking pathetic and helpless.'

I observe her closely. She's shaking.

'At one point, after the boat got the barrel back, I think he considered diving from the viewing deck, but you know Henry,' Matilda says, the words rushing out. 'All talk, no action.'

'Are you sleeping, Tilda?' I reach out and stroke my fingers over her cheek. She doesn't react.

'He just stood there, shaking his head and performing as if he were one audition away from being a great Shakespearean actor. He wanted all eyes on him.'

'Always more concerned with himself than anyone else.' A pause. 'Well, he can go jump in the Falls for all I care. I don't need him.'

Tilda nods. I watch her and it's like she's somewhere else entirely. She's distracted. I recognise fear. I think I might have terrified her.

'Everything feels different now,' I say. 'I've emerged better. Like I've no energy for being afraid and more for truly seeing and doing.' It's difficult to explain, but it's like the strange tension has dropped away. Hearing music through a wall, magnifying glasses, the word pebble, a child's hiccup, tiptoeing, potato peel: It's like there's more purpose and wonder in moments I'd previously dismissed.

She nods. Here eyes are wide and curious. I think she wants me to continue.

'My memories might have been stuck in here.' I point and my head. 'And in here.' I point at my throat. 'But now I can finally see why it wasn't me who died.'

Tilda's not looking at me. She's biting the skin around her thumb and staring at the bedroom door.

'Tell me,' I say. My eyes flicker with fatigue, struggling to stay focused on her. She shakes her head.

'Is it Nora?' I search the room as if she might suddenly appear. Why have I not asked about the child?

'No, no.' She hesitates and then, 'Mrs Lapointe … died alone.' She rubs at the back of her neck. 'I don't know if she was scared…' She sobs.

I swipe at my own tears with my fingers. 'Did you inform her church? They've been wonderfully efficient and kind. She was very loved.'

Her brow wrinkles, and then a range of emotions dance on her face until she settles on giving me the most determined look. 'Mr Hills took care of it all.'

'At least he's useful for something,' I say and Matilda smiles. 'We'll find a way to honour her, too. I promise.' Matilda leans over and kisses my cheek. The music downstairs seems to grow louder. 'Do we have guests?'

'About that,' she says, eyes looking back to the door.

I think I hold my breath, bracing myself for more bad news.

'I don't think—'

'What?'

'I don't think attracting paid guests to the boarding house is going to be a problem.'

I shuffle, gently shifting my weight about. 'I don't understand?'

Matilda's lips crinkle. 'There's been a queue of people outside. Every day since the stunt. Right now, a bearded lady and a strongman are entertaining a select group downstairs.'

'Lolly and Magnus are here?'

'And others,' she says. 'Mr Russell sent his travelling troupe here three days ago. Lolly's looking after Nora for me.'

I smile. This is a new chapter. 'Why didn't you travel to the stunt with me?' It's a niggle. Something I can't quite grasp.

Matilda shakes her head. She's not ready to share that with me. 'Mrs Taylor,' she says, 'the queue of folk outside all want to talk to you. They want to give you money for the privilege.' Her smile's so big it's practically stretching her skin. It's not reaching her eyes though. 'Mr Russell's charming them while they wait. But they're all here for you.'

'For me.' Repeating the words makes them real. I've done it. I've done something remarkable.

'He asked me to tell you.' She laughs gently and it tinkles. 'You're a heroine. An actual real-life heroine.'

I nod for her to continue, flattening my hair with my hands and looking down at my tatty nightdress. I can't let people see me like this.

'Hundreds died trying, but not the great Annie Edson Taylor.' A pause. 'How did it feel?'

I smile. 'In the moment … just before I toppled over the brink…' I begin, and Tilda nods for me to continue. 'That's when I realised, that David…'

She squeezes my hand this time; she read my letter.

'David.' She repeats my son's name without hesitation. 'I didn't know—'

'I didn't want you to think less of me,' I say. 'When David died…' I'm crying. A release. Relief. 'I realise now, though … to say his name is to honour him.'

'And when there's not a crowd demanding your attention, will you tell me all about your little boy? No more silence. I need you to tell me your story.' She stands, looking towards the door.

'So you're staying?' I say, and she nods.

'Going to be more Annie Edson Taylor.'

I can't help but smile at that. I want to ask more, but there are folk waiting to see me. This is madness. I look down at what I'm wearing. 'Can you help make me presentable?'

Matilda

29th October 1901

The pounding on the door vibrates through the boarding house. Her fanatics don't care that she's supposed to be recovering. They want to meet the woman who conquered the Falls. Each thud's a punch to me chest.

'Enough of your banging,' I shout as I step from me old bedroom. 'Mrs Taylor needs her rest. You need to speak to Mr Russell like everyone else.'

I thought the crowds had stopped turning up here. Mr Russell was arranging public lectures instead. Nora's on me hip again and giggling as I rush down the staircase.

'Open up, little girl.'

I stop. See him through the glass panel. Me breath comes in shallow gasps. The gravelly voice belongs to one of the burly men me uncle was talking to near the market. The one with the too-pale skin. Terror shoots its branches up me throat.

He sees me. 'Open up!' he roars. His voice is all menace. He's determined.

The shaking starts in me knees. I pull Nora closer to me. Fear roots me. Can't move from this spot. Me eyes dart to every corner of the hallway. I'm searching. Frantic. Need to escape. Dust motes in the dim light, the worn edges of the upholstered chairs, the ticking of the grandfather clock – everything's exposed. Why did I come back here? Of course they've found me.

The parlour door creaks open. 'Is there a problem, Miss Hamilton?'

Mr Russell's frame casts a long shadow across the floor. His dark eyes glint. He's doing what he does best – assessing and calculating. I've no doubt he's figuring out his gain. Mrs Taylor trusts him. She likes him, too. He helped her. Will he help me?

'Open the bloody door.' The man outside presses his face against the glass. His nose squashes and spreads. He's trying to see who I'm talking to.

'Do you know this man?' he asks, pointing to the main door. 'One of your clients.' He chuckles.

I know what he's implying, but right now I've bigger problems than Mrs Taylor's manager disrespecting me.

'There'll be reporters here to see Annie soon. We can't risk this kind of attention distracting them.' He waves at the door, turning to go back into the parlour. 'Surely you don't want to ruin Mrs Taylor's chance at fame and fortune, do you?'

'Wait,' I say. He's right, but also this isn't me fault. Not intentionally, anyway. 'Help me,' I whisper.

'Of course.' He beams in response. 'What does he want?'

'Me,' I say. 'Me uncle sent him to take me and Nora home.'

'And you don't want to go home?' He raises an eyebrow, curious.

'This is me home.'

He sighs, he shakes his head, he waggles his finger in the air. 'Of course, I can make this man go away, but your uncle knows you live here. He'll simply send someone else.'

I must grip Nora a little too tightly, as she wriggles in protest. 'It's not safe for me back with him. Me uncle's a bad man.'

His expression alters, but not to kindness. 'Mrs Taylor risked her life,' he says. His voice is stern, and I know he's right. 'This is her chance for success and you're bringing unnecessary trouble to her door. You're lucky you have a choice of homes.'

'But—'

'But nothing.' He turns back towards the parlour.

'Mrs Taylor made me want to be braver. To stay. To stand up for meself. I was leaving … but I stayed.'

'And that's commendable, Miss Hamilton,' he says. 'But if your uncle considers you and that child…' He glares at Nora, 'his property, then he won't rest until he regains his belongings.' He scratches his beard. Considers the problem I've caused. 'I can make this one go away now, but I won't always be around…

'Fine, fine.'

'You and that child of yours are attracting the wrong sorts.' He waves in the direction of the door and the banging starts again. It's frantic. It's peaking. Reckon he's going to bash the door in. 'And you don't want to be destroying all the good work Annie's achieved with her stunt… Or do you? Is that your aim?'

I don't. Of course I don't. Mrs Taylor risked her life. I've no desire to take success and achievement from her. Mama used to say that I made everything about me. That's what I'm doing here, and I need to stop.

'I'll get rid of him.' He steps into the hallway and the pounding stops when the burly man sees him. He turns to me, 'But only if you promise to consider others before your self-seeking needs.'

I can't make eye contact with him. I'm ashamed. An awful person. A bad mother, too. I nod in agreement. Walk to the staircase. Don't look back. Climb the steps to the sound of more banging.

'Magnus, come here,' Mr Russell shouts, and I hear the strongman's footsteps.

Nora wriggles; she wants to see what's going on. At the top of the stairs, I cower behind the bannister, like the coward I truly am.

The door creaks as it opens, and then, 'What do you want?' Mr Russell's voice is cold and unyielding.

'I'm here for the girl and the child.' I peek over the bannister. See him attempting to shove past Mr Russell. 'Her uncle sent me.'

Mr Russell doesn't budge. Magnus takes a step next to him. 'She's not going anywhere with you.'

The burly man hesitates, eyes narrowing. Reckon he's assessing Mr Russell and then Magnus. Trying to figure out if he can overpower them both. He can't. I swear the air between them crackles. There's an unspoken challenge that no one wants to back down from. They glare at each other. No one blinking. Seconds pass. All with fists formed by their sides. Finally, with a sneer, the burly man retreats. Takes a step backwards. And another. His eyes cast down. Then, as if sensing where I've been the entire time, he looks directly at me. There's venom in his eyes and covering his face.

'Uncle William says hello.'

'Bye bye,' Nora shouts. She's waving, too.

I duck back down with her. Invisible again. Me daughter giggles; she likes playing games.

'You can't hide forever.' That's all I hear him say. I run to me bedroom window, looking out and seeing him stomping down the driveway. He kicks the gate. Nora pulls at the net curtain.

'No, little one,' I say, jerking her away. I step out of sight and pop her into her cot.

I exhale, relief momentarily washing over me.

'What a selfish spoiled brat you are, Miss Hamilton.' Mr Russell blocks the doorway. His gaze fixes on mine. Deadpan. Domineering. Me heart had steadied, but now it lurches again. A new fear takes hold. He steps into me room and his presence fills the space.

'Annie didn't risk her life for you to put her in danger,' he says, his voice measured and smooth. He holds his gaze, entirely defiant. 'Your uncle has a right to his possessions.'

Me instincts scream. The room closes in around me. Shadows gather in the corners. 'He doesn't. We don't belong to him,' I say, me voice momentarily snagging in me throat. A cough. 'Get out.' It's a scream this time.

Nora screams, too. We're noisy, but he doesn't budge.

'Everything fine in here?'

Mr Russell pivots on the spot. His demeanour alters. He's all smiles as he rushes to Mrs Taylor. Places an arm around her shoulder. Her hair's wilder than wild, her eyes are conquering.

'What are you doing out of bed? It's not time for you to be up,' he says, his voice sugar and goo. 'Come, come, our heroine needs her rest before her reporters arrive. Miss Hamilton's a little emotional today, that's all.'

'I see you're practising your patronising tone again,' Mrs Taylor says. 'Perhaps one day you'll get it just right.'

Mr Russell stops in his tracks. Looks like his head might burst. He's furious. This is all me fault.

'I'm fine, Mrs Taylor. I promise.' Me words come out too quick.

She smiles at me but I turn away. Eyes on the net covering me window. Me chest visibly rises and falls in me dress. I won't make this about me.

Annie's Diary

30th October 1901

Six days have passed, and my feet are not yet steady on this ground. The thundering roar of Niagara Falls still fills me with a sense of awe and trepidation, and more. It reminds me of my love for the power of art and the beauty of nature; I've finally accepted that I deserve to live.

Perhaps I've shredded the dreamlike state that's covered me since David and Samuel died. A mist of sorts and all joyful memories were concealed in it. I truly worried about embracing good things. Troubled that would allow the weight of pain and grief that I feared my mind could not endure. I see that clearly – now that I've pushed my body, mind and soul to the brink.

Tilda and Nora have hurtled into my affection, like tiny rampaging bulls. That was unexpected. That caught me off-guard. That shifted something within. Combine with Heno's or God's decision – that I should live – and today the world shines differently. It's shifted and tilted, and here I am. Breathing, walking, surviving, but smelling and hearing and tasting and seeing for the first time in decades. By confronting fear in such a visceral way, it seems that I exposed the darker aspects of my own human nature. In that barrel I came face-to-face with the emotions I'd long buried. They were jiggled and tilted from me.

I'm alive though. I'm so very much alive.

That mist has lifted and now I breathe. At the moment of the drop I was free of the covering that's suffocated me since my loved ones died. Now, I take breaths without restriction for the first time in almost forty years. I'd even suggest that in the moment that the barrel tipped over the edge, the pain altered. It left me. Samuel and David joined the water fully – all of us free.

Matilda

31st October 1901

These past three days with Mrs Taylor home have made this place busier than I've ever seen it. Chatter from the boarding house's new occupants fills the air. The smell of fresh coffee and wet paint wafts through the parlour. Daily changes are happening around here. There's a question of ownership and a missing will, and this place's never been so busy. No lost women staying here in exchange for chores completed. Every guest must pay. Mr Russell said this is a business and not a charity. That's the rules now. The boarding house is unrecognisable, and I don't fit in here anymore. He's even got staff running it all. Workers I've not been introduced to. A stranger in me own home. Living here on borrowed time.

'Grabbing all the opportunities.' That's what I overheard him saying to Mrs Taylor this morning. She said something about how she wanted to talk to me about us finding someplace else to live. I heard her manager tut in disgust. Now Nora sits on me lap in the freshly decorated parlour. She's watching folk come and go. The piano's not here anymore; probably too old and battered to fit in now. There's excitement in the air, though, and me daughter likes it. Plays with a lock of me long hair and giggles. Our two bags are at me feet. Me heart aches, knowing we'll soon be leaving the only home me daughter's known.

Mrs Taylor walks through the open doorway. Her face's flushed with excitement and her eyes are tight with pleasure. She's stiff and bruised, but her warrior spirit has fully emerged. I swear she's lost twenty years in the last week. Power and determination ooze from her; she practically roars like a lioness. She scans the room. Spots me. Lifts her cup in a wave and hobbles forward.

'Awful stuff,' she says, tipping the liquid into a new potted plant on a stand. A smile hooks across her face from ear to ear.

'Mr Russell won't like—'

'What he doesn't know… Nora, sweetheart. I've missed you,' she says and me daughter squeals.

Nora holds her arms up for her and Mrs Taylor grimaces. Annoyed that she can't move faster. Her brain and her body aren't quite dancing together yet. She lifts Nora from me knee and me daughter puts her arms around Mrs Taylor's neck. I see the flinch, but she won't not hug me daughter. Their love for each other isn't bringing me comfort, though. Not today. Me fingers wipe a tear from me cheek.

'You should be in bed. There's a strict rest schedule,' I say. Me voice sounds tired. I untangle Nora from her and plonk her on the floor at our feet. Hook an arm through Mrs Taylor's and guide her to an armchair. She shrugs me off. She hates feeling old or in need of assistance.

'Journalists can't get enough of my story,' she says, tugging her wild hair into a knot at the base of her neck. The silver strands are coiled with perspiration on her forehead. 'And Mr Russell's been talking about us taking over this boarding house.' A pause and I nod for her to continue. 'But what about a little ranch in Texas for us, you, me and Nora?'

She beams at that. Her eyes shine with all the hope she's feeling. I force a smile. Struggling to quash the sadness and fear that whirl in me belly. 'That's wonderful,' I say quietly. Me voice trembles.

Mrs Taylor doesn't seem to notice. She's caught up in her enthusiasm. In the excitement that's been a bubble around her since her trip over the Falls. She moves to sit down and her face shines in the half-light. I crouch in front of her, Nora toddling beside me. Fidget nervously with the fabric of me skirt.

'Yes,' she says, 'and we'll be able to support ourselves. Live off the land. Maybe Mr Russell, Lolly and Magnus could visit.' She waves at a new guest passing the doorway and they smile with delight. 'We could perhaps take in boarders, too,' she says. Mrs Taylor's beaming. She's succeeded. She's survived. She's achieved something that no one else has. In an act that was deemed impossible. She changed that. Rewrote history, even. This is everything she hoped for.

'Oh, Tilda, it's going to be perfect.' Slowly, she edges her legs in front of her so that the heels of her new boots touch the rug.

I bite me lip. Tears sting the corner of me eyes. I can't stay with Mrs Taylor. I won't put her in danger being associated with me. Still, the thought of leaving the life we've built here…

I pull an armchair near to her. 'Remember when we didn't have much, but we had each other? There was always laughter in the house, the other women popping by for tea, sharing stories and helping each other out. We were poor, but we were happy.'

She nods, a small smile tugging at her lips. 'Those were good times.'

'Mrs Taylor.' Me voice trembles. Betrays the fear and uncertainty that gnaws at me insides. I avoid meeting her gaze. Unable to bear the thought of seeing the disappointment in her eyes. 'I … I must go away.'

She freezes. A stone statue in her armchair. Emotions flutter over her beautiful face like tiny butterflies. One sticks. She looks at me with curiosity and wide eyes. 'What's happened?'

I take a deep breath. Try to ground meself. I need to be brave like Annie Edson Taylor. 'Me uncle … he's found me.'

'Uncle?' She's confused. How could she know that's a bad thing. Me story's untold.

'Nora's father. And to the two babies that died first,' I say. I shake me head. Can't dig into that right now. 'Me mother's older brother. Liked alcohol and young girls more than he liked God.'

'Your mother's older brother.' She says the words slowly. I watch them being absorbed into her very soul. I hear the rise of anger in the way she says the final 'er' of brother. 'Does your mother know?'

I nod feebly. 'Blamed me and not him. He took what he wanted.'

'And you ran?' Her words are spoken in a staccato, but they're covered in emotion. Controlled.

She reaches over. Grabs me hand. Squeezes it. Mrs Taylor hears me. I'm believed. That hangs in the air.

'He's been threatening me… I can't put Nora in danger. I must go. Must take Nora and run.' I wipe me nose on me sleeve.

Mrs Taylor's expression turns fierce. 'If he comes anywhere near you, I'll kill him with the poker for the fire.'

I blink back tears. Force a brave smile. I can't be like me mother. I must be more. Must do more than she ever did for me. Me little girl feeling safe, her knowing she's loved, her being heard. She deserves more than I've known. The thought of Nora ever feeling as scared or as lonely as me…

'Does Mr Russell know?'

I nod.

'That what all the noise was about the other day?'

I nod again. 'Uncle William sent a man here to get what's his.'

'And Mr Russell made him go away?'

I nod. 'But Mr Russell warned me. Me uncle won't give up until he gets Nora. He's right'

Mrs Taylor's face stays neutral. She bobs her head slowly. 'Where will you go?'

'I'll figure something out.' Me voice is barely above a whisper. I push meself up in me chair, drawing in me knees and hugging them.

'Is there anything I can say to change your mind?'

I shake me head. 'I can't see a different way out from this mess.'

She nods. She understands. Her expression alters, too. 'Then I'll give you some money to help get you both started someplace else,' she says. 'You deserve a new beginning, away from your uncle and the past.'

I shake me head, trying to protest. 'You don't have to—'

'No, but I want to.' Her voice is firm. 'I need to… You and Nora are family. I need to make sure you're safe.' She's trying not to show emotion, but I can hear it. Her words are full of love. She reaches under her skirt and pulls a wad of bills from the hem. 'Take this.'

I shake me head. Hold up both palms in protest.

'It's my share from Mr Russell. I was going to use it on a new place for us all, but that doesn't matter now.'

'I can't—'

'It'll help you get started somewhere else.' She takes me hands and presses the money into me palm. 'Arrive broken, leave determined. Right?'

Tears stream down me cheeks. Unravelling meself, I lean over and hug her tightly. I've never known such love and kindness. No part of me wants to leave this wonderful woman. I wish, with all me heart, that I got to call her Mama.

This is what it is to be loved. I've searched me entire life for this feeling of unconditional affection. A mother's devotion. Never expected to find it in a rundown boarding house in Bay City. Now I must run again though. I gulp, attempting to swallow me emotions. I have no choice. Nora comes first. Always. This is about her needs, not mine.

Mrs Taylor tugs at me hands, urging me to look at her again. Her smile is soft, her eyes don't hide her pain.

'Thank you,' I whisper. Me voice chokes. I swallow. 'Thank you for everything.'

'You'll always have a home with me, Tilda. Always.'

'I promise I'll repay you,' I say. 'One day.'

Annie's Diary

1st November 1901

We said au revoir and not goodbye. That notion of us seeing each other again soon. In my heart, I know that's not true. I know that I won't ever see Tilda and Nora again.

Annie

1st November 1901

Mr Russell bursts into my room with all the subtlety of a bull in a china shop. He oozes confidence and self-assuredness. His presence fills my space, and the walls seem to bend inward as he paces back and forth.

'Annie, Annie, Annie,' he drawls, a hint of amusement in his voice. 'You're a sight for sore eyes.' He surveys my dishevelled appearance, and a smirk plays on his lips.

I laugh nervously, trying to flatten my unruly hair, but Mr Russell's critical gaze only intensifies. 'The loose hair … all of this…' He twirls his finger in front of my face.

'Triumph? Conquering what no others could? Victory?'

He shakes his head, as if that can dismiss what I've achieved. 'Makes you look old.'

'I am old,' I say, the words heavy with defiance. Mr Russell bats away my voice with his hand. He's consumed by his own agenda.

'Let's talk plans.' He plonks himself on the edge of my bed.

I shuffle a little, to allow additional space between us and for propriety. But even the smallest of shifts causes pain to shoot from my shoulders and down my arms. Recovery is taking longer than any of us want. Still, I've met every single person who has queued to see me, but the doctor continues to advise that I stay inside a few days more.

'Your newfound fame is everything we'd hoped for.' He beams with joy. 'There are public speaking engagements and photo opportunities already booked.' The words gush and rush. This is his job and he's good at it. 'I know that you're grateful for my role in your survival.' He bows his head as if praying. A pause.

Is he waiting for me to thank him? Is he attempting to convince me that he's the reason why I survived the plunge? I don't quite comprehend what's happening.

'We begin our tour in ten days,' he says, slapping the mattress. It causes me to wobble slightly. His enthusiasm is infectious, but I can see beneath his smooth exterior. There's a greed that I haven't quite measured yet. There's a layer of cold, calculating ambition there, too. His determination's rampant and free. This man will stop at nothing to get what he wants. That's going to make us very rich, and the prospect of earning back the money I gave to Matilda drives me.

'About this boarding house,' I say and his eyes widen with desire. 'I don't want to stay here. It's time to move on.'

He holds up his palm to shush me. 'Mrs Lapointe is sure to have left the property to you.'

'Her last will is still lost,' I say. He stands, He paces. He looks away, avoiding eye contact again. My suspicion grows daily. He's keen for me to fight for this boarding house and for his circus friends to run the business when we're on the road. He's adamant that I'd win in court – Mrs Lapointe had no children, no one has stepped forward to stake claim. Still, I know that my friend would have written a will.

'I don't want to live in Bay City.' I cross my arms over my chest. 'This is not my home. It's another barrel.'

'A barrel?'

I nod. I don't need to explain myself further. It makes sense to me.

'We'll discuss this matter further when you're less hysterical.'

I shake my head. 'Your attempts to diminish me only highlight your own insecurities.'

I won't change my mind on this one. Without Tilda, Nora and Mrs Lapointe, this Bay City boarding house is merely a stop along my journey. This property is not mine. I have no right to it. I don't want it. Since mentioning it to Tilda, I keep thinking about owning a small Texas ranch again.

'I'll send Lolly in to help with this.' He leans towards me and waggles a finger at my face again. He turns and walks from my bedroom.

The man must be exhausted from carrying around his massive ego all day. The weight of uncertainty doesn't press down on me, though. He doesn't intimidate me; I know who I am. The future doesn't loom ambiguous. Booked events, hundreds of folk wanting to meet me. The outlook is full of promise and potential.

'I wish Tilda was here to experience this, too.' I say the words aloud, but no one can hear.

Already, this new grief clings to me. I've not tried to shake it loose. I miss her. I miss Nora. I'm back feeling lonesome, yet this time I'm surrounded by shouts of my recent triumph. Why didn't Mr Russell make sure that Tilda's Uncle William never bothered her again? Magnus and he could have paid the man a visit. If I were stronger, I could have done that myself. I'd have shown him.

'Too late now.' It's a whisper. I shake my head to dislodge the sadness. Societal expectations have long sought to confine women like me to narrow roles and limited opportunities. The loss of Mrs Lapointe, the departure of Tilda and Nora, adds to that story too. This precarious position of women in a society that values our silence and submission above all else.

'Seems it's on my shoulders now,' I say. I nod to myself. I won't stay in a corner. Out of reach and out of sight. Hidden in the darkness that resides there. I challenged death itself, and I'll defy the expectations that seek to confine me too.

I shuffle my legs along the mattress and over the edge of the bed. Slowly, I allow weight onto them. I'm stiff. Still bruised and battered. Yet, my god, I am truly alive.

'Well, hello there, darling,' Lolly says, gliding into my bedroom with her usual air of grace and charm. 'How are you feeling today?'

'Sixty-three and acutely aware of the limitations that come with being old in a world that values vitality and beauty above all else.'

She chuckles. 'Ah, has Russ been charming you again?'

I laugh. 'Your wit is as sharp as ever. I suppose I should watch my step around you.'

Her burgundy-velvet dress is cinched at the waist with a satin ribbon. It flows elegantly as she moves about my bedroom. 'Hairbrush or comb? she asks, and I point to a drawer.

'I won't be bound by those manmade limitations,' I say.

'And neither will I.' She winks and strokes her well-groomed beard. It cascades down to her chest in gentle waves. A white blonde, it matches the colour of her long, braided hair.

'Age isn't a barrier to achievement,' I say.

'And neither is a beard.' She gives the tapered end a tug.

'Women of any age have the power to shape their own destinies.'

'I admire that you *believe* you can make that difference,' she says. She pulls two decorative combs from her braids. She holds them out to me for approval. They're encrusted with tiny gemstones. 'Let me fix your hair before Mr Russell skins me alive.'

'Do you fear him?' I ask, and Lolly shakes her head.

'He's just a man.' Her eyes are kind. They sparkle with warmth.

'Once you've shot the Falls, the water's fine,' I say.

She whistles and then clicks her fingers. 'Amen to that, darling.' She tugs at my hair and a bolt of pain shoots across my forehead.

'Ow.'

'Shush now, woman,' she says. 'Let's make you pretty.'

My sigh is loud and unapologetic.

Part VI: Mist-veiled Triumph

'I'll never forget her comforting presence and them stories of courage she told. That was way before she went over them Falls. Gave me hope during my illness, she did. Made me want to be stronger and better … and I am now. Left the boarding house with dollars for my train, too. Thanks to her I got me life back. I reckon her compassion and strength left an indelible mark right here, on me heart.'

Irene Johnson

Annie

2nd November 1901

No privacy for me in this boarding house. He charged into my room again last night, excited and clutching an oil lamp. He practically bounced off the four walls. I was just dropping off to sleep. Said that I needed to be dressed and ready within an hour.

'You've been invited to the Pan-American Exposition.'

'What?' I sprang out of bed. In that moment my body and my mind were youthful. Mr Russell clapped his hands with delight.

'We need to leave now. You can sleep during the journey there.'

'Didn't the doctor say I wasn't to go out yet,' I said, but he tutted my words away.

'Get ready. Carriage will be here in five minutes,' he said, rushing out of my room.

Now we're here and the 'Farewell Day' is in full swing on site. I've already met hundreds of strangers. It's both exhausting and exhilarating. I fear I've no more smiles left, though. Being constantly enthusiastic is more tiresome than I expected. I've answered the same questions – Were you scared? Why did you do it? Did you expect to live? – at least one hundred times. That's why I've retreated behind the warmth of the Temple of Music's fires. I rub my hands together like a prospector who just struck gold. Still, I've a chill in my bones and I'm desperate to be warmer.

'Annie?' Mr Russell appears, nodding his head for me to follow him back to greet more visitors. I spit on my hands and run my palms over my hair. Regular flattening of my wildness is needed. My hair hates being tamed. I grin at that thought. Everything back in place, I adjust my skirts, wiggle my wrists and catch up with Mr Russell. Time to smile again. Time to answer the same questions another hundred times. They've come all this way to meet me and they're willing to pay handsomely for the privilege.

'Ready to grab this opportunity and make us some money,' Mr Russell says, looping his arm through mine. Our strides match; his enthusiasm is catching.

I walk onto the esplanade, and I'm immediately surrounded by a sea of eager faces. I wave at the formed queue, smiling at their cheers.

'Thank you, thank you,' I say.

'Thank you for being here,' Mr Russell says.

The *Buffalo Evening News* reported my presence at the exposition. Throngs of visitors have come to pay their respects. They've caught trains and carriages to be here. More folk than expected want to check I'm not dead. I'm grateful to have piqued their curiosity, and keen for them all to remember my name.

'The anticipation in the air is palpable, don't you think?' Mr Russell says. He's thrilled. Delight gushes from him. He's seeing money everywhere he looks. I'm popular. People want to know Annie Edson Taylor. That makes him both fashionable and wealthier. He places his arm around my shoulder. It's perhaps to keep me upright, but still I welcome the support. I won't admit to him that I'm struggling with noise and light, my body not yet recovered from the distress of the stunt. I also won't admit that the thought of returning to my bed later is keeping me going.

The West Esplanade bandstand has been cordoned off with ropes, creating a path for the crowds to approach me, greet me and then to scuttle away. It's all very efficient. Mr Russell guides me back to my seat at the foot of the stairs. There's a huge sign next to me – *The Queen of the Mist*. My barrel's by my side; it serves as a reminder of the daring feat that's brought me here. I can't bear to look directly at it. Not yet. I worry that if someone offers enough money, Mr Russell will suggest I climb back in. I shiver at that thought. There isn't enough money in America to get me back in a barrel.

'Ready for round two?' Mr Russell asks, and I bob my head slightly. Large movements still send pain shooting through me. I'm entirely not myself, but there's no one around who would know. That thought stops me in my tracks. I tap the sides of my head gently to stop that from sticking.

'Ready and willing,' I say.

'Come, come, meet the fearless Annie Edson Taylor,' Mr Russell shouts, stepping away from me and towards the crowd. He thrusts his arms out wide and spins showily on the spot.

I greet the next visitor with a smile and a bob of my head, my appearance no doubt belying my being forty-three.

'Nice to meet you,' I say.

'Can't believe you're not dead.'

'Thank you,' I say.

'Did you even expect to live?'

'I did. I really did.' I shiver involuntarily. My teeth chatter, too. Still, I keep my smile broad and my back straight.

The Esplanade's bustling with hordes of excited visitors but their voices merged into an indistinguishable cacophony about two hours ago. It rebounds in my ears now. Despite the layers I'd donned to ward off the chill, that bone-deep coldness has settled within me. It seeps into my very core. I shouldn't be sitting outside.

'How much longer?' I whisper.

'Quiet.' It's almost a growl. Mr Russell stands beside me now. Tall and proud. Not of me, though. He grips my shoulder; he considers me his property. I slap at his hand, and he removes it.

'And this is the actual barrel,' he tells the next visitor. He practically sings the words. 'Alongside the straps and bicycle pump that aided in our journey.'

Our? He points to the artefacts. He's claiming a crucial role in securing my safe voyage inside the barrel. None of this feels tangible.

'I designed the barrel myself,' I say, my voice a little harsher than expected. 'Before employing men to assist my stunt. The items on show served *me* well.' I look up at Mr Russell and hold my stare.

'It served us well,' he says with a sternness that attempts to silence me.

I laugh. 'Forgive me,' I say. I smile broadly. 'I'm marvelling at how confidently you can speak while knowing so little.'

He blinks and turns away first.

More visitors continue to flow past. More and then more again. Their footsteps slap against the cold pavement. Increasingly, the sound is too loud. Some just want to gawk. That's when it would be more fun to detach myself and float away from the scene unfolding before me. Still, each face that passes offers a look of either curiosity, fear or admiration. That they're paying dollars for my greeting means that it's my job to respond to each of them. I begin winking at every fifth spectator. An added challenge being Mr Russell not witnessing the act. I'm a wild beast and the spectators' eyes are wide with wonder; I'm the woman who dared to challenge the mighty Niagara Falls. I'm unpredictable. I'm terrifying. I don't think any of them consider me sane.

'Roll up, roll up! Cast your eyes on the death-defying Annie Edson Taylor.'

Though the cold gnaws at my bones and I long for warmth, I remain stationed on the esplanade. This is important. To be invited to the Pan-American Exposition is significant. It's mammoth. It's the beginning of this new chapter in my story. Nonetheless, I'm a silent figure amidst the bustling crowd. A spectacle. A freak. An exhibit. The muscles of my back, between my shoulders, are particularly sore. I can't shake hands, fearing that the slightest touch would send tremors down my spine.

'Does she bite?' a woman asks Mr Russell. She's dressed primly in a high-necked, long-sleeved dress of fine lace, her hair neatly pinned beneath a fashionable hat adorned with ribbons.

I growl. The release is feral. She scampers away and Mr Russell glares at me. A warning? I shrug my shoulders, as if to ask, 'And?'

'You're truly remarkable, Mrs Taylor,' one woman exclaims, her voice filled with admiration. 'What you've done's a miracle.' Her eyes are alight with excitement.

I nod in response, offering a wide smile. 'Thank you,' I say, and she stares at me. Silence. Then, 'Did you know that the barrel was once full of pickles? Gave a whole new meaning to being in a pickle…' She walks away without responding to my best joke.

Mr Russell shakes his head as he bends down to speak to me. 'I'm going to have to give you lessons in how to hold an audience,' he says. 'You need to be better than this.'

'Thank you for your input. It's as valuable as ever, which is to say, not at all. I was a teacher. I know how to communicate.'

He waves his hand through the air, as if to remove my words. 'We have a plan to make us both famous,' he says. 'No more silliness.'

'Silli—?'

'Annie!' someone shouts. 'Mrs Taylor!' The voice verges on hysteria. I turn. He's practically bouncing on the spot, his excitement making him appear even more ridiculous. I stare, but I don't wave.

He beams with joy. 'I've been dreadfully worried about you,' he says. 'I was bothered that our future plans would be swallowed by those pesky rapids.' He's still impeccably dressed in a suit that hugs his lean frame, exuding an unwarranted confidence.

'Who is that?' Mr Russell asks, disdain dripping from the words. I like that he doesn't hide his contempt.

'We are to be married.' He's shouting at the queuing visitors. Bounce, bounce, bouncing along the queue. 'Annie Edson Taylor will be my wife.'

'For heaven's sake … Henry Hills. Mrs Winthrop's younger brother,' I say. I don't even have the energy to roll my eyes. 'Take me back to my lodgings… Now.' My tone offers no movement for negotiation.

I stand and walk away from both Mr Russell and Mr Hills.

THE MASTERMIND BEHIND THE BARRELL

Annie's Daring Feat Captivates Audiences and Reinforces Her Manager's Reputation as One of the Greatest

NIAGARA FALLS, NY - NOVEMBER 3, 1901

The world watched with bated breath as Annie Edson Taylor, a 43-year-old former schoolteacher, emerged victorious from a daring stunt that involved plummeting over the mighty Niagara Falls in a barrel. As the first person to survive such a feat, Mrs Taylor has earned a place in history – but behind her success is a strategic manager who played a crucial role in her fresh fame.

Mr Frank Russell, a shrewd businessman, and promoter, saw potential in Taylor's daring stunt and wasted no time capitalising on the public's fascination. His astute management of her affairs has led to an explosion of interest in Taylor's story, with eager audiences clamouring to hear first-hand about her experience.

Under Russell's guidance, Mrs Taylor will embark on a lucrative lecture tour, sharing her incredible tale and capturing the imagination of everyone she encounters. The pair's collaboration has already proven fruitful, with Russell expertly navigating the complexities of the entertainment industry and ensuring that Mrs Taylor's story reaches the widest possible audience.

In addition to managing Mrs Taylor's speaking engagements, Russell has organised a series of public appearances and promotional events, further cementing her reputation as a daredevil. His keen eye for opportunity and ability to generate excitement for Mrs Taylor's story will be instrumental in her ascent to fame.

'Annie Edson Taylor's bravery and determination are awe-inspiring,' says Russell. 'I am honoured to have played the main part in helping us achieve this goal. I have shown the world that with strong guidance anything is possible, and now is the time to ensure that my legacy produces future generations of daredevils and dreamers.'

As Mrs Taylor and Mr Russell continue to ride the wave of success, it is surely irrefutable that Russell's guidance has been the driving force behind this lady's transformation into a household name. Equally and indisputably, Russell proves that with the right combination of courage, determination, and skilled management, even the most implausible dream can come true. What a man!

Annie

3rd November 1901

Heading home from 'Farewell Day' and the rhythmic clopping of the horses' hooves on cobblestone streets offers a steady and comforting beat. The creak of the wooden carriage wheels and the occasional jingle of the harnesses adds to the symphony. I'd dance, too, if I were not so exhausted.

'Annie, Annie, Annie,' Mr Russell says, and I lift an eyebrow. Nothing complimentary ever follows when he addresses me that way. I remember the tales he used to tell – of his days as a trapeze artist, the glory of his first tightrope walk across the Mississippi, the night he saved a fellow performer from a burning tent. Those stories seemed to glow with an inner light. Did I imagine the early days when he was passionate about the circus? Wasn't he driven by the thrill of the performance then? Not by the glitter of gold.

'You're a sight for sore eyes,' he says. The sleeves of his shirt are rolled up his toned forearms. He's handsome; he knows that he is. He grabs my hands and looks me directly in the eyes. 'Let's forget all about your performance at yesterday's Pan-American Exposition. That departure… Say no more. All is forgiven.'

I shake my hands loose and focus on my surroundings instead. The carriage's interior exudes a sense of refined elegance and comfort. The seats are upholstered in plush, dark-green velvet. I stroke my palm over them; a richness that's both a soft and luxurious place to sit. These cushions are thick and inviting, with tufted buttons adding a touch of sophistication. This transport was provided for me. It's luxury I've not experienced for many years.

'There'll no doubt be crowds outside the boarding house when we get back.' He's smiling. 'Lolly and Magnus will have entertained them.' The intensity of his stare is unnerving. 'Lectures start in a few days … and I've been thinking.'

I nod for him to continue.

'Let's tell everyone that you died for a few minutes during the stunt. And that's what made you lose your mind afterwards.' His eyes glint with a mixture of excitement and dark ambition; it feels like a cold shadow creeping in.

I stare at him, confused. 'When did I lose my mind?'

'Consider it a new twist in the tale.'

I shake my head vehemently. 'A twist … a lie … I won't be adding.'

'Perhaps you had visions during your time in the barrel,' he says. He's staring at the carriage's ceiling. He's lost in his own world. 'We could use your newfound powers in magnet-therapy treatment.'

'What on earth are you talking about?' I ask. 'Are you possessed?'

This fame, this heroine status, the girls gone, Mrs Lapointe buried – my current reality is both unrecognisable and unexpected. A memory flickers – Mrs Lapointe's voice, warm and comforting, urging us all to gather for supper. Laughter and stories flowing freely around the table, a stark contrast to this hollow exchange.

'My life's been riveting enough not to have you fill in gaps with ridiculous stories,' I say.

'And you remember our plan?' he asks. He speaks slowly, as if I'm not quite capable of grasping the words. 'For your newfound fame. How that's more important than this madness.' He waves his hand in a circular movement in the air.

I grab his fingers. 'Disagreeing with your ludicrous ideas is not madness.'

'It is when queues of folk wait to meet you and you're incapable of sustaining their attention.' He opens the carriage's glass pane. Fresh air and dust travel through the window. He stands and leans his head out. 'Bellow if you want to see Annie Edson Taylor,' he shouts.

He laughs as he sits back down. He considers himself hilarious. I hold my stare. I observe him.

'I consider it fascinating how your perception of my abilities has no bearing on my actual competence.'

A slow nod, his eyes meet mine. 'Clearly, I've met my match in you.' A pause. 'Shall I carry on?'

I sweep my hand in front of me, giving my permission.

'So,' he begins, his voice smooth until its hard edges, 'we need to strike while the iron's hot. People are fascinated by what you've done. Hell, they wish to be charmed by you, by Annie Edson Taylor the stunter. So … we're going to give them what they desire.'

'I read the article about you this morning,' I say. I watch his face for a shift in expression or even embarrassment, but there's nothing. Instead, he shakes his head. His eyes are on me just as mine are on him.

'All part of the plan,' he says.

I observe him with suspicion. He's my manager and I need to trust that he's got my best interests in mind. I don't, though. This man's priority is himself.

'First, we'll have photographs taken of you with the barrel—'

'My barrel?'

'Possibly with the Falls in the background. They'll sell like hotcakes, and we'll make a pretty dollar or two.'

I nod again. Carlisle Graham gave me a photo like that. It makes sense. I shift in the carriage's seat. The tenderness of the bruises on my body a reminder. There's excitement bubbling in my stomach though. Mr Russell's enthusiasm is always contagious, and the fact that I need to earn back the money I gave to Matilda remains. Money makes everything easier.

'What else can I do?'

He looks puzzled. 'I have it all in hand. Recoup your energy and I'll instruct when—'

'I appreciate your concern, but I assure you, my success does not depend on your speaking for me.'

'Yet, it does depend on my management capabilities.'

I turn to look out of the window and he claps his hands together. He demands my attention.

'Your public needs you happy,' he says. There's a pause. 'Can you do that with this?' He twirls a finger around my face and offers an exaggerated smile, baring his teeth.

I bat his hand away. 'Your condescension is as charming as ever. Do tell me, how do you manage to fit such a large ego into such a small mind?'

He laughs from his belly. 'And you always know how to put me in my place.'

I nod, I can. Otherwise what's the point of all of this? Isn't this why I risked everything? I ask myself that, but I know the answer. It isn't. I did this for my family, too, but now they've gone. I'm alone again. I shake my head to dislodge those thoughts. Raindrops hit the roof. Mr Russell pulls the window closed. Rain streaks down the pane.

'We still need to fix this.' He points and waves his hand in my general direction. Clearly it's all of me that needs fixing and making presentable; my hand forming into a fist happens without me even considering why. 'Then, people will like you better.'

I sigh. I formulate a retort—

'I have finalised the dates for your public-speaking engagements,' he says, before I can speak.

'In Bay City?'

He shakes his head, beaming with delight. 'Your story's inspiring, and people will pay to hear you speak,' he says. He holds his right hand in the air, rubbing his thumb along the tips of his fingers as if he's trying to conjure wealth simply by the repetitive motion.

'Did you like teaching?'

'I loved it,' I say.

He claps his hands together again. I can't quite tell if glee or greed guides him. 'Then you must have it within you to be a performer.' He throws his arms out wide and bows from his waist. The movement is exaggerated. The words sound kind, but his eyes are cold and calculating. I've been around the block enough times to listen to my gut. It's currently screeching like a ghoul.

I shift on the seat, pulling a lap blanket over me. Its fine knit will provide the needed extra warmth. The pain in my body is momentarily forgotten as I consider the possibilities. I've been over the Falls in a barrel and survived. That makes me both remarkable and a freak. Unique, if I'm being kind. I have nothing else. Literally, nothing else at all. My friends are gone, the lost women are gone, the boarding house isn't mine. All I have is my stunt. I don't have contacts to gain from that, but Mr Russell does. That's his job and he's good at it. Money will make everything easier and, right now, I have none. My resolve must be to make the most of my newfound fame and my manager. He needs me as much as I need him; we are equals.

'I'm entirely committed to this,' I say, and he cheers. 'How about a memoir?' I suggest. I've so many stories to tell about my life. It'd be better than any tale I've read.

'Possible,' Mr Russell agrees, nodding his approval. He leans over, pushing his small trunk further into the storage compartments tucked beneath the seats.

'I could write it.'

He laughs from his belly at that. He considers me a hoot. 'We'll find a man to help you put it all down on paper.'

'Your lack of faith in me is truly inspiring'.

'I doubt you have that skill yourself.'

'But—'

He holds up his palm to stop me. 'You'll share your incredible journey with the world, and it'll be the most popular story ever written. No doubt about it. I remember hearing Charles Dickens at St James Hall.' He hesitates, perhaps waiting for me to react.

'In Buffalo?'

He nods. 'I was a child. There was a large throng, but my father sneaked me in. Mr Dickens was magnificent. I can still see him on stage.' He rocks from side to side, as if mimicking what he saw back then. 'Acting out his stories, making voices for his characters. Shame we can't find someone like him to write it for you.'

My heart quickens at the thought of my pain and my triumphs laid bare on the pages of a book. 'What about endorsements or advertising?' I ask. The bolder, the better.

Mr Russell smirks, clearly pleased with my eagerness, but there's something else, too. 'I've already got some ideas on that front. Companies are clamouring to associate themselves with the indomitable Annie Edson Taylor. But…'

I nod for him to continue.

'They had to retrieve your barrel.'

'Retrieve it?'

'From the Falls. Before the exposition,' he says. I must look confused as he sighs. 'It's the ultimate souvenir of the feat. Now we need to move it from the exposition to someplace else. Without it … there is no proof.'

I'd not considered why or how the barrel was with me yesterday, and no one had thought to offer further details. 'People won't take me by my word?'

He laughs as if I'm the most amusing person to have ever lived. 'Why would they?' he says, and I open my mouth to protest. 'Look at you.' He waggles a finger at me. He's shushing me. 'You're an old woman. The barrel is the proof you're not merely hysterical.'

I cross my arms defiantly across my chest and tilt my chin higher. 'I'll ask for testimonies from witnesses. Holleran will—'

'I want the barrel.' His voice is angry. I'm missing something here.

The hairs at the base of my neck prickle. I hold out my palms. He'll consider it submission; I consider it calming a tantrum. 'Fine, fine,' I say. 'Shall we request it's returned to the boarding house?' Perhaps he's right. I'd never considered that some folk might not believe me.

The driver's commands to the horses mingles with the distant sounds of city life. Mr Russell bows his head. 'Forgive me. What was I thinking?' His eyes crinkle with warmth and laughter. He's both hot and cold, and I'm unsure which version of him to trust. I've met men like him before; anger and cunning are a lethal combination. 'Now, what other schemes and money-making plans do you have?'

A pause. He's bouncing on the carriage's bench. He demands confirmation that I want this as much as he does.

'What about guided tours of Niagara Falls? The barrel next to me at the start and finish. I could tell visitors about the history, other daredevils like Carlisle Graham, and my own experience.'

'Brilliant.' His eyes narrow. 'You're a natural, Annie. Now… I want you to be presentable. I'll ask Lolly to help. We have a fortune to make and have wasted enough time already.' He taps the pocket watch in his breast pocket. 'We wouldn't want you to miss out on your share, would we?'

I turn and stare out of the window. Disquiet twirls and quickens around my torso. I can't quite chase it away.

Helped Her Into The Barrel

November 6th 1901

I, Mr Holleran, can confirm that on October 24th, 1901, I rowed Mrs Annie Edson Taylor to her launch spot and helped her into the barrel. She was brave, and we did our best to keep her safe. It was a day I will never forget.

Signed,

Mr Holleran

MARTHA WAGENFUHRER'S DISPARAGING REMARKS DRAW IRE OF ANNIE EDSON TAYLOR

NIAGARA FALLS GAZETTE - NOVEMBER 7, 1901

In a recent statement to the 'Niagara Falls Gazette', Martha Wagenfuhrer made disparaging comments regarding Annie Taylor's journey over the Horseshoe Falls. Wagenfuhrer was quoted saying: 'This woman, Mrs Taylor, I see by the papers, went over the Horseshoe Falls. Now everybody knows that there ain't much in going over them Horseshoe Falls. They ain't very dangerous. Of course, no one could go over Niagara Falls, them real Falls are 270 ft high, and it's most likely that if anyone went over that in a barrel, the barrel is going to clean the bottom and's never coming up, or else be smashed to pieces. Mrs Taylor never went through the whirlpool like I did, and everybody knows that's the worst trip there is. I'm the second one who's gone through the whirlpool and lived to tell the story. That's where the river narrows and the water spins violently. It makes a vortex that's swallowed many of us stunters up. Doing that is far more harrowing than a little plunge over them Horseshoe Falls.'

Annie Taylor, upon hearing Wagenfuhrer's dismissive remarks, responded with fervour and indignation. 'It is utterly despicable that Mrs Wagenfuhrer seeks to diminish the significance of my journey,' Taylor stated. 'Stunt performers have long been drawn to Niagara, each seeking to outdo the last. Since the early 1800s, daredevils have tried their luck, and most have been men. We are both women stunters and should be celebrating each other's successes. We have both achieved what men cannot and it is unjust to discredit the bravery and determination it took to navigate the treacherous waters of Niagara Falls. Contrary to Mrs Wagenfuhrer's assertions, the Horseshoe Falls are a formidable force of nature.'

Taylor's manager, Mr Russell, went on to emphasise the dangers she had faced during her daring feat, highlighting the uncertainty of survival and the sheer audacity it took to undertake such a perilous endeavour. He condemned Wagenfuhrer's attempts to undermine Taylor's achievement, calling for respect and acknowledgment of Mrs Taylor's courageous endeavour. 'We must refuse to let Mrs Wagenfuhrer's jealous and insignificant words detract from the significance of Annie's journey,' he declared. 'Perhaps if Martha had a manager like me, she too would have achieved a more daring stunt.'

Annie

8th November 1901

I've never been more furious. I spent the entire train journey reading and rereading what Martha Wagenfuhrer wrote about me and my response. Enraged. Steam practically shooting from my ears. I didn't once look out the window. Instead, my finger traced her words, and I scribbled little notes to myself. Additional retorts and comments. I glared at her photograph, drew a moustache and warts on her beautiful face. Then, I even walked along the dirt path, turning away and not taking in the view of Niagara Falls. Aimlessly and for an hour, repeatedly stomping out Martha Wagenfuhrer's disparaging remarks. Splashing through puddles and mud. Still livid. I didn't want to arrive here in a foul mood.

Now though, the damp planks of the viewing deck stretch out before me. Their sheen glistens with the icy mist of the Falls. The roar's a welcome back. They're excited I've returned. I am too. They're probably cross with Mrs Wagenfuhrer like I am.

It's here – my barrel. A true reunion.

'Finally!' Mr Russell bellows. 'Where have you been?'

I wave a hand in his direction. 'You must be very brave to speak to me like that. Either that or very foolish.'

He laughs and I step to my barrel.

'Hello, old friend.'

It's still in one piece. The cooper has fixed it up nicely. I don't know if that was before or after the exposition. The words are new, though. Painted in white, from top to bottom, *Annie Edson Taylor, Heroine of Niagara Falls, Oct 24th* in white paint. Then, *F.M. Russell Mgn* in lettering that's as big. Its staves gleam wet under the chilly haze of the Niagara.

'Looks like Mr Russell here wants to make sure his name is just as famous as yours truly. How considerate.'

'This barrel's as much mine as it is yours,' he says, his tone sharp at the edges of the words. 'I paid for it.' He moves to stand next to me and reaches out to stroke my barrel.

'You're mistaking your opinion for fact,' I say. 'You've received back all that you paid in advance and more.'

I place my hand on the barrel, too. Its presence is a stark reminder of the harrowing descent. I'm back in there again with the deafening roar of the water, the suffocating darkness within its belly. My heart pounds against my chest like it's attempting to match the thunderous rhythm of the waterfall. That rhythm was my sole companion in this oak tomb.

'Mrs Taylor, are you ready?' Mr Russell's voice cuts my thoughts. It's more of a command than a question though. 'Time is money.'

I steal a glance at him, seeing his expectant eyes as he waves a hand in the direction of the photographer. My manager's unconcerned about how this might feel for me, his mind only on the signed photographs and the coins they're sure to bring.

'What are we going to do about Martha Wagenfuhrer's—'

'Later.' He bats away my voice.

'The newspaper said I said—'

'Later.' A glare and a palm up to bounce back my complaint. 'Time is money. Step closer to the barrel.'

Martha's words stung, but what hurts more is the absence of my boarding-house friends' comforting voices. They were always ready with kind words and support. 'If time is money,' I say, 'you must be losing a fortune with all this interrupting. Now, about that barrel...'

It takes all my strength to stiffen my spine, to quell the Martha-related tremors and not to punch my manager on his nose. Three different emotions. Be more Annie Edson Taylor, I think. Focus on that right now. That makes me giggle. Inhale, exhale, I raise my chin and stand tall. I stare into the lens of the camera. The photographer fiddles with his equipment and the roar of the Falls grows louder in my ears; a magnificent crescendo. It demands and that makes my abdomen flip-flop. My body remembers. I think about the signed photographs. Think about the coins they'll bring.

I rock gently on my heels.

Martha's words echo. It's not just her dismissive comments that sting; it's the reminder of how fragile and rare true female alliances are. This world too often pits us against each other. Our worth is generally determined by men, and solidarity among women can be elusive. The camaraderie I had with Mrs Lapointe, Nora, and Matilda was precious and rare. We laughed together, shared our sorrows, and lifted each other up. Their unwavering support was my anchor, and without them I'm adrift in this sea of strangers and transient fame.

'Can't you make her stand still?'

'Annie.' It's a growl. He walks to me and takes my face in his hands. I try to turn my head away, but he pushes his palms harder against my face.

'Oi,' I say, shaking myself from his grip. I'm an old woman and not some immature child he can control. 'Do not touch me, young man.'

I glare until he turns and walks away. I'm as stiff as a statue.

'Stay like that,' the photographer says.

The camera flashes, and for a moment, everything goes white.

'Is it done?' I ask.

'No.' Stern, my manager has run out of patience with me.

I pull my cloak tighter around myself, taking solace in its thin warmth. My hands throb from the wind's touch, my feet are sopping from walking in the dirt path's puddles.

'No problem.' I smile. I'm getting better at pretending. It seems to be an essential skill these days. Eyes on the dollars. Money makes everything easier.

Still, the mist envelops me like a damp shroud and its tendrils threaten to release my hair from its tight bun. Gulls mew above.

'Are you ready?' He's young. His voice is almost drowned out by the roar of the Falls. Mr Russell stands beside him, his face like a thunderstorm. I smile my gentlest and most feminine smile.

'I am both ready and able,' I say.

'All right, Mrs Taylor.' The photographer peers through the viewfinder of his camera. 'Hand on the barrel.'

'Stand taller.' Mr Russell is angry. 'Let the world see the strength and courage that carried you over them Falls.'

I do as I'm told. My palm on the barrel and the memories surge through me: the roar of the water, the darkness that swallowed me whole, the violent pressure that threatened to tear me apart.

'I survived.' It's a whisper and then I hold my breath.

Mr Russell steps forward. 'Excellent work, Annie. That's a tiny bit of Niagara history captured,' he says, and it sounds genuine. 'Just think. This photograph will serve as a testament to your daring feat. We can share your story with the world through this single image.'

I nod. That's all that matters. 'Postcards, signed photos…' I say and Mr Russell claps with delight. Mentioning ways to make money is the way to his heart. Perhaps it's the only language we share.

I glance back at the photographer, then at the mighty Falls behind me, then at my barrel. I stand up taller, straighter, even. I smile wide and true. I survived. That barrel saved my life.

'Let's show the world that age is no obstacle to bravery and determination.' My voice is steady and clear.

The camera clicks again.

Annie

17th November 1901

November is proving a busy month. It's the fifth show in as many days, and applause spills over the heavy velvet curtain as the interval begins. Shadows, created by the dimmed lighting, dance on the walls. The air is thick with perspiration and a hint of sawdust. It's reminiscent of the theatre's old wooden structures. My pulse quickens. I'm backstage in the wings, standing in the shadowy quiet. Clearly, I'm far from the perilous roar of Niagara. Nonetheless, I'm on the brink of a plunge. It could be that I'm being dramatic. The town hall near Buffalo becomes silent. It brims with hushed anticipation. Whispers and rustles. I'm on next. They're waiting for me.

I adjust the lace collar of my high-necked dress against the curve of my throat. I feel the tight squeeze of my corset; a familiar pressure. White petticoats peek beneath my long, dark skirts; their silent rustle a kind of calming metronome amidst the mounting excitement. Apparently, when I'm nervous I notice details. I realised that yesterday. My hands move to my hair, tamed and pulled back into the tightest bun. I search for a loose strand to twirl but find none. I'm entirely not myself. I'm fully who my manager wants me to be. Waiting. In the quiet wings, I catch the low murmur of Mr Russell negotiating my fees. His words are punctuated by the chink of coins and the rustle of notes. It's a foreign territory for me, yet strangely exhilarating and growing in familiarity.

Payment made, Mr Russell nods towards me. He's loosening his tie as I step to the edge of the wings. I need to be more engaging than yesterday. That's my goal for today. The velvet curtain rises. My barrel, the worn oak glowing under gas lights, sits in the centre of the stage. A gasp as the audience sees it for the first time. I smile. That's happened at every show so far. The visual, the actual barrel, is a silent testament to our shared victory. The echo of Niagara's unrestrained symphony lingers in its hollow core.

The applause is louder than before, but then it cuts. Has there been a signal? The anticipation is palpable. The room is quiet.

'Ladies and Gentlemen, the Queen of the Mist, Mrs Annie Edson Taylor.' The strong voice pierces the silence.

Gathering my courage, I smooth my skirts, lift my chin, and step out onto the stage. A sea of faces greets me and, for a moment, I'm not an old woman. I'm not merely the woman who bested Niagara either. A cacophony of claps and cheers reverberates off the high ceiling. I lay a hand on the barrel and that excites the audience even more. Folk – of all ages – are on their feet, shouting and whistling with delight. What they don't realise is that I'm drawing strength from the sturdy staves. If I can survive what I did in a barrel, then I can achieve whatever it is that I'm going to do tonight.

I move to the lectern and place my hands on it. I feel the polished wood beneath my fingers, and it grounds me in the present moment. I clear my throat and glance at the audience.

'Ladies and gentlemen,' I say. My voice is firm and steady, despite the butterflies fluttering in my stomach. I think about teaching. About storytelling and oral tradition. 'I stand before you not as a mere survivor, but as a testament to human courage and resilience.'

A few chuckles ripple through the crowd, quickly stifled. I see Mr Russell, his brow furrowed, standing at the side and scanning the audience with a hawk-like intensity. He's on alert, ready to quash any sign of heckling. His vigilance soothes my nerves. That's his job, I need to do mine. I'm not alone.

'Not even four weeks ago,' I continue, my eyes scanning the sea of faces, 'I found myself on the precipice of the Horseshoe Falls, nestled within the confines of this pickle barrel.' I turn and point. 'Giving a whole new meaning to "being in a pickle",' I say but no one laughs. I glance at Mr Russell, and he shrugs. It's the fifth day of my joke falling flat, yet still I persist with it. Deep breath in. 'That day, I was not a woman facing a plunge into the abyss, but a human being, armed with faith and determination, challenging the unyielding force of nature.'

A murmur ripples through the audience; surprise and disbelief are etched on their faces. Three men in the front row, their moustaches twitching in disdain, exchange dubious glances. Yet, the women who accompany them, clad in their finest silks and satins, watch me with wide eyes and bated breath.

'Imagine … if you will,' I press on, my voice rising above the hum, 'the thunderous roar of the Falls, the terrifying drop, the violent churn of the waters. Yet, within the barrel, I found a peculiar serenity, a silence amidst the chaos.'

I've practised. There's a narrative shape. I know where my voice needs to rise, and where it becomes a whisper, too. The room falls quiet, the audience is hanging on to my every word.

'Yet before I continue, I wonder if I might tell you about two other women. One named Lelawala and the other Morgiana…'

I take a deep breath and continue.

OVER THE FALLS

ANNIE EDSON TAYLOR'S STORY OF HER TRIP

How the Horseshoe Fall Was Conquered

I am compelled to document the journey that has brought me to this moment.

Emotionally, the act of recounting my experience feels like a crossing, one that traverses the depths of my soul. With each stroke of the pen, I confront the memories that have haunted my dreams since that fateful day. The rush of the falls, the deafening roar of the water, the chilling embrace of fear – they all come flooding back to me with an intensity that leaves me breathless. Yet amidst the turmoil, there is solace in the act of putting words to paper, in finding meaning amidst the chaos.

Societally, I am acutely aware of the significance of my story. Not just for myself, but for women everywhere. In a world that seeks to confine us to the roles dictated by society, I refuse to be bound by limitations. My journey over the Falls is a testament to the resilience and strength of women, a rallying cry against the constraints of age and sex. Perhaps, through my words, I will inspire others to defy expectations and chart their own course, no matter the obstacles they may face.

Physically, the act of writing is both a labour of love and a preservation of memory. As the ink flows through nib and onto the page, I am keenly aware of the fleeting nature of time, of the memories that slip through our fingers like grains of sand. In documenting my journey, I seek to immortalise the details that have shaped me, to leave behind a legacy that will endure long after I am gone.

I pen the pages of this memoir, a testament to the triumphs and tribulations of a life lived on the edge.

January 1st, 1902. Written by Annie Edson Taylor

Annie's Diary

January 8th 1902

I asked Mr Russell what he thought of my memoir. He said, 'You're no Charles Dickens.'

I suggested that he let me know when he is ready to join the rest of us in the twentieth century.

Still, it's been brought to my attention that I'm living the life I wished for. It would be perfect, if not that it lacks the company of my friends, my loves lost, the women I once helped…

ANNIE EDSON TAYLOR OPENS SOUVENIR STAND NEAR NIAGARA

NIAGARA FALLS GAZETTE - JANUARY 19, 1902

Tomorrow marks a significant event near the State Reservation as Mrs Annie Edson Taylor, the intrepid woman who successfully navigated the Horseshoe Fall of Niagara, is set to open a fancy goods and souvenir stand in front of Mrs Davy's store.

Mrs Taylor's daring journey, undertaken on October 24, 1901, captured global attention and solidified her place in history.

Regarded by those who know her as a remarkable woman, the Queen of the Mist's stand will present a variety of items commemorating her historic accomplishment. Among the offerings will be miniature barrels, photographs of her courageous descent, and copies of her memoir that details the extraordinary feat she achieved.

Her manager, Mr Russell, stated: 'Positioned within earshot of the mighty cataract she conquered, Annie's presence near the State Reservation is expected to draw considerable interest from tourists and locals alike.'

It is noted that with her proximity to the awe-inspiring natural wonder, she is poised to become a noteworthy attraction in Niagara. All are welcomed.

Annie

20th January 1902

My teeth, my hands, my limbs – everything is icy. The biting January chill whistles. It plays a freezing counterpoint to the steady thunder of Niagara's rush. I'm bent over, attempting to regain both my breath and my energy. We've been struggling with this for over an hour.

'Even in winter's firm grip,' I say, 'the mighty Falls lose none of their terrifying majesty.'

I hear a cheer and look towards the entrance. There's a crowd forming outside. Two women wave enthusiastically. They're bundled in thick coats and scarves. I wave back and they huddle together for warmth. Their breaths mingle with the icy air.

Against this frosty backdrop, Mr Russell and I struggle with my barrel.

'Why didn't you ask Magnus to help us?'

'The strongman? He's busy.'

The unyielding chunk of Kentucky oak is as stubborn as the day I first laid eyes on it. Events have stopped transporting the barrel; the task of moving it falls on us now. My days of travelling in luxurious carriages are as distant a memory. The number of bookings is thinning, too.

'Mrs Taylor, shall we continue?' Mr Russell breaks through the cold silence with a stern tone. It's never Annie now. His eyes are questioning as they flicker between me and the barrel. His breath fogs up in the air, as he braces his hands against the barrel's icy surface.

I roll my eyes, grinning at his obvious scepticism. 'Already forgetting what I'm capable of, Mr Russell?' I quip, pulling my shawl tighter around my shoulders. 'I've conquered mightier forces than this.'

I give him a curt nod and move to the other end of the barrel. I roll up the sleeves of my dress and plant my feet firmly against the ground. My gloved hands rest on the cold, rough wood. The formidable chunk of oak stands tall and sturdy, almost mocking in its silent strength. At Mr Russell's nod, we heave together. Our joint effort makes the barrel groan and inch forward. The strain sings in my muscles; a harsh reminder of the vessel's weight. Yet, I push harder, my breath puffing out in white clouds. Mr Russell mirrors my effort. His grunts punctuate the winter air. My back protests the familiar weight. I hold my ground, pushing harder against the solid oak. The barrel submits. It teeters precariously for a moment before rolling onto its side. With a last, determined shove, we send it lurching into its designated spot, before tipping it upright again outside Mrs Davy's. We both step back, panting. Our breaths are visible, entwining in the early morning frost.

The barrel in position, Mr Russell straightens up and runs a hand through his dishevelled hair. We exchange a quick glance, a silent acknowledgement of the task accomplished, and then I brace myself for the day ahead. Despite the biting cold, the thrill of retelling my story to eager spectators sends a spark of warmth through me. Each clink of a coin, each gasp of astonishment will be a testament to my audacious plunge over the Falls.

I step next to my barrel. My fingers trace the staves. I glance at my manager.

'Remember to smile,' he says. 'Your face is too miserable and old to be liked.'

'Isn't it adorable how you think I need your validation? Now, if you'll excuse me, I have important things to attend to.' I laugh but without humour. He's watching me, waiting for my signal. There's a look of grudging respect on his face. The constant thunder of Niagara fills my ears. We have all the proof that I achieved the feat, and no one expects me to repeat the physical experience. Now its roar feels like a tribute instead, a thunderous applause for the woman who dared to dance with death.

'Quite the piece of craftsmanship,' he mutters, giving the barrel a solid pat. It's the closest he's come to a compliment these last few weeks. It's unexpected. There's been a shift I can't quite grasp – not in a good way – and it grows daily. He wants me to stay at the boarding house and I'm refusing. An unspoken threat simmers. Still, I take his positivity as a good omen for the day ahead.

We begin our routine – laying out the postcards, placing rocks atop to prevent them being swept away, setting up the small replicas of the barrel, readying the signed memoir of my plunge over the Falls – we're charging ten cents a copy. The business of capitalising on survival is as meticulous as the stunt itself. There's also a stereoscope, the Nielson photograph of me in the rowboat, and stereograph cards.

A photographer exits the store. 'If I could get a photo of Mrs Taylor sitting at the table in front of Mrs Davy's.'

I nod, moving to where he indicates. Various advertisements are around me: Fort Erie Races, Cataract Beer, Buffalo Co-operative Brewing Company, a trip to Toronto.

'If you could rest your face on your hand and look off to the right,' he says.

'Make sure to include the sign,' I say, pointing below the table. I like it. *Annie Edson Taylor, Heroine of Horseshoe Falls.* And, *This Is the Barrel which Mrs Taylor went over Niagara Falls.*

The photographer is quick. The shop bell tinkles as he returns inside.

'Ready, Mrs Taylor?' Mr Russell asks, glancing at the line of early arrivals. They're waving again, their eyes wide with anticipation. They've come to see the Queen of the Mist, to hear her tale, and perhaps carry a piece of my audacity home. Still, the bustling tourists blur into a characterless crowd. I miss the familiar faces of Mrs Lapointe, Nora, and Tilda. Their smiles were genuine; their laughter was a balm to my soul.

'As ready as I ever am.' I smooth out the wrinkles on my dress and adjust my feathered hat.

The first customers approach. Their coins clink against the wooden table. A surge of adrenaline rushes from my belly to my throat. It's warm and I embrace it.

'You are welcome, you are welcome, dear ladies and gentlemen,' I begin, my voice carrying over the roar of the Falls. 'Step closer to hear a story of audacity, a tale of a woman and a waterfall in a repurposed pickle jar.' I offer them my most charming smile, turning to my manager and raising an eyebrow.

'Some would say you were in a pickle Mrs Taylor,' Mr Russell says without enthusiasm, yet still the first customers giggle.

Old First Ward,
Buffalo, NY.
February 5th 1902

Dear Mrs Taylor,

I hope this letter finds you in good health and spirits. I regret to inform you that I have been quite ill for the past few weeks, suffering from severe chest congestion that has left me bedridden. As such, I have been unable to attend to my business affairs, including new bookings and correspondence.

Please be assured that as soon as I am well enough to resume my duties, I will be in touch with you regarding new engagements and any outstanding matters. Your patience and understanding during this difficult time are greatly appreciated.

Thank you for your consideration.

Yours sincerely,
Mr F. Russell

Traverse City,
Michigan.
February 18th 1902

Dear Mrs Annie Edson Taylor,

I am writing to inform you of a recent development concerning the Bay City property.

As Mrs Lapointe's cousin and rightful heir, I have come forward to stake my claim on the residence. In concluding the recent inheritance dispute, it has been decided that I will assume ownership and management of the boarding house, effective immediately. Consequently, I must inform you that you will need to vacate the premises by March 3rd, to allow for necessary renovations and administrative changes.

I understand that this notice is abrupt, and I apologise for any inconvenience this may cause. Please know that this decision was not made lightly, and I wish you the best in your future endeavours.

Sincerely,
Emil Lapointe

Bay City Boarding House,
Bay City.
February 28th 1902

Dear Mr Russell,

It is over one month since our last event, over three weeks since you wrote to inform me that you were ill. I've yet to receive response to my previous four letters. I trust your chest concerns are waning and that you're fully recouped. I'm beginning to fear that you have died.

As outlined previously, and given that Mrs Lapointe's cousin came forward with her claim for the boarding house, I've been given notice on this accommodation and must vacate in the next three days. Lolly and Magnus have helped me gain both work and temporary shanty lodgings with a travelling circus, but I am confused regarding missing payments owed by you, to me.

Transience has been a constant companion, a relentless force shaping the course of my existence. I traversed across states and cities, seeking refuge in the temporary nature of employment. Teaching in schools, imparting dancing lessons, I ventured from Texas to New York City, from North Carolina to Tennessee, Alabama, Michigan, each move driven by the necessity to stave off the encroaching tendrils of poverty. Yet now I'm Mrs Annie Edson Taylor. I've not done what no other had the nerve to do, only to become a pauper.

I'm the only person to survive going over Niagara Falls. Do you understand the point I'm making? Poverty should no longer be my companion. This part should be my reward for being daring. Transience has been a constant companion, but I yearn for the stability and warmth of my past. The company of my dear friends, lost but never forgotten, haunts me. Their absence leaves an ache no amount of applause can fill.

Have you news of additional adventures for us both? My barrel and I await instructions.

Yours sincerely,
Annie Edson Taylor

Annie

23rd March 1902

It gets worse. A mere five months since I conquered the Horseshoe Falls and I consider a dimly lit tent refuge from the bustling world outside. It's a cocoon woven from canvas and dust. The scent of damp earth and the faint aroma of medicinal herbs hang in the air. The flickering lantern casts dancing shadows on the tent walls My improvised sign *Annie's Marvellous Medicine Show* rests against my healing table.

Lolly bursts in, her eyes wide with urgency. 'Ready to heal?'

I nod, feeling a surge of determination. Magnet healing – a concept first suggested by Mr Russell, who suggested my plunge over the Falls could have unlocked a unique power within me. Lolly had remembered his words and saw it as another opportunity to sustain us. Now, I must make it real. Here goes nothing.

Magnus carries a woman into the tent. She appears miniature in his arms. He places her on my table. It's Lillian, an aerialist known for her breathtaking acrobatic performances. I watched her performance yesterday. Such incredible strength and agility, particularly on the swinging trapeze. I observed how she captivated the audience. She told a story through the air, but now is sprawled out on a makeshift table. Her face contorts as she clutches her lower back. I place my hand on her shoulder.

'What happened?'

'She fell,' Lolly says. I raise an eyebrow at my bearded friend, and she winks.

I remove my magnets from their cloth wrapping. Small, round and shiny. I allow them to warm in my hand.

'I'm fine,' she says, attempting to sit up but a jolt of pain has her prone on the table again.

'Stay still.' I press my fingers at the base of her spine, and she wriggles. Discomfort, but at least she can still move.

'Lolly said you wrote a memoir,' Lillian says through gritted teeth. 'What's it about?'

I smile, sensing her attempt to distract herself from the pain. 'What do you think I'd write about?'

'Your husband do something interesting?' she guesses.

I shake my head.

'But you wrote a memoir about him?'

'Not quite,' I say.

I fix my eyes on the group of four or five circus folk watching with Lolly and Magnus. Their stare is on Lillian. I doubt any of them see me. Freedom from erotic gaze brings with it loss, perhaps even grief, but there's independence, too. Here, I'm thankful that I can slip quietly in and out of conversations and crowds. I've had my taste of fame, but never expected it would be as fleeting. I'm formulating a new plan here.

This is temporary lodging for the transient. A travelling circus. A place that attracts wanderers and Lillian's been here a week. It's like the boarding house, but different. People stay here until it no longer serves its purpose. I shake my head at those thoughts. The nights spent at the boarding house are far from this experience. Laughter and shared stories were our true healers then. Will I ever stop longing for those simple, heartfelt moments? Outside this small tent, the glorious circus is in full swing. The distant murmur of the crowd's a familiar soundtrack now. The roars of laughter, the gasps of wonder, the thunderous applause – they're a world away from the quiet tranquillity of this tent. Dust swirls in the dim light and Lillian's waiting for me to heal her.

'Ready?' I ask.

The magnets feel warm and unfamiliar in my hands. I grip them tightly. I know I'm not a healer – not by any stretch of the imagination – but Lolly told me that the new residents don't need to see that.

Lillian grunts a delayed reply, her gaze fixed on a corner of the tent. I take a deep breath and place the magnets on her lower back. They sit on her leotard. It feels like I'm performing a charade, playing a part I didn't audition for. Wasn't that what going over Niagara Falls in a barrel was, too? A performance of courage and foolhardiness?

'Feel anything?' I ask, moving the magnets in what I hope is a convincing manner. Lillian grunts again, but this time, there's a hint of relief in her voice.

'Use words,' Lolly says. She's stroking her beard and observing what I do.

'Yeah,' Lillian mutters. 'Feels … good, I think.'

I hide my surprise, keeping my face neutral. Encouraged, I continue the treatment, growing more confident with each passing moment. If I can survive the raging waters of Niagara, surely I can pull off a little magnet therapy?

I move the magnets along Lillian's back. My hands are steady despite the uncertainty. 'You know, Lillian,' I begin, my voice echoing in the quiet tent, 'these magnets remind me of my barrel.'

She grunts, not turning her head to look at me. 'How so?'

She doesn't ask what the barrel might be. I suspect she's not really listening. 'Well,' I say, tracing the path of the injury with the magnet, 'both seem impossible, don't they? Healing an ariel acrobat like you with a couple of magnets, and surviving Niagara Falls in a barrel.'

'You know someone who went over the waterfall in a barrel?' she asks.

A murmur ripples through the onlookers. I smile at them; their eyes wide with curiosity. They see me now. Their interest is piqued, drawn in by the mention of my famed adventure.

'I remember the roar of the water,' I continue, my voice bold and loud.

'You were there?'

I bite my lip and nod. 'I was in the barrel.'

She turns her head. She observes me, wordless.

'The thunderous applause of Niagara as I plunged. It was deafening … terrifying.'

I mimic the motion with the magnets, a swift swooping movement down Lillian's back. She shivers, whether from my words or the magnets, I've no way of telling.

'And yet,' I say, moving the magnets in a slow, circular motion, 'just like these magnets on your back, that barrel carried me. It protected me, shielded me from the violence of the water.'

The tent is silent, everyone hanging on my words. I can see the awe in their eyes, the disbelief giving way to grudging respect.

'Where's your barrel now, then?' she asks.

'With my manager,' I say. 'And here I am.' I finish, pulling the magnets away from Lillian's back. 'The woman who survived the impossible.'

There's a pause, a collective breath held and then released. Lillian sits up, rolling her shoulders. 'Feels better,' she admits, a grudging respect in her eyes.

'Of course it does,' I reply with a wink. 'They don't call me Queen of the Mist for nothing.'

'You know, Annie, maybe you should start charging extra for a side of miracles,' Lolly says, stroking her beard.

I smile. My heart pounds with a mix of triumph and relief. I've no idea what I did there or why it worked.

The crowd beyond the tent roars with applause as the circus reaches its crescendo. But here in this dimly lit tent, amidst the dust and canvas, it seems I've found my own applause. Performer, survivor and now, perhaps, healer.

'If you could leave payment in that hat.' I point to a bowler I found in the circus tent earlier. It's on the floor beside my makeshift healing table. I push my shoulders back and take a deep breath. 'Next,' I say.

Annie's Diary

2nd April 1902

It seems that silence has become my manager's most eloquent response. Magnus and Lolly have moved on. They've left this circus shanty. I've looked for Mr Russell some more. Letters sent to last-known addresses, enquiries made, all met with the deafening absence of a reply.

In such moments of separateness, I can't help but reflect on the broader implications of such disregard. Is it merely a reflection of my worth as an individual, or does it speak to a larger truth about the place of women in this world? Are we destined to be silenced, relegated to the sidelines while our voices are drowned out by the clamour of men?

Yet, even as I grapple with these questions, I find solace in the knowledge that rejection doesn't define me. I'm more than the sum of unanswered letters and unfulfilled promises. I'm a woman of strength and resilience, capable of forging my own path in a world that seeks to confine me to its narrow boundaries.

I'll go and get my barrel. There are still folk who want to meet me – Annie Edson Taylor. Why am I waiting for a man?

Annie

14th April 1902

I'm sniffing my woollen coat as I step off the streetcar. The scent of tobacco clings to it, reminding me of a childhood lost. A whistle sounds. The clatter and hum of its motor trails off behind me and I spin on the spot to find my bearings. The spring weather is closer to winter today, and it's an unseasonably cold morning. I've a long walk ahead of me.

Cobblestones underfoot are slick and uneven. Walking's a tricky dance that needs careful navigation, especially in these high-button boots, but I don't slacken my pace. My right hand clenches tightly around the handle of my basket; the wicker edges press into my palm. The heavy coat had been a Christmas present bestowed by a former boarder. A paying one. She'd said I inspired her. Its weight is reassuring and familiar. It's the nicest piece of clothing I own, and the black buttons gleam under my touch.

A chilly gust sweeps through the street. It's a sharp contrast to the soft warmth of my coat. The brim of my hat wobbles with the breeze and I'm sure its feathers will be bobbing in protest.

Still, the air's chill tinges my cheeks and a sting is building inside my ear. My steps match the rhythmic clatter of horse-drawn carriages as they move. Each carriage, with its ornate designs and polished wood, tells a story of its own. Ferrying affluent ladies in their finery or transporting goods for the bustling businesses that line the street, I nod and smile as they pass. Fleetingly, I wonder if any of the passengers recognise me. Storefronts stand tall, their large windows showcasing an array of goods – from the latest fashions imported from New York or Paris to handcrafted trinkets and freshly baked pastries. My stomach rumbles. The air carries with it a medley of scents: the sweet aroma of fresh bread wafting from a nearby bakery, the tang of fresh produce from the grocer's stall, and the more robust smells of leather and iron from the local blacksmith.

'Hello, Mrs.'

'Nowt fresher.'

'Step inside.'

Shopkeepers – dressed uniformly in aprons and shirtsleeves – shout as I walk past. Each vying for my attention. Their voices blend into one.

Amidst this adult world, though, the joyous laughter and shouts of children playing pierce through. They dart between the carriages and stalls, their games simple yet full of imagination. A group plays hopscotch on a side street, while others chase a rolling hoop with a stick. I think about David. I shake my head. A simpler life echoes in those sounds; one that existed before barrels and waterfalls, before fleeting fame and before grief. Now it's a longing as distant as the retreating streetcar. Life persists.

Still, I miss the days when laughter was a constant companion. Nora's infectious giggle, Mrs Lapointe's hearty chuckle, and Tilda's expression of awe as we shared stories around the boarding house kitchen table. The noise of the city is no match for the comforting sounds of those evenings.

'Mr Russell.' I say his name aloud. It quickens my pace and focus.

I've been trying to reach my manager for two months now. No work for two months, even though he used to assure me that I was his best-earning stunter. Surely my act demands more than just transitory fame? It's not even six months since I was in my barrel. It's not like anyone else has survived the Falls since me. I've a gnawing churn building in my gut, though. Something's not quite right. Perhaps I shouldn't be here, perhaps I should simply wait for him to contact me, but patience isn't one of my virtues. My manager's refusing to communicate with me and so I've come to find out why. I've come to tell him that I'm going to venture alone and make my own bookings.

Rounding the corner of Elmwood Avenue, I hesitate. The stone-clad facades of the buildings loom and cast long shadows over the wet cobblestones. My target is in sight, the building at the end of the row. Its high brick walls dwarf the others. That's where Mr Russell stashed away my barrel after its time on the fairground. Its safety was assured under lock and key.

My heart hammers against my ribcage as I stride closer. My right hand reaches out as I walk, fingers pressing against the rough brick with each step. Steadying me, I trace the grooves of mortar and feel the grit on my fingertips. The hustle and bustle of the city has fallen away, replaced by this district's sombre silence. The only sounds are the distant clanging from the dockyards and the echo of my heeled boots on cobbles in this empty street.

'Mr Russell,' I call, my voice firm. I refuse to play his games anymore. His name bounces off the buildings and the echo returns to me as if mocking. The door is imposing in size; it makes me feel even smaller. Still, I rap my knuckles against the wooden surface and the sound punctuates the quiet street. No response. I wait. A knot of dread coils in my abdomen. I've tried the fairground and was told he'd stopped working there. They suggested I try here. I've nowhere else to check.

The noise of the city, the clatter of the streetcar, the bustle of Buffalo, all seem far removed from this lonely street. I need to get inside. I need to see my barrel. My life seems to have existed in circles of time and I can't shake the feeling that I've looped back to the beginning.

My boots crunch on the path as I look for a different entrance. 'Mr Russell?'

A scuffle of feet against gravel to the left of me. I spin around, squinting against the cold sunlight. A dog sniffs at my ankles, hesitates, then runs away.

'Mrs Taylor?' A familiar voice. It's Martin, a boy who helps Mr Russell with the storing of exhibits.

I step towards him, noticing the mud before I slip. One hand grips the wicker basket, the other's fingers clutch the edges of my skirts; the fabric bunches within my clenched fists. Martin's face is smudged with dirt, his hair matted with grease.

I suck in the air. 'Where's Mr Russell?' My voice is sharp, cutting through the tension.

He hesitates. He draws on a pipe that looks too big for his tiny head. He kicks at a pile of wet mud with his worn boots. 'Dunno.'

'Dunno, or won't tell me?'

Martin shrugs, his eyes fixed on the floor and my stomach drops into my boots.

I stride with a determined gait, shoulders back, and head held high. 'Stop with the lies, boy. Where is he?' The words echo against the brick walls.

His eyes widen, a spark of fear flickering.

'Take that ridiculous pipe out of your mouth.'

He does. He tucks it in his back pocket. 'I … I ain't lying, Mrs Taylor. He … he ain't here.' He chews on his thumbnail. His eyes still refuse to meet mine. He leans forward, picking at a splash of mud on his trousers as if it offends him. 'He's gone, ma'am. Left with the barrel.'

'Left?' I echo, the word tasting like vinegar. 'Left where?'

'On a tour, ma'am. Said he'd show the barrel around. For money.' He looks at me, wide-eyed and innocent, unaware of the blow he's just delivered.

'Where?' The word is screamed; I sound hysterical and the boy quivers. 'I don't care why. I only care where he's taken my barrel.' My voice trembles now with the force of my anger.

'Your barrel…' An echo; he's stalling, deciding whether to tell me the truth.

'Look at me.'

'He … he took it with him.' Martin stares everywhere but at me. I think he might be searching for an escape route.

'Took it with him?' I repeat. I'm struggling to grip hold of his words. What does that even mean? How? Where? Why? 'And where exactly did he go?'

A sigh. 'He … he's on tour, ma'am.' Finally, his eyes meet mine. 'He's taken the barrel on the road, selling tickets for folks to see it, but without … without you.'

The words hit like punches. My barrel – the symbol of my survival, my triumph – taken away by the man I'd entrusted with my career. With my finances. With my future, too. The world spins around me and I reach for the nearest wall to steady myself.

'Without me?' I echo, my voice breaking.

I went over the Falls. I survived, not him. I swear my heart constricts as the reality sinks in. Betrayed. By my manager. The fury and hurt bubble in my abdomen; a tsunami of emotion I'm struggling to keep at bay.

'And when is he due back?' My legs are trembling.

'Don't know, ma'am. He said … he said it might be a while.'

And there it is. The final twist of the knife. Betrayed and left behind. My barrel, my story, my survival – all paraded around for profit, while I stand here. Silenced. No one will remember my voice.

'Robbed of what little I had left,' I say.

The boy murmurs something I can't quite hear.

'Speak up,' I say.

'Er … he said that he paid for the barrel and it's his to do with as he pleases.' He holds up his hands in defence. Does he think I'm going to strike him?

'Go,' I say. He hurries away.

How could he? After everything…

My vision blurs. I can't cry, not here. Not now. It wouldn't be proper for the Queen of the Mist to be seen weeping in public. For the second time in my life – and in just five months – I find myself freefalling. Only this time, I've not got my barrel to protect me.

Part VII: Again Amidst Cascades

'Mrs Taylor's guidance and support shaped me into the woman I am today. Only had funds to shelter for two days, but she insisted I stayed longer. Said I needed to wait till me heart healed proper. I'd no idea she was struggling herself. She always put others first. A heart of gold. That boarding house was the first true home I had.'

Alice Thompson

Annie

26th April 1902

Mr Holleran's one of the few men I still trust. He put me on to the notion of a patron and said Mr Thompson was a true gentleman. Why am I this full of fear, then? I'm shaking like a horse and standing outside a bustling tearoom in Buffalo. For the last thirty minutes I've been trying to convince myself to step inside, and now I'm late for our meeting. There's a knot fully formed in the pit of my stomach. I'm being ludicrous. I'm not being at all Annie Edson Taylor.

I take the newspaper cutting from my pocket, scanning for the part that's relevant.

> *Having experienced the transformative power of opportunity, Mr Thompson is driven by a deep sense of compassion and a desire to give back to those in need. He believes that providing sponsorship and support to individuals facing adversity can empower them to change their lives for the better. Over the years, he's sponsored numerous people, offering them accommodation, financial assistance, and mentorship. He allows them to pursue their dreams and achieve their full potential.*

'There'll be a catch,' I say. 'He'll take advantage of me.' I'm talking to myself, and I bet my face is a mask of discontent. Still, I can't pass up this opportunity. Where's my courage? Sinking at the bottom of the Falls?

Mr Thompson's generosity and philanthropy have earned him a reputation as a benevolent and respected figure in the community.

I shake my head. He's too good to be true. I'm being repetitive.

He is well known for his altruistic deeds, and many people have been touched by his kindness and willingness to help those less fortunate than himself.

'I should go home,' I say.

My face tightens. Home? Do I mean that place that's currently imaginary? I don't have a home and I don't have a barrel, either. My fingers form into a fist. Decision made. I push the door to the tearoom, the bell tinkling, and step inside.

'I'm here to see a Mr Thompson.' I scan the room to try and guess what this gentleman might look like. The polished wooden floors gleam under the muted glow of overhead lamps. The walls are painted in a gentle pastel shade. Modest wooden tables are draped with white lace tablecloths that hang just above the floor.

'Beautiful,' I say, pointing at a small porcelain vase holding fresh wildflowers. It sits atop the table nearest me. This place isn't for poor people.

'This way.' The waitress swerves past chairs – cushioned and upholstered with floral patterns. They're neatly tucked under the tables and awaiting patrons. Two customers turn to look at me. I nod, and smile. They sit in a quiet cluster. Ladies in wide-brimmed hats, adorned with ribbons and feathers. A smile, a nod in return, before they return their attention to each other. I watch how quickly they become engrossed in a whispered conversation. Their gloved hands handle teacups, and the gentle clink of china.

'Ma'am?' It's the waitress again. 'Come on.' She's several steps ahead, waving for me to hurry up.

The grandmother clock in the corner strikes three and I shake my head. 'I'm so very late.' I quicken my pace as I follow the waitress' path. 'Sorry, sorry,' I say as I bang customers in my attempt to veer around chairs.

Finally making my way through the clamour of the main tearoom, I'm ushered into a separate space. I hesitate in the doorway; it's a sanctuary amidst the bustle. A wood-panelled dining haven with dark grains that reflect years of polish and care. At the room's heart stands a regal dining table – set for six – with polished silverware, pristine china, and gleaming crystal glasses that catch the light. A distinguished-looking gentleman sits at the head of the table. He's engrossed in his newspaper. His posture is relaxed, yet there's an air of authority about him. The gentle strains of music waft through the air, perhaps from a distant gramophone. I think it might be Tchaikovsky. It's a subtle accompaniment, but enough to give the room an aura of refinement.

'What is this place? I ask.

If he's startled, he hides it. Mr Thompson laughs.

'A buried gem.' He stands as I approach – there's an urgency in his movement – causing his shadow to stretch and leap against the white wall. 'I feared you'd decided against meeting.'

As I reach the table, he extends a hand, and his welcoming smile stretches from one ear to the other. His hair's white and his intense gaze makes me momentarily nervous; I like him instantly, though.

'The Queen of the Mist, in the flesh. Welcome.'

'Mr Thompson,' I say, offering a firm handshake. I grip tightly, looking directly into his eyes. 'Apologies for the tardiness. Call me Annie.'

His eyes pierce as he examines me. They might be the brightest blue I've ever seen. His neatly trimmed silver beard gives him an air of authority, yet kindness and warmth radiate from him. He's a tall, distinguished gentleman in his late sixties; a self-made businessman who's said to have accumulated considerable wealth over the years through his various entrepreneurial ventures.

'Do sit.' He gestures to a chair opposite him. 'Do you enjoy music, Annie?'

'Very much,' I reply, my voice softening as I wave my hand as if conducting. 'There was always music at the boarding house. We'd sing and dance, sometimes late into the evening.'

'Well,' he says with a warm smile, 'perhaps we can bring some of that joy back into your life.'

He motions to a nearby attendant, who nods and leaves the room. The music swells, filling the room with a lively waltz. For a minute or two, we sit in silence, simply enjoying the melody. It isn't awkward at all.

'The moment I heard about your incredible feat at Niagara… I must say, I was devastated not to have witnessed it.' He rubs the back of his neck. 'I understand that you're in need of assistance.'

Straight to business. I like him even more.

'I have a manager, a Mr Russell,' I say. 'I *had*…'

He nods for me to continue.

'He is a snivelling worm of a man and has absconded with my barrel.'

A pause. His lips twitch. I'm convinced he contemplates laughing. '*The* barrel?' he finally asks.

I nod. '*The* barrel.

'And you require my assistance to…?'

'Find my former manager, retrieve said barrel and, perhaps, offer stern *words* to prevent future misappropriation.'

He laughs then, rubbing his belly as he does. 'Well, that truly is the most unusual request I have yet received.'

I wait. He bounces his fingers off his chin as he contemplates my bid. Seconds pass.

'I am willing,' he says. 'Consider my participation in *the* barrel's retrieval a token of my admiration for your courage.'

I clap my hands in delight. 'I'm incredibly grateful for your generosity,' I say, my voice wavering slightly. It seems that my control over my emotions isn't as it was before my plunge. We've not even ordered drink or food and already he's offered me everything I hoped he would. 'I accept your agreement with sincere appreciation, but is there a catch?' I'm unable to shake off my nerves and suspicion.

Mr Thompson holds up his palms in surrender. 'I've experienced first-hand the struggles and hardships that come with poverty,' he says. 'Yet through a combination of hard work, determination, and a few lucky breaks, I've managed to rise above the circumstances assigned to me at birth. I've built a successful life.' His voice is calm.

I nod, still wary.

He smiles. 'When you know me, you'll understand.'

I return the smile. It appears that what Mr Holleran told me is true. That despite his success and the admiration he receives from others, Mr Thompson remains grounded and humble. Perhaps he is a gentleman, in the truest sense of the word.

'I live by the principles that have guided me throughout this life,' he says, then pauses. 'You know…' He leans in conspiratorially, 'there was a time when I, too, did something quite daring.'

'Oh?' I raise an eyebrow, intrigued.

'Yes.' He chuckles. 'I once climbed the clock tower in the middle of town on a whim. Nearly gave my mother a heart attack when she found out.'

We both laugh, the tension easing away. For a moment, it feels like we're old friends sharing stories rather than two people bound by business.

'I'm sorry,' I say, holding up a palm in surrender. 'For doubting your motivation.'

Mr Thompson reaches over, squeezing my hand in reassurance. 'I treat everyone with respect and empathy, regardless of their social standing or background, Annie,' he says, patting my hand before withdrawing his. 'I see myself in you. But I do have one condition.'

'Ah, there it is,' I quip with a smirk. 'The fine print.' I cross and then recross my legs. My ankle bangs against the table's leg.

'Two conditions actually.' His grin is broad and contagious.

I nod for him to continue.

'My first is that you stay with me while we solve this riddle.' A pause and I bob my head enthusiastically again. 'My final condition is that if you ever do another daredevil stunt, then you tell me in advance.'

My exhalation is loud. He laughs.

'That way I can either talk you out of it or come along and watch.'

'That's all?' I say and, this time, he bobs his head enthusiastically.

'Do we have an agreement?'

SCANDAL UNFOLDING

DAREDEVIL ANNIE TAYLOR ALLEGES MANAGER STOLE HISTORIC BARREL

BUFFALO EVENING NEWS - MAY 27, 1902

In an astonishing turn of events, our beloved local heroine, Mrs Annie Edson Taylor, finds herself embroiled in controversy and claims of betrayal. The 63-year-old – famed for her audacious plunge over the roaring Niagara Falls in a wooden barrel in October 1901 – is now battling storms off the waters.

Mrs Taylor's manager, a former circus promoter named Mr Russell, who was entrusted with the custody of her feat's key symbol – the iconic barrel – stands accused of a grave act of treachery. According to Mrs Taylor, Mr Russell has absconded with the barrel, capitalising on her daring exploit in an unsanctioned tour. It would appear that ill luck is a persistent follower of our Queen of the Mist.

Emerging from her quiet Buffalo lodgings, Mrs Taylor's outrage was palpable. The barrel, she says, symbolised more than her survival, it was a testament to her audacious triumph over the Falls. Without it, she is bereft of the tangible proof of her historic endeavour.

This news has shocked the city, with Mrs Taylor's patron, Mr Thompson, expressing his deep disappointment in the turn of events. 'We had faith in Mr Russell to honour the trust Mrs Taylor placed in him,' said Mr Thompson, adding that he shared Mrs Taylor's sense of betrayal.

This unforeseen scandal has cast a long shadow over the legacy of our city's recent heroine, leaving her fans shocked and disheartened. However, Mrs Taylor, who stared down the perilous Niagara, is far from defeated. As she bravely proclaimed, 'I faced the Falls, I'll face this, too.'

A full investigation is expected to follow.

Annie

28th May 1902

One month living here, and the study in Mr Thompson's sprawling home feels safe. I don't think I've seen a piece of furniture that shines quite so much as those in this room. It's fast become a cocoon of quietude and order amidst the perpetual chaos of my life. Not today, though. Papers are strewn over the mahogany desk.

Equally, Mr Thompson – until now a model of composure – looks ruffled as he paces. He arranged a time for us to meet in his study, insisting we needed to strategise and plot our next move. He's just suggested that I 'perhaps forget' about the barrel.

I look around his room and it's clear that, in this study alone, he has an abundance of precious and valuable items.

'If I asked you to close your eyes, could you name every exquisite thing in here?' I ask.

'Annie, dear, that's not what I'm—'

'I only have that barrel. That's it. That's my only exquisite item.'

'And he'll say he paid for it.'

'I've explained that he supplied the initial funds, but I paid that money back to him. By going over the Falls. He knows that was our arrangement,' I say. 'My design, my stunt, my barrel.' My tone is firm. I'm repeating myself.

He hesitates, then he shuffles the documents on his desk and pulls out a piece of paper. He perches his spectacles on the bridge of his nose and reads. 'I request that you remain calm.' Our eyes meet and he chuckles; the notion of associating me with calmness is ludicrous. He regains his composure and breathes in. 'There's been word from Chicago.' His eyes barely look up from the telegram in his hand.

'And?' I'm on my feet. Excitement.

'My contact there spotted an advertisement in the local Gazette. Russell's going to exhibit the barrel at a sideshow, charging people to see it. Next month.' A pause and I nod enthusiastically for him to continue. 'Seems he's part of a show troupe known as The Game Keeper Company.'

Chicago. A twinge of disappointment flickers, but it's quickly quashed by a surge of determination. 'So we know where he will be,' I say. I take a sip of tea, eyes glancing at him over the porcelain. 'We should act.'

'Calm, Annie,' he says, still reading the telegram.

'Were you not going to tell me?'

Mr Thompson shakes his head, sinking into his leather-seated captain's chair. 'I considered that giving the man additional attention…' A pause and I wave my hand for him to continue, but he refuses to meet my gaze. His eyes are locked on the telegram.

'The man's a crook. We can't let him get away with it.' I stare at my patron, demanding an answer, but he's still not looking at me. 'I'm exhausted by the notion that a man assumes he can take whatever he wants from a woman.'

A gentle bob of his head. A sigh. 'I've hired a private investigator,' he says.

I'm pacing his room and unease is swirling in my gut. I'm at the mercy of too many men – for money, for employment, for the return of my property.

'Someone who is tracking Russell discreetly. Meaning that, if he moves the barrel again or not to Chicago, we'll be able to keep tabs on him … without him knowing.'

'I suppose that's an acceptable course of action,' I say, sounding ungrateful, when really I'm experiencing a twirl of shame and thankfulness. My fingers fiddle with my dress' cuffs as I pace. I can't keep any part of me still. I want to confront Mr Russell immediately, to let the world know that he's a thief. 'Do you know where he is now?'

'Rochester.' Mr Thompson nods. 'And there's more…' He pauses, and I hold my breath. 'It seems our man tends to follow a certain travel pattern, visiting cities where he's previously experienced success.'

I exhale. 'Well, isn't that convenient. A travelling snake-oil salesman with a predictable routine. How utterly surprising.' My brow furrows at this revelation. Still, a pattern, that's something we could potentially exploit to our advantage. 'So…' I'm still pacing and Mr Thompson's watching me intently. I wonder if he's ever met another quite like me. He's a kind soul and I confuse him. 'We have his trail, and we know his modus operandi.'

'Yes.' Mr Thompson bobs his head as he steeples his fingers. 'We're getting closer. We just need to stay patient and vigilant.' He stands and moves to a decanter, pouring himself a drink. He doesn't offer me one.

I raise an eyebrow, feigning nonchalance. 'Well, I suppose that's one way to stay patient,' I say, gesturing towards the alcohol. 'Though I've always found a good book to be a more sober alternative.'

He laughs, raising his glass to me and then taking a sip.

Patient and vigilant. Ridiculous notions, and easier said than done when your life's greatest achievement has been stolen. Still, I understand the necessity. We've the beginnings of a plan, and that's more than I had earlier today. He's given me hope.

'I understand your anger.' Mr Thompson sits down, leaning back in his chair again, swirling the glass of amber whisky in his hand. 'That man's like a three-cornered tart and full of puff.'

'I want to squash the worm under my foot.' I stomp on the spot, then think perhaps I see fear in Mr Thompson's eyes. 'It's not just about the barrel. It's about what it signifies.' My fingers have curled into fists and I'm digging my nails into my flesh. I'm trying to curb the erupting anger. 'That barrel's my proof, Mr Thompson.' There's desperation creeping into my voice. 'It's my ticket to future lectures and talks. Without it, I'm just another madwoman telling tall tales.' I pause to regain my composure. 'Folk won't believe me without that barrel.'

'That's not true.'

'With respect, men tend not to believe women. We're either mad, hysterical or emotional. Sometimes all three.'

'Not all men are—'

'Enough men. It's always been that way. Has it not?' I'm angry. Frustration gushes from me like water over the Falls.

He sighs, setting the glass down on his desk.

'I'm a stunter.' I shouldn't be shouting.

'Yes, yes.' He lifts his hand as if to wave me on.

'A daredevil. A heroine.'

He claps his hands together. 'Yes, Annie, you are,' he says, leaning closer. 'Let's squash that worm together.'

Annie

2nd June 1902

Of course, I find myself in Rochester. There was no way I would risk my former manager altering his plans for Chicago. Strike while the iron is hot, as they say. That's the only way to get things done. The carnival is a spectacular explosion of life. It's raucous. It sprawls. I think it might stretch endlessly.

'It's a cacophony of sights, sounds, and scents,' I say. No one listens to me.

Mr Thompson will consider my impatience improper, but I doubt he'll be surprised. I'm spinning on the spot, just below the entrance's huge sign. A riot of colours encompasses me. Brightly painted stalls and tents are pitched side by side. Vibrant banners flutter in the breeze. Twirling dancers in layered skirts of every hue, jesters with jingling bells, and mysterious fortune-tellers draped in shawls – they all beckon, they all tease. I feel at home here.

'Showtime,' I say, my fingers forming into a fist.

My stomach grumbles. I've not eaten since yesterday. Now the air's thick with the mouth-watering aroma of carnival treats. The buttery scent of freshly popped corn wafts through the lanes. It competes with the sugary allure of cotton candy and caramel apples. Nearby, a vendor sings the praises of his hot roasted chestnuts.

'Can't think about my stomach,' I say, taking a step into the crowd.

The constant hum of chatter envelops me. It's punctuated by spontaneous bursts of laughter and the occasional shriek from thrill-seekers trying out the rickety rides. No choice but to move with the pack. The melancholic tune of a calliope provides a beat. Its nostalgic notes weave through the sounds of excitement. Mr Thompson would argue that I shouldn't be here, but I'd offer that he's incorrect. This is exactly where I should be.

I stride forward. Picking up pace. It seems the balmy evening has driven people from their homes. They hurry around me but – without my barrel – I'm invisible again. Their laughter and chatter offer a strange backdrop to my tight knot of determination. It's wound into a ball in my chest. My cheeks will be the reddest they've ever been.

My breath catches. I spot it.

My barrel.

It's perched grandiosely on a makeshift stage. My barrel. Not his. That wiggly little worm of a manager. Its familiar hoops of Kentucky oak gleam in the afternoon sunlight. My name's still written on it, though. Why? That makes no sense. And why is it so polished? That it's battered and torn is part of my story. Part of its journey.

Clusters of people mill around my barrel. I understand why. It's as enticing and beautiful as the first day I laid eyes on it. Their voices brim with curiosity and disbelief.

'Did she really…?'

'In this barrel?'

'Are they married?'

'Over the Falls?'

'He's handsome.'

'She's full of luck.'

The questions and compliments flutter around like startled birds. The thrill is contagious.

'Mr Russell!' I shout. I wave.

He's at the centre of the crowd and I don't think he hears me. The picture of ease and charm. All smiles as he strokes spectators' arms, charming and entertaining them, basking in their curiosity, making each of them feel important. His tailored suit lends him an air of authority, and his smile is as captivating as ever. The audience practically swoon with every word he says. He's reeling them in. He's ensnaring them into his net. He can hear the jingle of the coins in their pockets. He talks animatedly, gesturing to the barrel behind him.

A woman moves next to him. Who is she? He places an arm around her. A tailored bodice with a high collar, adorned with delicate lace or embroidery. She looks the part. She's all smiles and fawning. Her skirt's floor-length, with a slight train, accentuating her slender waist and flowing with every step she makes around the platform. Completing her ensemble is a wide-brimmed hat adorned with feathers. It's perched atop her carefully styled hair. She radiates sophistication and poise. Smiling and nodding to her audience, she waves her gloved hand. I'm intrigued. Who is she and why does she keep touching my barrel?

I hold my breath and inch my way through the gathered crowd. How could he do this to me? How could he steal from me? Did I think he was a friend? No. Never a friend. Did I ever like him. He's smiling that confident smile. He's selling my bravery as his own.

'Thief!' I call, raising my voice above the crowd's hum. People turn to look at me. I smile at them. I wave. They're my audience now, too. Their expressions range from surprise to annoyance. Mr Russell's heard me this time. I watch him searching the crowd.

His eyes meet mine. A flicker of recognition, followed by a knowing smirk. He doesn't look shocked or concerned. On the contrary, he appears almost pleased and calm. 'Mrs Lapointe,' he says, sweeping an arm in a flourish. 'What brings you to Rochester? Have you come to hear about Annie's adventures with Niagara Falls?'

'Lapointe? You imbecile,' I say. Has he lost his mind? How has he forgotten my name? It's on the barrel right next to him. 'You know who I am.'

The crowd parts, their curious eyes now trained on the confrontation before them. I grip my skirts and step onto the stage. Me, him, the barrel, and the beautiful woman.

Was this my plan? I shrug my shoulders. It's begun, and there's no turning back now.

'Mr Thieving Scoundrel Russell,' I say, stepping forward. I wag a finger at him. My hands shake though. I clench them into fists, hoping no one notices. 'You must return my barrel.'

A gasp. It's the crowd and his beautiful companion in unison.

The sound that emerges from his mouth is nothing short of a scoff. He stands still, hands on hips. A pause. I wait.

'Your barrel?' He laughs as though I've just performed a slapstick routine. 'Is this your barrel…' He moves to it and strokes the oak. 'The barrel paid for by my hard-earned money?'

'Yes, but—'

'You dare to call me a thief?'

The crowd boos. Roasted nuts hit my nose. Someone has thrown them. They bounce off my chest and shoulders, too. I turn to the gathering, searching for the culprit and am met with a sea of angry faces.

'We had an agreement,' I say. 'It's my story, my adventure.' I try to keep my voice steady; that doesn't work. My emotions have escaped. This is not unfolding as I practised in my head.

'Oh, an agreement, you say?' He smirks. He's playing a game, and the rules are entirely his. 'Doesn't ring a bell, I'm afraid. Can I see the documents?'

'I have testimonies.' I rummage in my handbag and pull out the letters I've collected. 'Newspaper men, a captain, a first mate, a—'

'They are not documents,' he says. 'There is no evidence that you didn't write those yourself.'

'And photographs of me next to *my* barrel.'

'Any tourist could have those taken.' He laughs. 'Many did.'

My cheeks flush – I imagine them, purple now – both from the biting wind and my rising anger. 'You're exploiting me, Mr Russell. This is my barrel, my feat. You can't simply steal it.'

He holds up his hands, as if to protect himself. 'You're hysterical, Mrs Lapointe.' He's calm. Infuriatingly calm.

'I'm Annie Edson Taylor.' I scream the words.

'*I'm* Annie Edson Taylor.' The beautiful woman steps forward, waving her hand in the air. Is she performing? She looks vaguely familiar. I've seen her face somewhere…

The crowd stirs. Whispers weave through the sea of people. Their faces are etched with scepticism and disbelief. A woman confronting a man, let alone a woman of my age. It's outlandish. Are they scared of me? Do they fear for their lives?

'*I'm* Annie,' I say. 'Not *her*.'

'Go away,' someone shouts.

'Didn't come here to see this mad woman,' another says.

'Look at her hair.'

'She really is hysterical.' Another one.

'Lock her up.'

Why am I crying? I'm distraught. I'm frustrated. Bewildered, too. I'm standing on a makeshift stage and frozen to the spot.

'Ladies, gentlemen.' Mr Russell raises his voice, opening his arms wide. He's a seasoned performer. 'I apologise for this spectacle. It seems Mrs Lapointe here is a little … disoriented. Age does things to a woman's mind, after all.' He's played his best card. 'The poor woman's confused. If we could all applaud her … perhaps she'll leave the platform.'

'Your attempt to belittle me is as transparent as your understanding of my capabilities,' I say.

Laughter. Mocking. Cruel cheers resonate through the crowd. I feel myself stranded on an unfamiliar shore. I'm displaced again. My knees quiver under my skirt. Perspiration dampens my neck. Tears skulk at the corners of my eyes. Still, I've no barrel. I've no proof.

'Mrs Lapointe,' he says, turning back to me, his voice dripping with feigned sympathy. 'Perhaps it's best if you go home and rest. Leave these matters to the men folk.'

The crowd cheers and Mr Russell turns back to them. He waves and then applauds their support. He's relishing their amusement and I'm frozen to the spot. Dumbfounded. 'After all,' he says, patting my barrel, 'who would believe that a woman my grandmother's age could survive this ordeal?'

'The newspapers reported—'

'That Mrs Taylor was forty-three years old. Does *this* woman look like our Queen of the Mist?'

A fresh wave of laughter washes over me. It fills my ears and my mind. The ridiculousness of the situation dawns on me. If they had to believe a woman could survive a plunge over the Falls, of course she'd be younger and beautiful. No one trusts me. They're not listening.

'That's right,' Mr Russell says, his voice loud and clear. He leans against my barrel, with his hands in his pockets. His shirt sleeves are pushed up his tanned forearms. He's entirely at ease. 'The beautiful Annie here was the one who conquered the falls. In this barrel. That hysterical old woman wants to steal her achievement.'

I can hardly hear the cheers and applause over the pounding in my ears. He's stolen the story. My story. My voice. He's hired someone younger, prettier, better, to pretend to be me. Why am I shocked?

It hits me. I recognise her photograph from the newspaper article. No moustache or warts in real life. 'Martha. That's Martha Wagenfuhrer,' I say, wagging my finger towards her. 'She navigated the rapids and whirlpools. Not *my* Falls.'

Martha winks, then laughs.

With a final, helpless glance at the smirking Mr Russell, I turn, striding away from the jeers and laughter echoing behind me.

'Don't mind me,' I call back over my shoulder, my voice laced with anger. I swipe at my tears with my fingers. 'Age might be a sign of time passing, but dignity? That's something you can't take away, no matter how hard you try.'

Annie

6th June 1902

Mr Edwards clears his throat. 'From what you've explained, Mrs Taylor, you had a verbal agreement with Mr Russell. He would manage your affairs and profits from the exhibitions, yes?' He doesn't look at me as he speaks, instead his fingers lightly skim the papers.

The wood-panelling is as stifling as my corset. The smells of aged wood, musky books and cigar smoke are heavy in the air of Mr Thompson's library. I sit across from the stern-faced Mr Edwards, a reputable attorney in Buffalo. The austere set of his features are softened only slightly by the spectacles perched precariously on his nose.

I give a curt nod, but he doesn't see. His seriousness has me stifling a giggle. I worry about my maturity. He looks at me then, waiting for a voiced response, and I nod again. 'Yes,' I say. 'And he paid for the barrel too. But the agreement was that I'd be the one to exhibit it. Not him. Plus, it was my understanding that he would take the cost of the barrel from the profits.'

'And you're saying he's been withholding a large percentage of the proceeds from you?'

I nod again. 'I received two-hundred dollars for appearing at the Pan-American Exposition and another two-hundred for the lectures I gave. After that he started paying me about fifteen per cent of what was earned.' My voice remains firm and steady, a mask of strength that conceals the grief weighing heavy on my heart.

Mr Edwards sits back heavily in his chair, and it creaks under the strain.

'And you didn't realise?' That's Mr Thompson. He's shaking his head.

'I was too trusting. Thought he was my ally in all this.'

Mr Edwards sighs. I'd describe his expression as pained. His spectacles have been set aside now, and he's reviewing a stack of papers with focused intent. He pauses, rubbing his eyelids with his fingertips and then pinches the bridge of his nose.

'Mrs Taylor, while the deceit is clear, the fact that he funded the barrel complicates matters. However, the verbal agreement and his subsequent actions do lend weight to your claim.'

From the corner of my eye, Mr Thompson shifts in his chair. His unease mirrors my own. He's been the silent supporter, the quiet investor, a kind man, but it's shifted slightly to the right. My little trip four days ago did that.

'Mr Thompson told you not to go to Rochester,' Mr Edwards says and my sponsor refuses to meet my eyes. 'Yet you disobeyed him.'

I scoff, my anger simmering beneath the surface. 'So now I'm taking orders from Mr Thompson, am I?' I say, my tone sharp and biting. 'Forgive me if I missed the proclamation declaring him king of my decisions. Last time I checked, I was the mistress of my own fate.'

'You deliberately—'

I raise my eyebrows, daring him to continue. He looks away. Another man who seems to think he knows what's best for me? I need not to explode. The rage bubbles in my gut though. I'm property, just like my barrel.

'Edwards, what are we looking at here?' Mr Thompson breaks my spiral. His voice is deep and calm, unlike the rage that's formed a bubble around my being. 'In terms of time, options and costs?'

Mr Edwards replaces his glasses and leans back, folding his hands in front of him. 'We swore out a warrant for the arrest of Mr Russell this morning. Mrs Taylor charges that Russell has stolen her barrel in which she made her famous journey.' A pause and both Mr Thompson and I nod. My foot is poised and ready to squash that worm. 'Still, a case like this … it could drag on for months, even years. As for costs, between court fees, my services, investigations … it will be expensive.'

The room falls into a tense silence. The figures he's subtly hinting at, the time he's predicting, it's daunting. Is it unspoken that they consider this a waste of their time and money? Still, I remain quiet, holding my nerve. The echo of the Falls is in my mind; my barrel, my proof, in the hands of that betrayer.

Mr Thompson looks to Mr Edwards. A pause. They're communicating wordlessly. Mr Thompson turns to me and gives me a bob of his head. It's a silent show of support.

'Mrs Taylor,' Mr Edwards begins. His voice is measured, as he shuffles through a stack of papers again. 'I know some *suitable* men … let's call them workers…'

'Workers?' I say and he nods.

'Who have located your barrel and await a decision.'

His words stir a strange mix of satisfaction and unease within me. 'Go on,' I say, my gloved hands clasping and unclasping in my lap.

Mr Edwards removes his spectacles again, setting them aside, his gaze meeting mine. 'I believe we stand an excellent chance of those workers *retrieving* your barrel.'

There's no air left in this room; only words and cigar smoke linger. I muster up a nod, meeting his serious gaze with my own determined one.

'They'll steal it back?' I ask, and then a playful smile dances on my lips. I turn to Mr Thompson and he smiles, too. I understand. I clap my hands with delight.

'Can I join in the robbery?'

'No,' the two men say in unison.

'You would be recognised, and the legal implications would be…' Mr Edwards scribbles notes.

I chuckle, shaking my head. 'Imagine that, a sixty-three-year-old woman attempting a barrel theft. I'd make the headlines again!'

'This is a serious matter,' Mr Edwards says. The pen drops from his hand and rolls across the desk. He makes a grab for it but is unsuccessful. I watch the pen fall to the rug.

'That is not the kind of headline I encourage,' Mr Thompson says. He's smiling though.

'Then I'll stick to being invisible until my barrel makes its grand return.' A pause. 'It will return, won't it?'

'On my word,' Mr Thompson says.

'We are all in agreement?' Mr Edwards asks. He's observing our exchange. His voice and face are stern.

'Let's set those glorious *workers* to work,' I say, with a wink that surprises even me.

Mr Thompson raises his glass in a toast. 'To justice.'

'And to thievery done right,' I add.

The Western Union Telegraph Company June 10th 1902
From: Chicago
To: Mr Thompson, Bay City

GRAND HUNT UNDERWAY. STOP.
MEETING TONIGHT WITH PARTNERS. STOP.
GOOD NEWS EXPECTED SOON. STOP.
LIONS PROVE TRICKY. STOP.
STOP.

The Western Union Telegraph Company June 13th 1902
From: Chicago
To: Mr Thompson, Bay City

EAGLE SECURED. STOP.
OUR FEATHERED FRIEND SAFE. STOP.
FLIGHT TO NIAGARA SOON. STOP.
KEEP KETTLE READY. STOP.
STOP.

The Western Union Telegraph Company June 16th 1902
From: Chicago
To: Mr Thompson, Bay City

PACKAGE EN ROUTE. STOP.
DELIVERY BY DAYBREAK. STOP.
CELEBRATIONS EXPECTED. STOP.
PREPARE TEA AND BISCUITS. STOP.
STOP.

MYSTERY SURROUNDS THE RETURN OF FAMOUS NIAGARA BARREL

THE BUFFALO GAZETTE - JUNE 17, 1902

In a bizarre turn of events, the iconic barrel used by Mrs Annie Edson Taylor in her historic plunge over Niagara Falls has mysteriously reappeared.

The barrel, which had been missing for several months, amidst accusations and confusion over its ownership, was discovered early this morning by two unidentified residents walking close to the viewing deck at Niagara Falls. Authorities were promptly notified, and the barrel was recovered with no sign of damage. It had been cleverly concealed behind a rocky outcrop, nestled in a crevice overlooking the thundering cascade, as if waiting for its courageous occupant to return.

Mrs Taylor, formerly known as The Queen of the Mist, who had been hoping for the return of her cherished barrel, expressed her bewilderment upon hearing the news. 'I have no idea how my barrel ended up back there,' she stated. 'Yet it is a true miracle. I am thrilled that it will, once again, be in my rightful possession.'

Her former manager, Mr Frank Russell, had been touring with the barrel and a former stunter portraying Mrs Taylor. A warrant for his arrest had been sworn. Mr Russell has refused to comment on the unexpected turn of events. However, sources close to the situation speculate that his inability to pursue the matter further, allegedly due to legal complications and veiled threats from unknown sources, has left him seething with frustration.

The sudden reappearance of the barrel has reignited public interest in both the stunt and the controversy surrounding its disappearance. We are told that there is to be no further investigation and the truth behind this perplexing mystery will remain elusive.

Only time will tell what secrets the barrel may hold, and what revelations may yet come to light, but for now, the return of Mrs Taylor's barrel reminds us of her triumphant story. It is a persisting symbol of resilience and perseverance in the face of adversity, and we eagerly anticipate the tales that Annie Edson Taylor – the daring adventurer herself – will share with the world. Her storytelling prowess has captivated audiences before, and now, with the barrel back in her possession, the public eagerly awaits the opportunity to hear her firsthand account of bravery and survival.

Annie

18th June 1902

A blast of summer heat hits me as I step outside Mr Thompson's house in Buffalo. I pause, removing my hat and shaking my hair loose. It's untamed. It's free. As am I. I close my eyes, tilting my face in the direction of the sun. The heavy door clicks behind me with a sense of finality. I open my eyes. I smile.

'I did it.'

There's no one here. No one to share this moment. Yet, saying the words aloud makes it all seem real. I want to jump and punch the air. I don't, though. Instead, I stay as still as a statue, smiling my biggest and widest smile.

'It's over,' I say. 'I have my barrel again.'

Sunlight bounces off the cobblestones, rendering everything with an unflinching clarity that mimics how I'm feeling inside. My voice was heard. Mr Thompson listened. They stole back my barrel. Life is good. I think about the telegrams, each one more thrilling than the last, and how Mr Thompson and I giggled like schoolchildren.

Squinting against the glare, I start down the granite steps. The heels of my boots click against the stone. The city doesn't pause for my small victory. Buffalo moves on. Its rhythm is as unchanging as the path of the Niagara. Horse-drawn carriages clatter by, their riders indifferent to my little drama. Ladies chatter as they pass, their parasols bobbing like delicate mushrooms amidst the bustle. Street vendors shout out, their cries braiding into the city's complex soundscape. Each comforts me. Each brings me additional joy.

As I walk, a group of children playing nearby catch sight of me. One of them, a little girl with bright eyes and a wide smile, runs up to me, clutching a handful of wildflowers.

'Are you the lady who went over the Falls in a barrel?' she asks, eyes wide with wonder.

I nod, crouching down to her level. 'I am.'

'You're so brave,' she says, thrusting the flowers into my hands. 'These are for you.'

I laugh, accepting the flowers. 'Thank you, dear. That's very kind of you.' She rushes off, waving but not turning to me again. It's simple, pure happiness that warms my heart.

'Mrs Taylor,' a voice calls from behind me.

I turn. He's a young man; spectacles perched precariously on the bridge of his nose, tie askew. He has paper clutched in one hand and a fountain pen in the other. I don't recognise him. He jogs to catch up.

'Clarence Tremblay, *Buffalo News*,' he says. 'How does it feel, Mrs Taylor?' He bends over, panting. I keep walking. 'Justice being served, and your barrel being *found* yesterday?' He's fishing to find out what happened with my barrel. He's a third of my age and still he struggles to keep up with my strides.

I hesitate for a moment. There's much that I'd like to say, but instead I bounce the words inside my head first.

'It's not about feelings,' I say, tucking my hair behind my ear. I think about putting my hat back on but decide against it. 'It's about right and wrong. It's about reclaiming what's mine.'

His nib scratches against the paper. 'Did you arrange for the barrel to be stolen from Mr Russell?'

A slight beat; does he notice? 'Look at me, Clarence,' I say. I laugh from my stomach, shaking my head. 'I'm almost sixty-four. An elderly woman. Do I look like I have the strength and determination to steal a barrel?'

The reporter hesitates, his expression sombre. He tilts his head, his eyes narrow as he looks me up and down. He hesitates and then he shakes his head.

'Is that all?' I say.

He panics. He flips over his paper frantically. Looking for notes made in preparation.

'I do have a request,' I say, using a sickly-sweet tone. 'Perhaps you could write in your newspaper that if anyone were to try and spirit my barrel away from me again…'

He waits, he nods, pen poised.

'They'll end up with a chunk of lead in their rear.'

He gasps. Too shocked by my impropriety to write down what I've said.

'Good day, Clarence.' I smile what might be my happiest smile ever. I'm sure I sparkle with genuine delight. With a final bob of my head to the reporter, I turn and continue my walk away.

Part VIII: Falls' Echoes Fade

'I've never forgotten her storytelling and how it transported us women to faraway lands. In Mrs Taylor's care, I felt safe and supported; feelings I'd not had before. Folk underestimated her. Not me, though. She was full of magic. All she wanted was for us women to heal. And we did … thanks to her.'

Mary Landry

Niagara County Infirmary,
Lockport,
New York.
April 29th 1921

Dear Mrs Matilda Forster,

I trust this letter finds you well. My name is Dr Matthew Hoffman, the doctor here at the Niagara County Infirmary and I write to you with a heavy heart.

Mrs Annie Edson Taylor, who has been under our care since February 23rd of this year, passed away quietly in her sleep today, April 29, 1921. After being transferred here from Niagara Falls Memorial Hospital, her health declined steadily. Her spirit seemingly dimmed along with her eyesight. Annie, as you might not have known, had been battling with blindness in the later stages of her life.

Among Annie's sparse belongings, we found a bundle of letters, all penned by your hand. Each one was carefully kept; evidence of a bond that remained strong despite time and distance. They were preserved within a book. The blue cover is worn, but it feels important that I send 'The Blue Fairy Book' to you, too. Your words, I believe, brought her a great deal of comfort in challenging times. I hope that this bundle brings you similar comfort now. Additionally, I have found a letter addressed to you from Mrs Taylor that was unsent. I have enclosed it too.

Sadly – I feel it necessary to inform you, given the caring sentiments expressed in your correspondences – Mrs Taylor died with little to her name. As per standard procedure, she is to be placed in a pauper's grave here in Lockport. It is a heartbreaking reality, and I share this news with deepest regret. Her memory will be cherished here and, I am sure, it will be equally treasured by you and your family. If you can assist, do let us know, with immediate effect.

Please accept our most sincere condolences for your loss. If there is any further information you require or any aid we may provide, do not hesitate to contact us at your convenience.

Yours sincerely,

Dr Matthew Hoffman, Niagara County Infirmary Lockport

1338 Elm Street,
Lafayette.
October 24th 1904

Dearest Mrs Taylor,

My darling friend, I hope this letter finds you in good health and that you are celebrating your birthday.

I've missed you every single day since I left three years ago. I pray the address I found for you is finally correct. You won't believe the wild chase I've been on to find you for over a year now. Your old friend or sponsor (is that correct?), Mr Thompson, proved to be less helpful than I had hoped. He told me that he had lost touch with where you were residing. He tried to find out, but his failing health kept his proprieties elsewhere.

What glorious new adventure are you having now? Tell me everything.

I write to you from a small town in Indiana – 1338 Elm Street, Lafayette – to be precise. It's peaceful here, a world away from the chaos and noise of Niagara Falls. A different state, a different life.

I read in the newspapers about the theft of your barrel. I wish I'd known earlier. I'd have provided evidence to support your claims. I was there after all! That scheming manager of yours, Mr Russell, I never trusted him. Perhaps that's a tale for a different day? I do hope you are faring well now though. I trust your spirit is undaunted as always.

Nora and I are managing, Mrs Taylor. More than managing really, we are flourishing. Nora's a charming little girl, full of life and laughter. Four already, and I swear that some days she's wiser and bolder than I could ever be. It's like she's all the best bits of me, you, Mrs Lapointe, Olive and Sarah in one. She's the brightest spark; inquisitive, kind and demanding. I love her so very much. She's everything that I wasn't. You'd be proud of her. I am – every single day. And me? Well, I have news, too. I'm educated now. Reading, writing, speaking – bettered myself for Nora. The more time and distance between me and Newfoundland, and the easier it's becoming to be someone else. Learning's been my entire focus since leaving. I reckon I sound like a cultured lady now, and perhaps that's how I've become one? We become and we attract what we feel we deserve?

Also, and quite by chance, I've found someone. Only six months ago, but it feels like a lifetime already. A gentle gentleman by the name of Walter Forster. He's shown us such kindness and warmth. He's made us feel welcome in this new world. He wants us to be a family, Mrs Taylor. A proper one. He loves Nora as if she were his own. I just know that you'd love him, too.

Can you believe that it's already three years (today) since your journey over the Horseshoe Falls. I tell my Nora about it almost daily. We have your photograph postcard on our mantle. I found it quite by chance in Niagara last year. She waves you good morning and goodnight each day, without fail. I'm determined that she never forgets you. I think about your son David often, too. We include both him and you in our prayers each evening.

I need you to know, Mrs Taylor, that I love you dearly. You remain like a mother, a sister, and a friend to me. Your courage and determination are inspiring, and I hope that wherever you are, whatever you're doing and whoever you're with, that you remember that. You saved me at my darkest moment. You gave Nora and me back our lives. I'll remember your kindness until my dying breath.

My other happy news is that Uncle William is dead. That's why I feel confident writing now. I don't fear him finding this letter. The message of his passing reached me and I cried with relief for an entire week. A weight has been lifted. Nora is safe. I no longer search each room as I enter. I no longer scan marketplaces for his face or fear flickers of movements in shadows. I'm finally free from him; I'm finally alive.

Please, write back to me when you can. I long to hear your voice again, even if only through ink on a page. I want to know how you are, what you're doing, and most importantly, I need to know that you're safe. Perhaps, even, you could move here? I've spoken to Walter, and he welcomes news of you, too.

Your loving Tilda

325 Elmwood Avenue,
Santa Barbara, CA.
October 24th 1907

Dearest Mrs Taylor,

Happy Birthday, to you! My annual letter, and another year without hearing from you; six since you conquered the Horseshoe Falls. I do hope this letter finds its way to you, wherever you may be. I've got to the stage where I don't expect a response, but still I long for one.

It's been an elongated and eventful year since I last corresponded, and I've thought about you every single day. Oh, how I wish for a letter from your hand – even a list of how I may have offended you – to know that you are well and still carrying the spirit of adventure that defined you.

So much has changed in our lives. Nora, our precious Nora, has blossomed into a remarkable young girl of seven years. She's bright and inquisitive, excelling in her studies already. I can see traces of your fiery determination, and I'm certain that she carries a piece of our Morgiana's indomitable spirit within her. I adore her. Some days, I watch her playing and I am overwhelmed with a need to protect her from the world. She's a gift. One that I can't quite determine I deserve.

Still, Mrs Taylor, this letter has a different purpose too. I must share with you the joyous news of the newest addition to the family. I have been bursting to tell you. A son – last month! Our little boy - born from the love between Walter and I – has been named David. We chose this name in honour and remembrance of your beloved son who left this world too soon. We named him in tribute to you, too; in saying his name we send our love to you. Already, our boy brings us immeasurable happiness and fills our home with love. In his eyes, now, I see a glimmer of the courage and zest for life that defined you. We are forever joined – as mothers to Davids; yours and mine.

Walter's job, as it always does, has taken us on a journey across this vast country. From Lafayette, where we bade farewell to our dear friends, we find ourselves settling in the charming town of Santa Barbara. The ocean breeze and the picturesque landscapes provide solace and tranquillity.

We're making cherished memories in this coastal haven, embracing the beauty of the Pacific and the warmth of a tight-knit community. Will you join us, Mrs Taylor? Will you complete our little family? That invitation remains open and until my dying breath.

My dear friend, I write this letter filled with both hope and trepidation. I'm uncertain if the address I have is still accurate, if my words will reach your hands. Still, hope drives me. You, Sarah and Olive gave me that hope and I've danced with it since. I implore you, if by some miraculous chance this letter finds you, please write back to me. Let me know that you are well, that life has treated you kindly.

We miss you, Mrs Taylor. Your presence is sorely lacking in our lives. Your absence leaves a void that no other could ever fill. I pray that this letter serves as a bridge between our worlds, and that you will once again be a part of our journey.

With unwavering affection and a persisting au revoir,

Your loving Tilda

325 Elmwood Avenue,
Santa Barbara, CA.
October 24th 1909

My dearest Mrs Taylor,

The season turns, the russet leaves fall, and I'm always reminded of the day we said goodbye in 1901. It seems a lifetime ago, and yet, I recall the heartache as vividly as if it were yesterday. Still, my mind fills with the warmth of your kindness and bravery every day, even if I've not heard from you those eight long years since.

Life, as it is wont to do, has been full of surprises and changes. Our spirited Nora, now nine, has developed a love for books that I'm sure you'd be proud of. She reads by lamp, under her bed covers, her face illuminated with the thrill of the stories she delves into. Her retelling of 'The Forty Thieves' is quite something to behold. Last week she decided that she would write her own story. Unsurprisingly, it's the tale of a brave woman who ventured over the Horseshoe Falls. The first person ever to survive. She's titled it 'Grandma Annie' and is illustrating the pages as I write this to you. She cherishes your memory, locking it to her chest and dreaming of being as brave and as daring as you when she grows.

And then there's our little David. He's now two, can you believe it? He's grown into a spirited toddler, radiating joy and enthusiasm in everything he does. His laughter fills our house with a warmth that's truly irreplaceable. His early strides bear the promise of an adventurer, a wanderer; your spirit living through him too.

Walter has received a promotion and we plan to move again, this time, to San Francisco. The idea of a new beginning in a city vibrant with life and full of promise fills us with a delightful excitement. The thought of the sea's bracing air, the eclectic city life and the charm of the painted ladies beckon us. Yet, the thought of being even further away from you causes an ache in my heart. I implore you, once again, and as I do each year, to consider joining us, Mrs Taylor. Our family, your family, is incomplete without you.

I can't express enough the magnitude of your absence. It's like a phantom limb; I feel your presence even though you're not here. Your courage, your spirit, your essence – it's woven into the very fabric of our family. Each day that goes by without a word from you is a day that lacks the complete joy of knowing you're well, that you're safe. I fear my words will always be inadequate when talking about you – the woman who gave me life.

Please, if these letters find you, if my words reach your heart, give us a sign. We're always here for you, always waiting for you. You're our heroine, our guiding star. Our place, ever warm and inviting, awaits your return.

Wishing you every happiness on your birthday, and waiting for the day we meet again.

Your loving Tilda

1432 Haight Street,
San Francisco, CA.
October 24th 1920

My dearest Mrs Taylor,

Another year has passed. Another year without word from you. Another birthday wish being sent to you. I hope this letter both finds you and finds you well. Some days I wake in the night, fretting about your passing. That you may no longer be with us and that I might never know – those thoughts terrify me. Will you let me know about your life? I won't ever accept that your reasons for not responding are negative. Until I'm told otherwise, I'll keep writing annually and I'll keep hoping for a response.

Another year in San Francisco, and it's as if we've been here our entire lives. Walter works as a foreman at the bustling shipyard. His hard labour has made our life here possible. I'm so very lucky. Our home's a refuge of love and laughter, and he's the kindest man I will ever know.

It's hard to believe it's been nearly twenty years since I arrived on the doorstep at the Bay City boarding house. That frightened young woman with child is unrecognisable now. Today, Nora stands beside me, a strong and beautiful woman of twenty. She adores teaching and, yes, as suspected last year, her wedding day is fast-approaching. Joshua's a kind man. Diligent and determined. They're a handsome couple. Our boy, David, has turned thirteen. He's grown hearing the stories, asked about you, about the lady who went over the Falls and lived to tell the tale. We debate often about your audacious bravery, your strength, the seeming recklessness that, somehow, spoke of an immense will to live.

Last week I even mentioned the many unfortunate souls who have since attempted to follow your lead, and how they've perished. Hundreds who haven't survived. We look at your feat with a strange mix of admiration and concern; the line between bravery and folly is indeed thin. You're remarkable. I knew that from the moment I met you. I fear though – with my determined inclusion of you in our daily life – that he might become a stunter one day. He talks about following in your footsteps. May the good Lord help us all.

He knows all out your David, too. His memory lives on, darling Mrs Taylor.

Recently, I've been thinking about when I left the boarding house. How I ran, even though every ounce of me longed to stay near you. When you gave me the money from your stunt, you gave me the gift of experiencing a mother's love and unconditional love that I'd never known. From that day, I stopped searching for what my mother would never give me; I accepted my loss. I never contacted her again. You gifted me so much more than the money for a new life – you gifted me the sense of being enough, of being lovable too. I truly became a mother that day.

Now, I've found comfort in work as a seamstress. As I stitch and mend, I often think back to our time in that old boarding house and those hours that I spent attempting to embroider in the parlour. Do you remember that pillow with the heart embroidery I made for your birthday? I wonder what became of it. Life seemed so much smaller then. Now, my world's here in San Francisco, with Walter, Nora, and David, but a part of me is still there, in the memories we shared. In that feeling of belonging that has expanded and evolved and become me over the last twenty years. Does that even make sense? I wonder about Sarah and Olive often, too. Do you even remember them? Or me? I wonder how many lost women you have helped over the years.

I miss you dearly, Mrs Taylor. I miss you every single day. Your bold spirit touched our lives. I know that you've achieved greater things in your life – and I can but imagine the greatness you've experienced since I left – but still I hope that you remember Nora and me. How I wish you would meet Walter and David, see how Nora has grown. My offer still stands; you have a home, should you ever need us.

I don't know if you'll respond to this letter, or if you even receive them. Regardless, I'll keep writing and I'll keep letting you know the address of your home. Know that you've left an indelible mark on our lives. You are, and always will be, part of our family.

With unwavering affection and an enduring au revoir,

Your loving Tilda

24th October 1920

My dearest Tilda,

I am writing this letter with the understanding that it will perhaps reach you upon my death. My eyesight fails but my mind is sharp. Still, death edges nearer each day and I'm writing now, before my capacity fails entirely.

I do hope this letter finds you in good health and high spirits. I'm aware that it has been many years since we last spoke, or rather since I last communicated with you, and I regret deeply that I could not find the strength to reply to your many heartfelt invitations. It is with a heavy heart that I now write to you, knowing that it will be read in my absence. Knowing this will be too little and too late.

Firstly, let me assure you that my silence over the years was not borne out of a lack of affection for you or a desire to harm you. On the contrary, it is because of the deep love I have for you and the life you have built, that I chose to remain silent and removed from it for all these years.

When we first crossed paths on that fateful day in 1901, when you turned up on our doorstep at the Bay City boarding house, I had no idea of the impact you would have on my life. The love I felt for both you and for little Nora was instant. You were suddenly family and there was little I would not have done to keep you both safe from harm. As you know, I was fortunate to survive that perilous journey over the Falls, and the money I earned from it allowed me to support you and provide for your well-being. It was an act of love and kindness, one that I will never regret. Helping you is one of my proudest achievements in this lifetime. You are a story that bristles with success, my darling girl.

But, my dear Tilda, life is a complex tapestry, is it not? It's woven with joys and sorrows, hopes and regrets. The pain of losing a child is a burden that only a mother can truly comprehend. Sharing my David with you was almost accidental. Did I truly expect to survive a trip over the Falls? I was the first. The odds were not in my favour. Yet, even with the tragedies experienced, I always lived a life expecting a positive outcome. Perhaps I even demanded it. I'd argue then that I wanted to share David with you. I wanted you to expose that piece of my soul, so that you could know me entirely.

That you say his name, that you have honoured his legacy by naming your own son after him – those are the truest and purest of gifts anyone could ever bestow on me. You repay me every single day. I'm truly grateful.

Still, in my heart, I've always believed that you deserved a life far better than what I would bring by being in yours. I was your past and you were living in the present. You were young, full of potential, and always destined for greatness. When you wrote to tell me that you had met Walter, I squealed with joy. You found a kind and loving man who saw the beauty in your heart; I knew that he could offer you a life beyond my grasp. The life you deserved. I wavered then. I almost replied. But why would I seek to pull you back in time or expect you to play a role that you should no longer fit? My part in your life was to help you heal. You didn't need to see or hear about the life of squalor and poverty that I was living. You see, my life didn't quite turn out as I'd hoped it would after winning back my barrel.

As the years passed, and you welcomed David into your family, I rejoiced silently from afar. I watched (or, rather, enjoyed reading) you build on your loving home, filling it with even more laughter and warmth. Each snippet of your life fed joy into my soul. I knew in my heart that you had found the happiness I always wished for you. It was then that I made the difficult decision to stay silent for the rest of my days, to allow you the space and freedom to fully embrace the life you had created. A present bursting with life and love. Please know, that the thought of a home with you has, over the years, kept my mind safe. You and Nora will always be my happy place. But to love you is to lose you – and once was enough. I made the choice not to allow you or anyone else close to me. A choice, darling Tilda. I chose not to expose my heart again.

Instead, I wanted you to let go of the past, to release the hold it had on your spirit, and to focus on the present and the future. Does any of what I'm writing make sense? Sorrow is an infectious and incurable disease. It rots from the inside out. In leaving you to your own devices, I hoped to offer you the chance to live a life untouched and not infected by the tragedies of my past.

After my barrel was stolen, a newspaper once said that I was persistently followed by ill luck. I've thought about that often. I wanted you to savour every precious moment with Walter, Nora, and David, to create beautiful memories that would overshadow any lingering ghosts from long ago. It was my way of loving you, my way of protecting you, my chance to give life. Survival takes many forms, Tilda. This was mine.

Now, as I write these words – knowing you will receive them from beyond the veil of my life – I hope that you can understand my intentions. I hope that you can forgive my silence and know that every letter left unanswered was a testament to my love for you. Still, I read them all, again and again. I treasured each and I looked forward to every single word that you shared with me. You were my beacon of light and joy. You've persisted with grace and, like our Lelawala, you've been rewarded for your bravery. You've been gifted a life that you never imagined, but look at all that you have. Look at the mother you became. We survived differently, you and me. Not all survivals are equal. I fear that I have no legacy. That my journey over the brink and quest for fame are irrelevant now. Fame is transient; I am already forgotten.

Please understand that I've always held you close to my heart, and I will forever cherish the memories we shared. You are my daughter. My longed-for and chosen daughter. You brought light into my life and, for that, I will be eternally thankful.

Keep living. Keep finding joy. Embrace Nora for me and ask David to live grand and achieve the world for my boy, too. If I may, though, can I have one final wish? If your response is positive, then know that my desire is that folk will one day know my name. I would like to be known as more than being 'the woman who went over Niagara Falls in a barrel'.

With all my gratitude and blessings. With unwavering affection and a last goodbye,

Your loving Annie Edson Taylor

Part IX: Women Resurfaced

MAY 1921

Matilda

8th May 1921

'I had the privilege of treating Mrs Taylor during her final days. Her sight was reduced to mere shreds of blurring light and shadow by the end,' the doctor tells me.

Dr Matthew Hoffman – the attending physician – is a middle-aged man with a calm and reassuring demeanour. I am already relieved; Mrs Taylor will have been cared for here.

'She was eighty-two, and she relied on the gentle pressure of either mine or a nurse's hand guiding her when she walked,' he says. He waves his palms towards me, as if to illustrate their strength.

And now I'm walking through the stinking corridors of Niagara County Infirmary in Lockport, New York. I'm looking for Mrs Taylor, but she's not here anymore. I'm too late. The smell of unwashed bodies lingers in the air. It seeps into my cotton dress. My legs quiver. I'm not sure if that's the cold or my grief.

'My office is this way,' he says, flattening his dark hair and striding ahead. He's in a hurry to be out of the corridors. I note that his hair's flecked with touches of grey at the temples.

'Do sit.' The doctor points to a leather chair as he moves behind the mahogany desk. The focal point of the room. It's adorned with intricate carvings and polished to a gleaming finish. There's money in this room but not elsewhere in this poorhouse. Behind the desk, Dr Hoffman's leather-upholstered chair sits upright; its high back conveys authority and confidence. A row of medical reference books line one side of the desk, while a brass desk lamp illuminates the surface, casting a warm glow over the papers and documents meticulously arranged upon it. Everything points to the fact that he's a good man. He cares about his patients.

'Did you like her?' I ask and he smiles.

'We chatted often during her short time here,' he says, sitting down and wriggling until his body has fitted into its groove. 'But by the end, she rarely remembered the topics of our conversations.' I think I detect an air of respect. Maybe it's humour. He's recalling their stories in his mind. 'She was the woman who went over the Canadian Falls…' He doesn't suppress his awe. It dances over his facial features.

I smile. I shuffle to sit a little taller in the chair. 'She was the first person to survive.'

Seconds pass. He's bobbing his head in agreement and contemplating. 'Do you think it was worth it?' he asks.

I shrug. 'How do you measure what is of value in another's life?'

'In a barrel, wasn't it?'

I nod. 'I guess she doesn't still own it?' Not that it matters, not that I'd have any idea what to do with it.

The doctor's sympathetic gaze meets mine, and I can sense his understanding of my grief. 'I truly am sorry for your loss,' he says, his voice soft but professional. 'She was quite a remarkable woman.'

I nod again. I can feel tears at the corner of my eyes. I push my tongue to the top of my mouth. 'Thank you,' I manage to murmur, my voice shaky with emotion.

He flips through some papers on his desk, a stethoscope hanging within reach. 'Mrs Taylor was a fighter, that's for sure. Determined till the very end.'

A faint smile tugs at my lips as memories of her resilience flood my mind. 'Yes, she was,' I agree softly. 'She never backed down from a challenge or an argument.'

'I recall one particular conversation we had,' he says, his expression thoughtful. 'She mentioned a circus performer and how he stole her barrel.' The doctor nods, jotting down a few notes as he speaks. 'She seemed troubled by the mention of him,' he explains. 'Spoke of betrayal and loss.'

I furrow my brow, trying to make sense of Mrs Taylor's cryptic words. 'Not the weasel manager, Mr Russell?'

'This was after him,' the doctor continues, his gaze distant as if lost in thought. 'Something about the barrel being stolen twice.'

I nod. 'She defeated her manager, got the barrel back the first time,' I say. 'It was in the newspapers.'

His eyes widen in surprise. 'How?'

I shrug my shoulders, a smile playing at his lips. Mrs Taylor was a determined soul. Did he experience that side of her too?

'She was full of surprises,' he says.

I nod in agreement, feeling a swell of pride in my chest. 'Whatever she set her mind to, she pursued with unwavering resolve.' Even if that was not replying to my letters. 'She told me about Lelawala,' I say. He looks confused, but I've no time to explain. 'Mrs Taylor was my Heno. I met her when I was truly broken and she ministered to me. Stayed with me until my heart healed.' A pause. I push my tongue to the top of my mouth again. Must control my emotions. 'Her last letter said I was rewarded for my bravery by being gifted a life I never could have envisaged.'

For a moment, we sit in silence, lost in our memories of Mrs Taylor. Then, the doctor's gaze drifts to a photograph on his desk. I wonder if it's his wife or children. The mischievous part of me hopes it's a framed postcard of Mrs Taylor and her barrel. 'She left quite an impression on me.'

Tears threaten to spill from my eyes once more as I search for a handkerchief in my small clutch purse. I'm sure I popped it in there. Lipstick, a compact mirror, a small notebook and pen.

'I assume you know that she worked as a clairvoyant in later life? Gave magnet therapies?'

'I didn't.'

'She lived in poverty,' he says. 'She said that without proof, no one believed she'd conquered the Horseshoe Falls.'

'Did Holleran and Trusdale not come forward in support? They saw it all,' I say. 'I could have helped…'

Dr Hoffman stands and leans over his desk, a handkerchief in his hand. I take it.

'Thank you.' My voice is barely above a whisper. 'Thank you for taking care of her.'

I open the compact, dabbing at the corners of my eyes with the handkerchief. Golden hair with a side part and styled with finger waves. Kohl-rimmed eyes, and bold plum lipstick. Would I be unrecognisable to Mrs Taylor?

'Amongst her meagre belongings, I discovered letters written to her by other women. She kept them all.' He hesitates and I nod for him to continue. 'I wrote to each of them. Forty-three women. Informing them of her passing. Many replied.'

'And?'

'Needless to say, Annie need not have worried about her life's legacy.' He slides some sheets of paper across his desk to me. 'It seems she lived her life saving others.' There are names on the top sheet.

Evelyn Sinclair: stayed in Bay City Boarding House, October 1900
Minnie Montgomery: stayed in Bay City Boarding House, January 1901
Rose Baker: stayed in Bay City Boarding House, March 1901
Margaret Chen: stayed in Bay City Boarding House, May 1901
Irene Johnson: stayed in Bay City Boarding House for 3 weeks, paid for 1, March 1900
Alice Thompson: stayed in Bay City Boarding House August through October 1900
Mary Landry: stayed in Bay City Boarding House February 1901

'Best read it later.' He gestures towards my handkerchief.

'Thank you,' I say, dabbing at my tears. He's right. His kindness is welcomed.

'Mrs Forster, I do have a sensitive issue to discuss,' Dr Hoffman begins, his voice gentle yet solemn. I freeze with the handkerchief and compact mid-use. 'As outlined in my letter … Mrs Taylor, passed away in our care. Unfortunately, she had no money or resources to cover her expenses, and as such, she has been laid to rest in a pauper's grave.'

'Yes, you told me in your letter.' My voice trembles. 'But surely, there must be something we can do to give her a proper farewell.'

He offers a sympathetic nod. 'I assure you that we handled her arrangements with the utmost dignity and respect. However, without any means to cover the costs, our options were unfortunately limited...'

I wish I wasn't crying. 'She deserves more.' Compact back in my clutch, I blow my nose like it's a trumpet.

'Wait…' There's a shift in his disposition, in his energy, in both. He's almost excited. 'I might know someone who can help,' he says. He laughs. 'I really do.' He grabs a piece of paper and writes a name: *Miss Charlotte Ledger.*

Matilda

9th May 1921

It's under the bright sun of afternoon that Nora and I find ourselves outside Miss Charlotte Ledger's office. She's a woman well-known in these parts, mainly for her dedication to preserving the heritage of Lockport. Clutched in my hand are all my letters to Mrs Taylor, and all the newspaper cuttings, photos and souvenir postcards I've collected since 1901. I don't know why I'd thought to bring them with me on receiving Dr Hoffman's letter, but they're proving essential. I grip that bundle, now etched with her loss and my determination. My heart hammers in my chest; it drums out a cadence of hope and of fear. I'm a grown woman, but right now my head's back in 1901; I'm scared, carrying a weight of fear on my shoulders. I'm praying that the person on the other side of this door will help me. I need to be heard. I'm feeling all the emotions I did the day I knocked on the door of the boarding house.

'Mama?'

I turn to Nora. She was with me that day, she's been my unconditional. I love her so very much. She's twenty-one now, and a full head and shoulders taller than me. She has the confidence of both youth and her profession. She's everything I hoped she would be.

'Quick thinking and an ability to stay calm under pressure,' she recites. She's prompting our chant.

I smile. 'Embrace the courage of Annie Edson Taylor and the cunning of our Morgiana to conquer this challenge,' I say, just like I have so many times through our journey. A quick look in my compact to check my hair, kohl and lipstick. All fine. 'Ready?' I ask and my daughter's fingers find mine, connecting our hands into one. She gives my hand a squeeze.

'For Grandma Annie,' she says.

I give the open door a firm rap with my knuckles; the sound echoes in the quiet corridor.

An internal door creaks open and a head pops into the corridor. We're greeted by Charlotte's warm smile. Her greying hair's tied back neatly; her spectacles are perched on the end of her nose.

'Mrs Forster?' she asks, striding along the corridor towards us. She looks from me and then to my daughter.

'In the flesh.' I thrust out my hand. I offer a firm handshake, gripping tightly and looking directly into her eyes. Like I saw Mrs Taylor do many times. 'And you must be Miss Ledger. Thank you for fitting us in at such short notice.'

'Call me Charlotte.' She shakes my hand firmly. She smells of cigarettes and lavender.

'Tilda.' I point at myself. 'And this is Nora, my daughter.' They shake hands, too. Charlotte turns back towards her office, signalling with a wave of her hand for us to enter and follow her.

As Nora and I step into the room, she gasps with joy. The office is a curious spectacle – a maelstrom of books, paper, and maps. It's as though time's stood still here and there's a testament to the past in every corner, on every inch of the tables and even in piles on the floor. This is my girl's idea of heaven. I see her fingers itching to touch and read all that's surrounding us.

'I feel we should get straight to the matter,' Charlotte says, nodding to the bundle of papers I'm clutching. Formalities are swept away by the urgency that's the heart of our visit. I look at Nora and see her instant disappointment switch into renewed focus. We are here for a very specific end purpose.

We gather around a small wooden table, an oil lamp casting a soft glow over us. I place the bundle of papers in front of me, staring at them as if to separate them would be harmful. Miss Ledger's office has fallen into weighted silence. The air's thick with anticipation. All eyes are on me. Nora reaches over and gently squeezes my hand again. I glance at her, but her gaze is fixed on Charlotte. They're both waiting. I clear my throat.

'As I explained when requesting this urgent meeting, you may have heard of her – Annie Edson Taylor?' There's a tremble in my voice. Charlotte lifts an eyebrow in intrigue, inviting me to continue. 'Mrs Taylor wasn't just a boarder at Mrs Lapointe's house. She was also the first…' I pause. Grief catches in my throat. I push my tongue to the top of my mouth and pinch the bridge of my nose, desperately trying to distract my emotion. 'She was the very first person to survive going over Niagara Falls. A woman was the first. Not a man. It was both intentional and in a barrel of her own design, no less. She was sixty-three years old, but everyone thought she was forty-three.'

Charlotte gasps, her spectacles slipping from her nose. She pushes them back up, leaning forward into her chair, surprise etched across her face. 'A woman … her age … that's … incredible.'

'She was the first to do what no other human in the world had the nerve to do,' Nora says. Her words are glistening with pride. 'And, in the twenty years since Grandma Annie, on average twenty to thirty people attempt to conquer the Falls each year. Only one other has survived – a Bobby Leech in 1911.'

'I'd heard of Bobby, but not of Annie.' Charlotte shakes her head. She's disappointed in herself.

'She saved our lives,' I say. The grip of Nora's hand tightens. 'We had nothing, and she gave us everything.' I look at my daughter and she nods in agreement; her lips are set in a determined line. 'There were others, too. Lots of us. I've got names and addresses.'

'She was remarkable,' Nora adds. 'I owe her everything.'

Charlotte's silent for a moment. She's studying our faces. She doesn't ask why we needed saving; that piece of gossip is irrelevant to her. Finally, she sighs, leaning back in her chair. 'Women supporting women,' she says. Her voice is a soft whisper. 'That's exactly what we should be celebrating, don't you think?'

'Absolutely.' I reach for the bundle and find the photo of Mrs Taylor next to her barrel. I slide it across the table. 'We can't let Mrs Taylor be forgotten. Her story deserves to be heard. Her bravery, her survival…'

'You said it was a timely matter. Can I meet her today?'

The guttural sound I release surprises me. My body shakes with my sobs.

'She died,' Nora says. 'They've put her in a pauper's grave.'

'What?' Charlotte's face is shadowed by anger. 'A pauper's grave? No, no, no.' She's stomping around the room. 'She needs to be in the Stunter's Rest section of Oakwood Cemetery.' She leans over the table, frantically scribbling notes onto paper.

'Grandma Annie was the epitome of strength and courage,' Nora says. I twist to look at my daughter. Her gaze is intense, but she's smiling. She's embracing the courage of Annie Edson Taylor and the cunning of Morgiana to conquer this challenge. My daughter's strength inspires me; it always has. 'She deserves a grave fitting of her legacy.'

Charlotte nods, her face thoughtful. 'We should start a fundraising campaign immediately. Raise awareness and raise money.' She hands me a silk handkerchief from her sleeve. I'm still crying. 'It's clean.'

'Do you really think folk will be interested?' I ask. I blow my nose and Charlotte nods enthusiastically.

'There are many in this town, in this state, who would be willing to contribute to this cause.' She hesitates, looking at us with a newfound resolve. 'We can do this. Together.' Her arms extend out. Her wide sleeves like magnificent wings.

'What's the plan?' Nora asks. She's mesmerized. She stares at Charlotte with urgency, hungry for all advice on offer.

Charlotte's nodding again. 'A pamphlet, and then we go door to door.' She's been scribbling notes and seems to have a list of steps we need to take. 'Obtain permission, acquire permits, coordinate cemeteries, exhumation process, reburial…'

I smile at her list-making. Mrs Taylor would have liked her.

Charlotte takes a cigarette from a silver box and lights it. 'Do you smoke?' she asks and I shake my head. 'Right, then let's get to work.'

The words hang in the air on cigarette smoke. Tears roll down my cheeks, relief floods my heart. I should have come back here years ago. I should have hunted Mrs Taylor down and forced her to come and live with us. I never repaid her for saving us. I glance at my daughter, her determination and focus matching mine.

I won't let Mrs Taylor down again.

The Legacy of Annie Edson Taylor Pamphlet
Annie Edson Taylor

Adventuress, Teacher, Fearless Soul, Queen of the Mist

Do you know her name? You really should! The very first person to conquer the mighty Niagara Falls in a wooden barrel and live to tell the tale. Her brave spirit personifies the audacity of hope, of resilience, of defiance against the odds. Her incredible journey from teacher to stunter offers a beacon of courage and inspiration, an example of the potential every man and woman holds within them. Yet on April 29, 1921, Mrs Taylor breathed her last at the Niagara County Infirmary, blind and penniless. She was buried in a pauper's grave. A tragic end for a woman whose bravery will echo through time.
We, the undersigned, refuse to let her story end in obscurity, forgotten in a pauper's grave. We are on a mission to raise funds for a befitting stunter's grave. A memorial that will stand testament to her indomitable spirit and inspire generations to come.

Stand with us. Let's honour Annie Edson Taylor's legacy together.

Donations of 50 cents or $1 accepted. Help us preserve the memory of a true heroine. Contributions can be made in person to Charlotte Ledger and Matilda Forster, who will be visiting homes throughout Lockport. Or you can send them to 34 High Street, Lockport, NY.

Women Supporting Women – Because Together, We Are Unstoppable.

Paid for by the Remaining Friends of Annie Taylor and the Community of Lockport, for the Honour and Memory of Annie Edson Taylor.

Matilda

10th May 1921

The sun's dipped below the horizon, washing the town in dusky pink and lavender hues. We're a peculiar pair. I'm entirely motherly, in a dropped waistline, loose dress with a flowing silhouette, whereas Charlotte's entirely poised in her sophisticated waistcoat and long skirt. She's an emblem of the modern woman.

'Permission and permits acquired.' She ticks her list as we walk. 'Now we need to coordinate cemeteries and fund the exhumation process.' A small stack of pamphlets peeks out from her leather satchel.

'People need something tangible to read after our visit,' she said earlier. I liked that.

Nora's back at Charlotte's office, ready to collect donations. Our plan to save Mrs Taylor is progressing.

Charlotte takes a final drag on her cigarette, before dropping it to the pavement. Stepping onto the stoop, her gloved hand reaches out to the ornate knocker on the first door. It creaks open slowly. She turns to me, shrugs, then knocks again.

'Hello?' A man in his mid-forties. His eyes question us from behind a pair of wire-rimmed glasses.

A pause as she considers him. She smiles. 'Good evening, sir,' Charlotte says, her voice clear and unwavering. 'I'm Miss Ledger, and this is Mrs Forster. We're part of a fundraising initiative here in town.'

His eyebrows crease in a frown. 'Fundraising for what?'

I step forward, standing tall and straight next to Charlotte. 'For Annie Edson Taylor, sir. She made history by being the first person to survive a plunge over the Horseshoe Falls in a barrel.' I force my voice to be steady, mimicking Charlotte. I'm quivering under my skirts.

Recognition sparks in his eyes instantly. I watch as it spreads across his face. 'Annie Taylor? The daredevil? I saw her do it. It was a miracle she survived.'

His excitement is infectious. I want to jump up and down on the spot. 'Yes, sir, that's her,' I say. 'You were there?'

'On the viewing deck. Told my son about her just last week.' A pause. 'I forgot her name though…' I see his embarrassment.

'I was there, too,' I say. I want to squeeze him tightly and kiss his forehead. I wish Mrs Taylor could hear how her story's persisting through families and generations.

'She passed on April twenty-ninth.' I stumble slightly. A gulp. 'And we're looking to give her the burial she deserves. Not in a pauper's grave where she is currently resting, but a stunter's one.' I grip at the cotton of my dress, twisting it within my fingertips. I can't cry; not now.

'I'm sorry for…' He hesitates. He's trying to figure out if I'm related to her. I nod.

I glance at Charlotte, and she extends a pamphlet towards him. Her movement is enthusiastic. She's excited; her plan is working. 'Her bravery must not be forgotten, sir. We're women supporting women, even in death. Your contribution will help preserve her legacy.'

He holds the pamphlet, a thoughtful silence settling between us as he reads the words. Finally, 'She was brave…'

'Will you help?' I ask.

He nods enthusiastically. 'Yes, yes, I'd be honoured to contribute.'

A small smile tugs at the corners of his mouth, as he takes out his wallet.

'Thank you,' I say, my smile echoing his.

Charlotte holds out a cloth bag and he places his donation inside.

'To the next house,' Charlotte says, turning away. She lights another cigarette as she marches down the pathway.

'Let me help, too.' His hand reaches inside his house, grabbing a bowler hat and closing the door behind him. 'Perhaps a cemetery plot could be donated by trustees of Oakwood Cemetery. My father is one of them. Let's head there now.'

NIAGARA FALLS COMMUNITY RALLIES TO HONOUR UNSUNG HEROINE, ANNIE EDSON TAYLOR

NIAGARA FALLS GAZETTE - MAY 11, 1921

The local community of Niagara Falls is rallying together in a touching display of empathy and admiration for the late Annie Edson Taylor.

Taylor, who passed away on April 29, 1921, lived her later years in relative obscurity and poverty, her incredible feat largely uncelebrated during her lifetime. Upon learning of her passing, the Niagara Falls community, filled with a sense of sorrow and regret for not having celebrated The Queen of the Mist's achievements more during her lifetime, swiftly organised a campaign to raise funds in her memory. The initiative, led by local philanthropists and historians, aims to ensure that Taylor's contributions to the area's history are recognised and that her memory is enshrined for posterity.

'Annie Edson Taylor's incredible feat is a poignant reminder of the human spirit's ability to push boundaries and face the unknown,' said Charlotte Ledger, a local historian and one of the organisers of the fundraising effort. 'It's our responsibility as a community to honour her memory, express our gratitude for her bravery, and ensure her story is not lost to future generations.'

The funds raised will cover Taylor's exhumation expenses and her reburial, the installation of a commemorative plaque at Niagara Falls and the tombstone at her final resting place in Oakwood Cemetery's Stunters Section. A cemetery plot has been donated by trustees of Oakwood Cemetery. The plaque will tell the bittersweet tale of her life, her daring act, and the indomitable spirit that was overlooked for far too long.

The outpouring of support and heartfelt emotion from the Niagara Falls community serves as a testament to the impact Annie Edson Taylor's story has had on the area. It is a poignant tribute to a woman who risked everything in pursuit of adventure, and a promise that her bravery and determination will be remembered and celebrated for generations to come.

FUNERAL NOTICE

A funeral and reburial service for Mrs Annie Edson Taylor [Queen of the Mist] will be held at 2 o'clock on May 15, 1921, in the Dykstra funeral chapel on Main St, at Michigan Ave. The Rev David H. Weeks of the Episcopal Church will officiate. Followed by burial in Oakwood Cemetery's 'Stunters Section'. All are welcome.

Matilda

15th May 1921

The iron gate of the cemetery creaks in protest as I push it open. Perhaps the rusted hinges sing a melancholy tune. The sound echoes across the expanse of granite and marble. A cool breeze carries with it the delicate scent of lilacs from a nearby tree, greeting us as we step onto the gravel path. I stay as still as a statue there, taking a moment to acknowledge the sea of gravestones. Each weathered, each worn; I've aged years in the last two weeks. Our silence stretches.

'Mama?' Her hand finds mine and our fingers lock together with ease. Magnets. We've travelled this path as one. Side by side. Our connection unbreakable, our bond unwavering. Always together. My daughter, my friend, my compass. I am so very lucky.

'Each one's a testament to a life once lived,' I say, pointing to the graves. Springy moss decorates the simple tablets.

Nora nods. She lifts my hand to kiss it and then loops her arm through mine. She's hesitant, watchful in her mourning black. Some days it overwhelms me to think how we have grown from her as a babe on my hip turning up at Bay City Boarding House, to here, now. That heartache and fear is out of my reach these days. I can but hope that my daughter never experiences the loneliness and fear that I once ran from. To think there were days I hoped to die, when I questioned why I was still alive. I never dared to imagine I'd be living a life so very full of love and opportunity. I blinked and we became older though. Two women standing tall. Two survivors, bonded by love. We've grown up together, she and I. And now, today, I realise that I'd have it no other way. I'd endure my childhood a thousand times if it meant a lifetime with Nora by my side.

My daughter is the picture of grace and solemnity in her wide-brimmed hat; its dark lace veil offers an illusory barrier against the finality of our visit. I don't know if we'll ever come here again. My life is back in San Francisco, with Walter and David. Nora will marry this year; they plan to start a family, too. They're my home. I've been straddling two worlds for too long. It's time to let this one go.

'Ready?' I ask and she nods again. She wipes a tear from my cheek with her fingers. I'd not realised I was crying.

The path's uneven under our boots, a result of years of exposure to the elements and the procession of countless mourners. We walk slowly, passing elaborate mausoleums and modest tombstones alike. The names and dates etched upon them whisper tales of joy, of loss, and the inevitable passage of time. Life is so truly short. Fresh flowers adorn some graves. They offer a vibrant contrast against the stony greys and greens. Mourning rituals, I note, have changed little since my childhood, the traditions persisting even through the upheaval of the Great War.

The sign reads *Stunters' Rest Section*. Fresh flowers decorate it. The newly turned earth of Mrs Taylor's grave comes into view. Nestled among a copse of towering oak trees, it's a solemn but dignified site. Befitting. Here she'll bask in the dappled sunlight. I smile as it filters through the rustling canopy above.

'Grandma Annie will love it here,' Nora says. I bob my head in agreement; she really will.

'The transience of life,' I say. My daughter doesn't respond. Perhaps she nods.

I'm so happy we came back here. I don't mean today; I mean the way we rushed here on receiving the letter from Dr Hoffman. The grandeur of Mrs Taylor's final resting place is in stark contrast with the pauper's grave she'd been so unjustly assigned. For the hundredth time in the last few days, I'm hit with a wave of gratitude for Charlotte's hard work and focus. None of this would have been possible without her. Perhaps, though, I'm glad I never gave up on Mrs Taylor. I wrote every single year, never knowing if she was receiving my correspondence or if she was still alive. Still, I persisted. If I hadn't…

'We did it, Mrs Taylor,' I say, and Nora squeezes the top of my arm.

The letters on the headstone are crisp, etched with a precision that defies human hands. Silently, Nora reaches out to trace the name. Her touch is gentle, almost reverent. The grave of a woman she can only remember through my recall.

'I know that name, too.' I point to the grave next to Mrs Taylor's. '*Carlisle D Graham. First to go through the whirlpool rapids in a barrel and live.* He was her friend. Met him. In the boarding house.'

'She has a friend to keep her company,' Nora says.

'We've finally repaid our debt.' My voice breaks. I wipe a tear on the sleeve of my mourning coat.

The reality of my loss and the love I had for the audacious Mrs Taylor rushes through me. It's as bold, as fresh and as raw as the day I left her in 1901.

'Grandma Annie…' Nora whispers. She turns to me, eyes wide and brimming with tears. 'She… I wish she'd come home to us.'

My heart is crushed. A lump forms in my throat. It's hard and uncomfortable. Regret tastes bitter. So many letters sent and unanswered. So many missed opportunities to push for answers. My tears flow freely.

'Thank you for writing to me. For explaining,' I say. 'I worried you hated me.' It's a confession meant only for the breeze and the cold stone in front of me. 'And, thank you for always putting Nora and me first. For protecting us.' I gulp back my tears, aching at the thought of being separated from Mrs Taylor again. 'You showed me unconditional love for the first time in my life. You taught me that I was worthy of happiness and joy. I'm a better mama because of you.' Nora places her arm around my shoulder and pulls me to her. 'I've so much love to give, Mrs Taylor. It bursts from every pore. And I understand why you stayed away. I wish though … I still wish you hadn't.'

'Excuse me.' It's a shout behind us.

Turning slightly, I see two figures approaching quickly.

'Tilda?' A voice breaks through the quiet. They draw closer and a surge of recognition mingles with surprise. 'Is that really you?'

'Sarah?' The word is a whisper. My voice is thick with emotion. She nods. Her eyes meet mine. Tears spill from them. I recognise the gentle waves of her hair, no longer the vibrant chestnut I recalled when I thought about her, but still as soft and welcoming as ever.

'Tilda!' The other figure rushes forward. Her vibrant energy fills the space between us.

'Olive?'

Before I can fully comprehend what's happening, she envelops me in the tightest embrace. Her still petite frame feels familiar against mine, her curls tickling my cheek as she holds me close. My once best friend; I'd forgotten to miss her.

'You're here? How?' I say. I can hear my confusion. I pull out of the embrace, as if to check on their presence. I look from Sarah to Olive. 'Had you seen Mrs Taylor since you left?' I ask and Olive shakes her head. Her sadness matches mine.

'Mom wrote, but we never received a reply…' Her left hand reaches for the pendant hanging from her neck. It's a familiar, a comforting gesture. 'Dr Hoffman wrote to us after she passed, and we came.'

I nod. A mix of emotions swirling within me.

'And you must be little Nora,' Sarah says softly, her voice tinged with nostalgia. A pause as she observes my daughter. 'You look just like Tilda did when we were friends.'

I meet Sarah's gaze. There's a pang of recognition as memories of our past friendship flood back. 'I never got to thank you,' I reply, my voice quivering.

'Thank *me*? For what?'

'You made me realise that not all mother-daughter relationships are neglectful,' I say, fighting with my desire to curl on the floor and sob.

'Gave me hope that maybe one day I could have a relationship like yours…' I look from Sarah to Olive. 'With Nora.'

Sarah pulls me into an embrace. A sob catches in my throat; its sound louder than necessary.

'I've heard so much about you both,' Nora says and then I hear her squeak. Sarah and I both look to see Nora wiggling out of Olive's tight clinch. I can't help but giggle.

'We thought about you both often,' Olive says.

'I think about Mrs Taylor every time I waltz,' Sarah says. '*Lift your chin. You're not a turtle retreating into its shell.*' She mimics Mrs Taylor's voice.

A lump forms in my throat as I meet their earnest gazes. There's a brief pause as the weight of our shared history hangs in the air between us. There is always joy in darkness.

'I've longed to tell you both that I'm fine. That we're fine. Better than fine,' I say.

We, these three women and I, have shared history and a bond that time will never erode. In this moment, surrounded by their warmth, I understand the sense of homecoming, as if a missing piece of myself has finally been restored.

'We owe Annie our lives,' Sarah says, and I nod. We do. 'Today's about her, let's reacquaint fully later…'

Murmurs behind us distract me. I turn. A sea of mourners walks towards Mrs Taylor's grave. They're strangers but somehow friends. Their black forms appear like crows against the greying sky. It's a crowd larger than any I've seen at a funeral, and they're all gathering here to honour Mrs Taylor one last time. The money, raised by this community, has provided her with this dignified spot. This is her legacy. She won't be forgotten. Is it thanks to them or because of her courage? Both even? I honestly don't know, but I'm truly grateful.

I feel Sarah's arm around my shoulder. Her embrace is both strong and comforting. I reach for Nora's hand again. The sound of her sniffing causes reassurance. Olive has moved to stand beside my daughter. This is our shared sadness. Walter and David don't exist in this world; I'm glad that they don't. So, instead, we stand here together, my daughter and me alongside the other lost women that The Queen of the Mist saved. We stand amongst a sea of mourners we'll never know. We stand united in grief and thankfulness. Together, we bow our heads to her stunter's gravestone in Oakwood Cemetery.

ANNIE EDSON TAYLOR
FIRST TO GO OVER
THE HORSESHOE FALL
IN A BARREL AND LIVE
OCTOBER 24, 1901

Author's Note

It is significant that Niagara Falls in 1901 was a breathtaking natural wonder, composed of three main waterfalls: the Horseshoe Falls, the American Falls, and the Bridal Veil Falls. The powerful Niagara River, flowing from Lake Erie to Lake Ontario, created these majestic falls. The Horseshoe Falls, the largest and most famous, curved in a horseshoe shape on the Canadian side, while the American Falls and Bridal Veil Falls were located on the American side. The river's intense rapids and swirling whirlpools added to the dramatic landscape, and several small islands, such as Goat Island and Luna Island, dotted the river near the falls, providing scenic viewpoints and contributing to the area's unique geography.

Thus, among the annals of human encounters with nature, Niagara Falls is a distinct place. It embodies both awe-inspiring beauty and inherent peril. The history of these falls is interwoven with tales of daredevilry, but one narrative must stand out prominently and be celebrated – that of Annie Edson Taylor.

Since 1850, it is noted that over 5,000 individuals have plummeted over Niagara Falls, whether that be deliberately or inadvertently. The undisputed fact remains that on October 24th, 1901, at the age of sixty-three, Annie Edson Taylor, a teacher by profession, became the first person to survive a plunge over the Niagara Falls. That is to say, that before and since that time thousands had been sacrificed there, had taken their own lives or had even failed to conquer the Horseshoe Falls. Encased in a barrel of her own design, she not only survived the mighty Falls but also set an unparalleled precedent as a woman and as a woman of advanced age accomplishing such a perilous feat. This singular event underscores the often-underrepresented narrative of women and elders undertaking extraordinary acts of daring.

In 1901, Annie Edson Taylor emerged as a pioneering survivor. Despite the multitude of other attempts over the subsequent 123 years, a mere sixteen individuals have reportedly survived the perilous drop, all of which took place over the Canadian Horseshoe Falls. Among these survivors, only two other women are known to have intentionally gone over the Falls and lived to tell the tale. On June 18th, 1995, Lori Martin, alongside Steve Trotter, braved the Falls, marking Trotter's second successful attempt. On March 10th, 2009, an unnamed thirty-year-old woman survived going over the Horseshoe Falls. Consequently, three of the sixteen survivors of the Falls have been women. This striking number of female survivors, particularly when contrasted with their male counterparts, points to the disparity in the gender representation among those who have dared to challenge the Falls. It also brings to the fore the exceptional nature of Annie Edson Taylor's, of Lori Martin's and of the unnamed woman's achievements.

That said, the narratives of these survivors should not obscure the inherent danger and illegality of such attempts. Following a tragic incident in 1951, the risky feat became illegal with steep fines reaching up to $25,000. It is crucial to underscore that the act of navigating the Falls is not only perilous, often resulting in severe injury or death, but also contravenes local laws. Thus, in recounting the story of Annie Edson Taylor, this text serves not just to highlight an individual of extraordinary courage and resilience, but also to illuminate the broader narrative of women and elders confronting the raw, untamed forces of nature. This account is a tribute to the rare few who have survived the might of the Niagara Falls, but it is by no means an endorsement of such dangerous endeavours. The overwhelmingly low survival rate stands as a stark testament to the merciless power of the Falls.

Finding Annie

My editor, Charlotte Ledger, brought Annie Edson Taylor to me. The very best email. *Meet Annie Edson Taylor*, she wrote. I'd not heard her story before, and I've not stopped thinking about her since. Annie remains an enigmatic and intriguing figure from our past and her daring stunt over Niagara Falls is etched into the annals of history. Yet, much about her remains little known and shrouded in incorrect or false facts.

What *is* known is that Annie Edson was born on October 24th, 1838, in Auburn, New York, one of eight children in a financially comfortable family. Unfortunately, the death of her father (in 1850) led to a sharp decline in her family's fortunes; a circumstance that perhaps shaped her future resilience and adaptability.

She married Samuel Taylor in 1856, when she was eighteen. Her only son was both born and died in 1861. Two years later, Annie's husband was killed in Gettysburg. As a consequence of her trauma and before her stunt, Annie held a variety of roles – a testament to her tenacity and resourcefulness. From schoolteacher to dance instructor and clerical worker, she defied the traditional expectations for women of her time. She was even held up by Jesse James! However, her claim to fame was undoubtedly her daring venture over Niagara Falls in a barrel on her sixty-third birthday. It is noted that she lied about her age, convincing everyone that she was forty-three. Remarkably, she survived with only minor injuries, but the financial security she had hoped to secure from this stunt eluded her. Her manager did abscond with her barrel, and her earnings from public appearances and souvenir booklets fell short of her needs.

My work, as a novelist, was to ask questions to try and understand Annie's motivation. Why did she risk her life? Why did she lie about her age? Why would she think that she could survive a feat that had taken the lives of thousands before her? And, perhaps, did she even care if her attempt failed? What did Annie have to gain? And what did she have to lose?

My response is this fictionalised account of Annie's life, grounded firmly in recorded facts. As stated, there is much about this courageous woman that remains unknown, and that allowed creative freedom around the gaps in her story. My academic research focuses on the author's ethical responsibility, when writing fiction based on real lives, and creative decisions were made with that in mind.

In her memoir, Annie claimed part of her reason for attempting the stunt was to raise money for two friends – one battling illness, the other struggling to care for a child. Taking this given fact but no other details, within this novel, Tilda, Nora and Mrs Lapointe are fictional characters. Additionally, the locations where Annie lives are based on fact, but are fictionalised.

After the Falls, Annie did write a memoir and she did later offer magnetic therapies. She spent her final days in the Niagara County Infirmary in Lockport, New York, admitted in February 1921 due to deteriorating health. It was there, on April 29, 1921, that she passed away at the age of eighty-two, penniless and largely forgotten. Originally given a pauper's grave, community fundraising did lead to her resting place in the 'Stunters' Rest' section of Oakwood Cemetery in Niagara Falls, New York.

Thus, while this novel uses a degree of creative license, it is rooted in the fragments of Mrs Taylor's story. Her life, as unconventional and daring as it was, serves as a reminder of human tenacity, resilience, and the lengths one might go to alter one's circumstances. She lived to tell her tale. Annie Edson Taylor, the first person to survive going over Niagara Falls in a barrel, was a remarkable woman. This is my, fictionalised, love letter to her.

Dr Caroline Cauchi

Acknowledgments

This novel is for the thousands of readers who consume stories that centre women's voices like it's the air they breathe! It is for those who wish to shout and celebrate the successes of the remarkable women who navigated this world long before us. We stand on their shoulders now. Dear Reader, thank you for spending your precious time with Annie. I am grateful that you have.

I hope that through this novel, I have initiated a conversation about Annie Edson Taylor, ensuring she takes her rightful place in history. The bravery of other stunters is unquestionable, but this story is Annie's. Thank you, Mrs Taylor—it has been a privilege and an honour to spend time devoted to researching and retelling your story. Before writing this novel, I was in a metaphorical barrel of my own, and writing about you has taught me much about myself. Like all my novels, this one reflects a very specific chapter in my journey too. I like that our narratives are forever joined.

Special thanks to HarperCollins UK and the fabulous team at One More Chapter, especially to Charlotte Ledger, the editor of my dreams. Thank you for introducing me to Annie, for trusting me to tell this story and for giving me the much-needed permission (kick up the arse!) to write into those gaps. It is fair to say that you toppled that barrel over and forced me to climb out (I am possibly labouring this notion!). Your excitement, vision, and belief in my writing mean more than I can express. Lydia Mason and Emily Thomas—thank you for your editorial wizardry and boldness. You are both incredible. Love and gratitude also to Arsalan Isa, Lucy Bennett, Chloe Cummings, Emma Petfield, Bethan

Moore, Caroline Scott-Bowden and Francesca Tuzzeo. Equally, a special mention to the brilliant HarperCollins UK foreign rights team, who have been incredible champions of my writing. I buy a smurf (I know!) for every deal received and my shelf is looking super crowded. Much gratitude for your amazing efforts in bringing this story to a wider audience. You're all ace.

To the HarperCollins Canada Team—I am taking this opportunity to thank you for bringing my writing to Heather Reisman's attention and for your infectious enthusiasm about Mrs Taylor (even before I'd finished writing the novel). I am in awe of your publishing brilliance, but your support/cheerleading of my writing has been invaluable in toppling me out of that barrel (yup!). Special thanks to Cory Beatty, Lauren Morocco, Cindy Ma, Brenann Francis, Peter Borcsok, and Colleen Simpson.

To my colleagues at the University of Hull—I am so very thankful for your enthusiastic welcome to the university this last year. Working alongside such talented academics (whilst attempting to write this novel) has been a joy. Special thanks go to Edmund Hurst, Catherine Wynne, Jenny Macleod, Chris Westoby, Kath McKay, Anna Turner, Jo Metcalf, and Charles Prior.

To Tom Poehnelt, Jonathan Milner, and Hazel Gaynor. Thank you for your expertise and generosity of time.

To Jackie Jardine—thank you, for more than I can reveal here.

To my glorious friends and family. Ramon Azzopardi Fiott, Matty Busuttil, Steve Spiteri Fiteni, Alex Brown, Elsa Williams, Keith Rice, Emily Hills, Wendi Surtees-Smith, Rachael Lucas, Paula Groves, Richard Wells, Margaret Coomb, Ryan Groves, Clare Christian, Kat Nokes, Bernie Pardue, and Johnny Vegas – thank you for your advice, encouragement, and your belief in me. Love to you all.

To my Cauchis—Jacob, Ben, Poppy and Lauren. Thank you for loving me constantly, unconditionally, and deeply. For staying, for roaring, for giggling inappropriately—thank you for the persistent and unreserved love. How blessed am I to have you as my family? Exceptionally.

Lastly, to Nathan. That invisible thread stretched and tangled, but it never broke. Thank you for finding me again, darling man. Holding your hand brings with it magic. I'm truly excited to live this adventure with you, with Ron, and with our air fryer (you promised!).

The author and One More Chapter would like to thank everyone who contributed to the publication of this story...

Analytics
James Brackin
Abigail Fryer
Maria Osa

Audio
Fionnuala Barrett
Ciara Briggs

Contracts
Sasha Duszynska Lewis

Design
Lucy Bennett
Fiona Greenway
Liane Payne
Dean Russell

Digital Sales
Lydia Grainge
Hannah Lismore
Emily Scorer

Editorial
Arsalan Isa
Charlotte Ledger
Bonnie Macleod
Lydia Mason
Jennie Rothwell
Caroline Scott-Bowden
Emily Thomas

Harper360
Emily Gerbner
Jean Marie Kelly
emma sullivan
Sophia Wilhelm

HarperCollins Canada
Cory Beatty
Peter Borcsok
Brenann Francis
Cindy Ma
Lauren Morocco
Colleen Simpson

International Sales
Bethan Moore

Marketing & Publicity
Chloe Cummings
Emma Petfield

Operations
Melissa Okusanya
Hannah Stamp

Production
Denis Manson
Simon Moore
Francesca Tuzzeo

Rights
Vasiliki Machaira
Rachel McCarron
Hany Sheikh Mohamed
Zoe Shine

The HarperCollins Distribution Team

The HarperCollins Finance & Royalties Team

The HarperCollins Legal Team

The HarperCollins Technology Team

Trade Marketing
Ben Hurd

UK Sales
Laura Carpenter
Isabel Coburn
Jay Cochrane
Sabina Lewis
Holly Martin
Erin White
Harriet Williams
Leah Woods

And every other essential link in the chain from delivery drivers to booksellers to librarians and beyond!

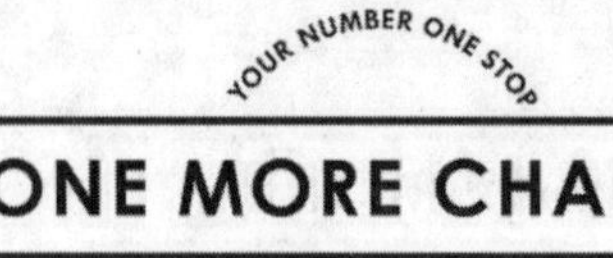

One More Chapter is an award-winning global division of HarperCollins.

Sign up to our newsletter to get our latest eBook deals and stay up to date with our weekly Book Club!
Subscribe here.

Meet the team at
www.onemorechapter.com

Follow us!

 @OneMoreChapter_

 @OneMoreChapter

 @onemorechapterhc

Do you write unputdownable fiction?
We love to hear from new voices.
Find out how to submit your novel at
www.onemorechapter.com/submissions